TOO HOT FOR COMFORT

TOO HOT
FOR COMFORT

Andrew Bibby

GRITSTONE
PUBLISHING

Published in 2020 by
Gritstone Publishing Co-operative,
Birchcliffe Centre,
Hebden Bridge HX7 8DG

Gritstone Publishing Co-operative is jointly owned by its members, some
of Britain's best-regarded authors writing about the countryside and the
natural world. Look out for our other titles.
http://gritstonecoop.co.uk

ISBN 978-1-913625-01-6

Printed in the UK by Imprint Digital, Exeter

PROLOGUE
(A Tuesday in May)

1.

Joan had taken a decision. It was time to leave the Lake District behind. Tomorrow she'd take the campervan down the M6, down maybe to Devon. She had friends in Totnes.

A long drive would help recharge the van's leisure battery. The gauge was showing that it had almost nothing left. But, anyway, she had come to recognise that her stay in the Lakes had become disastrous. The past few days had been hard, having to move the van every night to some new hidey-hole on a back road among the hills just in case. The abuse and the threats on social media had been getting worse - it was really quite disgusting what some people felt they could say - and for almost the first time in her life she felt unsure of her physical safety. How was it possible, she asked herself, that she could be freaked just by some online trolls? She'd felt no fear confronting police on the anti-fracking demos in Lancashire, no fear at all when taking part in the Extinction Rebellion direct actions in London. But now, she had to admit, her life in the campervan was just a little too solitary for her liking. She missed Goldie enormously. Ever since Goldie had been killed, she had felt vulnerable.

She'd driven the van that day over the Wrynose pass from the Duddon valley where she had stayed the night before. She had made her way along Langdale and had finally found a little pull-in to park up on the back road on the lonely side of Grasmere. The lights of the cars of the tourists who were hurrying back from a night out to their hotels and B&Bs could be seen far away across the lake. Nobody came this way at this time of the evening.

Except, it would seem, very occasionally. The first thing she heard was the noise of car doors slamming. There were men's voices, close at hand, at least two of them, sounding like they might have been drinking. She tensed involuntarily.

Then came the sound of breaking glass. She became aware that one of the van's windows had been shattered. Something had been thrown through the passenger side window of her van and was on the floor below the steering wheel. A brick, she thought. No, she looked more closely, it was a glass bottle. And something appeared to be burning at its neck.

For a long moment, everything was silent again, as peaceful and still as the beautiful Lake District countryside all around. Then came an explosion. The darkness was immediately transformed into sharp white light by flames which leapt up, engulfing the van. The curtains caught fire, then the carpet and the seats, and the cupboards below the kitchen sink, and the pull-out mattress for the bed. It was astonishing how quickly a fire could take hold.

For perhaps ten minutes the flames had their way. Finally there was an even larger explosion, as the fuel tank under the vehicle went up. The fire began to die away. Only the charred metal skeleton, bent by the heat, remained to show what had once been a campervan.

But by this stage there was nobody left to see it. The car which, a few minutes earlier, had pulled up alongside the van had gone again. Its occupants were somewhere near Keswick, safely on their way to their own homes.

On the far side of Grasmere, away from the main road, wisps of dirty grey smoke climbed slowly into the night sky. All was returning to darkness.

(The next afternoon)

2.

It was a pitiful turn-out to mark a death. The Cumbrian Enquirer had been serving its readers for the best part of two centuries. Week after week the paper had faithfully recorded the joys and the sorrows of the people who lived among the mountains and lakes in this part of northern England.

And now what had once been a local legend was no more. Nick Potterton had helped Molly Everett, the last of the long line of Enquirer editors, put the final edition of the paper to bed that afternoon, pushing the 'send' button one last time to mail the digital files over to the printers. Then they had made for the upstairs room of a nearby local pub.

Booking the room had been a mistake. There was enough space there to hold seventy or eighty, or more perhaps for a sweaty Saturday disco. Nick looked around and counted fifteen people, huddled in groups around the side of the room, chatting and drinking wine in a perfunctory fashion.

Evidently, few people had bothered to come to mourn the Enquirer. Nick knew most of them of course. There was Petra, who had staffed the Enquirer's switchboard, in her own words, for yonks. There were three residual members of the news team, a couple of staffers from the sports desk and two others who, like Nick, were freelances. That was it, in terms of the office. The last few weeks as the paper's fate became obvious had been difficult, but surely the other staff who had worked at the Enquirer could at least have made an effort?

Few others had taken the trouble, either. Nobody senior had shown up from the council, although there was a very young employee tucking into the crisps. There were a handful of other people there, almost at random. A couple of Rotarians. Somebody from the local history society. The vicar. The President of the local chamber of commerce.

The Cumbrian Enquirer hadn't even been able to die with dignity. The family which owned most of the shares had sold the rights to its name to a newspaper group based up in the north of the county. A journalist up there would be charged to bring out a paper called the Enquirer, putting together the copy as best they could from forty miles away in Carlisle. Molly and Nick knew what would happen. It would be a pitiful product which would carry on for a year or so until the very last of the Enquirer's loyal advertisers had got the message and abandoned ship.

Nick took a gulp of beer. The room had gone quiet as Molly had begun to say a few words. This was, after all, not just an event to mark the passing of the Enquirer, it was also Molly's retirement bash. Only in her late fifties, the job she loved so much had been snatched from under her.

Still, she was a professional. She'd gone back through the paper's archives and dug out a few choice stories. She began with William Wordsworth's attempt to stop the building of a new railway to

Windermere in 1844. "The Sabbath day in the towns of Bowness and Ambleside would be subject to much additional desecration," Wordsworth had said. Molly paused, and the laughter she'd anticipated duly came.

And then, embarrassingly, Molly's mobile phone had suddenly rung loudly. She hurriedly dug the phone out from her bag and passed it to Nick. "You deal with it," she said under her breath.

Nick retreated to the doorway to take the call. "Hello?" he said.

There was a moment of silence at the other end.

"Ah, I was expecting the illustrious editor," said the caller.

"It's Nick Potterton here. Molly's busy at the moment."

"Ah dear boy, it's George here."

The information was unnecessary. Nick had immediately recognised the tones of George Mulholland. An old school friend of Molly's, George had joined the Cumbrian police, risen through the ranks, been promoted eventually to be Detective Superintendent - but then, a year or so earlier, been given the heave-ho. Like Molly, he had been retired before he wanted to be. From what Nick knew, the last few months had not been an easy period of adjustment.

"I just wanted Molly to know that I have some news for her," Mulholland went on. "Front page next week, perhaps."

"But George, you're too late. We're at the Cumbrian Enquirer's funeral wake at the moment. Molly told me she'd invited you."

"Ah, it's today. I seem to be forgetting things these days," he replied.

"Anyway," Nick went on, "what is your news?" Nick might not have anywhere left to take his stories, but by instinct he remained a journalist.

"It's about Joan Arkle."

"Ah. St Joan of Arc."

"Eh?"

"Sorry, that's Molly's private name for her. What's the story?"

In recent months, the actions of Joan Arkle had sometimes seemed to fill the Cumbrian Enquirer's news pages all by themselves. There'd been her demonstrations and pickets to report. There'd been her magistrates' court appearances. There had been the time she had been sent down to the cells for contempt.

More laughter reached Nick Potterton from across the room, where Molly was still speaking. Nick tried to focus on what George Mulholland was telling him.

"Her campervan appears to have been firebombed late last night on a by-road somewhere between Elter Water and Grasmere. Hell of a mess." Mulholland paused. "Of course, pretty well everyone in Cumbria hated her at one time or another for something. But still…"

There was a moment as Nick absorbed this information. "God. Is she OK?"

"Forensics are at work. But I gather my erstwhile colleagues are gearing up to do some work."

"What sort of work, George?" Nick asked.

"Not clear at present. But, well, it might be homicide." George replied, quietly.

There was the sound of clapping as Molly came to the end of her speech. She came across to Nick, beaming broadly.

"Right," she said, "who was that trying to reach me?"

PART ONE
(Six weeks earlier)

3.

Joan was up first. Pete, whose flat and whose bed she had been sharing for the past few days, was still asleep. She was supposed simply to be sofa-surfing, just for a short time while her van was having a new clutch fitted, but somehow he had persuaded her to move from the living room into the bedroom. Pete was a nice guy and she liked him a lot, even if – she told herself - these days her sexual orientation wasn't even supposed to be heterosexual.

Still, he wasn't an early riser. She looked at him, suddenly feeling irritation towards the sleeping body stretched out under the duvet. She'd never liked long lie-ins, certainly not on Mondays. Early mornings were the time of the day she enjoyed most. Her work often meant getting up in the dark and seeing the sky gradually lighten as the English countryside turned with the earth towards the sun.

Today, in any case, she couldn't afford to be tardy. Tediously, she had an appointment in Workington for ten o'clock and it was one of those occasions where, all in all, it was better not to show up late. Before she left, Goldie would need her usual morning walk.

Joan looked at yesterday's clothes which she had left lying on the floor the previous evening. There was a black T-shirt, the red check woollen jacket which she was wearing these days almost all the time, a pair of faded skimpy jeans with a tear at one of the knees and her workaday bra and knickers. Her black boots and thick woolly socks were there as well.

She pondered the question of what to wear. Really, most people would dress at least a little smartly on a day like today. She'd been at magistrates' courts before where some of the male members of her activist group had even put on jackets and ties, not that it ever really did them any good. She long ago had learned the way that the system seemed to work, from the point of view of magistrates. They simply had to find you guilty, work out which column to look at in the Sentencing Council's tariff of fines, and then – wham! – tell you how much you would have to pay. It was all supposed to be linked to your weekly income, but it was always hundreds of pounds. Fortunately, crowdfunding could sometimes come to the rescue.

She looked again at her clothes, and took a decision. She pulled out a T-shirt, dragged it on over the previous day's bra she'd put back on and then hurried into the knickers and jeans. She had chosen the T-shirt specially for the occasion. It was one some friends in Lancashire had had made a year or so back. The slogan on the chest ran *You must be fracking stupid.* It would do just fine for Workington magistrates, she decided. It might be a little creased but it was clean. What more could they ask for?

4.

Monday was perhaps the busiest day of them all in the Cumbrian Enquirer's newsroom. Somehow, in the time remaining before Wednesday afternoon, a twenty-four page newspaper had to be put together from scratch. Somehow a powerful front page story had to be researched and written. Somehow the news pages, the features, the leisure pages and the sports coverage at the back had to be filled too. It was the same every week.

Molly Everett was talking through story ideas at the regular weekly news conference. Nick Potterton was perched on a table in Molly's office and two news reporters were also in the room, one standing and the other cross-legged on the floor. There was the usual friendly banter before the meeting proper got under way.

"Did you spend much time in magistrates' courts in your days at the Sunday Times?" Molly asked Nick.

Nick laughed. Molly was back on what was familiar ground between the two of them. It was true that Nick's journalistic career, the trajectory that had brought him now in his early fifties to be freelancing part-time at the Cumbrian Enquirer, was not precisely an orthodox one. After his Masters in journalism at City University and a short spell in the provincial press he'd got himself a plum job as part of the Insight Team at the Sunday Times, working on some really cutting-edge stories at a time when the press still put proper resources into investigative reporting. And after the Sunday Times came The Independent. That's where he had met the woman who had stolen his heart, who had brought their daughter Rosa into the world, who had lived with him for eighteen years – and then who had left him abruptly to go back to Barcelona and shack up with a Catalan called Jordi. It was all because of her departure that Nick had turned his back on London, turned his back on the national press and retreated licking his wounds to the Lake District.

Now, of course, he wouldn't want to live anywhere else.

"We broke a story which ended up at the Old Bailey," Nick replied to Molly's question. "Somebody else did the tedious work of sitting in the court, though. Why?"

"Just wondered if you were up to speed on what journalists need to know about the law. I spent months learning it all when I was a junior reporter but I expect you lot in London considered it was beneath you."

Nick pulled a face.

"Exam time," Molly said. "Get your notebook out. Question 1. How should interruptions from the public gallery be reported? Question 2. When might the court refuse to allow reporting? Question 3. What is an either-way offence, and what reporting restrictions might apply? Question 4…"

"OK, that's enough. Any reason for all this?"

"Magistrates' hearing at Workington this morning on the anti-nuclear protest the other week down at Drigg. Criminal damage charges, I think. There are two women up before the beak, and I'd like to run the story. And, guess what, it just so happens that the Cumbrian Enquirer has its very own Nuclear Power Correspondent."

Nick grimaced again. After moving to the Lakes, he had laboured for several years on a book which tried to uncover the secretive big business interests behind the resurgence of nuclear power worldwide. It hadn't been easy research but for the first time since his Sunday Times days he had felt he was uncovering really important new information which needed to be told. Finally his book, titled *Nuclear Power: Yes Please?*, had been completed. It was, Nick knew, a very competent piece of work. It had been worth the hours of research, and it was a topical issue as well. After all, wasn't a new nuclear power station already under construction, with a little help from the French and the Chinese, at Hinckley Point in Somerset? Twenty billion pounds and more were being sunk into the ground on a headland on the Bristol Channel to try to make sure the lights didn't go out across the UK sometime in the 2020s.

The final text of the book had been emailed by Nick to his London publishing company eighteen months or so back. And after that something had gone wrong. Whether the publishers had got cold feet Nick couldn't tell, but they had done almost no marketing work for the book. It had come out the previous June, one of the quietest times in the publishing calendar, priced at a ridiculously high cost of £19.95. Unsurprisingly it had barely received any reviews and had now had sunk without trace. Nick would keep the advance, of course, but there was no chance that there would be further royalty payments coming his way.

"I am not sure I ever want to hear the words nuclear power again," Nick said.

"Of course you do," Molly replied. "It'll take you some time to drive over to Workington, so you'll need to leave soon. Find out what you can about the demonstrators. Who are they, where are they from, and why haven't we come across them before at the Enquirer? I'm thinking an inside page lead, so say 600 words. As always, I let you have my juiciest stories."

5.

Elizzabeth had been brought up to tell the truth. Today it still wasn't seven o'clock and she had already told two lies.

Her husband Baz had returned pissed the previous evening, long after she'd taken herself off to bed, but had woken her by galumphing around the bedroom and then – once he had finally got himself into bed - had wanted sex. A little resigned, she had rolled over and tried to get in the mood. Instead she found herself pondering whether their money would last out until the month end. Now this morning as her alarm had sounded she had felt his hand sleepily make its way across her breasts, obviously interested in a repeat of the night before. She had firmly pushed him away. "Sorry, love, no time. Work have asked me to go in early," she had said.

That was the first lie. The second came ten minutes later when she texted her employer. She had written: *Really sorry Dawn I've woken with a raging toothache. Will come as soon as I've managed to get the dentist to see me.* Dawn might not believe her, but too bad, Elizzabeth definitely wasn't going to tell her the real reason why she'd be late.

It was, she told herself as she washed, all the fault of bloody Joan Arkle. Joan had a way of cajoling you so that you ended up doing things you didn't really mean to do. Although that wasn't quite fair, because in some sense you did want to do them.

She went across to her wardrobe and picked out the most modest clothes she could find. Her work uniform was already bundled into a shoulder bag she'd got ready the night before. Somewhere between Workington and the cut-price supermarket in Keswick where she worked on the tills she would have to find a place where she could change. Maybe there would be women's toilets in the court building.

Of course she hadn't told Baz she had been arrested. God knows what he would have done. God knows what he would do now if he knew the real reason she was up an hour earlier than usual. There was a bus from Keswick bus station just after eight o'clock which would fetch her up in Workington an hour or so later, unnecessarily early but the only option because if she missed that bus she'd be late. Perhaps she'd find a café and treat herself to a bacon butty while she waited.

It was Joan who had persuaded her to go on the demonstration she'd organised down at Drigg, close to the coast near Seascale. Drigg's high security fences told you that this was the place where the radioactive waste left behind after more than sixty years of nuclear power generation in west Cumbria had been buried. Stuff from Britain's nuclear bombs apparently, too. Radioactive waste, even the low-level waste which was all that Drigg was supposed to be taking in, had a habit of hanging around. Drigg would presumably need those security fences a very long time.

Unless climate change had other ideas. Joan Arkle had got hold somehow of an old report from the government's Environment Agency which had talked about the high risk of coastal erosion on this stretch of the coast. "It's here in this document in black and white," she'd said. "Rising sea levels and storms are predicted to eat away at the coastline and the waste dump's only a few metres above sea level. There's a real risk of an environmental catastrophe."

Joan had decided that a demo was needed. "We have to demonstrate that climate change affects absolutely everything, even the toxic muck we've buried in the ground and have tried to forget about," she'd said. "It's time for a little bit of NVDA." Elizzabeth had by now learned that this meant non-violent direct action.

It was David Attenborough who was probably to blame for the fact that Elizzabeth had got herself involved with Joan Arkle. She'd watched his programmes on the risks of climate change and the desecration of the natural world with increasing alarm. Some time, not just yet but certainly sometime in the years to come, she hoped she would have children. She wanted them to come into a world that was full of promise and hope, not one which was on its last legs and heading to become an inferno. So when she had the chance, when Baz had planned evenings out with his mates, she began to start going to the meetings about climate change which Joan Arkle was organising.

And then, by some happy or perhaps unhappy coincidence, she discovered that the Drigg demo had been fixed for the same day as a home match at Carlisle United. Baz would be off as usual to Brunton Park, leaving early on Saturday morning in time to get in a pint or two before the match and then staying on afterwards to celebrate Carlisle's success or to drown his sorrows, depending on how the fates had treated the team. The day was hers to spend as she wished. She told Joan she was coming. Joan gave her a lift across to the coast in her campervan. It was Elizzabeth's first demonstration.

6.

Nick's day in court, when he finally got to Workington, had been a lesson in patience. Perhaps patience was the main attribute they were looking for, he thought, when they were appointing new magistrates.

There had been a seemingly endless series of cases of people being found guilty of failing to buy TV licences or of not paying their Council Tax. No wonder that these days few local newspapers had the resources to have journalists monitoring the courts. Eventually, some time just before midday, the cases Nick had come to hear came up. He reached for his notepad.

The younger woman's case was taken first. She had straggly bleached hair and was dressed in what looked an uncomfortably Mumsy two-piece suit. She appeared disorientated by the experience of finding herself in court but at the same time determined not to allow herself to be intimidated.

Curiously her name was given on that day's court list as Elizzabeth Bowes with two 'z's, a careless typing mistake by some junior court official, Nick assumed. He would have guessed that she was in her late twenties, so when she gave her date of birth to the court he was surprised to find that she was only 24. He noted down her address carefully when she confirmed it to the Clerk of the Court. It was a street name he didn't know, somewhere in Keswick.

Her time in front of the magistrates ended quickly. The Chairman – an older woman, who was wearing her own two-piece costume rather more comfortably than the defendant – told her to stand up as the charge against her was read out. Was she guilty or not guilty of Aggravated Trespass? She pleaded guilty.

A man in a rather nicely tailored suit whom Nick realised was there from the Crown Prosecution Service then briefly outlined the case. Nick's shorthand pencil made its way rapidly across the notebook. On Saturday February 3rd, from approximately 2pm until shortly after 3pm, there had been a demonstration of around fifteen persons at the Drigg licensed nuclear site, one of whom was the defendant Ms Bowes. The demonstrators carried placards, alleging that the facility was at risk of flooding as a result of climate change. Ms Bowes was seen by police officers present to be weaving coloured wool into the fencing surrounding the site, and joining in with the singing of a number of songs.

Twenty uniformed police officers – the Prosecutor went on – were present during the demonstration. At approximately 2.27pm the officer commanding, Sergeant Graves, advised the demonstrators by loudspeaker that the Drigg licensed site was a Protected Site under Sections 128-131 of the Serious Organised Crime and Police Act and that trespass on Protected Sites was a criminal offence. At this point most of the demonstrators withdrew behind the police line, where they continued singing and chanting. Ms Bowes, however, did not withdraw at this point, but continued with her work of weaving wool to the fence. At 2.42pm she was arrested by PCs Shipton and Monkton, and taken to Whitehaven police station where she was questioned, before being released under investigation. She is a person of previous good character.

The prosecutor sat back in his chair, job done.

"Ms Bowes," the Chairman of the magistrates said, "we shall be retiring in a moment to discuss the sentence we will impose. But you have the opportunity now to tell us anything relevant in mitigation." The young woman looked blank. "I mean, anything which you feel you would like us to know which might make us consider imposing a more lenient sentence. Have you anything to say?"

"Not really," she paused, speaking quietly. "Well, only that I was weaving a spider's web with the wool and I just wanted to finish it before I had to leave. I didn't think I was doing any harm." She stopped again, and then continued with more firmness to her voice. "But I do feel very strongly that we're doing terrible things to our world. I mean, I can't understand why nobody seems to be taking climate change seriously. That's really all there is to say." She stopped abruptly.

The magistrates left the court room, returning almost immediately to impose their sentence. It was a fine of £250 fine, plus prosecution costs, plus the statutory surcharge. It came to just under £400.

The young woman visibly blanched. "I can't pay that much," she said in a small voice.

"The court will accept payment by instalments. What offer can you make?" the Chairman said.

There was a muffled reply. "I don't know. Maybe £50 when I get paid each month."

"Your offer is accepted. The court officers will discuss the arrangements with you." The woman remained where she was. "You may leave now," the Chairman prompted.

The court moved on immediately to the next case, and the young woman with the bleached hair was replaced by a second woman, somewhat older, also charged as a result of the Drigg demonstration. She had short spikey hair, which was probably naturally brown but which she had dyed light pink. She was facing the charge of Aggravated Trespass but also a second charge of Criminal Damage, which it turned out was for writing slogans on the official warning signs which surrounded the site. Her name was Joan Arkle. She was 34, Nick learned, and the address she gave was in Maryport, an old working town on the coast to the west of the tourist part of the Lake District.

Joan stood up as the charges against her were read out, her face set with an expression which could be interpreted either as boredom or aggression. Before she could enter a plea, however, Nick noticed a quiet conversation taking place between the Clerk of the Court and the Chairman of the magistrates. It was the Chairman who spoke.

"It is suggested that the clothing being worn by you Miss Arkle could be considered offensive and disrespectful to the court." Eyes, including Nick's, swivelled round to inspect Joan's T-shirt more carefully.

Joan responded, firmly fixing the Chairman in her gaze.

"I don't find my T-shirt offensive. In fact, in my opinion it is fracking which is the really offensive thing that's going on." She paused. "But I can easily remedy your concerns. I'll put the T-shirt on inside out."

As she spoke Joan Arkle was reaching down with crossed hands to the bottom of her shirt, pulling it over her head. She was left dressed in just her bra, with her bare shoulders and bare midriff facing the magistrates. It was impossible not to notice the tattoo of a large blue whale, smiling cheerfully and complete with a little badge reading 'Save the Humans', which appeared across her chest from inside the left cup of her bra.

There was a ripple of displeasure from the bench.

"Miss Arkle, this is quite unacceptable behaviour." The Chairman of the magistrates turned to address the court usher. "This woman is in contempt of court. Call for security and have her taken to the cells. We will not resume this hearing until the defendant has found something more appropriate to wear in court. Case adjourned."

And Joan Arkle was bundled unceremoniously from the court room down the stairs to the cells below, a uniformed private security officer at her back. The magistrates moved on to the next case on their schedule for the day and Nick took the opportunity to slip out.

It was good timing. Emerging from the women's toilet into the main entrance hall was the first of the two women, now dressed in what was obviously her clothes for work. Nick saw his chance.

"Hello, I'm Nick Potterton from the Cumbrian Enquirer," he introduced himself. "You had a long wait this morning for your case to come up."

She nodded. "Yes," she said.

"Your first time too, I gather".

She nodded again. Nick pressed on.

"I shouldn't admit this, I suppose, but I've no idea what Aggravated Trespass actually means," he said.

"No, I've no idea either."

Nick looked at her in surprise. "But you pleaded guilty."

"Yes," she shrugged. "Joan wanted me to plead not guilty. But that would have meant coming back here all over again and missing work again. And they'd have found me guilty anyway and probably fined me more."

"That seemed a large fine for a first offence," Nick suggested.

The woman looked at him helplessly. "Yes," she said.

"Can you afford to pay £50 a month?"

Again she shrugged. Her hair tumbled over her eyes. "Of course I can't," she replied quietly.

Nick had a sudden desire to reach into his pocket and pull out some bank notes. He resisted the urge. He was there professionally, he reminded himself. "Tell me why you went on the demo."

"Like I said. The world's in a mess. Somebody has to do something. I don't think we can leave it to politicians. Everyone knows all they do is argue with each other."

"You care about the risks of climate change?"

"Of course I do. Why don't your newspapers explain this to people better?"

"Well, perhaps we should." Nick paused. "By the way, is it really true that you spell Elizabeth with two 'z's? That's what the list of court cases said."

"Yes. I think my parents got themselves confused when they registered me. It gives me no end of problems whenever I have to spell my name." She paused, and suddenly looked worried. "Why are you asking?"

"Well, when I come to write my news report I need to make sure all the details are right. I can't have your name spelled wrong."

Elizzabeth Bowes' attitude had suddenly changed. "But you can't print my name. That would be terrible." She was almost shouting.

Nick tried to look sympathetic. "I understand. But your name and address are in the public domain now. That's how courts work. And that's how newspapers report court cases."

The woman looked stunned. "But you don't understand. I could lose my job. And my husband... Really, he'd go ballistic. Nobody knows I'm here today."

"Elizzabeth, I admire your courage in standing up for your principles but perhaps you needed to think of that before you got yourself arrested."

The woman looked up at him. "You don't care, do you, you don't care at all what happens to me. My personal life is just fodder for your bloody newspaper. When I was a kid I fancied being a journalist, you know. I was good at writing and I liked the idea of the job. It seemed quite glamorous. But maybe the truth is that journalists are all bastards." She paused. "I've got to go to work."

She marched towards the exit, and then abruptly turned back. "OK, so I'm in the shit. But I don't blame Joan for any of this. Joan's a good person. Don't forget it."

7.

It had been a lost afternoon. Another one. Of course, the court system was under a lot of pressure, but the cost to the economy of all the time which people wasted just hanging around must be astronomical.

Detective Inspector Chrissy Chambers had hoped that her days of having to appear regularly at Magistrates' Court hearings as a police witness were coming to an end when she had got the career move she had been working towards and had been transferred from the uniformed branch to the CID. But justice moves slowly. She had been called back to Workington magistrates for the trial of three likely lads who were up for breaking into a newsagents' shop in Cockermouth and stealing cigarettes. She'd been the arresting officer who'd been called to the scene that evening when she was still a Sergeant in uniform. Now, many months later, the case still hadn't come to trial. And this time, at the last minute, the magistrates had run out of time to hear the case and yet another adjournment had been given.

She sighed as she got ready to leave the court building. If only the public realised just how much time the police had to spend on the bureaucracy that accompanied any successful charge, they might be more tolerant when, let's say, a police constable failed to show up immediately to catch the culprit who had scratched somebody's car bonnet.

She'd missed a training course too in order to be in court. It was on SOCMINT, or social media intelligence if you wanted to be formal, a topic that really interested her but one which – even though she was only in her early thirties – she felt she was almost too old to properly understand. Britain's police forces had realised rather later than big business the value of the low-level information which people voluntarily shared with the world on their Twitter or Facebook or Instagram accounts, but just recently there had been a flurry of interest from CIDs in the topic. If detectives had once upon a time had to cultivate low-life characters on the edge of the underworld the answer to catching criminals these days seemed to be something called behavioural analytics.

This didn't normally mean overworked CID officers laboriously poring through individuals' social media offerings. Increasingly it meant buying the right SOCMINT monitoring software from one of the private companies in the market and letting the algorithms do the hard work for you. SOCMINT had already proved its worth in several high-profile cases nationwide, but as Chrissy was aware the legal basis on which the police could go poking around in individuals' personal lives in this way was by no means clear. She knew she needed to get herself up to speed on the issues.

There'd been quite a change in the CID since Chrissy had started going to work in plain clothes. Detective Superintendent Mulholland, one of those old-school police officers who had been with Cumbria

Police ever since school, had finally been persuaded to retire. Chrissy had respected Mulholland's way of working and liked him as a man. He'd strongly supported her when she had first considered moving across to the CID, at the time when she had been in uniform and swotting for the National Investigators' Exam.

Mulholland's retirement had turned out in some ways to be an advantage because it meant that there had been a series of promotions up the ladder. Chrissy's hard work had paid off: she was one of only a small number of candidates awarded an 'exceptional' score when her answers to the questions in the NIE were totted up. Her success went noted by her superiors. Only a few months after joining the CID as a DS the Board interview for promotion had come up. She was promoted to the rank of Detective Inspector. It felt right. Many of the friends she had known twelve years earlier at Newcastle University, those who had gone into the private sector, had already started to move into senior management roles; it was time for her, too, to move ahead.

If there was one consolation of the wasted afternoon at Workington it was hearing the gossip which had gone round the court building of the woman defendant who had stripped off down to her bra in one of the courts earlier in the day and who had been sent down to sweat it out in the cells. When something like this happened it provided a welcome diversion for court staff from the usual daily routine. In this instance, the woman had only been left locked up for a few hours. The magistrates were obviously feeling generous: they'd called her back later in the afternoon and after the woman had offered a muttered apology for her behaviour the case had been progressed. A little. The woman had firmly declared that she was not guilty, which had meant that nothing more could be done there and then and that a trial would be necessary. Once again police officers might have to take time off from catching criminals to hang around in the Magistrates' Court waiting for their moment in the witness box.

Chrissy would never had said a word to her colleagues, but privately she was by no means convinced that it had been in the public interest for the Drigg protestors to be brought to court. The nuclear installations on the west Cumbrian coast were the most sensitive sites in the whole of the area covered by Cumbria police and her force regularly undertook exercises with the other emergency services to prepare for an accident or a terrorist incident. So it had certainly been significant news when the word had come through that someone was planning a demonstration down there. But in reality only been a handful of people had turned up and they'd apparently done little more than the usual singing and chanting.

She'd have been inclined to persuade the demonstrators to accept a formal Caution. Or maybe she'd have arrested them, interviewed them at the station and then let them go without charge. Hauling two of them up weeks later in the courts meant that there was the opportunity for more media publicity, and in the circumstances publicity wasn't necessarily all that desirable. A reporter from the Cumbrian Enquirer had been at the hearing, too. Damn: the best thing that could happen to Drigg and its nuclear waste was probably to let it alone, out of sight and out of mind, mouldering away quietly in the Cumbrian countryside.

Still, the decision had been to prosecute. Chrissy suspected it might not be the end of the story. Joan Arkle: that was the name of the woman with the T-shirt and the whale tattoo. Chrissy made a mental note to remember the name.

8.

It was a glorious evening to be out on the fells. The weather was unusually warm for March and they reckoned they had another hour or so of light before they needed to be safely off the hills. They'd met in Little Langdale, close to the Three Shires Inn, and had initially taken the track up to Knotts and High Tilberthwaite. On summer weekends Little Langdale and the countryside around it would be heaving with visitors. Tonight, they reckoned, they'd have the fells to themselves.

Lindsay Maddens had rung Nick Potterton's mobile as he was driving back from Workington and left a message, and Nick had rung her back as soon as he got home to Grasmere. Lindsay and Nick were old friends, both signed up as volunteers with one of the

Lake District's Mountain Rescue Teams and both members of their local running club. They'd be out together again a few days hence, when Coniston and Hawkshead Harriers held its usual weekly pack. But Lindsay had suggested that the Spring weather that Cumbria was experiencing was too good to squander. Did he fancy an early evening run?

Fellrunning was what Nick had discovered when he had moved ten years or so earlier from Kentish Town in north London to make a new life for himself in the Lake District. Back in London, when he was living with his partner Ana and their daughter Rosa, he'd hardly had the time for all the things you needed to do just to keep ordinary life going, let alone time for any sort of sport. There's been a little token jogging on Hampstead Heath and once a charity 10K race that Ana had persuaded him to enter, but nothing more.

But the Lake District mountains cried out to be explored, and what better way to get to know them than to run over them, skipping lightly across the turf and finding all the little sheep trods and hidden paths? Nick parked his car opposite the pub, opened the boot and changed into his fell shoes. He'd already put on running kit in the short time he'd spent at home.

Lindsay arrived a minute or two later, on her road bike. In recent years, Lindsay had become almost as experienced a cyclist as she was fell runner and climber, and she was proving to be a half-way decent swimmer as well. The previous summer Nick and others from the Harriers had cheered her on as she'd undertaken the Windermere triathlon, completing the 1500 metre swim, the 47 km cycle ride around the lake and the 10K race in a total time which had made her the third woman in her V40 age category. She'd also raised a very useful £600 in sponsorship for the Mountain Rescue team.

"Hope you hadn't planned anything else tonight," she said to Nick as she got off her bike and changed into her own fell shoes, taking them from the pannier. She had also come already dressed for running.

"Nothing. This is a good idea."

"Tilberthwaite and Wetherlam?"

"Why not? We've just about got time."

They set out at a steady pace, Nick matching Lindsay's stride. A buzzard circled high over them as they reached open ground.

"Nesting season is getting under way," Nick said.

"Yes, the birds know the seasons better than we do," Lindsay replied.

Together they picked their way up Tilberthwaite Gill, before swinging round to approach the summit of Wetherlam from the north-east.

"I like Wetherlam," Lindsay said. "It's a very workaday sort of mountain. It's seen life."

"It's had its insides bashed around for centuries for the copper deposits and the slate," Nick replied. As they both knew, the flanks of the mountain were riddled with old shafts and levels left from copper-mining days, as well as numerous old quarries.

"Wainwright claims that there are a hundred holes of some kind on Wetherlam, all of them left from the mining," Lindsay added.

They stopped briefly at the cairn on the summit.

"It's a great view," Nick said. "There's Skiddaw. And Helvellyn. And is that Fairfield?"

"You can just see the line of the Pennines across Windermere," Lindsay replied. "And Morecambe Bay in the other direction."

"This is the time of day I love being out. When the sun is low in the sky and the views are really special."

"Yes, but we need to get back. Half an hour to go before the sun goes completely."

Fortunately, running down mountains takes less time than climbing them. Nick and Lindsay took the direct path down to Greenburn Beck, emerging on the road in Little Langdale at Fell Foot Bridge.

"Nick, I've got a suggestion. How about having something to eat in the pub? I've got good lights on the bike and I don't mind cycling home in the dark. And actually I've got something I want to say."

"OK. Your bike will go in my car anyway, if we just take off the front wheel. I can run you home later."

Lindsay ordered the drinks at the Three Shires bar, a modest round of a lime juice and soda for her and a half of bitter from the local Hawkshead Brewery for Nick. They settled down, and waited for the food to arrive.

"Well?" said Nick. "You've something to say?"

Lindsay laughed. "I want to ask a favour. I've decided to do one of the Lakeland challenges this summer, and I need people to recce the route with me and support me on the day."

"Aha," said Nick. "I know what you have in mind. You're planning to do the BG."

The Bob Graham Round must be the most famous Lake District challenge for fellrunners. It involves running a 66 mile circuit of over forty of the highest mountains in England, starting at the old Moot Hall in Keswick's town centre. It includes about 27,000 feet of climbing and there is a time limit too: if it takes you a minute more than 24 hours to get back to the Moot Hall, you've failed the challenge. Every year around a hundred runners try to do the BG, first undertaken back in 1932 by the Keswick runner and hotelier whose name the challenge now carries. Every year more than half these attempts fail. It's not easy.

Lindsay smiled. "I've thought about the BG, although it's getting so ridiculously popular that I'm a little put off. Maybe next year. No, I've got in mind something else. The Frog Graham."

"Sorry?" Nick responded.

"You've not heard of it? It was thought up about twenty years ago by a guy called Peter Hayes and it's becoming increasingly popular. There's thirty-something miles of running and around 15,000 feet of climbing, but you also have to swim across four of the lakes. Bassenthwaite, Crummock Water, Buttermere and then Derwent Water. Like the Bob Graham, you start and finish in Keswick. Reckon I can do it?"

"I'm sure you can. And I'll be happy to support you. Maybe not on the swimming bits." Nick knew his limitations.

"OK. It's a little present to myself. Before… Before I settle down to married life with Phil."

"What?" Nick responded.

"OK, I need to tell you properly. Phil and I have decided we might as well go legit. It's been five years now we've been together. Marriage on a Saturday in mid-May. There'll be a party, of course."

Nick reached across, kissed her and at the same time gave her a very large hug.

"Congratulations," he said.

"You're pleased for us?" Lindsay asked.

"Of course I am."

Nick told himself not ever to remember that, before the kiss and the hug, his first thought had been a little less generous. The first thought, unspoken, that had come into his head had been a selfish one. It was, in broad terms: Lindsay could have been my partner.

Nick had met Lindsay for the first time shortly after his separation from Ana and his move to England's north-west. Lindsay, too, had at the time recently extricated herself from an unhappy marriage to an ambitious young accountant who had left her at their home in the Lakes to be a housewife while he plied his trade, and played the field, around the country. Nick and Lindsay immediately got on well, and there was a time when they could have become lovers. But somehow it had never happened. Nick was ten years Lindsay's senior, and that perhaps had been a factor. Instead they had become simply very good friends.

"Second time lucky for me marriage-wise, I think," Lindsay had gone on. "Phil's a lovely guy."

"He is." Nick had pulled himself together. Phil was a chartered surveyor, living up in Carlisle, and Lindsay herself was a planning officer by background. It was a good match. And although Phil wasn't a runner he was a keen cyclist, a veteran of the Lake District's best known cycling event, the Fred Whitton sportive.

"We're thinking of getting married at St Bega's church on Bassenthwaite Lake. Do you know it? A tiny Saxon church all by itself in the fields near the lake. Osprey territory." Lindsay paused. "Actually the first leg of the Frog Graham Round goes past the church, so that's sort-of why I was attracted to the idea of doing it."

"Sounds really beautiful."

Their conversation was interrupted by the arrival of the food, two portions of beer battered haddock with, of course, the essential Northern addition of mushy peas.

"Bon appetit," said Lindsay, reaching for the little pot of tartare sauce which had also arrived. "Wish Phil and me lots and lots of happiness."

"I absolutely do," Nick replied. "Bon appetit."

9

Elizzabeth came home from work with two pepperoni pizzas and a rather brightly coloured trifle for pudding which she had bought using her staff discount. Most of their household food shopping was bought the same way: the money she saved with the discount really helped see them through to the month end.

Unusually, she had made another purchase too: a bottle of prosecco which had been on special offer beside the tills and which she had been eyeing up all afternoon. She felt she'd earned it.

Surprisingly, given how the day had started, she found herself feeling very positive about things. Dawn, her manager, had been understanding when Elizzabeth finally arrived some time after two. "You could have taken the whole day off, you know. Toothache's a horrible thing".

The customers who, god knows, could sometimes be a grumpy bunch seemed to be matching her mood, chatting with her cheerfully as she swiped their items through the till.

She was relieved that the magistrates' hearing was over, of course, but it was more than that. She felt satisfied with what she had done. The demonstration and its aftermath had turned into a significant event for her. It was silly that she hadn't yet shared the story with Baz, but she'd do that tonight. They'd break open the prosecco together, have a good chat and then head off together to carry things on in the bedroom.

Baz eyed up the prosecco with unconcealed delight. "Bloody hell, babes, you come in to some money or something?" he asked.

"The shop has it on special offer this week. I've been selling it to loads of customers and I thought we deserved a bottle too," she replied.

Baz took the bottle, removed the foil, carefully took off the wire holder and popped the cork. Elizzabeth had already found two glasses.

"Here's to us," she said. "I've had quite a day. I've got loads of things I want to tell you."

"Me too," he said. "I went to the pub for a pint or two after work and Terry was there. He's given me a web address for a video which he says we really have to look at. Once we've had tea I suggest we cuddle up together under a rug and see what we think."

Terry's web address, as Elizzabeth well knew, would lead to a porn site. There was a time when Baz had come back with DVDs which Terry had lent him – or perhaps sold him, who knew? Now it tended to be all online. The films seemed to be getting a little more hardcore, too.

There was no secret between Elizzabeth and her husband about his use of porn. He'd started, he'd told her, when he was about 14 and he had begun showing her his films when they'd started going out together. There was no harm in it, was there?

Certainly the porn almost always had the desired effect on Baz. Elizzabeth's reaction was not so straightforward. There was no disputing that sometimes she found the stuff titillating. She and Baz would mute the sound and get down to business themselves. But other times the on-screen fucking seemed to her very mechanical. The women all had the same attributes: ridiculously big boobs and a cold expression on their faces. There were times, too, when she felt that the men were treating the woman in an unkind way, just as some sort of inert body to play around with – the two-on-one scenes for example. There was nothing very loving about any of it.

The prosecco was drunk and Elizzabeth saw her moment. "OK, Baz," she said, "I need to tell you about what's been happening to me."

"Sure," he replied airily. "Let's just get this film on first." The screen sprang to life, and Baz pulled Elizzabeth closer to him on the sofa, his right arm curled around her body. "Let's give it a score out of 10. See if we can pick up any new techniques, eh?" he said.

Elizzabeth sighed, allowed herself to be cuddled and reached down with her hand towards Baz's crotch, in the way that he always liked. But somehow she was in no mood tonight for the film. It seemed to be veering off into BDSM territory, too, which wasn't something she was particularly into.

"Turn it off," she said. "We can do better than this stuff ourselves."
"Sorry?"
"Take your kit off."
"What, now? In the lounge?"

"Yes, go on. Don't be shy."

"Only if you do the same," he replied.

"OK," she said. They both pulled off their clothes, leaving them on a pile on the floor.

"What now?" Baz enquired.

"Lie on your back. Hands behind your head, I think. You've got a beautiful body. I want to record it."

Baz did as he was told, smirking slightly. Elizzabeth switched on the video camera function on her mobile phone and, very slowly and steadily, ran the camera across his naked body, starting with his head, panning down to his nipples and chest, then on to his cock and then finally down to the toes at the end of his feet. She pushed the stop button.

"OK, want to see yourself?" she asked.

Together they watched the replay. "Wow," he said, "that's good. Your turn now."

She watched him as he reached for his mobile phone. She sat herself cross-legged on the floor, facing him.

"I could blindfold you," he said. "That would be sexier."

"No thanks," she replied.

"OK, but we need to think up some business for you to do." His gaze fell on the bunch of bananas which Elizzabeth had put on the coffee table. "That's it. I could film you giving head to this banana."

"I don't think I want to pleasure a banana," Elizzabeth replied.

"I'd really like it. It would turn me on."

Baz was smiling at her in a way she found endearingly boyish. She found herself smiling back. "Go on then. Got the camera on?"

She half-unpeeled the banana, puckered her lips and got to work. The banana had a slightly strange texture but she found herself getting into the part, bringing her tongue out of her mouth now and again to lick the banana, before pulling it back inside her mouth. She was conscious of Baz's mobile phone pointed at her as she did.

Finally, and abruptly, she took a large bite out of the banana, and stopped.

"That's enough," she said.

"Fucking hell, babes, you had better not try that last bit with my cock," Baz said. He turned the phone round and together they watched the video he had taken. His camerawork, she felt, was rather shakier than hers had been, and all in all she found it unsatisfactory. She had tried to celebrate the beauty of Baz's body. But somehow he hadn't reciprocated. His video was just about his idea of sex.

Her mood changed. "Baz, let's talk," she said.

"Later. Because first I want you to kiss me long and hard." He turned round, positioning his naked body over hers. "First things first." And his lips were against her lips, his tongue against hers.

10.

Joan Arkle left Workington magistrates court in a foul mood. The day had been utterly pointless. There had been nothing to do in the cells except ruminate on the unjust nature of the British justice system. That, and on the fact that at a time when the world was in need of radical change almost everyone seemed content to go through their lives as if everything was just fine.

The magistrates had eventually consented to hear her plea (not guilty, of course) and, as she'd known, her case was then immediately deferred until a trial could be arranged. It was a pity in many ways, she thought, that she hadn't been charged with doing more expensive criminal damage at Drigg, because at least then she could have chosen a Crown Court trial with a jury. As it was, she was stuck in the magistrates' court and they apparently didn't appear to have a slot for her for over five weeks. God, how tedious all this was.

She had to admit that she'd felt let down by Elizzabeth's decision to plead guilty. She understood the reason, but it meant that she was now once more on her own when it came to facing the courts.

And then, to cap a lousy day, just as she'd been leaving the Workington court she was accosted by a journalist from the local rag, presumably sniffing around for a story. She'd given him short shrift.

But her irritation lasted only until she arrived back at Pete's flat and was given an ecstatic welcome, as always, by Goldie.

"Good girl. Have you been bored? Let's go for a walk."

As if intuiting what Joan had said, the dog bounded across to the front door of the flat. Joan hurriedly grabbed a light jacket for herself, a fully biodegradable plastic bag for clearing up anything Goldie might want to leave behind, and the dog lead. As she had done each day since staying at Maryport with Pete, she headed through the streets of terraced houses towards the sea, turned north along the path beside the sea-wall and then continued up towards the cliffs. She relished the wind in her hair, coming straight in off the Irish Sea. The hills of south-west Scotland were in view across the water, looking enticingly close at hand.

Goldie had been her companion for over two years. A black Labrador, or more precisely a mongrel for whom there must have been quite a number of Labradors somewhere in the family tree, Goldie had come from the dog rescue people when she was still a puppy. Joan had taken considerable effort to train her properly.

"I've had a shitty day," Joan told Goldie.

The dog wagged her tail in sympathy.

"But on the other hand the garage has just texted to say that the van's fixed. We'll be back on the road tomorrow. That'll be good, won't it?"

More wagging.

"The bill's pretty horrendous, but we'll manage. We always do."

Joan stopped at a bench, leaving Goldie to run free along the hillside, and pulled out her mobile phone to check activity on Twitter. She'd had to give up her phone when she was in the cells, but had tweeted immediately she was outside the court. She'd sent a photo of the Fracking Stupid T-shirt, with a note saying "Do you think my T-shirt is offensive? Workington magistrates do. Have just spent most of the day locked up because of it."

As she'd expected, she had already had more than fifty 'Likes' and a host of comments. She quickly scrolled through to find a load of supportive messages waiting for her. Twitter was turning out to be an important campaigning platform, Joan felt, and she had now acquired over 5,000 followers, mostly other activists but also all the main environmental and climate change organisations. In turn, she made a point of always following them as well. She quickly retweeted something that had come through from Extinction Rebellion and another from Greenpeace about the overfishing of European fish stocks. As usual, she added the hashtags #ClimateEmergency and

#ClimateChange.

The dog returned to her, putting her head on Joan's knees.

"Don't move, Goldie. I want to take a photo of you."

The photo was taken and sent out to the world, accompanying another tweet which Joan quickly typed. It read: "Here's my gorgeous dog Goldie. Goldie has been fully #vegan for the past three months, and is thriving on her diet." The dog food came from a specialist online company and was admittedly considerably more expensive than the supermarket tins of dog food, but Joan had long stopped eating dead animals herself and Goldie seemed content to do likewise. Joan completed her text with the hashtag #VeganLifestyle.

Joan checked her new Twitter followers. They included a climate change group in Nova Scotia and an anti-nuclear group in Normandy who somehow must have heard of her. There was also a new individual follower, somebody with the handle @nickpott254. She added this to the list of Twitter accounts she followed herself.

"Goldie, Pete's been very sweet, but I'll be sleeping on the sofa tonight," Joan told the dog. Pete had been one of the small group of demonstrators at Drigg, though he'd managed to avoid getting arrested. Joan was grateful for the use of his flat, but she'd never intended to get into a long-term relationship with him. He might be disappointed, but he'd get over it.

"Maybe I'll call by the co-op and buy Pete a bottle of wine as a farewell present," Joan said once more to Goldie. "What do you think? Something on special offer that's cheap but vegan." The dog again wagged her tail.

11.

"There's no story."

"Nothing at all?"

"Well, not a sizzling 600 word page lead, if that's what you were hoping for."

It was Tuesday, and Nick was back in Molly's office at the Enquirer. Technically Nick freelanced two days a week at the Enquirer, leaving the rest of his time free for other freelance commitments or for book writing. In reality, since *Nuclear Power: Yes Please?* had bombed, he had excess time on his hands. Molly appreciated his help, and was able to find at least something to offer him from the scrapings of the fast-disappearing freelance budget.

"The main person behind the demo is a woman called Joan Arkle. She's interesting and we definitely need to cover her in due course, even if she did tell me to fuck off." Nick went on to tell Molly briefly of the episode in court with the T-shirt and Molly laughed. "But she's pleaded not guilty, so I'm not sure we can say anything much about yesterday until the trial's over, can we?"

Nick knew that Molly would be better briefed on the risks for newspapers of being in contempt of court.

"No, it'll be best to wait. Pity. You could at least cover the woman who pleaded guilty."

"Yes, although it's only worth a couple of paragraphs."

"A couple of pars is better than nothing. But listen, I do have something else that's come in. How would you like to interview a King this afternoon?"

"What sort of king?"

"The King of Rheged, to be precise."

"Rheged is that visitor place and conference centre near Penrith?"

"Yes it is, but Rheged is also the name of the old Celtic kingdom hereabouts which disappeared when the Saxons moved in. We all used to speak some form of Welsh and recite epic poems to each other. It was just a little before my time, you understand."

"And somehow the Rheged monarchy has survived centuries of Saxon oppression?"

"Actually the King of Rheged is self-appointed. His name is Phillip Petherton and his life work appears to be to reclaim our Celtic roots. I did a feature on him a few years back, when he tried to set up a sort of eisteddfod for Cumbria. I seem to remember white bed-sheets were involved as costumes. Anyway, pleasant enough chap, and just another in the fine line of English eccentrics who help fill our newspapers."

Nick laughed.

"Actually he'd probably accept he was eccentric but he'd hate being accused of being English," Molly said, after a pause. "He'll probably try to talk to you in Cumbrian, by the way."

"Dialect?"

"No, a separate language very like Welsh. There was some linguistic research done some years ago to see if the language could be recreated, but basically it couldn't. But what did get created was a complete new language based on what Cumbrian Welsh could have been like. It's called Cumbraek. There are some sensible language experts involved in this story, by the way, even if the King of Rheged isn't one of them. You could check back through our cuttings. I've covered the development of Cumbraek a few times over the years."

"I'm not sure my T-line shorthand works for Cumbraek. Anyway, what precisely is Mr Petherton wanting to tell us?"

"Mr Petherton has decided it is time for a local voice at the polling stations. There may be one established Cumbrian regional political party already but apparently we need more. He's launching a party called A New Voice for Cumbria in time for the May local elections. He rang me yesterday afternoon to tell me. You could do a phone interview but somehow I think you'd enjoy meeting him in person. He told me he was available all day today."

Obviously history had not been kind to Rheged royalty. Nick found himself stopping the car outside a very modest semi on a 1970s estate on the outskirts of Kendal. A flagpole, from which was flying what Nick realised must be the Cumbrian flag, dominated the small front garden.

The front door was opened by a young woman who was dressed in a short green dress, the top half of which comprised a close-fitting laced-up bodice. The woman was either about to head off for a Morris dance rehearsal, Nick thought, or audition as an extra in a remake of Game of Thrones.

Nick was shown in to the front room and asked to take a seat. "The king is not quite ready for you, but I'm sure he will see you soon," she said, leaving the room and firmly closing the door.

Nick sat down as instructed and eyed up the room, which was unremarkable. A rather amateurish oil painting of what Nick recognised as the outline of Blencathra hung over the fireplace and another small watercolour, of what was probably Brougham Castle, the mediaeval fortress a little way outside Penrith, was on the wall behind the sofa. A bookshelf held some popular biographies and a few illustrated books about Cumbria and the Lake District.

Time passed. Nick looked at his watch. He had been left alone now for approaching ten minutes. More time passed.

Nick had a hunch what was going on. In his career for the national press, Nick had on a few occasions been deliberately and unnecessarily kept waiting to meet an interviewee. It was some sort of power game, and it wasn't a game Nick was prepared to accept, certainly not from a cod royal in Kendal.

He got up, opened the door to the hall and then immediately opened the closed door facing him behind which, he guessed, he would find Mr Petherton. He found a man dressed in a curious mediaeval-style gown behind a low wooden table, flanked on his right by the young woman who had opened the front door and to his left by another, older, woman who was identically dressed. Mr Petherton's wife and daughter, Nick guessed. Behind the three of them was a bright green banner on which someone had embroidered the words A New Voice for Cumbria.

"Oh, ah, I'm afraid we're not quite ready..." the man began, looking startled.

"My apologies, Mr Petherton, I'm sorry but I only have a few minutes left before I have to dash off to cover another story. Tight deadlines, I'm sure you understand," Nick said.

"Yes, of course. Well. *Bore da, hoadh cuvarvot genich,*" the man responded, trying to regain the initiative.

"Thank you, and my apologies for not being able to conduct this interview in Cumbraek. Tell me about your manifesto."

Nick had expected Mr Petherton to launch into demands for bardic recitals, compulsory Cumbraek on the curriculum and saluting of the Cumbrian flag by all local authority workers each morning when they started work. This would have made his job of writing up the article afterwards a real joy. But Mr Petherton was not quite so obliging.

"We just think Cumbrian people get a raw deal," he said.

"Go on."

"Well, take housing. One of our slogans is *Local homes for local people.*" Phillip Petherton turned to the younger woman at his side.

"Go on, Paula, you've done the research on this, you explain."

"We need decent social housing," Paula took over. "There's a chronic shortage of homes for local people, particularly local young people on low incomes and we know that the wages in Cumbria are low. Of course we're not against tourism, but second homes and holiday homes are stopping people from affording their own homes as well as stifling community life."

She stopped briefly and then continued. "Your own paper had that report recently of almost 7,500 second homes in Cumbria, and you said that was probably an underestimate. One in four homes in Borrowdale. Forty percent of all the homes in Patterdale. Primary schools closing because there are no longer enough children growing up in the villages. I've read that, in the heart of the Lake District, the house price to income ratio is over twelve to one. I mean, it's completely unsustainable."

Nick nodded, his pencil making marks on his reporter's notebook.

"I think the issue is well known," he said. "But what I want to know is what you intend to do."

"Make sure new houses have covenants which restrict them to locals. Push up the taxes second home owners pay," Paula said. "Help villages where the community itself wants to build new homes for their young people. There's plenty that could be done."

"That sounds pretty anti-tourist to me."

"Of course it's not. This whole county would be broke if we didn't have holiday-makers. What we need though is a tourist tax on overnight stays which wouldn't be noticed but could help generate useful revenue."

Nick nodded, simply by way of encouragement.

"Then there's farming. Our traditional upland farmers have been struggling to make ends meet, when the vast bulk of the agricultural subsidies have been going to the enormous landowners down in the flat lands. We've got to find ways of supporting hill farmers. And of helping young people who want to take up farming and can't even afford a farming tenancy."

Paula came to a halt.

"Some of your policies are those that mainstream parties might well support. A New Voice for Cumbria sounds unnecessary. And"

- Nick gestured towards the table – "I'm not sure many people will take your party seriously if you dress up in strange costumes. Or when it is led by someone who calls himself a king."

Mr Petherton sighed. "I know, but it attracts attention. And what's wrong anyway with a little make-belief? Our old history is important to me. *Yr Hen Ogledd*, the Old North, that's what they called our part of Britain."

"You really want to be a serious political party? This isn't another Monster Raving Looney initiative?"

"We're deadly serious about trying to tackle the problems that Cumbria faces today," Paula replied. "A New Voice for Cumbria isn't a joke. You'll be surprised. We're going to be in the news a great deal from now on."

12.

It was good to have a few drinks on a Friday night, to celebrate the arrival of the weekend, Baz believed. Admittedly, tonight was Thursday not Friday, but on the other hand it didn't hurt to get a little practice in whenever you could.

He was at the bar of his usual pub in Keswick buying a round. He and Mick had come direct from work, and had been joined shortly afterwards by Horsey. Terry was the last to arrive.

"How did you like the video?" Terry asked when Baz had returned to their table with the drinks.

"Yeah, good. Although Elizzabeth made me turn it off halfway through."

"Too steamy for your missus?"

"No, she told me to stop watching the screen and to get my clothes off."

There was laughter from the others around the table.

"A sudden attack of shagitis, eh?" asked Mick.

"Who said anything about shagging?" said Terry. "Everyone knows that Baz and Elizzabeth just gaze lovingly into each other's eyes. That's married life for you."

Baz had first met Terry five years back when they'd both been students at the Lakes College in Workington, studying to qualify as electricians. Baz had stuck it out, now had his Level 2 Diploma and was making half-way decent money for a local firm that mostly did commercial contracts. Terry hadn't been able to stomach the course, had had a spot of trouble with the law and had disappeared from the scene for a time. Now he was back in town, running a vaping business from a small shop in a side street. Baz wasn't sure quite how well the shop was doing, but at least Terry always had enough money on him when it was his turn to get in the drinks.

"We haven't been told yet whether you did obey your wife and take your clothes off," went on Horsey.

"He always obeys his wife," said Terry. "Love, honour and obey, those were the vows he made."

Baz was the only one of his mates to be married. He and Elizzabeth had got together when they were fifteen and had stayed together ever since, leaving aside those times when they had both checked to see what else, and who else, might be out there. The marriage, which had happened a year previously at Cockermouth's registry office, had come shortly after one of Baz's other girlfriends had given him the shove. He and Elizzabeth had decided that first love was true love.

"Shut up, Terry, I asked Baz a question. Did you take off your clothes?"

"May have done," said Baz.

"And what about Elizzabeth? Did she take her clothes off?"

"May have done," repeated Baz.

There was more laughter around the table.

"Anyway, she said we could do better than the porn film," Baz added.

"Oh yeah?" This was Terry.

"Want to see Elizzabeth practising her technique?" Baz wondered momentarily as he got out his mobile phone whether he was sharing something that Elizzabeth would have preferred to have kept private but, what the hell, Terry, Mick and Horsey were good mates. It was just a bit of a laugh anyway.

One by one the others watched the short video which Baz showed them.

"Mm," said Mick. "You'd better discourage that biting habit she's got."

"I'm not sure my girlfriend would allow me to film her like that," said Horsey.

"Would that be your imaginary girlfriend that nobody's ever met, Horsey?" said Mick.

Horsey made as if to punch Mick's face and Mick gave a pretend punch back. Horsey, technically speaking, answered to the name of Rick when he was at work in the kitchens of one of Keswick's less fancy hotels, but Terry had once a long time before told him that he was a dark horse and the nickname had stuck. It was true, Horsey often kept his cards close to his chest.

The conversation moved on to a new subject, Carlisle United's forthcoming match at the weekend. All four had been kids when Carlisle had had a long run in League One and they had stayed loyal even after the club was relegated down a tier when they were teenagers. There was talk of how the last few matches in the season would go, and how much they'd be asked to pay for a season ticket for the following year.

It was Mick's turn to buy a round. Four full pint glasses were put on the table, joining the twelve empty ones which still hadn't been cleared away.

"Look at this," said Terry, once again changing the subject. "Someone is speaking some sense for once."

An earlier drinker in the pub had left that day's edition of the Cumbrian Enquirer on the neighbouring table and Terry had been idly flicking through it. "Cumbrian homes for Cumbrians. They'll get my vote when the election comes."

"Terry, you've never voted in your life. I shouldn't think you're even on the list of voters," said Horsey.

"That's because all politicians are shite. I'd vote for somebody who promised to get rid of the Poles and all the other refugees. The reason why there's no decent housing in Cumbria is because they've been given it all."

"I don't think Poles are refugees," suggested Mick.

"Well, whatever. Migrants, then."

"Your grandparents came from Ireland."

"Yeah, but that was years back." Terry stopped, his eye caught by a news item lower down the page. "Fuck me, look at this."

He showed Mick and Horsey what he'd found, shielding the paper so that Baz couldn't read what it said.

"I see your missus has been busy, Baz. You're obviously not giving her satisfaction in the bedroom. Bananas aren't enough," Terry went on.

"Let me see," Baz said, snatching the paper. The news story carried the headline *Anti-nuclear demonstrator fined*, and under it he was astonished to read the name of Elizzabeth, her age, and their home address.

"Fucking hell," he muttered under his breath.

"I don't think you even knew," said Horsey.

"The fucking bitch," Baz muttered again to himself.

"It's obvious, really," Horsey went on. "There was this really cool activist guy there, with dreadlocks and a peace badge and a knitted woolly hat and mucky jeans…"

But Horsey was speaking to an empty chair. Baz had drunk his full pint in one swig and was already on his way to the door. "The bitch," he repeated. "Wait till I see her."

13.

Joan reached for her phone and, as she always did, took a photograph of the meal she was about to eat. Today it was a simple chickpea curry, made with a tin of chickpeas she'd picked up from the supermarket in Keswick where Elizzabeth worked, but spiced up with some fresh ginger, some coriander seeds that she had crushed with a pestle in her mortar, and some fresh coriander leaves as garnish. With it she'd cooked plain basmati rice. She thought it looked pretty bloody good. The photo went on her Twitter account, along with the message *Here's tonight's meal Yum yum,* and the usual #VeganLifestyle hashtag. Her daily posts, along with the accompanying photos were attracting considerable comment from her followers. What had begun as an occasional set of tweets had become a fixed part of Joan's life.

She was cooking just for herself again, after the time staying with Pete when she'd cooked for him as well. She'd picked up the van from the garage on Tuesday morning and since then had been parked up on some land up a quiet back road between the A66 and Ullswater. The land was close to outhouses attached to a smallholding which was being run by a couple on the fringes of the environmental movement who had told her that she wouldn't be in their way. Even better, there was a basic outside toilet she could use beside one of the barns and there was cold running water.

Life was getting back to rights, she felt. She'd got up very early the past two mornings, both times driving the van to Threlkeld and wandering down to the banks of the river Glenderamackin just as it was getting light. Otters had recently been reported there on one of the local wildlife sites on Facebook and Joan was sure she identified otter spraint close by the water, black and coarse and – when she opened the droppings with her fingers – full of tiny fish scales and crayfish parts. The otters themselves had not appeared, however. She would try again, of course.

Goldie seemed contented, too, at being back in the van with her. The dog knew the routine. She knew that she had to remain in the van for Joan's early morning forays, but she also knew that her morning walk wouldn't be long delayed. Now she was curled at Joan's feet, looking up as the chickpea curry began to be eaten.

Joan turned on the phone's camera again, took a snap of the dog, and sent out another tweet. *Not enough curry for you, Goldie, but don't worry because your scrumptious vegan dinner is on its way #VeganLifestyle.*

There was still some residual chat on her Twitter feed going on about her Fracking Stupid T-shirt, but in general the conversations had moved on. She retweeted a link to a new report on how plant-based proteins were being grown to look and taste like meat. In twenty years' time, the report's authors had claimed, the livestock industry would have gone the way of horse-drawn carts. Twenty years? Joan wasn't sure the world could wait that long.

Aimlessly, she stopped to read a comment which had just come in in response to her last tweet. *I don't give a toss if you kill yourself eating rabbit food. But your dog needs meat. You people claim to love animals but you are killing the dog.*

Before she had thought it through, Joan had responded. *Dogs can thrive on #vegan diets. Why don't you check the facts before tweeting nonsense?*

Whoever had tweeted her was obviously still online. An immediate reply, slightly misspelled, came through: *You stupid twat. Dogs are carniferous. They're descended from wolves. I hope you have your dog taken away from you.*

Joan involuntarily shuddered, turned off the Twitter feed and reached down to stroke behind Goldie's ears. "There are nasty people out there," she told the dog. "But we're OK together, aren't we?" The dog licked her outstretched hand.

But her mood had changed. She pushed away the half-eaten curry and picked up the tin whistle which she in the process of learning. It had got dark outside an hour or so previously, and even though it wasn't yet eight o'clock she'd probably practise for an hour or so and then have an early bed. She'd try Threlkeld again first thing tomorrow and see if her luck changed.

Her phone rang just as she was half-way through tackling King of the Fairies, trying to make her fingers sound as effortlessly Irish on the D whistle as she possibly could. She sighed and reached across to answer the phone.

"Hi Elizzabeth," she said, looking at the name displayed on the screen.

"Hi Joan. Listen, I don't want to be a nuisance…"

There was a moment of silence. "Baz and I have had a bit of an argument."

"Shit. Are you OK?"

"I'm in Keswick bus station. I've realised that all my money and cards are back in the house."

There was another pause.

"I don't suppose you're anywhere nearby? Could you come and get me?"

14.

Thursday evenings were, by long tradition, the evening when Nick's running club met up for the usual weekly packrun. The club ran on the Coniston fells in the summer when the days were long, but at this time of year made do with road running. Nick bagged a lift with a friend down to the village of Hawkshead for the rendezvous at the Kings Arms at seven o'clock. Lindsay led the run that evening, down the eastern shore of little Esthwaite Water to Near Sawtrey, then on to Eel House before turning back again to Hawkshead via the western side of Esthwaite Water. In all, the group ran about eight or nine kilometres, not so very far perhaps but enough to justify a drink in the bar.

Lindsay bought Nick a pint of the locally brewed Hawkshead bitter, ordered a glass of red wine for herself, and together they found a table.

"I'm planning a recce of the first leg very early on Sunday, the leg over Skiddaw and down to Bassenthwaite," Lindsay said. As Nick immediately knew, she was talking again of the Frog Graham Round. "I wondered if you were interested?"

"How early?" Nick replied.

"Well, when I do it for real in the summer I plan to leave Keswick at three in the morning, so that it will be getting light on Skiddaw summit. I thought if I left about 5am that would be about the equivalent time for this time of year. The route from Skiddaw is back to Carl Side and then there's a bit of a scree scramble down through Dodd Wood to Mirehouse and the little church. I reckon it will take us two hours, maybe a little longer. If you came, we could take two cars so we could get back to Keswick. You'd be able to be home again by nine."

"OK, let's do it," Nick said. "If you drive to my place in Grasmere for four o'clock we can go up the A591 in convoy."

They clinked their glasses, a decision made.

"Lindsay, in exchange let me show you something which came in the post this morning. It's from Catalonia. From Mataró to be precise."

Lindsay raised her eyebrows. "Isn't that where you told me Ana was living these days. With her fella."

"Yes, with Jordi," Nick replied, trying hard not to sound bitter. "The letter appears to be from Ana, but there's something odd about it."

"Has Ana been in touch recently?"

"Not at all. We last saw each other when Rosa got married when we both did the adult thing and made polite conversation." Rosa and her partner Becky had married in an old Georgian mansion on Hampstead Heath a couple of summers earlier, and of course both her parents had been required to be there, and to be on their best behaviour. "It sounds pathetic, I know, but we use Rosa as an intermediary if we need to communicate. We have each other's addresses but no mobile phone numbers or anything like that."

"And now Ana has written to you directly?" Lindsay asked.

"Yes. If it's a genuine letter. Look."

Lindsay read the letter which Nick had produced. It read:

Hello Nick. I hope you are well and I am sorry that we do not keep the contact. I am well. I have left El Periódico and moved to La Vanguardia. Did you know they publish an edition each day in català as well as spanish? I hope you are also finding journalistic work. Rosa told me you had written a very good book, I hope it has been successfull. I need to ask you something important, but it will be difficult to spell out in a letter so I have asked Rosa to contact you very soon and explain. She says she will try to visit you. Please help me if you possibly can. Una abraçada, Anna

"A bit mysterious, I agree," Lindsay said. "What's that bit at the end?"

"She's sending me a hug. It's like saying 'love' at the end of a letter. I'm not taking it personally. But what's odd is what comes after that. The name. Ana's only got one 'n'."

"Are you sure?"

"I should be. We lived together for eighteen years and had a daughter together."

"Yes." Lindsay had detected the edge of bitterness in Nick's voice. "Have you contacted Rosa yet?"

"I've tried to several times, but I can't reach her. I think she's on a business trip, possibly Singapore." Rosa was a commercial lawyer, working for one of the large international consultancy companies. "I imagine she'll ring when she's back in a European time zone."

"OK, so until she does you'll just have to stifle your curiosity. You can tell me the full story on Sunday morning. Still sure you can get up that early?"

"Still sure," Nick replied.

15

Molly Everett arrived at the Enquirer's office on Friday morning a few minutes before ten, and was greeted by Petra at the reception desk.

"Oh, hello Molly, your ten o'clock visitor has already turned up. I've shown her to your office."

"What ten o'clock appointment?" Molly replied, surprised.

"A youngish woman with pinkey hair. She said she was here to see the editor."

"Did she?" Molly replied, and headed straight for her office. Inside, sitting at Molly's desk on her swivel chair, was indeed a woman with short-cut hair coloured pink. Not only was she sitting on the chair, she appeared to have decided that she intended to remain in it. She had a chain attached to a cuff around her left wrist which she had threaded around the metal legs of the chair and then reattached to the cuff with a large padlock.

"I'm Molly Everett, the editor of the Cumbrian Enquirer," Molly said immediately. "Perhaps you can tell me who you are."

"My name is Joan Arkle, and I've been waiting to talk to you," came the reply.

"Well, I'm here now. I am always happy to talk to readers of the Enquirer, although normally people don't feel the need to chain themselves up."

Joan shrugged. "Just a precaution," she said.

Molly looked more closely at her visitor, recalling Nick's account of the Magistrates Court hearing at Workington. Unless she was badly mistaken, this was the woman with a large whale tattooed somewhere in the region of her left boob.

Molly pulled up a spare chair. "Would you like a coffee?"

"No," Joan replied firmly. There was silence. "Take a look at this," she went on.

Joan pulled out her mobile phone, passing it across to where Molly was now sitting. On the phone was a photograph of a woman in her twenties, with two black eyes.

"Perhaps you can explain why you are showing me this?" Molly asked.

"Yes I can. This woman's name is Elizzabeth Bowes and it's thanks to the Cumbrian Enquirer that she has two black eyes and a possible broken cheekbone. I spent most of the early hours of this morning with her at A&E in Whitehaven."

Joan pulled out from her shoulder bag a copy of the week's edition of the Enquirer already open at one of the inside pages, and passed it across to Molly.

"You wrote a news story giving Elizzabeth's name and address, and her arsehole of a husband reads it. OK, so maybe Elizzabeth should have chosen who she was going to marry more carefully, but I think you carry the bulk of the blame. And what's more Elizzabeth expects to lose her job as well now. She told me that she'd pleaded with your journalist not to include her name. So go on – justify yourself."

"I'm sorry, but there's a public interest in reporting what happens in the courts."

"Public interest? Don't talk such crap. Where's the public interest in seeing a young woman suffer domestic violence and get the sack?"

"I understand your anger but –"

"You understand nothing. And while we're on the subject, when did you last run something in your paper about the epidemic of domestic violence that women suffer in our society? Did you know on average the police receive a hundred calls relating to domestic violence every hour? Three women are killed by their partners or ex-partners every week? Go on, when did you last report any of this in your paper? Probably never, because you are just an establishment rag propagating the idea that everything in society's fine and dandy and there just a few little people like me on the margins with funny ideas trying to stir up trouble."

"I am not prepared to be preached at," Molly replied. "The Cumbrian Enquirer has always been proudly independent and I decide as editor what I think is sufficiently of public interest to go into my paper. And that's why people choose to buy the Enquirer each week."

"You appeal to people's basest instincts. You still haven't explained to me the journalistic ethics of reporting Elizzabeth's name and address."

Joan was interrupted as Nick came through the door into Molly's office. It was not good timing.

"Oh sorry, Molly, I'm interrupting. I'll drop in later," Nick said.

"No, you'll stay and listen to me," Joan immediately replied. "You're the toe-rag journalist who's most to blame. You wrote the bloody news story."

Nick and Molly exchanged glances.

"As I said, as editor I take full responsibility for everything in the paper, so any complaints come to me, not to any of my journalists," Molly replied. "I am trying to listen carefully to what you are saying. What I would like to know is what precisely you are demanding of me which will allow you to remove the padlock from that chain and permit me to begin my day's work."

"I want you to run this article on climate change in next week's edition," Joan said, passing a typed sheet across to the editor. "By way of penance."

Molly laughed. "I'm sorry, we do not print any editorial written externally. If we did, you really would be legitimate in claiming we had sold out on our independence. People with the biggest wallets would rapidly decide what people could read."

There was a pause while Joan absorbed this information.

"You ran a stupid feature this week on a man who pretends he is King of Cumbria. I'm asking for a similar amount of space next week on something which is deadly serious, and that's climate change. On why some of us are prepared to go on demonstrations and get ourselves arrested and have to pay ridiculous fines because actually the future of the world is very much at risk. That's what my article tries to say."

Molly read through the article which Joan had offered her, and then passed it to Nick to read.

"This is a good piece of writing," she said eventually. "But the principle remains that we don't run editorial copy we haven't written ourselves. But I can offer you a compromise. If you are happy for us to interview you, we'll set up an interview and run a feature length article on climate change next week. I'll ask Nick to write it. He's our most experienced writer."

"I'll need to approve the text after it's written," Joan said.

"Impossible," said Molly. "That's not the way papers work. But, despite what you think, the Enquirer believes in ethical journalism.

Nick will write the piece in a way that allows you to express your views. Won't you, Nick?"

"Yes," Nick replied. "When can we schedule the interview? Where do you live?"

Joan appeared to be pondering. Eventually she reached down and removed the padlock, unthreading the chain.

"I live in a campervan, and let's say that I'll be at the pull-in beside the old AA box at Dunmail Raise on Monday at 11 o'clock. But remember this. If I don't like what you write, I'll be back. I'll be very happy to chain myself into your office for days on end if I have to."

"Of course, but I'm sure it won't be necessary," Molly replied, extending her hand towards Joan. Joan reluctantly shook it, glared at Nick, and left the room.

"Well," said Molly, "that was interesting. I hope you don't mind handling the feature."

"It'll make a change from the King of Rheged," Nick replied.

Molly didn't immediately reply. "I rather liked her, you know. A woman on a mission."

"Yes," Nick replied. "Gutsy".

"She's obviously genuine. She needs to be careful, though. Societies don't always like individuals who come along and tell them what they don't want to hear."

"Hmm," was Nick's reply. "Should we have printed that story?"

"The other woman's name and address? It's a court report."

"Yes. Even if it led to unpleasant consequences. Probably best not to think too deeply about this journalism business."

"Talking of which, I need to tell you what I've got coming up at lunchtime. Another visit to the accountant," Molly went on.

"Things still not looking good for the Enquirer?" Nick said.

"No," Molly replied. "Advertising disappearing online, readers disappearing online, income in freefall."

"Anything I can do?"

"I don't think so. Not at the moment anyway."

"Will we pull through?"

There was silence from Molly.

"If you want my honest opinion, I think we have a few more weeks left. And after that – well, who knows?" she eventually replied.

16.

It was turning into an unusual Saturday night. Elizzabeth's face was a mess but nothing had been broken. Even so, she didn't want to go out and she certainly didn't want to be seen by any of her friends. So a quiet night in, in a flat in the out-of-the-way town that was Maryport, was perhaps the best thing in the circumstances.

Joan had made the necessary arrangements with Pete: Elizzabeth would stay for a day or two on the sofa in his place. She'd go back to Baz very soon, she had decided, but she just needed a few more days by herself to think things through. And Joan's campervan frankly had been a little too cosy. She had stayed there for what remained of Thursday night after the hospital had let her go, and on Friday night too, but she'd found it hard to get any sleep. Goldie the dog occupied the floor area behind the front seats, whiffling quietly to herself as she slept. That left just what Joan called her rock-and-roll bed for Joan and herself. There was one double duvet to share, although Joan had also rustled up a sheet and rug for Elizzabeth's side of the bed. Still, Joan slept, it appeared, without wearing any clothes and had unselfconsciously stripped before getting into the bed.

Joan had turned out to be a good friend and had helped her through the A&E experience but Elizzabeth felt uncomfortable at being quite so close to a naked woman, and one who she had to admit she found quite intimidating. She kept on her bra and knickers and tried to keep firmly to her side of the bed. She could hear Joan breathing peacefully in her sleep, and once or twice had felt Joan's hand reach out unconsciously towards her. Briefly, Elizzabeth thought of responding and turning towards Joan's body. God knows she needed some human contact and affection just at the moment. But instead she crammed herself even further into the edge of the bed.

Ever since Thursday evening, the phone calls and texts had been coming in almost incessantly from Baz. Elizzabeth had decided not to answer any of the calls, but she read the texts each time her phone pinged. You could tell immediately what Baz was up to.

Most of the time he was full of remorse, pleading with Elizzabeth to forgive him and promising never to lay a hand on her ever again. On early Friday evening, though, the tone had become more maudlin. "I love you and miss you loads, Betty-lizz," he wrote, using the pet name he called her. "You've got to come back."

By later that evening, the mood had changed again. "You're a cold cow," he had texted. "You don't care for me at all. I'm your husband and I've a right to have my wife at home. What the fuck are you playing at?" Almost certainly, he was in the pub with his mates.

She had written just one text back, in response to the stream that had arrived. "Baz, I love you too but you hurt me badly and I need a little time to recover. We'll be OK again, you and me, but just be patient."

There'd be a lot of rebuilding work to do before her life was fully straight. She had had to cancel two shifts at the supermarket, for Friday afternoon and all day Saturday, and this time Dawn was unsympathetic. There were too many other people, it seemed, living in Keswick and desperate for a boring job on the check-outs for crap pay. Elizzabeth found herself, as she'd feared, jobless. Joan had tried to cheer her up. "There's lots of ways to get by," she'd said. "You can be self-employed like me. Lots of flexibility and we can have time to organise more demos together." Elizzabeth said nothing. She could think only of the £50 a month which Workington Magistrates were waiting to receive from her.

Elizzabeth had been driven in Joan's van across to Maryport on Saturday morning. She'd known Pete only a little, from the planning meetings and then from the Drigg demonstration itself, but he seemed a nice enough guy. A bit younger than her, perhaps. To her surprise, she found that she had become something of a celebrity in his eyes.

"I really admire your courage," he'd said. "Getting arrested, and all that. I found the police a bit scary."

She hadn't liked to admit that she hadn't planned to get arrested, that she was just trying to finish off the ball of wool she was weaving into the fence.

"And what was it like at the magistrates' court?" Pete had gone on. "Were they really horrible?"

Elizzabeth, despite herself, found his attention endearing. He was easy company, very different from Baz of course, but the sort of person who – had they met before Baz and she had decided to get back together and do the marriage bit – she just might have wanted to get to know better.

"Want to see what I had done the other week?" Pete had said, after they had shared a vegan pasta dish together and he had broken open the bottle of white wine Joan had given him. He rolled up the left sleeve of his T-shirt to show off a tattoo of the Extinction Rebellion hourglass logo. It was, he admitted, his first tattoo.

Elizzabeth rolled up the right leg of her jeans to show off the chain she had had tattooed above her ankle, where an ankle bracelet would be worn.

"Is that your only tattoo?" Pete asked.

Elizzabeth laughed. "Just one other at the moment. On my back, below my neck."

"Let's see."

She pulled up the back of her T-shirt so the tattoo was visible. It had been well designed. It showed a bird of prey, its wings half outspread and claws extended to seize its quarry. It had cost Elizzabeth money she'd not really been able to afford but even though she could only see it in a mirror it gave her confidence to know the tattoo was there. Sometimes, when she was feeling particularly vulnerable, she thought of the bird riding on her back and felt stronger.

"That's amazing," Pete went on, moving his hand across it. "Still, you've got space on your arms for an Extinction Rebellion tattoo like mine if you wanted." He reached across to stroke her upper arm in the place where the tattoo would go. It felt like a caress.

They had been sitting together on the sofa, and had found themselves gradually moving closer together. Pete's arm made an exploratory move around her shoulders. They exchanged a kiss.

"I don't want to push you, but… a shag would be very pleasant," Pete said eventually.

Elizzabeth responded by pulling off her jeans and unfastening her bra. Pete responded by taking off his T-shirt and the shorts he had been wearing. They kissed again, more intently.

"That's nice," Elizzabeth said, as their lips parted.

From the other end of the room came a ping from her phone, as another message arrived. Elizzabeth broke away from the kiss. The moment was lost.

"Sorry, Pete, this isn't what I want. I'm really sorry."

"That's OK, I understand," he said after a moment. He turned away and pulled his clothes on again. "I'll - I'll put the kettle on."

17.

It was not the best of days to be on the mountains. After leaving Lindsay's car at Mirehouse, a little way up the Bassenthwaite road from Keswick, Nick had driven them both to the informal parking place at the foot of the Skiddaw path, round the back of Latrigg. It was about five o'clock and still dark as they started out.

"I don't think we'll see a beautiful dawn from the top of Skiddaw today," Nick said. "The clag is well and truly down."

Immediately they had left the car they had been swallowed up in a thick wet white cloud. Tourists to the Lake District may buy souvenir guidebooks showing sun-bathed mountains above beautiful lakes of aquamarine but in reality the Cumbrian clag is just as likely as the sun to welcome anyone venturing on to the fells.

"My head-torch is pretty ineffective in this stuff," Lindsay said.

"At least it's a well-beaten footpath," Nick replied.

They ran steadily, confidently picking their way among the rocks which lay at their feet. Two eyes from a surprised sheep showed up at one point, reflected in their head-torch lights.

"Thank you for agreeing to this. We must both be crazy," Lindsay said a little later. They had reached the summit of Skiddaw, pausing there briefly before turning back to the smaller summit of Carl Side. Night had passed, but the daylight merely served to reinforce the whiteness of the cloud they were in.

"There's a path down the hillside into the woods somewhere here, I think," Lindsay went on. They skittered down the hillside on a small stony path to emerge at a stile where the fellside gave way to woodland. "Bull's eye. This is Dodd Wood. My car should be just at the bottom, I think."

The area of parking where Lindsay had left her vehicle would, later in the day, almost certainly be full of visitors' cars, come to try to see the Bassenthwaite ospreys from the two viewing areas that had been created in the woods. Although the Lake District normally attracts several pairs of breeding ospreys it is the Bassenthwaite pair who have celebrity billing, at least as far as the Cumbrian tourism industry is concerned.

"Mind going on a little further? Down to the lake edge? We can visit St Bega's chapel and see where the nuptials will be happening," Lindsay said. The clag lifted as they emerged from the wood and there, sure enough, was her car, parked where they had left it more than two hours earlier. A white campervan had in the interim been parked nearby, but otherwise everything was deserted. It was still only just after seven.

"Nuptials? Is that what you're calling it? Very fancy!" Nick asked. Lindsay laughed. They knew each other well.

"So where are you and Phil planning to live? Will you keep your own places?" Nick continued. Phil had a Victorian terrace house in Carlisle while Lindsay lived in a pleasant first floor flat she had bought in Ambleside.

"I'm going to rent out my place, I think. Move up to Carlisle," Lindsay replied. "In fact, I'm planning to move very soon. No need to wait for the wedding certificate."

"OK. You'll be missed round here."

"I'll give up Mountain Rescue in due course. But I'll stay with the Harriers if I can. It's not too far to travel."

"It's far enough," Nick replied, feeling again a pang of self-pity. Carlisle was a good hour's drive north of his home in Grasmere village.

"Anyway what's your news?" asked Lindsay as they took the field footpaths down towards Lake Bassenthwaite, making for the church. "Anything come through from Rosa?"

"She texted yesterday from Seoul. Just a short message which said 'Sorry to be elusive. Is it OK if we come next weekend? Any chance of Oxenholme, Saturday, 12.21pm?'"

They both laughed. Oxenholme was the mainline station for the southern Lakes, and Nick could usually be persuaded to take the car across to pick up Rosa from the London train.

"It sounds as though Becky is coming as well. That's good,"

Lindsay said.

"It is, yes," Nick replied. Rosa and Becky had met in their first term at Warwick University, had fallen for each other immediately and been together ever since then. Their marriage almost two years previously had simply formalised their relationship. Nick had grown to love Becky almost as much as he loved his own daughter, although usually it was only Rosa who made the long train journey north to see her father.

"I've not seen Becky for ages," Nick went on. He hesitated. "I've been just a little worried about how they've been getting on."

"Have you?"

"Nothing definite to go on. Probably unnecessary parental anxiety. Probably nothing at all." He stopped, changing the subject. "So who precisely was St Bega?"

They had arrived at the church and were standing looking across the churchyard to the lakeside beyond. The cloud had given way to early morning sunlight.

"Daughter of an Irish chieftain, about to be married off against her will to a Viking prince. Boo, hiss. So she left her father, did a runner across the Irish Sea and landed in Cumbria. And then she dedicated her life to the church and ended up becoming sainted, or whatever the word is. That's what Wikipedia told me, anyway." They both laughed.

They ran the short distance between the church and the lake. "This is where you'll have to put on your wetsuit when you do the Frog Graham?" Nick said.

"Yes, this is lake Number One. After this it's Crummock Water and Buttermere. And then the final slog across Derwent Water. Plus thirty-six miles of fell running in between, of course."

"You'll be fine." Nick stopped. He had suddenly noticed, a little over to the left, the figure of a solitary woman, standing motionless beside the lake. He pointed her out to Lindsay, gesturing and without saying anything.

"Weird. It's pretty early on a Sunday morning to be out here alone," Lindsay responded, in a low voice.

"What do you think she's doing? It's not a very obvious place to be a tourist," Nick replied.

The sound must have carried, for the woman turned round to look at them. Despite the distance, they could see that she was scowling aggressively.

It was at that moment that Nick realised that he knew the woman, and that she had recognised him.

"Bloody hell," he said.

Lindsay looked at him curiously. "What's up?"

"I know that woman," he replied.

"Yes?"

"I've got to interview her tomorrow. Joan Arkle. It's Joan Arkle."

18.

Horsey was cradling his pint, biding his time and saying nothing as the others talked. It was Sunday evening, and they were back in the pub for the fourth evening running. Baz needed company. His friends had rallied round.

Eventually the conversation around the table petered out. Horsey saw his moment.

"Want to know about the woman who's really to blame? I mean, for what's happened to Elizzabeth?" he said. He passed his mobile phone to Baz.

"What's this?" Baz replied.

"The Twitter feed from a woman called Joan Arkle," Horsey replied.

"It says Joan Sparkle here."

"That's her Twitter handle, stupid."

Baz scrolled down through the entries for the Twitter user called @joan_sparkle. Terry and Mick moved round behind him, so that they could see the screen as well.

"Loads of stuff about saving the world. Climate change stuff. Surprise surprise she's a vegetarian."

"A vegan," Horsey corrected.

"OK, OK. Lots of pictures of weird food. And she's got a scruffy dog who is a vegan too, poor bastard dog. What the fuck was Elizzabeth doing associating with her?"

Horsey didn't reply. Baz spoke again.

"Horsey, nice one! You got me! You're winding me up! I really believed you for a minute."

Horsey smiled his enigmatic smile.

"You're wrong," he said. "It was a piece of piss to track Joan Arkle down. The Cumbrian Enquirer talked about a demo at Drigg, so I just did a Google search on 'demonstration' and 'Drigg' and Joan Arkle's name lit up the internet. And it wasn't precisely hard to find her on Twitter either. It's not much of a fake name she's using."

"Well done, detective chief inspector Horsey McHorseface," Terry interjected.

"Fuck off," Horsey replied.

Baz was still looking at the Twitter feed. "Keep looking," Horsey went on. "Found the stuff yet about the planning meetings for the demo? Found the mention yet of someone called Elizabeth with two 'zz's? – there are not many of those in Cumbria."

Baz put Horsey's phone down and sat quietly. It was Terry who picked it up.

"Right, let's give that bitch a few choice responses to her stupid tweets," he said.

"Not on my Twitter account," Horsey said quickly. "Anything we say needs to be difficult to trace. I'll set up a new account. What user name do you want?"

"Proud patriot," Terry said.

"It's taken," Horsey said after a few key strokes. "In fact, there are loads of users called @proudpatriot something. Think of something else."

"Proud Brit," Mick suggested.

"Proud meateater," said Baz.

"That's not taken," Horsey said. "We'll use that."

The account was activated and one after the other they took turns in responding to Joan Arkle's tweets. Terry was the last. "*You're a cunt and you don't deserve to live. Or your fucking dog,*" he typed. "There, that's enough for now. We can do more tomorrow. In fact, every time she tweets we can answer."

There was a sense of satisfaction around the table at a job completed. They all reached for their pints again.

"So let's have a look at your own tweets, Horsey," Terry said eventually, picking up the phone again. "Bloody hell, why are you retweeting all this stuff from something called A New Voice for Cumbria?"

"We discussed them a few days ago, you muppet. Cumbrian homes for Cumbrians. You said you'd vote for them, Terry. And you can, because guess who is going to be their Keswick election candidate in May?"

Terry looked mystified.

"It's me," Horsey replied. "I thought A New Voice for Cumbria sounded like they were talking sense so I got in touch with them. I got in touch with the young woman who's basically running it. Paula signed me up as a member and we talked things through and next thing I knew she asked if I wanted to be their candidate here."

"Horsey, what did I say, you really are a dark horse. Tell us more about this mysterious Paula. Have you slept with her yet?" Terry asked.

"Fuck off," Horsey replied. "I'm serious about this. I thought we could organise our own rally in town sometime soon. Decent homes for decent Cumbrian people. Get some Cumbrian flags and some St George flags. Want to take part?"

"I'll be there," said Baz. "Let's drink to it. To Horsey's political career. May it be happy and glorious. Long may he reign over us. God save the Horsey."

They drank their pints dry.

"My round next," said Mick.

19.

"So what do you want to know?"

It was, Nick thought, as though Joan Arkle had spat the question at him. There had been no attempt at any initial pleasantries, no pretence of politeness.

Nick had half expected the Dunmail Raise lay-by to be empty of campervans when he had driven there on Monday, making sure he arrived a little before the eleven o'clock time that he and Joan Arkle had agreed. But, whatever else she might be, clearly Joan Arkle was not unreliable. Her white campervan, immediately identifiable from the stickers which plastered the back window as belonging to an activist, was already there.

Joan had opened the sliding door to him and gestured to one of the seats at the table at the back of her camper van. "You'd better sit there," she instructed him. Then she had ostentatiously made herself a mug of what looked like herb tea in the little galley area at the side of the van and brought it across to the other side of the table, where she sat down. He hadn't been asked if he would like anything to drink. He would decline if he was offered something now, he thought to himself.

"Do you mind the digital recorder?" Nick asked her, placing a small machine beside her mug. "I'll be taking shorthand notes too." Joan said nothing, simply responding with one of her trademark scowls. Nick took this as a signal to proceed.

"You said last Friday that our newspaper needed to increase our coverage of climate change. Tell me why this issue is important to you."

This time Joan sighed. "You read my article," she said.

"I did, and with your permission I want to quote some of what you wrote. But I'm interested in hearing from you directly, in your own words. Lots of people have a broad idea of what climate change means, but most people don't go on to campaign about it in the way that you do. Why do you?"

Another sigh. "Where do I start? You won't have heard of the IPCC, of course."

"The UN's Intergovernmental Panel on Climate Change? Yes, I've read the latest Assessment Report. It's an impressive scientific review of the issue," Nick replied. He had read the summaries of the main IPCC reports some years back as part of his research for *Nuclear Power: Yes Please?* but he had also made sure he was adequately prepared for the morning's interview, revisiting the relevant websites and skim-reading the key documents.

"We've basically squandered the last thirty-plus years. The IPCC was set up by the UN in 1988 when there was first international concern about the risks of climate change and when there was time to do something about it. Instead, nothing has fundamentally happened and the planet's in the shit." Joan noticed Nick's pencil making marks on his notebook. "You can quote me on that, not that you will," she said.

"Were you at the Paris summit in 2015?" Nick asked.

"Of course I was at Paris. Well, for the fringe events and the demonstrations. The Copenhagen summit in 2009, too. I was young then and really optimistic that finally things were moving. Copenhagen was exciting. But then the governments got together and, guess what, the summit achieved fuck all."

"But Paris did achieve something, perhaps?"

Somehow Nick would have the task of turning all this into acceptable copy, into a feature which the Cumbrian Enquirer's audience might actually want to read. He already had a shrewd idea of how he would do this, and it certainly didn't involve focusing on high-level international conventions, however important they might be. But if the interview was to achieve anything at all, he had to persuade Joan Arkle to be more forthcoming. At this stage of proceedings, a question on the Paris Agreement was what was called for, he thought.

"Well OK, I suppose it was a step forward that almost two hundred countries did actually manage to sign an agreement on climate change. Even if it's all promises and nothing that represents firm commitments. And even if the Agreement isn't to bring down carbon emissions, merely to try to keep the increase in carbon emissions under control. And even if the target of keeping increases to 1.5 degrees Centigrade above pre-industrial levels will still mean devastating effects on the environment. And even if the US has now reneged on the Agreement and none of the major industrialised countries has actually met the emission reduction targets they pledged. I mean, no serious scientist challenges the main IPCC findings any more, so why are we being so blind to the future of our planet?"

Joan Arkle was at last talking. She told Nick of the predicted effects of a 1.5 degree increase in global temperatures. She talked of the climate implications, of the increased likelihood of severe weather events such as floods and droughts, of the melting of the arctic ice caps, of the rise in sea levels and the effect on coastal areas, of the risk to plant and animal life of species loss as their habitat changed, of the problems of water supply and food security for humans. She paused.

"And that's with a 1.5 degree increase in temperature, which may be the Paris target but which nobody shows any sign of actually being able to achieve. We're heading at the moment for a 2 degree increase as a minimum, and some reports are suggesting the world will be 3 degrees or even 4 degrees warmer than it was around 1800. That's quite unsustainable for a planet in which people can continue to live. Humans are an unbelievably stupid race."

Nick had been taking copious shorthand notes. "You're very well informed," he said when Joan finally came to a halt.

She looked up at him. "Don't patronise me," she said, her eyes suddenly flashing with anger.

As if in response to the raised sound of Joan's voice, the large dog who had been lying quietly under the table stirred and made a short growling sound.

"It's all right. Lie down. Good girl, Goldie."

So the dog was called Goldie. Nick looked at the mass of black fur at his feet and decided to say nothing. Instead he persevered.

"Joan, please, you don't need to be so aggressive," he went on. "I need your help to make this article as powerful as possible."

Joan made a non-committal noise.

Nick moved on to one of the questions he had prepared. "Tell me more about your own involvement in the campaign. How did you first get interested?"

"I don't see why my story is relevant. Your article needs to be about the risks of climate change, not about me."

"Yes, it will be. But journalism always has a challenge to meet. It has to try to make complicated issues interesting to people. To do this we bring in the human interest angle. We need stories of individuals, just to connect with readers' own lives."

"I don't want to talk about myself."

"I'm sorry, but I thought you wanted a feature which was effective. If I don't mention you, and your passion for the issue, and your determination to do something to stop runaway carbon emissions, I'm not sure anyone will read a word I write. And my editor will give me a bollocking."

Joan gave a half-smile. "I've never trusted the press," she said.

"So it would appear. And yet you understand that you need to use us," Nick replied.

"Yes. Reluctantly."

"OK, let me ask you another question for you to answer reluctantly. I know you were involved in the anti-fracking movement before you moved to Cumbria. Tell me about that."

Joan was silent, and then began replying. "I was down at some of the protests in Lancashire. In North Yorkshire, too. Fracking is just amazingly stupid. It means extracting fossil fuels, which is the last thing we should be doing at the moment, and there's all sorts of environmental hazards. But of course it's profitable and it's big in the US and these days we do what the US tells us."

"You were arrested several times?" Nick asked. He had done his research, having read the newspaper reports of Joan Arkle's many court appearances on one of the online databases that he could access from the Enquirer's office.

"Getting arrested the first time may be a big deal for some people, but I've stopped worrying. We know from our history that it is only by breaking the law that things ever get achieved. Think of the suffragettes. Before them, there was the fight by the Chartists for the vote. Then there were the Diggers who squatted on common land during the English Civil War and got fucked over by the magistrates for their efforts. I mean, it's disgusting that the police are used to protect the profits of big business by arresting demonstrators. And that magistrates spend their time punishing people who are actually trying to bring about a better world."

"Don't we need laws?"

"We need laws that help protect ordinary people. That's not what we've got at the moment."

Nick felt that, finally, his article was going to work. This was the material he needed. He tried another question. "And before fracking became an issue, were you active in other campaigns?"

"The Heathrow protests, yes. And my first big NVDA set-piece was at a bloody enormous power station in the Midlands that was burning coal and pushing out tons of greenhouse gases into the atmosphere all the time. It was an amazing event, so empowering. Mind you, a police dog bit me and I got a nasty wound. I got arrested too although in the end I wasn't one of those they charged. They were eventually all acquitted, of course, although it had to go to appeal. It turned out that there was a Metropolitan Police spy with us, basically an agent provocateur. Bastards."

"Do you come from a politically active family?"

There was a pause before Joan Arkle replied. "I grew up in care. They couldn't find anyone who wanted to adopt me," she replied.

"I see," Nick replied carefully. "Where did you grow up?"

"Down south. It really doesn't matter. Can we get back to the subject?"

"OK, Joan. So let's see, you've moved from the anti-fracking protests in Lancashire to Cumbria. What's good about Cumbria?"

"Isn't it bloody obvious? It's beautiful here. I don't spend all my time in prison cells, you know. I love the natural world. The outdoors is my life."

"But campaigning is important to you too. You organised the Drigg protest. What now?"

"Climate change is going to have a devastating effect on upland farming, but most farmers haven't really realised it. So a few of us have decided to organise a public meeting in Keswick. We hope lots of farmers will come. I've arranged a really good speaker, it won't just be me."

"I can mention this, I assume?" Nick asked. The intro to his article was rapidly taking shape in his head.

"Yeah, I guess so. It's Sunday week, at 7.30pm. We've booked a local church hall. Apparently they let it out for this sort of thing."

Joan Arkle had become almost friendly. She reached for her tablet from across the table, and called up the Facebook page which was advertising the event. Nick read the title: Cumbrian Farming and Climate Change. He made a careful note.

The interview was coming to an end. Joan's tablet had switched back to the screen saver, a beautiful photograph of two otter cubs, one with a small fish clasped in its mouth.

"That's a great image," Nick said. "Where did the photo come from?"

Joan looked at him. "I took it of course. On Saturday morning, in fact, down at the river's edge at Threlkeld."

"You're a good photographer."

"Wildlife photography. It's how I make my living. Animals and birds and plants."

"You're freelance?"

"Yes. Almost all my sales come from one of the online agencies. It's not great income but it's enough to live on."

Nick suddenly made a connection. "I saw you yesterday at Bassenthwaite, by the lake and I wondered what you were doing. Were you taking photographs?"

"Checking out possible otter activity on the lake. Yes, I saw you. That was your girlfriend you were with, I assume."

"Just a friend," Nick replied quickly.

"I think the two of you scared away every living thing for several miles but never mind. Just try not to get in my way every time I'm out working."

Nick laughed. "I'll do my best."

Joan's mood suddenly changed again. "Listen, I need you to piss off now, I've got things to do. I've trusted you. I hope I haven't trusted you too much. Tell your editor I know where her office is."

"I know you do. I will try to be as fair as I can."

"Be warned. I'll be out to buy a copy of the paper first thing Thursday. It better be good."

20.

DI Chrissy Chambers sighed. It was Wednesday, work was piling up, and she wasn't sure how she would clear everything that needed doing before she headed off for the leave she'd booked in from Friday. She loved her work, but they were hopelessly understaffed. She was juggling an ever-increasing work load, and she had two fewer DSs and several fewer DCs working on her team than she really needed.

She and her husband Tony had arranged to have an extended weekend break in Prague, and she was looking forward to some good meals and some good Czech beer. But actually she'd still be thinking about work, and particularly her career, while she was away.

Her line manager, a woman Detective Chief Inspector only a year or two older than her, was going off on maternity leave later in the year, and Chrissy felt she had a good chance of being lined up as her cover. A few months acting up would give her the springboard to move her career on to the next level to become, she hoped, a DCI in her own right. She was in any case a long way through the College of Policing's Senior Investigating Officer Development Programme, which – all being well – would get her the necessary Level 3 professional recognition and the chance to lead her own major enquiries.

But all this meant more work. There was the revision she needed to do on the course's organised crime module, and somehow she also had to squeeze in the time to get her professional development portfolio up to date. The PDP would have to be submitted in a couple of weeks' time, when she'd be interviewed on exactly what professional experience she already had under her belt.

But in the meantime, she was enmeshed in Cumbria's drug problem. Like everywhere else in the country, her area had its share of users of illegal drugs, and that meant in turn a criminal hierarchy of street dealers, regional suppliers, drug transporters and the odd bent accountant or solicitor prepared to add their support. It was big business, a multi-billion pound industry which in terms of turnover, Chrissy had once read, was already approaching half that of the legitimate alcohol industry. Massive profits could be made if you were happy to break the law and live in a culture where violence could sometimes be an aspect of business life. And if you could avoid the attention of Chrissy Chambers and her colleagues, of course.

The task facing Chrissy and DS Peter Blackford, the Detective Sergeant who was working directly under her on this, was to try to unpeel, layer by layer, the infrastructure of the trade which ultimately led to the drugs being available on Cumbrian street corners to a rag-tag collection of end users. It was relatively easy to pull in the street-level dealers, but it could be frustratingly difficult to get to the big boys higher up the chain.

Of course, the public had no idea of the amount of investigative work which went on. Well-intentioned citizens who were alarmed to see drugs being sold openly in their neighbourhoods were ringing the police all the time to report what was happening, and Chrissy knew that they couldn't understand why nothing seemed to be being done in response. Just the other week an old school friend of hers who had bumped into her in Booth's in Windermere had complained that he'd taken down the number plate and the make of car of two guys who had been dealing near his house. "I rang the police but I don't know why I bothered. Sorry, Chrissy, but nothing's been done. The same car's been back several times since then," he'd told her.

Chrissy had tried to sound reassuring, suggesting that the police were doing things behind the scenes. But she had to admit to herself afterwards that what they were able to do was a little like mopping up a torrential flood with a dish-cloth. And for each dealer successfully sent down there were others to take their place. Most people didn't set out deliberately to work in the drugs business, they simply got drawn in through family members or friendship groups.

Still, little by little, piece by piece, the evidence could build up. At the moment, DS Blackford was in Chrissy Chambers' office, giving his DI a briefing on a back-street shop in Keswick which had recently attracted his attention.

"It sells vaping equipment and oils but it seems remarkably lacking in many regular customers," he told Chrissy.

"Who's the owner?"

"Young guy called Terry Venables, boss. No, not the footballer."

"Anything on him?"

"Yes, a conviction for actual bodily harm three years back. Basically a Friday night fight after closing time, by all accounts. 80 hours community order. Nothing else on the PNC."

"OK. So?"

"We think he might be using the shop for storage purposes. And/or laundering some of the cash. Or he might be simply running a retail business."

"We're a nation of shop-keepers, after all. Keep me posted," Chrissy said. DS Blackford took the cue, and left her office.

21.

Goldie shifted restlessly.

"All right, old girl, I'll give you your lunchtime walk soon. Just give me five more minutes. The world's gone mad this morning," Joan Arkle told the dog.

Thursday had started quietly enough. Joan had got up shortly before dawn and, in what was becoming almost a daily ritual, had driven the van once again to the car park at Dodd Wood. For the past couple of days, her focus had been not on otters or ospreys but on the wildlife in the woodland itself. More precisely, she was on the track of Squirrel Nutkin.

Britain's native red squirrel has lost out badly to the grey squirrel, which was introduced into the country from North America in the late nineteenth century and is now firmly established in most of the woodlands where once red squirrels had held sway. But there are still corners of England where red squirrels cling on, and the Lake District is one of these.

Perhaps it's thanks to Beatrix Potter's children story of the impertinent red squirrel and his narrow escape from an owl called Old Brown that there's quite so much public affection for the animal. Certainly, Joan knew that there was a seemingly endless demand at the online picture agency she used for photos of red squirrels, particularly if they could be photographed nibbling acorns and looking cute. Joan disliked this. She considered herself a serious wildlife photographer and rejected the sort of cosy approach to nature represented by Beatrix Potter's tribe of imitators. On the other hand, Joan needed to make a living and red squirrels helped bring in the pennies.

Today, though, there had been no red squirrels. What she had managed to photograph, and in close-up too, was a treecreeper. She'd spotted the little bird with its beautiful slender bill hurrying its way up the trunk of one of the trees in the wood, on the look-out for insects. She'd managed six or eight shots before the bird had flown away to the base of a second tree. A couple of the photos worked well, she thought. Next time she had access to a fast internet connection she'd upload them to the agency website.

On the way back from Dodd Wood she stopped in Keswick, and – with a certain amount of dread – went into a newsagent to buy the new edition of the Cumbrian Enquirer. The chain and padlock were ready in the van, in case they were needed.

She took the paper in to her favourite vegetarian café, ordered a mug of Rooibos tea, and opened the paper to find a photograph of her face looking back at her from one of the inside pages. She read the article alongside carefully. It was much too focused on her as an individual for her liking, but on the other hand it did set out the climate change case succinctly. She noticed some of her original article being used, parts of it converted into direct speech which had been attributed to her. Her own article was definitely superior, she thought, but what the journalist had done was, she supposed, acceptable. Just about.

On the plus side, he'd given plenty of useful publicity to her forthcoming public meeting. *Cumbrian farming must change, says climate change activist* read the headline. The opening paragraphs of the feature were also focused on the event:

Local farmers and environmentalists will be able to debate the effect of climate change on the future of Lake District farming, at a public meeting to be held in Keswick on Sunday week (14th). The meeting, organised by local climate change activist Joan Arkle, will discuss how current agricultural practices are contributing to greenhouse gas emissions.

"The way humans use the land contributes about a quarter of all greenhouse gases worldwide, and half of this comes from animal production. We can't continue farming with the same numbers of cattle and sheep in the countryside if we want to stop runaway global warming," claims Ms Arkle.

She took out her phone, photographed the article and added it as an attachment to her Twitter feed, along with the hashtags #ClimateEmergency and #ClimateChange. If she was going to get a decent audience for the public meeting she knew she had to use Twitter as often as she could, although increasingly she found her account was attracting all the wrong sort of attention. One user in particular had become particularly active in the past few days with tweets which were becoming more and more abusive. Sure enough a few minutes later a new tweet came through from this account. *Vegans make a particularly tasty alternative to beef. A good butcher will know the best cuts. Chop chop chop. Rump, breast meat, delicious! You have been warned.* The tweet ended with the hashtag #climatechangehoax.

She sighed. Many people, she knew, would report this sort of stuff straight to the police. That was the last thing she was going to do. Should she notify Twitter itself? Yes, she probably should. Would doing so stop the endless vomit of filth coming through? Probably not, she thought.

The mug of tea was drunk, the smartphone temporarily put away and the campervan driven back to its current home near Ullswater when the first phone calls started coming through. Obviously other people had begun to read the article in the Cumbrian Enquirer. Two of the rival regional newspapers were the first to ring, in both cases wanting more information about the Keswick public meeting. What was she planning? Who was speaking? Was she expecting hostile questions? Was she anticipating trouble?

With mounting levels of irritation, she batted back the questions. A few more minutes passed and the phone rang again: it was the newsdesk at the BBC regional TV station. Could she get across to Newcastle that evening for a live interview on Look North? No? Well, perhaps she could get to the Carlisle regional newsroom? All right, could she at the very least do a recorded interview that afternoon? They would take her up to one of the Cumbrian fells, they said, and arrange for a nice flock of Herdwick sheep to be somewhere in the background.

It was arranged that she would meet the BBC reporter in Threlkeld at two o'clock with the plan being to walk a little way up Blencathra for the filming. She rang off, hoping this had been the right decision. She was feeling uncomfortable at the way that the media were focusing in on her individually. On the other hand, years back, when she had undertaken training ready for her first non-violent direct action, the group she was with had talked through the reasons why they were prepared to do NVDA. They'd agreed that they were doing it to raise the public's awareness of the issue of global warming. Appearing on the BBC early evening news would certainly help do this.

"Goldie," she said to the dog. "Am I doing the right thing?"

The dog wagged her tail. Joan took that as a yes.

All was quiet for at least fifteen minutes. Then the phone rang again. This time it was a man who introduced himself as the representative of the National Farmers' Union locally.

"I'm not against you organising this meeting, but I confess I'm surprised that the NFU isn't invited to take part. After all, we represent 55,000 farmers in England and Wales," he began. "Don't you think we should have a speaker?"

Joan Arkle was caught wrong-footed.

"All the speakers are fixed already," she ad-libbed. "But people can speak afterwards from the floor."

"I'm sure a great many of my members will be there and will have things to say," he replied ominously.

"Farming is responsible for terrible amounts of greenhouse gas emissions. We've got to stop."

"Farmers are committed to doing their bit. I'm sorry, Miss Arkle, but I don't think that picking on hard-working Cumbrian hill-farmers, who by and large survive on very low incomes, is going to advance your cause."

"We're not against farmers. We just need to have fewer cows and fewer sheep on our hills."

"Most people eat meat and the food system couldn't cope if they suddenly all stopped. And it's the cows and sheep which you seem not to like that help keep the Lake District landscape looking so beautiful."

"Landscapes change. What Wordsworth saw in the Lake District is very different from today's landscape," Joan responded. She'd read this a few days earlier in a specialist academic article she had come across.

"Perhaps, but the Lake District is an UNESCO World Heritage Site mainly because of the importance of its historic landscape. Let me ask you again. Will you allow a farmer to address your meeting?"

"Sorry," Joan replied. "This is my meeting. Why don't you call your own meeting?"

After she'd rung off, she wondered if perhaps she had handled the call as well as she could have done. But the man had irritated her. He'd spoken with a sort of confidence which always brought out her hackles: he'd been to public school, probably, and then a decent university. And no doubt he had a brother who was a police inspector and an uncle who was a magistrate. People like him were part of a smug establishment which was bringing the country and the world to the brink of disaster.

"You agree with me, don't you?" she said to the black fur at her feet. Goldie looked back at her lovingly.

22.

Horsey was the last to get to the pub.

"Any of you see the local TV news this evening?" he asked.

"Nah," said Terry. "I never watch that stuff. Why?"

"The best friend of Baz's Elizzabeth was featured," Horsey replied.

"What?" Baz said.

"Joan Arkle, Cumbria's own communist activist and mad tweeter."

"Oh, her," Baz replied. "Elizzabeth's no longer got anything to do with her."

"Are you sure?"

"Yes, Elizzabeth and I talked everything through yesterday. I said sorry and gave her a bunch of roses. She's come home."

"Shouldn't she have said sorry to you?" Terry asked. "She was bang out of order."

"Yeah, but I was out of order too. I shouldn't have been angry with her in the way I was. So, anyway, we've both said sorry. End of story."

Baz took a slurp from his pint.

"Why was Joan Activist on telly?" Mick enquired of Horsey.

"She's saying that cows are burping too much and the nasty methane they produce is wrecking the world. Hundreds of litres of methane from each cow each day. Well, it was something like that."

"That's a bit random," Mick responded.

"Yes, and then the BBC interviewed a hill farmer who said basically that she was talking bollocks."

"Good for him," Terry replied. "Put that woman in her place."

"Read this, everyone," Horsey said. He pulled out the new edition of the Cumbrian Enquirer and put it on the pub table.

"Any news stories this week about Baz's Elizzabeth?" asked Terry when he saw the paper.

"Shut it," Baz replied.

"No, just a big feature about you-know-who. And that's what I need to talk to you all about."

"Why?"

"She's organising a public meeting in Keswick on Sunday week, for her climate change friends. All about how Cumbrian farming has to change. I'm going to be there and I want you there too."

"You're going to her meeting?" said Baz in astonishment.

"No, I'm organising a rally outside. It's on the theme Defend Cumbrian Farming. I've talked to A New Voice for Cumbria, and they're up for it. It'll be the first rally of my election campaign. Remember, I'm going to be on the ballot paper come the May elections."

"Isn't there a home game that Sunday?" asked Mick.

"Yes, but it's an early kick-off. We can get back to Keswick in time. There'll be time for a few jars, too. I think demos go better if you've got a few beers inside you."

"What do you have in mind?"

"Like I said, St George's flags, posters with slogans, that sort of thing. Make a bit of noise, frighten off the climate change wallies. Are you up for it?"

"Sure. Why not?" said Terry. "I could get the word round to a few other people I know, too. They'd come along."

"OK," said Horsey. "That's agreed. I'll buy the next round, so we can drink to its success."

Terry had his smartphone out. "I think it's time for another tweet," said Terry. "Time to take the sparkle out of Miss Arkle."

23.

Rosa had texted her father from the train to say that it was running twenty minutes late. "Sorry, Dad, we're somewhere the far side of

Preston at the moment. Wrong type of snow on the tracks, I think," she'd said. The day was unseasonably warm, another Spring day of clear blue skies and not a hint of rain.

But the text had arrived as Nick was already on his way to Oxenholme station to meet her and Becky. It was, he thought ruefully after he had arrived, parked, and put on Radio 4 to while away the time, a little like the way he'd had to wait endlessly in the car for her to emerge from a friend's house or a party when she was a teenager in north London. And now she was married and was almost certainly earning far more than he could have dreamed of in his days working for the national press.

Of course he didn't really mind the wait. He was looking forward enormously to having the weekend with Rosa, the first time for more than three months that she had been able to come up to visit him. And with Becky, too, how good that would be. He'd put clean bedding on the single bed in his spare room which normally acted as an office and an untidy store for his research notes when he was working from home. He'd move in there, leaving the double bed for Rosa and Becky. And he'd booked a table for three, for a meal that evening in an up-and-coming restaurant in Ambleside which Lindsay had recommended to him. They'd get a taxi from his place to Ambleside and back again to Grasmere village at the end of the evening, so they could enjoy a bottle or two of wine with the meal. All in all, he was anticipating a really enjoyable weekend.

Eventually the train pulled in. Nick left the car and wandered on to the platform as the first of the passengers began to get off, his gaze sweeping the far end of the train as he waited for Rosa and Becky to appear. A cheerful voice behind him almost made him jump.

"Hello, Dad," it said. Nick turned round. There was Rosa, his much-loved daughter, standing just behind him, obviously having just emerged from one of the first class carriages.

But there was no Becky with her. Instead, Rosa was accompanied by another woman whom Nick had never seen before. Nick guessed that, like Rosa, she was in her early thirties, and she was wearing a cream-coloured hoodie and close-fitting jeans cut in a style that somehow looked different from the usual. She was dragging a large suitcase on wheels behind her.

The words were out before Nick could stop himself. "Where's Becky? You said she was coming too."

"No. I didn't," Rosa replied, sounding surprised. "Becky was never going to be able to come. She's over with her parents this weekend. I'm not sure what it is, maybe an aunt's birthday or something like that."

Nick tried to absorb the information. "You used the word 'we' when you said you were coming up. I thought that meant…" He tailed off.

"I meant I was coming with Lluïsa, of course." Rosa turned to speak to the woman, changing into the language which was both her own mother's and Lluïsa's native tongue. "Et presento el meu pare, Lluïsa. És periodista també, com et vaig dir. Parla una mica de català però necessita que li parlis a poc a poc!" She and Lluïsa laughed.

Nick had been taught Catalan more than thirty years before by the woman who had swept him off his feet and won his heart. He had first met Ana when he was working at The Independent and she was the London correspondent of El País, working from a desk near his in the office in City Road which The Indy had occupied at the time. Later, after Rosa had been born, Ana and he would sometimes speak Catalan together at home, particularly when they didn't want their daughter to know what they were discussing. What happened was that Rosa learned Catalan almost as quickly as she learned English. She soon became much more proficient than Nick.

So the strange woman must be Catalan too, he realised. With a terrible feeling in the pit of his stomach, he deduced that this must be Rosa's new girlfriend. He'd suspected things weren't going well with the relationship with Becky, but this was still horribly unexpected. It was a shock too that Rosa had felt able to bring her girlfriend up to meet him without at least giving him a little more warning.

There was something else bothering him too. He wasn't sure that he liked the coincidence that both he and Rosa had fallen for women from Catalonia. How disconcerting that was.

Rosa was continuing to talk to him. "Don't worry, Dad, Lluïsa has pretty good English, so you won't need to polish up your old language skills. And of course she wants to improve her English while she's staying up here."

"Sorry?" Nick replied, now even more confused.

"I mean, just talk to her as you would to anyone else. What she needs is the practice of hearing colloquial English spoken."

Lluïsa offered her hand to Nick. "I'm pleased to meet you, Mr Potterton," she said.

"Yes, pleased to meet you too," he replied, adding as an afterthought the appropriate greeting in Catalan. "Molt de gust."

"Encantada," she replied.

"Dad, it's almost one o'clock." Rosa had pulled out her smartphone and was looking intently at Google maps. "There's a pub just beyond the station here that says it does bar food. Shall we go?"

The careful preparations Nick had made for the weekend with Rosa and Becky had included the light salad he had prepared for lunch and which was waiting for them on the kitchen table back in Grasmere. All his plans were evaporating fast. "Good idea," he found himself saying.

They settled down in the pub, Rosa going to the bar to order two glasses of dry white wine for Lluïsa and herself and an apple juice for her father. She brought back a copy of the lunchtime menu.

"I've booked a table for a meal out tonight. I mean, if that's what you think you want to do." Nick was no longer taking anything for granted.

"Sounds ideal," Rosa replied. "OK, so we'd better have something light now. Ciabattas maybe? What about the Cumberland sausage and red onion marmalade ciabatta, Dad, since we're in Cumberland?"

"Actually we're in what was Westmorland, but yes, go for it. I'll have the brie ciabatta."

"I will take the brie ciabatta too," Lluïsa said. And then, politely, she added: "Excuse me, I need to visit the washroom."

Nick found himself alone with Rosa. "I'm pleased to meet Lluïsa, of course," he began. "She seems a very nice person. It would just have been good to know that you were bringing her. And, you know, that you'd started a new relationship."

Rosa looked dumbstruck. "But Lluïsa and I aren't lovers, don't be silly. And you knew Lluïsa was coming, Mum wrote to you and explained everything, didn't she."

Nick pulled out the letter from Ana which he had brought with him and passed it across to his daughter. "Your mother did write to me, but I had no idea what she was trying to say."

Rosa took the letter and skim-read it. *I hope you are well... I have left El Periódico... I hope you are also finding journalistic work... I need to ask you something important, but it will be difficult to spell out in a letter so I have asked Rosa to contact you very soon and explain. She says she will try to visit you...*

Rosa put the letter down. "Oh shit," she said.

24.

The woman who took the bookings for the church hall in Keswick rang Joan at lunchtime on Saturday when she was in Penrith. She was in a café in the town centre, partly to have a bowl of vegetable soup but mainly in order to take advantage of the free wifi on offer to upload her most recent photos to the internet.

Purportedly, the telephone call was to enquire how many chairs Joan wanted putting out for the meeting the following weekend. "Theatre style, or would you prefer them arranged more informally? And a top table presumably for the speakers?" had been the first questions.

But it rapidly became obvious that there was another agenda behind the call. The church, it appeared, was becoming apprehensive about the booking it had taken.

"You've had a lot of publicity for the event," the woman said. "All the press have been ringing me, because they said they couldn't find your number anywhere. Fortunately I was able to pass them all on to you. Good thing you gave me your mobile number."

"Oh yes, thank you, I'm so sorry if that put you to any extra work," Joan said. "Did you see the BBC feature last Thursday?" she added as an afterthought.

"Yes, I did." There was a pause in the conversation. "Are you sure our hall will be suitable? You may want to think about booking somewhere else."

"No, I'm sure your hall will be fine," Joan replied.

"Have you... Have you enough stewards? I mean, will you have enough people on the doors?" The note of concern in her voice was unmistakeable.

"Oh yes," Joan replied, hoping to sound confident. In reality she had yet to give this side of the arrangements for the meeting much thought.

"And a chairman, or a chairwoman of course, who can keep order?" the woman had gone on.

"Yes, there will be an experienced chair," Joan replied. "We're looking forward to a really useful meeting, with lots of discussion and debate. I hope you'll be there yourself."

"That's good." The voice on the phone sounded anything but convinced. "Well… If you need to discuss anything with me before Sunday week, you have my number. Or if you find that you would prefer another venue, just let me know." She rang off.

Joan toyed with her phone, had another bite of the sourdough bread which had come with her soup, and then came to a decision, using the 'call' button for one of the numbers stored in her phone.

"Pete," she said when her call was answered. "I need your help a week tomorrow at our meeting. I think I need you to chair it," she said.

"To chair the meeting?" Pete replied, sounding surprised. "Why me? I've never had to chair a public meeting before. I'm not sure what you do."

"It's quite straightforward. You welcome people, introduce yourself and then introduce the speakers. That'll be the climate scientist woman from Lancaster University who's agreed to speak, and the second speaker is me. Then afterwards all you need do is handle the Q&A and the discussion. And finally thank everyone for coming. Oh, and mention the bucket collection at the door to help meet the costs."

"Joan, can't you find anyone else? I mean, a local vicar or a retired bank manager or someone like that who has loads of experience of chairing meetings?"

"You're not serious? It's bad enough that we're having to meet in a church. The last thing I want is any vicar barging in."

"OK." There a moment of silence. "Well, I suppose I could do it," Pete said eventually.

"Good, I knew you'd agree. Better arrive a bit earlier. Say 6.30. I'll meet you outside the main doors."

That was one thing organised. Now she just had to find a few people to be on the doors. Joan called up on her phone the alphabetical list of activists who had been with her for the Drigg demo, ringing the first name that was on the list.

The call was answered by a voicemail message. "It's Elizzbeth here," said the voice. "I can't take your call now, so please text or leave a message."

Joan rang off and texted. *Hi, Elizzbeth. I need your help for the meeting next Sun. Can you be on the doors to welcome people etc? 6.30pm please.* The message was completed with a smiley face.

Back in her house in Keswick Elizzbeth had her phone in her hand. She had chosen not to take the call from Joan when she had seen who was ringing, but she wasn't surprised when almost immediately her phone pinged to tell her a message had arrived.

"Who's trying to reach you?" Baz asked her from the kitchen.

"Not sure," she replied. "Some marketing company perhaps."

Elizzbeth read the text and immediately replied with another of her own:

Sorry, Joan, something's cropped up. Can't get to the meeting. Hope it goes OK. Elizzbeth.

25.

"Lluïsa's planning to *stay*?" Nick said incredulously. "Where?"

Rosa looked at her father. "Dad, I'm really sorry. I thought you and Mum had discussed it all. It's probably my fault for being abroad so much recently."

"OK, start at the beginning. Who is Lluïsa?"

"She's the daughter of Jordi's younger sister Patrícia. So she's Mum's sort-of niece. She's good. She's got a Master's in journalism and communication at one of Barcelona's universities, and she's been working for the local press at Girona for the past few years. Mum thought it would be a good idea if she spent a few weeks in Britain to see how the British press operates, and she thought you could fix it up. She'd be an intern, that sort of thing."

"OK, but she needs to be in London, not hidden away up here. Get her to talk to the national press."

"Actually, she does need to be hidden away, as it happens."

"Sorry?"

"Well, the reason why Mum didn't necessarily tell you all this in her letter is that Lluïsa is in a spot of trouble with the Guardia Civil."

"The *police* are after her?"

"The Guardia Civil, not the Catalan police. It's not what you think. She's not done anything wrong, apart maybe from being a little too active in the Catalan independence movement."

"What has she done?" asked Nick firmly.

"You know that the Spanish state has come down very hard indeed on anyone who suggests that, actually, Catalans should have self-determination to decide their own future. Or who tries to point out that the Spanish state is a collection of different nations and languages. Or who reminds people that Catalonia had independence in the 1930s, before Franco won the civil war and got himself power."

"Just spare me the history lesson and tell me why Lluïsa is on the run."

"She's an experienced climber, and a few weeks ago she and a mate free-climbed up the side of the Guardia Civil's barracks in Girona, removed the Spanish flag from the flagpole, replaced it with the Catalan flag and for good measure put up a banner demanding the release of Catalan political prisoners. Everyone locally thought it was a hoot. Except obviously the Guardia Civil who weren't at all amused, and are now trying to arrest her on a charge of high treason, or something like that."

"So your mother hatched the idea of sending her off to England, to hide in an old slate mine in the Lake District until the heat dies down?"

"Um, I think Mum was hoping that Lluïsa might be able to be found a bed, rather than a hole in the ground. Of course, in an ideal world, you and she would have had the chance to discuss the arrangements."

Nick decided not to respond that, in an ideal world, he and Rosa's mother would still be living happily in north London, and that he would never have heard of Jordi, or of Jordi's niece either. He shrugged, partly because at that moment Lluïsa returned to their table from the toilet.

"I like this bar," Lluïsa said. "It is how I picture an English country pub."

"I've been telling my father about why you're here. I've told him that… I've told him about some of the climbing you have done."

"Yes," Lluïsa smiled. "Normally I prefer mountains, you understand."

"There are plenty of mountains to climb here," Rosa replied.

"That will be enjoyable," Lluïsa replied. Nick said nothing.

"However, there's been a slight problem in communication between my Mum and my Dad," Rosa went on. "El meu pare no sabia res de la teva acció a la caserna de la Guardia Civil," she explained, changing back into Catalan.

"No?" responded Lluïsa. "Hi ha algun problema?"

"Espero que no. Però… Dad, what do you think? Can you have Lluïsa working at the Cumbrian Enquirer for a little while? Jordi's sister has given her plenty of money, so there's no question of her needing paid work."

"I suppose I can ask my editor Molly. It's never been done before."

"Obviously you would say she was here just to improve her English. No need to say anything else."

"I don't normally lie to Molly."

"Not lying, just not necessarily telling the full story," Rosa replied.

"Hmm," Nick responded. And then, quite unexpectedly, he burst out laughing. "Your mother really is quite mad. Mad and incorrigible. That's why I loved her so much, you know."

"I know," Rosa replied.

"I'll try to help Lluïsa. Not because I want to please your mother, and certainly not because I want to please Jordi or his sister. But simply because of the memory of the eighteen good years I spent with her, and how we tried together to bring you up to be an independent young woman who had the self-confidence to make her mark on the world. I think we succeeded."

Rosa smiled. "You did," she said.

"Mind you, in eighteen years I never managed to get your mother to pronounce my name correctly. I was always *Neek.*"

Rosa laughed. "I know that too. She still calls you Neek."

"OK," Nick said. "The first problem we've got is to find somewhere where Lluïsa can stay."

"Any ideas?"

"None at all."

26.

"No dressing up this time, Dad." Paula Petherton was adamant.

"I don't see that it does any harm," her father replied. "It gets media attention, too."

"Yes, but very often the wrong sort of attention. I think we were lucky with the Cumbrian Enquirer that the journalist was as restrained as he was. You know I wasn't happy to agree to the fancy dress. We want to demonstrate that we're a sensible political party, not a load of nutcases."

"I don't see why we have to be hidebound by today's fashions. Why is it OK to wear jeans but not the sort of gowns which our ancestors wore when we were an independent kingdom?"

"Believe me, there is not a great demand for mediaeval gowns in menswear shops these days."

"What's wrong with being radical and starting a fashion?"

They had had arguments like this regularly, ever since Paula had broken up with her boyfriend, had found herself struggling to find somewhere she could afford, and had asked her parents if she could move back temporarily with them. It was not easy. Paula was in her late twenties, and much as she loved her parents she found them still tending to treat her like a sixteen year old.

"Nothing wrong necessarily, but we've already agreed what the priority has to be," Paula said. "A New Voice for Cumbria is campaigning for a fair deal for native Cumbrians, and we want to get the maximum votes we can in the May elections."

The King of Rheged made a face.

"Look, Dad, you're happy to wear normal clothes when you go to work," Paula went on.

"Only because I'm made to."

"Here's a proposal. Once the election is over you've got free rein. Why don't you think about organising another eisteddfod later in the year?"

"Maybe I will," Phillip Petherton replied. There was a pause. "Anyway, what precisely is it that you're organising for next Sunday?"

"I've told you. It's a rally to support Cumbrian hill farmers. There's a meeting being called in Keswick by a group who say that farmers have to completely change the way they work the land. We'll be there to say that this isn't on."

"You'll take Cumbrian flags?"

"Yes, we'll take some Cumbrian flags. Rick, who's going to be our candidate for Keswick, has promised to bring some flags and placards too. St George's flags, I think."

"That's the flag for England, not Cumbria."

"Oh for god's sake, Dad, leave this to me. We're going to have a nice peaceful rally in front of the hall where the meeting's being held, we'll have a dirty great banner saying A New Voice for Cumbria, and we'll tip off the TV stations so that we get maximum coverage. What's not to like?"

Her father said nothing for a moment.

"Have you told the police?"

"No, of course not. We won't be blocking the road or anything, just staging a rally."

"And who is this Rick?"

"I've told you. He got in touch, saying he supported our aims. He's a chef in Keswick and needless to say he's living in shitty rented accommodation because he can't afford to compete with the second-homers for a place of his own. We need a Keswick candidate for the elections and he's got lots of local connections. He's bringing his friends along to the rally, too."

"Does Rick want to learn Cumbraek?"

"I shouldn't think so for a moment. That's not a condition of supporting our party."

"I hope you know what you're doing. So you want me and your mother just to be part of the crowd and to wear our ordinary clothes?"

"That's exactly what I want. But you can bring all the Cumbrian flags you can find."

"I certainly will," Phillip Petherton replied.

27.

The Ambleside restaurant had been understanding, prepared to change Nick's booking from three people to two. Lluïsa had stayed behind at Nick's house in Grasmere, where they had gone after leaving the pub at Oxenholme.

"Rosa, Nick is your father and you don't see him very soon," she had said. "You should eat the meal just the two of you."

She had pointed to the box of eggs which was sitting on the work surface in Nick's kitchen. "I make an omelette for myself," she said.

And so it had been agreed. Rather than call a taxi, father and daughter had jumped on the 555 bus for the short journey into Ambleside. They were now ensconced at a table in a quiet corner of the restaurant, both attacking the piled bowls of mussels they had ordered as starters.

"I've got a client with a head office in Lille and I was over last September at the time of the city's *braderie*, "Rosa said. "The whole city is in the streets looking at the stalls of antiques and second-hand tat, and eating mussels. There are mounds of mussel shells on the pavements almost as big as old slag heaps."

Her father nodded, popping another mussel into his mouth. "These are from the Solway Firth, just up the road," he said.

"For all I know, that's where the Lille ones come from, too," Rosa replied.

"So work is going well?"

"Very well. In fact -" Rosa paused, "they've offered me a senior management position in the Barcelona office, if I want it." Rosa's firm of commercial lawyers, although officially London based, spanned the world.

"And do you want it?"

"I've said yes. It's a big promotion."

"Loads more money?"

Rosa laughed. "Yes, but that's not the main thing. I like my job and I'm good at it." She paused. "Although the money's fine too. I'm going to treat you tonight, by the way."

Her father smiled. "OK," he said. "So will Becky move too?"

"Let's say we're talking it through."

"Everything all right?"

"So-so. Becky's got her own career to think of." Becky worked as a manager in a major publishing company specialising in online legal bulletins. "Actually Becky is talking about wanting a family."

There was a moment of silence between them.

"Dad, Becky and I are agreeing to live in separate cities for a while, just to see how it feels. We both feel OK about it, don't worry."

"I don't think parents ever stop worrying," Nick replied. "It was such a delight to be at your wedding."

"I know." The conversation was dropped.

The restaurant specialised in fish, and they had chosen a bottle of Chablis to accompany the meal. Rosa topped up her father's glass.

"I'm really sorry to spring Lluïsa on you," she said.

"I wasn't even sure the letter I got from your mother was genuine. She signed it Anna with two 'n's."

"Yes, that's the way she does these days. It's the Catalan spelling. In Franco's day people couldn't have Catalan first names, so her parents had to spell it with just one 'n'. Didn't you know?"

"Obviously not. Anyway Lluïsa seems nice enough. About your age?"

"Younger. Not yet thirty. 28, I think she said. Oh, and just to reassure you given what you thought in the pub, she's heterosexual."

Nick laughed. "We need to find her somewhere permanent to stay." They had agreed that afternoon in Grasmere that Nick would stay in his usual bed, Lluïsa would stay in the spare room and Rosa would bed down downstairs on the sofa. But they'd also agreed that the arrangement was only for the weekend.

"Do you know anyone with a spare room? Someone who is looking to rent out a flat? Maybe someone in your running club?"

Nick abruptly put down the glass which he had begun to raise to his mouth.

"Brilliant idea. Lindsay. I'll talk to her first thing tomorrow."

"I remember you've mentioned Lindsay."

"Yes, she's moving in with her soon-to-be husband in Carlisle. Her place is just round the corner from here in Ambleside and she told me she was set to rent it out."

"Excellent."

"Lindsay does some climbing too, so that could work well."

The mussels had been cleared away and the main courses arrived. The fish, according to the blackboard in the restaurant, had all been landed at Fleetwood docks, a short distance south across Morecambe Bay. Nick had ordered Atlantic codling, served on a bed of Puy lentils with braised endives and tiny sautéed potatoes. Rosa had chosen the special, a mixed plate comprising Fleetwood-landed plaice, brill and turbot which were served with lightly cooked green vegetables and a handful of scallops. It looked almost too good to eat.

"Bon profit," Rosa said, using the Catalan for bon appetit.

"Bon profit," her father replied.

"Any good stories on the go?" Rosa asked, after they had both had a few mouthfuls.

"A local climate change activist chained herself in the Enquirer office the other day."

"No! What had you done?"

"Among other things, she complained that we'd not carried enough stories about climate change. She's organising a public meeting next weekend which I suspect may be a lively affair."

"On climate change?"

"On climate change and farming. The paper's had no end of farmers ringing us up about it. Cumbrian farmers can be forthright in their views."

"I can imagine. What's her name?" Rosa had pulled out her mobile phone.

"Joan Arkle. She calls herself Joan Sparkle on Twitter."

Rosa's attention turned momentarily away from her plate of fish to her screen.

"Bloody hell, Dad. Have you been following her Twitter feed?"

"Now and again. Probably not as much as I should. I'm old-school when it comes to journalism."

"Look at this filth."

Rosa passed her phone across. Nick scrolled through the

comments which Rosa had found on Joan Arkle's account. There were offensive tweets referring to her appearance, but these were mild by comparison with the rest. There were several tweets threatening her with rape. There were three which told her that she had to prepare to die.

"I cannot believe human beings feel able to write this stuff," Nick said.

"I hope she's had the good sense to report it all to the police."

"I wonder. Joan Arkle seems to have a difficult relationship with the police. She's been arrested rather too often on demos, perhaps."

"Hmm." Rosa shuddered. "This talk could put me off my food. Tell me something else you're doing at the Enquirer that's less nasty."

"OK, I'll tell you what happened when I met the King of Rheged."

Nick described in detail his interview with Phillip Petherton. Rosa laughed. "That's more like it," she said. "How do you say 'cheers' in Cumbraek?"

"No idea!"

"Well, whatever. Let's finish up this bottle."

28.

They'd made love and were lying in bed, chatting inconsequentially. The sex had been good, Elizzabeth decided. Baz seemed pretty contented too. She knew her way round his body well.

He'd apologised, she'd come home. It was Tuesday. A new week was under way and it had brought with it a new start. They'd agreed new rules. Baz had promised never ever to use violence against her. He'd promised too to rein in the number of times he used porn. Elizzabeth had told him that she found some of it unpleasant. The compromise had been that they had agreed they'd stop watching Terry's videos together. Elizzabeth knew she had no control over what Baz might do when she wasn't there but maybe that didn't matter. A wank was, at the end of the day, only a wank.

She turned back towards him, finding his mouth with hers. "Come on, lover boy, how about another go?" she asked him when their lips had separated.

"Bloody hell, Betty-lizz," he replied. "I'm shagged out."

She laughed. "No stamina," she said. "I'll get you some nice blue pills from the chemist next time."

Baz propped himself on his elbow and turned to look at Elizzabeth. "I didn't know I'd married a nympho," he said.

"Not quite," she replied. "Still, we've got some catching up to do. Did you miss me?"

"Of course I missed you," Baz replied.

There was a comfortable silence between them.

"Have I told you about Horsey getting into politics?" Baz eventually said.

"No! What for?"

"He's going to be the local candidate for A New Voice for Cumbria. You and I will have to get ourselves on the electoral list, or whatever."

"Who are A New Voice for Cumbria?"

"Some new party that wants to do things right for proper Cumbrian people. I think it makes a lot of sense."

Elizzabeth shrugged. "I've not heard of them," she replied.

"You will soon. Horsey's planning his first demonstration in Keswick. I've told him we'll both be there."

"I thought you didn't like me going on demonstrations."

"Only if you don't tell me first. And only if you're stupid enough to be arrested."

She stuck out her tongue at him in response.

"So go on, tell me the details," she said. "Who knows, I may already be committed to several other demonstrations at the same time."

"As if," Baz replied. "It's on Sunday evening in Keswick. We're protesting at a public meeting. It'll be awesome. A bit of shoving and pushing maybe if anyone tries to go in. It'll be great craic."

Baz was still smiling but Elizzabeth rolled away from him. It felt that it was if he had slapped her hard once again on her face.

"Fucking hell. You don't mean the meeting Joan Arkle's calling?"

"That's right."

"I'm not demonstrating against Joan."

"You told me you were having nothing more to do with that woman," Baz responded.

"Maybe, but what she's doing is good. Tell Horsey to call off his demonstration."

In a brief moment the mood in the bedroom had turned sour.

"Horsey will do what he likes, and so will I," Baz said, almost spitting out the words. "And you'll be there, arm in arm with me. Joan Arkle is mad. What she needs is a good screwing from me and my mates, and then she'll start seeing some sense."

"Don't you dare talk about my friend like that," Elizzabeth found herself saying.

"Oh, she's your friend again now, is she? Feel free to snog her any time you like, don't mind me, I'm just the husband."

Elizzabeth, naked, rolled out of the bed. Slowly and methodically she went to the bathroom and washed. She returned to the bedroom, put on her clothes and then, equally slowly, went through her wardrobe putting most of the items into a suitcase. Baz looked at her, saying nothing.

"I loved you, Baz," she said. "I really loved you."

"You still do," he replied. "And I love you."

"No, I hate you. It's over. Fuck off out of my life."

She took her case, marched to the bedroom door and shut it firmly behind her. A short time later the front door closed.

29.

PCSO Greg Czarnecki looked across at his colleague PCSO Debbie Winters. This was turning out to be a little more unruly than they had been led to expect. Sunday evenings could be lively in Keswick, but not normally this early. It was only about seven o'clock.

Debbie shrugged back in response, gesturing to the radio. Greg followed her suggestion, put the radio into call mode and called for back-up.

They were at the doors of one of Keswick's church halls. Around them were perhaps twenty-five people, mainly young, mainly male, and mainly waving St George's flags. These were complemented by a handful of Union Jacks as well as by another flag, blue and green and white, which neither of the PCSOs immediately recognised. An older couple, who looked as if they could have taken a wrong turning on the way to a whist drive, were the ones who were primarily waving the mystery flags.

The protestors had come with banners too, almost all home-made. Hands off our farmers, read one. Cumbria needs a better deal, read another. And, bizarrely, one (being held by one of the whist players) pronounced in careful handwriting *N'estungen bith*.

This wasn't quite the sort of policing incident which they had role-played during the PCSO training courses. And on top of that no less that two TV crews were present. Greg recognised one of the reporters from the BBC's regional news programme. At that moment she was interviewing the young woman who had previously identified herself to the PCSOs as the organiser of the demo. The other TV crew were busy doing vox pops, primarily of some of the younger men. By this stage several of them had broken into raucous singing which it sounded as if they had practised earlier on the football terraces.

The singing died away and was replaced by chanting.

"Cumbria -" began one of the young men.

"For ever!" came the reply.

"Cumbria -"

"For ever!" they repeated.

"What do we want?"

"Homes for locals"

"What do we want?"

"Jobs for locals."

The chanting grew in volume, and changed tack.

"Hippies - "

"OUT!"

"Vegans - "

"OUT!"

"Foreigners - "

"OUT!"

Greg Czarnecki called over the young woman organiser.

"You need to quieten things down," he warned her.

"I'll do what I can," she said. "I'm afraid – it's turned out a little noisier than I expected."

Greg saw her have a word with the young man who had been

leading the chanting. He appeared to shrug, and the chanting continued.

"Hippies - "

"OUT!"

"Vegans - "

"OUT!"

Meanwhile, a bemused group of men and women had been arriving at the church hall and filing past the two PCSOs on their way into the meeting. They were a mixed bunch. Some were young and might have been the very hippies and vegans that the demonstrators apparently disliked so much. Some were completely different: older men, several wearing caps and waxed jackets, who looked as if they could have come straight from tending sheep on the fells. And then there was a neatly dressed woman, probably about forty, who announced herself as one of the speakers and asked if there was any reserved parking for her car.

Inside, Nick Potterton had taken his place at the back of the church hall. He had agreed with Molly that he would cover the meeting for the Enquirer. It made sense. He had interviewed Joan Arkle and had written the story ten days ago about the meeting. But he had come with company. Alongside him was Lluïsa, enthusiastic and keen to see what a political meeting in Britain was like. It was only a week that she had been in Cumbria, but already she seemed well-embedded in local life. She'd relocated to Lindsay's flat the previous Tuesday, moving into Lindsay's small second bedroom while Lindsay got herself ready to make the move to Carlisle. "I like her," Lindsay had vouchsafed to Nick by text message. "That's a relief," he'd texted back.

Lluïsa had begun working in the Enquirer office on the Wednesday. Molly had been surprised at Nick's request on Lluïsa's behalf, but had not raised any objection. "I'm not saying no to a free extra pair of hands, provided she doesn't want to be paid and doesn't get in the way," had been the response. "Is this something you've arranged with your ex-?" she asked Nick. Molly knew the Catalan connection to Nick's past love life.

"Sort of," Nick replied, not offering further details.

It was approaching twenty-five past seven, five minutes before the meeting was due to start and around thirty people were in the church hall waiting patiently for things to begin. Nick noticed Phillip Petherton and his wife come in and take their seats in the back row, carefully folding their Cumbrian flags and putting them on their laps as they did. Paula followed a few moments later. The other demonstrators obviously had slipped away, probably to a nearby Keswick hostelry.

No longer dressed in the bizarre Morris-girl costume he'd seen her in at her parents' house, Paula Petherton looked both older and tougher. He'd taken the opportunity to interview her outside the hall, while the demonstration was in full swing. Was this, he'd asked her, the sort of activity they could expect from A New Voice for Cumbria in the election period? Some might see it as uncomfortably close to a far-right rally, he suggested. She'd answered tight-lipped: "We'll do what's needed to get our message across," she'd told him.

Nick had turned his attention to the King of Rheged, close by her side. How did he feel his party's initial demonstration had done? Mr Petherton looked uncomfortable. "No comment," he said. Nick had tried again. Are you pleased to see so many younger people here supporting you?, he asked. "You need to talk to Paula," came the reply a second time. A New Voice for Cumbria was, Nick thought, having a few teething problems.

Meanwhile, the hall was quietening down in anticipation. A trestle table had been set up on the stage at the front of the room, and three people took their seats behind it. Joan Arkle was there, of course, her short-cropped hair now dyed a bright blue colour. Alongside her was a second woman, smartly dressed in a white blouse, neat jacket and navy skirt, who was looking down at the audience before her over half-rimmed glasses. The other person at the table was a younger man whom Nick hadn't previously met, but who Nick guessed was a fellow activist of Joan's. He was dressed in a check-shirt and jeans.

It was the man who called the meeting to order. He looked nervous, and his first words came out falteringly. He then over-compensated by speaking too fast. Still, in the end he found his rhythm, welcoming his audience and introducing himself as the Chair of the meeting. His name, he said, was Pete Rawlinson. He was sure they were going to have an interesting and productive evening. Nick got his shorthand notebook ready.

Pete started by introducing the first speaker, the woman in the jacket and skirt. She was, he said, from the University of Lancaster, where she lectured in environment and land resource studies. They were lucky to have her with them. She had driven up to Keswick from the other side of Lancaster specifically to be at the meeting. Please give her a warm welcome.

A polite ripple of applause greeted this last comment, and as the woman rose to her feet an opening slide appeared on the drop-down screen which hung behind the top table and which had up to then been blank. The slide gave her name as Dr Jennie Hetherington, and her subject as Climate Change and Upland Land Usage. Nick noted down for future reference the university email address that was on the slide.

"Thank you for the introduction," she said briskly. "I have a lot of slides I want to get through tonight and time is limited, so let's crack on. Next slide."

Nick noticed a woman operating a laptop near the slide projector. The slide-changing was, he was pretty sure, being undertaken by the woman called Elizzabeth whom he had met that time at Workington magistrates' court.

The opening slide disappeared, and a graph appeared, showing a line climbing sharply towards the right hand side.

"This will probably need no introduction," she said. "This is how global surface temperature has increased worldwide from 1850 to 2020. We tend to call 1850-1900 the pre-industrial period, although obviously Britain industrialised earlier. You'll see that temperatures are now about one degree up from where they were back then. Of course, it's not a steady line but the trend is unmistakeable. Next slide."

"This shows how land is used worldwide. About 12% of the land surface is used for growing crops and a little under 40% for pasture. We don't need to spend long on that. I'll talk about Britain later on. Next slide."

Almost before it had appeared, the slide was removed.

A new graph appeared. "This is interesting," Dr Hetherington said. "Cereal yields have gone up 200% worldwide since 1961, but look at that top line. That shows use of inorganic nitrogen fertiliser usage, up almost 800%. Fertiliser is a major cause of nitrous oxide in the environment. It's a particularly problematic greenhouse gas, far worse than CO_2. Next."

The slides came in quick succession. There was no doubt that Dr Hetherington knew her stuff, Nick said to himself. He was taking shorthand notes as she spoke, but he would also make sure afterwards that he could get hold of the slide handouts. The problem, though, was that she had misjudged her audience. She was talking, he realised, as if she was lecturing to a room full of undergraduates. Her audience tonight occupied a different world. They weren't stupid. Nick knew that the men a few rows ahead of him were undoubtedly highly knowledgeable sheep farmers. They knew exactly how much to expect from the sales of the gimmer shearlings they took each year to Penrith livestock market, or just how far they would push the bidding at auction for a good pedigree Herdwick tup. They were listening politely, but communication was clearly not taking place.

"My slides, by the way, are taken from the UN IPCC report on Climate Change and Land which came out in 2019 and which I expect you're familiar with," Jennie Hetherington went on. Her students continued to show blank faces.

"So let's try to summarise what I've been saying so far," she continued at one point. "According to the IPCC around 25% to 30% of the total greenhouse gas emissions are attributable to the food system. These are from land use and agriculture and also from food transport, packaging, processing, retail and things like that. Crop and livestock activities in farms are responsible for about half that total of greenhouse emissions. Say 10%-12%, some people say more. It's a major contributor."

"So let's turn our attention to the Lake District," she went on. Nick noticed her audience try to pull itself together. "This is a beautiful area and one where farming is integral to the landscape. But farmers in this room will know that much of the land has been officially designated as a Severely Disadvantaged Area, agriculturally speaking. An average hill farm will have around 250 hectares of rough grazing, perhaps 100 hectares of better-quality in-bye land and maybe a little woodland. It's likely to carry over 800 breeding ewes and a much smaller number of suckler cows. Of course, that's the average, all farms are different."

The audience had become noticeably more attentive. "The problem we all face is that hill farming is not commercially viable." A new slide popped up. "This is taken from a recent academic study," Dr Hetherington said. "The piechart on the left shows income for a typical Lakeland farm, coming in at around £100,000 a year. You'll notice that 40% of this income is farm subsidies of various kinds, or in other words the replacement for the European farm subsidies. On the right the piechart shows the fixed and variable costs of the farm. It's just a little less, just below £100,000. So – that's good, you're thinking, thanks to public subsidies hill farms are at least making a profit."

"Except that the right-hand piechart doesn't include farmers' labour. Add on labour and things become dire. Research suggests that Lake District farmers manage on average to survive by paying themselves under £10,000 a year."

"Hill flocks of sheep have their own carbon footprint, as do cows. Cattle are worse than sheep, but of course there are more sheep than cows. I could give you the CO_2 kilogram emissions per kilogram of animal liveweight, but you'd fall asleep." She looked down over her glasses. Nobody appeared to be asleep yet, although it might just be a matter of time.

However, she was clearly reaching her peroration. Her opening slide reappeared.

"So traditional farming is potentially in crisis. And at the same time the planet is certainly in crisis. If we're not careful, our world will very soon be much too hot for comfort. My message is that we can't carry on in the same way. I congratulate the organisers for arranging such a timely meeting, and I thank you for your attention." She sat down, to somewhat underwhelming applause.

Pete the Chair took over. "Dr Hetherington has a long journey home so has to leave us very shortly unfortunately, so before we turn to our second speaker she has agreed to answer a few questions. Anyone?"

There was silence in the hall. Eventually, one hand was thrust upwards. The hand belonged to a well-dressed man, a few rows from the front.

"I'm sorry, but I just don't buy this climate change propaganda," he began. There was scattered clapping from around the room. "Our climate's always been changing. Sometimes it gets hotter and sometimes it gets colder. It's normal." He sat down, and more clapping broke out around the room.

Jennie Hetherington looked down at him over her glasses. "Yes, of course we've always had fluctuations in climate," she said, as if to a very dim first-year student. "Britain was a warmer place in Roman times, for example. That's probably why they could grow vines in the north of England. And then around 1500 AD the temperature dropped and for some hundreds of years we had what's sometimes called the Little Ice Age."

There were murmurs around the room. Dr Hetherington had appeared to have scored an impressive own goal.

"But that is not the point," she went on. "The point is that human activity in the industrial age has led to a dangerous increase in temperature. Directly. As a direct result of what we as humans have done and are doing. No reputable scientist contradicts this, and believe me there are a great many scientists working in this field. I don't think we'll ever get temperatures back to where we were pre-industrialisation. We'll be lucky to escape with a 2 degree increase in temperature. Trust me, this is a crisis."

She sat down. Another hand went up.

"I'm here from one of the Cumbrian farmers' co-operatives," he said. "You're right that these are challenging times for local farmers but you've painted a very one-sided picture of the environmental impact of livestock. What about the environmental benefits they bring?" he asked.

"Yes, I wouldn't deny that. Cattle can help keep moorland vegetation varied, for example. And then there's tourism. You can put a monetary figure on the benefits from tourism, and of course tourists like to see sheep grazing peacefully on the fells. But I'm sorry to have to say it. The studies show that the environmental negatives of livestock farming far outweigh the positives."

"You'll tell me next that it's because my cows fart too much," said a voice with a local accent from near the back of the hall. His intervention was greeted with widespread laughter.

Dr Hetherington maintained a severe expression. "No, not flatulence. That's a common misapprehension. Burping is the main problem. Approximately 95% of the methane produced by bovines comes from belching, and methane, like nitrous oxide, is another greenhouse gas that's more damaging than carbon dioxide. Cows can't help it, it's how they digest grass by regurgitating the cud. You can help reduce the methane emissions in the burping, though, by changing the animal feed you use. There's plenty of written material about this."

The room had fallen silent again.

"Well," said Pete Rawlinson. "If there are no more questions, perhaps we can show our appreciation to Dr Hetherington for her presentation." There was some further polite applause. Jennie Hetherington left her seat, picked up her briefcase, shook hands with Pete and Joan Arkle on the platform and made her way off the back of the stage. "My apologies for having to leave early," she said as she did.

With her departure there was, Nick thought, a definite shift in the mood of the meeting. The academic had been treated with a certain amount of respect. Now, however, the platform held just two young people, one of them with dyed blue hair. Joan Arkle and Pete the Chair suddenly seemed vulnerable. Nick was there professionally: his job was to report the event objectively for the Cumbrian Enquirer. Nevertheless he couldn't help hoping that Joan Arkle was up to the task ahead of her. He had a premonition that the rest of the meeting could be a car-crash.

Joan Arkle started well.

"Here are a few photographs you'd probably rather not be reminded of," she said. The photos were of Keswick in the immediate aftermath of the serious flooding in early December 2015. There were scenes of streets under water, businesses flooded, people's homes several feet deep in mud and sludge.

"I know that people in Cumbria won't forget Storm Desmond for a very long time," she went on. "And it wasn't just December 2015. If anyone is here from Cockermouth you'll recall the November 2009 flooding, when the flood waters took over most of the centre of the town. Workington too. That was the flood which cut Workington in two."

"Cumbria has had it tough recently. The problem is that it isn't just an accident of fate. You remember Dr Hetherington's first slide showing the way surface temperatures have increased since industrialisation. Climate scientists tell us that extreme weather conditions, such as floods and droughts and devastating wild fires, are just what they can predict from rising temperatures. We're bringing these changes on ourselves."

There were murmurs from the audience, although it was impossible to know if people were showing agreement or disagreement with Joan Arkle's assertions.

"Now here's a more pleasant photograph. It's one I took just last Thursday, in fact, when I was on Wether Hill south of Ullswater." The photograph was of a brightly coloured medium-sized bird, with a bright ruddy-coloured belly and a white chest band. "This is a female dotterel, of course, our beautiful mountain plover. They're not common, it's always a delight to see one," she went on.

"I'm showing this picture because we may very soon find that dotterels are no longer found in Cumbria. They are birds of the high mountain lands and as temperatures go up all our montane flora and fauna is at risk. Climate change threatens the arctic saxifrage and the purple saxifrage and the lovely mountain ringlet butterfly which you can't find anywhere else in England except the Lake District. Lots of other things like these."

Joan Arkle's blue hair was bobbing up and down as she spoke. There could be no gainsaying the passion she brought to her campaigning. Lluïsa at Nick's side was clapping loudly.

"So what can we do? Well, one thing we can all do is eat less meat. Better still, eat no meat. I'm proud to be vegan, and I'm proud that hundreds of thousands of other people in Britain have become vegan in the past two or three years."

There was no doubting that the muttering from the audience was now primarily hostile.

"We've heard about the greenhouse gas emissions from livestock, and I could mention all the other problems: the chemical pollution of our fresh water supplies, the pollution from antibiotics fed to livestock, the overgrazing and loss of forest cover, and everything else."

"But I'm just going to focus on food. Almost half of the world's crops are fed to livestock, which are then in due course slaughtered to give us meat. It's really wasteful. We end up with much less protein than if we'd just eaten the plants. On average ten grams of vegetable protein gets turned into one gram of animal protein. Beef is worse than average: about seventeen grams of vegetable protein go to produce one gram of animal protein."

"We've got to change the food we eat, and the way we farm it. And if you don't believe me, then what about believing the 15,000 scientists around the world who signed the Warning to Humanity statement in 2017, telling us to drastically reduce the amounts of meat we eat and the fossil fuels we use?"

A middle-aged man rose to his feet a few rows back.

"I'm not prepared to sit here and listen to local farmers being criticised in this way," he said. There were some 'hear hears' from behind him. "Farmers work hard to produce the food we all need, and if we stopped farming the supermarket shelves would rapidly empty. The speaker doesn't have a clue."

Pete Rawlinson tried to intervene. "There will be time for questions and comments…" he began. But he had begun to lose control of the meeting. An older man, clearly a hill farmer, had also got to his feet.

"My grandfather farmed Herdwicks, my father farmed Herdwicks, and I farm Herdwicks," he said. "My daughter will farm Herdwicks here after I've gone, so we don't need any offcomer to Cumbria telling us what to do."

Pete looked desperately at Joan Arkle, who was still on her feet, trying to make herself heard. It was a forlorn effort. Another man was by now also standing up.

"Bracken," he boomed. "I'll tell you what will happen. Bracken will invade our fells. Take away the yows and you'll be left with scrub and bracken. And wait and see how much the tourists will like that."

A conversation began to develop between several of the men in the hall.

"They all talk about rewilding the fells, these environmentalists, but it just means letting the land go to waste."

""You're right, Jem," his neighbour responded. "Wolves. Wolves and lynx. That's what they want to introduce. Have you heard?"

"The first wolf that arrives in the Lake District, I'll take my shotgun and shoot it through the head. I don't care what the law says. I'll go to prison."

"I'm going home," said one of the waxed jackets, getting up and heading for the door. Several other people, including the Pethertons, joined him.

But as they were leaving, at the same time a group of four younger men came in and sat themselves down in chairs half way down the hall. Nick recognised them as some of the demonstrators who had been outside at the start of the evening. They had obviously used the time profitably since then to have a number of pints and – judging from the fact that they were all eating - to visit a takeaway.

"You'd better not eat that beefburger too noisily, Terry," said one of the men in a deliberately loud voice.

"Yes, sorry," Terry replied, equally loudly. "How is the donner kebab?"

"Lovely and *meaty*," came the reply.

"So's my *beef*burger."

"Keep your voice down, Baz, there may be *vegans* here for all we know."

"No, there are no vegans in Keswick. Or if there are, they need to leave town" he raised his voice " – very very soon."

One of the other men burped loudly.

"Oh, pardon me," he said, to the whole hall.

The public meeting which Joan Arkle had called had disintegrated in a matter of minutes. She and Pete looked down helplessly as the bulk of the audience made its way out. Eventually the men with the takeaways also sidled out, although not before they had spotted the woman by the slide projector.

"Well, hello, Elizzabeth," the man called Terry shouted across. "I hope you've had an arousing evening. If you're looking for some night-time company, Baz is busy but uncle Terry here will be happy to oblige." His comment was greeted by guffaws. Elizzabeth turned away.

Nick and Lluïsa made their way forward. Nick needed to get a few final quotes for his piece for the Enquirer. A small group, clearly Joan Arkle's fellow activists, had gathered around Joan and Pete at the front of the hall.

Joan she was almost in tears. "I'm *not* anti-farmer," she was saying to Pete. "I wanted to hold the meeting because I wanted to help farmers. Why don't people understand when you tell them the truth?"

The woman from the church hall committee who had stayed in the small kitchen at the back during the meeting also came forward. She looked relieved that her chairs and tables were all still intact.

"Is it you who I need to ask for the £50 rental fee?" she asked Pete politely but firmly.

Pete looked shocked. "Oh god," he said, "I completely forgot to mention the collection buckets. We've got no money." He looked around helplessly. "Joan, we need to pay the church."

The group beside him started dipping into their pockets and gradually some bank notes and coins began to be assembled in a pile. It didn't much look like £50, Nick thought. He reached for his wallet and contributed a ten pound note. It might be unorthodox behaviour for a reporter but... well, the meeting would provide copy for next week's paper.

Meanwhile Lluïsa and Joan had begun to talk together animatedly. Lluïsa's English, if not completely fluent, was competent enough but it was clear in any case that there was mutual understanding between the two women. It took one political activist to know another, Nick thought.

"And of course we have Fridays for Future days in Girona, too," Nick heard Lluïsa say to Joan. "Outside the Girona Town Hall on Friday afternoons. The school students take over the streets to campaign against climate change. I am writing many many newspaper articles about them."

Nick collared Pete Rawlinson for the quote he needed. "I'm disappointed people didn't let Joan finish but we're not going away. There will be plenty more climate change actions in Cumbria in the weeks ahead," Pete told him. The words, converted into T-line shorthand shapes, went into Nick's notebook, ready for Monday morning in the office.

The few people still there were drifting away. Nick had offered to give Lluïsa a lift back to Ambleside, so he waited for her conversation with Joan Arkle to come to an end. Joan's tears seemed to have dried, and – despite the way the meeting had finished - she was almost back to being her usual confident self.

"Right," she said, "I'll just go and pick up Goldie and then we can go. I left her on her lead on a rug in the side room so she wouldn't feel she'd missed out on the meeting."

Joan briefly left the main hall. Almost immediately there was a terrible cry, a noise that must have come from Joan but which barely seemed human.

"Goldie's gone," Joan said, rushing back in. "Goldie's not there."

There was a moment of complete silence.

"Somebody's taken Goldie," she said.

PART TWO

30.

It was the sort of Monday morning which makes the humdrum routine of so much policing work worthwhile. DI Chrissy Chambers had called DS Peter Blackford into her office. Both were smiling broadly.

"Three cuckoos caught in one nest, ma'am," Peter Blackford said to his boss. "The heroin has a value of about £14,000 street price, so a tidy haul. It was a proper little distribution centre they there. There were weighing scales and a load of packaging. They even had a stack of business cards with a mobile phone number to ring."

"Where are they now?"

"Still in custody. All three have given addresses in Newcastle, which of course Northumbria Police are checking out for us. It's classic county line stuff, I think. We had a strong hunch that some of the Cumbria drug trade was being supplied from Tyneside."

"Ages?"

"Three white guys, aged 22, 21 and 20. Two are brothers."

"And who was living in the nest that they occupied?"

"A single woman in her thirties with a drugs habit and almost certainly mental health problems too. The classic sort of background for a victim of cuckooing, as we well know. The house was an ex-council house which was being privately rented to her."

"Did they turf her out?"

"Apparently they arrived last Wednesday, barged past her at the front door and told her from then on only to stay in her bedroom and the bathroom. She's not in a good state."

As both detectives knew, police forces across Britain were regularly having to address the issue of cuckooing, the latest manifestation of the illegal drugs trade. Drugs gangs based in cities across Britain were building new supply networks to bring illegal drugs through to local drug suppliers and street dealers in rural areas and they needed unobtrusive houses to work from. The easiest way to get a house in a new area was simply to take one over for a while.

Victims of cuckooing were almost always vulnerable. They might be drug users. Or they might simply be older people living alone, or people with a drink problem, or with physical or mental health issues, or just people who were very poor. Their house would be used for a few days, or perhaps for a week or two, after which the cuckoos flitted to somewhere else.

"We've found that the three men had a house they were using across at Cleator as well, and that they'd taken over an AirBnB holiday flat on the coast near Flimby. Quite entrepreneurial, I think you'll agree."

"Hmm, yes," DI Chambers replied. "How did we get them?"

"One of the neighbours rang 101. They said there were lots of strange people going in and out of the house and unfamiliar cars parked outside and that they hadn't seen the woman for several days. I got a couple of DCs to wander past, in their scruffiest sweatshirts and jeans of course, and frankly what they saw fitted the classic cuckooing scenario to a T."

DI Chambers looked down briefly at the papers on her desk. "What's the approach now, in your opinion?"

"It's an opportunity to mop up some of the small fry. But we know very well that there will be new operators trying to muscle in on this patch soon. Cumbria has already had attention from gangs from both Manchester and Liverpool, so the chances are that they will now try to build a stronger base up here."

"So we look for signs of things being disrupted, of people doing unusual things?"

"I think so, yes."

"The never-ending war against drugs. Still, every victory is sweet. Make sure all your DCs know that I'm very pleased with everyone's performance."

"I will. Thank you, guv."

DS Peter Blackford slipped from the office. Chrissy Chambers sat quietly, looking at the mounds of work before her on her desk. The long weekend in Prague had been wonderful, a real rest-cure. She and Tony had enjoyed the sight-seeing, had enjoyed the restaurants and had even had time to take a day-trip by train to Karlovy Vary, the beautiful old spa town that had once been known as Karlsbad. But Prague seemed an age away now. Since getting back, she had been plunged straight back into work. Somehow she had to find time as well for her College of Policing development programme, she told herself. There was a phone call she had promised herself she would make about this, which she still hadn't got round to. She had ten minutes now she could spare.

The phone rang in the lounge of a semi in a pleasant residential area on the outskirts of Cockermouth. A familiar voice answered it.

"George Mulholland speaking," the voice said. The former Detective Superintendent had at that moment finished the Sudoku in his daily paper and was eyeing up with considerable scepticism the cryptic crossword.

"It's DI Chambers here, sir."

"Chrissy, dear girl. How very good to hear you. And, please, none of this formal address now I'm no longer in the force. You must call me George. But, goodness, first I must congratulate you on your promotion!"

"Thank you... George," Chrissy replied. She had been a uniformed Sergeant when George Mulholland, as a Detective Chief Inspector, had first drafted her in to help him on an enquiry into the death of a charity walker who had tried and fatally failed to undertake Britain's Three Peaks challenge in a weekend. The fact that she was now in the CID and holding the rank of Inspector was, she felt, at least in part thanks to the support that she'd received from George Mulholland back then.

"So, what brings you to liven up the afternoon of an old man who is now in his retirement?" George asked.

"I hope I'm not disturbing you?"

"Certainly not. My better half is out at the shops and it is far too early in the day to enjoy a little taste of the golden waters of the Isle of Islay." Mulholland drank moderately, but when he did drink he liked drinking well. There were bottles of the produce of all eight whisky distilleries on Islay lined up neatly in his living room. It was always Islay single malts.

"How you would feel about meeting up some time? A coffee or lunch perhaps? I could come to Cockermouth. I'm close to finishing the Senior Investigating Officer programme, and I just wondered how you would feel about talking things through with me. As a kind of informal mentor."

"Absolutely delighted to be asked, dear girl. If you really feel an old man like me has anything relevant to say."

"George, I vividly remember that there was a whip-round in the police station a few months before you retired, and that was to celebrate the fact that you had just turned fifty-five. So I'm not particularly convinced by all this old man talk."

"Ah, I am pleased to see that there are still sharp brains at work in Cumbria police who are prepared to focus on the facts," he replied. Chrissy laughed.

"What about a week today?" she went on.

"One o'clock, perhaps? We have a nice new café that's opened in South Street. I'll email you though the details."

"Thank you, George. I'll see you then."

31.

"St Joan," said Molly Everett pensively. Nick was in the office and had been giving his editor a full account of what had happened the evening before at the public meeting. Then, apparently at random, she added: "Do you know many of Bernard Shaw's plays?"

Nick laughed. "None. Shaw's a little out of fashion these days. And anyway, my degree was in history."

"Yes, you were one of those clever clogs who went to university. Shaw wrote a play called St Joan. About Joan of Arc, of course. Our local AmDram players performed it a few years back, and Paul had to play the part of the Archbishop of Rheims." Paul was Molly's husband of long-standing, a local solicitor whose practice operated from an office above a shop in Cockermouth.

"Mm?" Nick replied questioningly.

"He wandered round the house for weeks trying to learn his lines, saying things like 'Woman, they will drag you through the streets and burn you as a witch'. By the end, I knew his part as well as he did himself."

Nick laughed.

"You're worried that Joan Arkle is somehow turning into a Bernard Shaw character? There were plenty of farmers there on

Sunday night, but I didn't see any archbishops."

"In the play, Joan of Arc saves France from the English, tells the wimpy Dauphin to get his act together and be crowned King, and finally for her pains gets burned at the stake. You think that must be the end of the story. It's a ridiculously long play, anyway. But Shaw wrote an Epilogue to the play, set years later, which he was adamant couldn't be cut. Basically it shows how twenty-five years on it suited the political establishment of the time for Joan to be pardoned and canonised as a saint. The moral I think is that nobody wants to be told what's right, particularly not by a woman, until it's too late. And then, when they're safely out of the way, everyone agrees what a wonderful person they were.

"Joan Arkle undoubtedly has a certain je-ne-sais-pas-quoi. She still appears to hate me, by the way."

"Treat it as endorsement of your professionalism. How are you going to handle the story of the meeting? Better be careful. She'll still have that chain and padlock."

They both laughed.

"I don't yet know. We could run the story in very different ways. Public meeting ends in chaos and confusion. Near-riot as audience walks out of climate change meeting. Those are both possible headlines. Or we could run with, Different opinions aired at public meeting on climate change. That's equally truthful."

"I know. There are very different ways of seeing the world. Journalism has a frightening amount of power sometimes in how it reports events," Molly replied. "By the way, there's already a Letter to the Editor come in from the National Farmers' Union."

"That's quick. What does it say?"

"Basically that farmers are committed to doing their bit. The NFU has a target of zero net carbon emissions from British agriculture by 2040."

"That's a conveniently long way off," Nick replied.

"You're sounding like Joan Arkle now."

Nick laughed again. "She gets on well with Lluïsa. If I'm the horrible nasty hack as far as Joan is concerned, Lluïsa is the journalist who can do no wrong."

"Oh well, bad cop, good cop, it's a long-established technique. Is

Lluïsa alright for coming in tomorrow?"

"I think so," Nick said. The arrangement Molly and he had agreed was that Lluïsa would come in to the Enquirer office for two days a week, on Tuesdays and Wednesdays. "She's out with Lindsay today, I gather. Open water swimming or climbing, I'm not sure which. Lluïsa and her landlady have rapidly become buddies."

"That's good. Sometime, Nick, you must tell me exactly what Lluïsa's doing here. I don't think I've been told the full truth."

"God, Molly, you're just too good at sniffing out stories. OK, I'll tell you what I know when we've got a moment."

"I suggest we do lunch today. I was going to suggest lunch anyway."

"Oh no," Nick responded. "We only normally do lunch when you've been to the accountant and there's yet more grim news about the Enquirer's finances. That's not the reason this time, I hope."

Molly paused before replying.

"Nick, I'm sorry. That's exactly the reason. I'm running out of ideas."

32.

Elizzabeth had stayed on Sunday night squashed once again on Joan's rock-and-roll bed. It was obvious that Joan was in no fit state to be on her own. Somebody had to be with her.

When the public meeting had eventually finished, when everyone had gone from the church hall, the lights had been turned off and the doors shut, Joan had broken down. "Goldie," she had cried despairingly. "Goldie, where are you?"

Several times in the fifteen minutes or so it had taken Joan to drive her van back from Keswick to her little patch of land near Ullswater Elizzabeth had feared for both their safely. Joan should not have been at the wheel. The van had been driven erratically, all over the road.

"You don't know for sure she's been kidnapped," Elizzabeth had tried to reassure her, once they were safely parked up. "Goldie may have slipped her lead. We'll put out notices tomorrow all round Keswick. She's a distinctive dog. Someone will have seen her."

Joan appeared beyond consoling.

"Please, Joan," Elizzabeth tried again. "Get some sleep. Things always seem better in the morning."

Eventually, Joan had turned in under the duvet, leaving all her clothes on and just kicking off her boots. Elizzabeth sat quietly at the front of the van, near where Goldie herself should have been sleeping, until she heard Joan's breathing become regular. Then she undressed down to her underwear and took her place under what remained of the duvet.

The alarm on Joan's mobile rang at five the next morning. Both women stirred. Elizzabeth looked at the time on her watch. "Joan, for god's sake," she said sleepily. "It's 5am. Why has your alarm gone off?"

"Oh, this is when I normally get up," Joan replied. "Do you want to carry on sleeping?"

"Of course I bloody well want more sleep," Elizzabeth answered.

"OK, I'll be quiet."

Elizzabeth rolled over, grabbing the side of the duvet which Joan had been occupying and pulling it over her ears. But it was impossible. She heard Joan pull open the sliding door of the van to go to the outside toilet, heard her come in a short while later, heard the kettle being put on for the usual breakfast mug of herb tea, and then heard Joan tapping away on her mobile phone. What's more, she realised she needed to go to the toilet herself. She reluctantly pulled herself out of the bed and put on her previous day's shoes.

"God, Joan, you're weirder than I thought. Nobody gets up this early."

"Best time of the day," Joan replied. She was munching a cereal bar in her left hand, her right hand cradling the mug. "Anyway we need to find Goldie as soon as we can. I've put out messages to my all my Twitter followers, and I've done Facebook too. And I've been typing up the text for a notice we can put up this morning everywhere in Keswick."

Joan pointed at the screen of her laptop. Elizzabeth read the text:

STOLEN

(OR LOST)

DOG

Black cross-breed, answers to Goldie

Taken from Keswick town centre, late Sunday evening

£100 reward for recovery

Under the word 'DOG' was a picture of Goldie, with her tongue hanging out in an endearing fashion. At the bottom, Joan had added her mobile phone number and a note saying 'or tweet #wheresgoldie'.

"Can you afford the reward, Joan?" Elizzabeth asked.

"No, but I'll borrow it if I have to."

"I'd love to lend you it, but - ." Elizzabeth stopped herself continuing. She was about to add: "But I have to pay £50 a month from now until eternity to Workington Magistrates' Court". In the circumstances, that wouldn't have been helpful.

"Are you really sure you should say Goldie was stolen?" she said instead.

"Listen, there were people who were there last night who hated me. They can't bear to have their comfortable lives challenged. I know it, somebody took Goldie just to spite me."

"You should go to the police then, if you really think that," she answered Joan's last comment.

"Don't be bloody stupid. That's the last thing I'd do. The police are too busy at work building up the paperwork to make sure that when my Drigg trial finally happens they can nail Joan Arkle good and proper."

"Even so…"

"Forget it. In this world you have to do things for yourself. There's nobody out there you can rely on," Joan responded. She pulled out a small portable printer from one of the van's cupboards and linked it up to the laptop. "How many of these posters do we need?" she said. "Forty or fifty?"

"That's a lot," said Elizzabeth.

"Fifty," Joan replied decisively. "We need to blanket the whole of

Keswick. Hurry up, grab a tea or something. There's a banana too if you're hungry. I'm ready to go."

An hour later, almost every lamppost in central Keswick had a new poster taped to it.

Two hours later, the trolling began.

33.

Baz awoke about seven-thirty. He was still having to get used to being alone in his bed.

Generally speaking, he preferred sex in the mornings to sex last thing at night. He liked the feeling of waking up all sleepy, reaching across with your hand to the naked woman sleeping beside you, waking her up too, stroking her breasts, reaching down to her groin, turning her on. Starting the day with a bang.

As the days went by, he found himself being crosser and crosser with Elizzabeth. She'd flounced out on him, not giving him a second chance. Hadn't he said he was sorry? Hadn't he promised he'd look after her better? Frankly, she had a nerve to walk out. Good riddance. There would be other women who would jump at the chance of letting him get inside their knickers. It was early days yet, although it was a pity that, just at the moment, he hadn't met anyone. Still, Terry had promised to introduce him to one of his friends. A girl called Michelle. Michelle ma belle.

He reached for his phone. A good way to start the day would be to take Joan Sparkle down a peg or two with a few choice comments about her crappy public meeting. He and the lads had managed to set up about a dozen Twitter accounts, all safely anonymised, so you could alternate which accounts you used. In fact, you could pretend to have a conversation between the different accounts, so that it sounded as if lots of people had the same opinions, and all of them thought that Joan Arkle was a twat.

But @joan_sparkle had obviously got up before him. His Twitter feed was full of tweets from her about her bloody dog, which apparently had got itself lost. Baz got to work with some choice replies.

'Goldie has left home to get a decent bowl of dog meat. @joan_sparkle #wheresgoldie', he tweeted.

'Goldie has asked for sanctuary in the Penrith dogs home. Can't stand life in a van with a vegan any longer. @joan_sparkle #wheresgoldie', he continued, from another account.

'Goldie's shagged out after a night being rogered by a randy poodle. @joan_sparkle #wheresgoldie'. Really, Baz thought, this one offered endless opportunities.

And then he had one of his best ideas ever. He had a few minutes before he needed to leave for work. He hurried into Keswick town centre. Another hour and the shops would be opening and people starting to appear but at the moment the roads were almost deserted. Now was the ideal time.

Getting out his mobile phone, he took photo after photo of Keswick street scenes. The Moot Hall. The Golden Lion. The King's Arms. The sports bar. The parish church. The bridge over the river Greta.

Contented, he strolled back to his place and got his phone connected back on the wifi. Then, one by one, he posted the photos on Twitter, accompanying each with a suitable comment.

'Goldie's round the back of the Moot Hall, having a shit. @joan_sparkle #wheresgoldie.' This went with a photo of the front of the town's most famous landmark.

'Goldie's scrounging a cooked English breakfast with bacon and sausages inside the breakfast room. @joan_sparkle #wheresgoldie'. This was posted alongside a photograph of the outside of one of the town's main hotels.

'Goldie's praying God to find her a better place to live. @joan_sparkle #wheresgoldie.' This was sent with a photo of Keswick church.

'Goldie's hiding behind the lamppost. You can't see her because she's got so thin. Not been eating enough meat. @joan_sparkle #wheresgoldie'.

'Goldie's slipped down the cracks of the drain in the gutter. Bark, bark, bark, let me out. @joan_sparkle #wheresgoldie'

'Goldie has borowed an invisibility cloak from Harry Potter. She's just in front of the park bench. @joan_sparkle #wheresgoldie'

These last were attached to photographs of empty streets. Exhilarated at his creativity, Baz sent round texts to Horsey and

Mick and Terry, asking them to join in. Frankly, he wanted to give Joan Arkle as hard a time as he possibly could. He blamed her more than anyone for Elizzabeth leaving him, and he felt that each tweet he sent was in some small way a gesture of revenge. Besides, it had been impossible in Keswick not to notice the posters which Joan Arkle had been out posting about her bloody dog. If she wanted publicity for the dog, then who was he to deny her a little extra coverage?

Mick responded almost immediately, and Baz saw his efforts appearing on Twitter. Mick had raided the internet for implausible photographs, so that the messages were rapidly becoming more and more surreal. A picture of Buckingham Palace bore the message *'Goldie's been up to London to visit the Queen'*. One of a Scots Guardsman playing the bagpipes came with *'What does this Scotsman have under his kilt? It's Goldie, who's playing hide and seek'*.

Together Baz and Mick carried on in like vein for another quarter of an hour. Horsey hadn't got back in touch; fair enough, Horsey usually had to do the breakfast shift in the hotel where he worked. Terry also hadn't replied: he was also obviously tied up.

Baz knew he needed to get ready for work. His firm currently had the electrical contract for a hotel refurb job just outside Ambleside, and it would take him half an hour or so to drive down there. What a pity. How many tweets did you need to do, he asked himself as he reluctantly put his phone in his pocket, before a hashtag started trending? They surely couldn't be far off now.

34.

Every one of the fifty flyers had been put up.

"Do you think I should print off some more?" Joan asked Elizzabeth. "The art-work's on the laptop."

"For god's sake, fifty's enough. Everyone will see them."

Joan shrugged. They were back in Joan's van, which she had parked in a car park at the back of the shops in Keswick. She was drinking another herb tea and dipping into a bag of dried apricots. Elizzabeth had insisted on a coffee and had also bought herself two croissants from one of the supermarkets. Joan had told her firmly that the croissants had butter in them. Elizzabeth had told her firmly that she didn't care.

Since finishing the leafleting and parking up, Joan had been monitoring her mobile phone. Her tweets about Goldie were now attracting a seemingly endless number of trolling responses. She passed the phone across to Elizzabeth. "Look at these," she said.

"God, Joan, that's just awful. You have to go to the police."

"We've had the conversation about the police already," Joan replied. "Same answer". The tears of the night before had gone. She was back to her usual self. Joan Arkle, the woman with a mission and the determination to see it through, had returned from the dark place she had been to the previous evening.

Elizzabeth, munching her second croissant, reread one of the #wheresgoldie tweets more carefully. *Goldie has borowed an invisibility cloak from Harry Potter*, it said. She had a sudden intuition that she knew who was tweeting. More than once when she'd lived with Baz he'd left her a note saying things like 'Have borowed £10 from your purse. Hope that's OK'.

There must be thousands, millions, of people in the Twittersphere who couldn't spell 'borrowed'. But still. Elizzabeth recalled what Joan had said about someone taking Goldie out of spite. She thought back to the previous evening. There had certainly been a lot of hostility about. There had been rows and rows of unhappy farmers. There had been the journalist there whom neither she nor Joan liked. And right at the end of the evening Baz had been there with his mates, pissed of course. But surely not…?

"Since I'm in Keswick, I've got a few things I may as well do," she said to Joan, having come to a decision. "Leave me here. I'll ring you later." Joan was talking of taking the van back to Bassenthwaite that morning, hoping for a further tryst with red squirrels.

"OK."

"And don't be too downhearted about Goldie."

"I'm angry. I'm never downhearted," Joan replied.

Elizzabeth opened the sliding van door and headed back towards Keswick's main shopping street. Her relations with Baz had completely broken down, there was no point contacting him, but she had decided that she would see if she could track down Horsey in the hotel where he worked. Of the four of them, he was probably the most sensible, she thought.

But first, she was going to disobey Joan. She was going to the police.

Or she was going to try to. Once upon a time, Keswick had a traditional police station. But, as everyone knows, the police service in Cumbria as everywhere else has faced swingeing cuts. The police station has been sold and now local police officers operate out of the Keswick Town Council building in Main Street. Elizzabeth made her way there, entering apprehensively.

"Oh no, love, sorry," said the woman receptionist who greeted her. "There's no public facilities here to talk to the police. It's just their private base, see."

"So how do I talk to them?" Elizzabeth asked.

"In an emergency you ring 999. Otherwise you ring 101. It's quite simple."

Back on the street outside, Elizzabeth found herself a bench to sit on, pulled out her phone and dialled. The 101 number rang and rang with no reply. She tried again and this time found herself speaking to a tired-voiced woman, who sounded as if she was a long way away.

"I'm ringing up on behalf of a friend," Elizzabeth began. "Her dog was stolen last night. Or at least probably stolen."

New calls to the police have to be logged properly. Elizzabeth got no further before she was interrupted and asked for her full name and her date of birth. "But it's not my dog, I'm just ringing up for someone else," she replied, without success. With considerable reluctance she gave her personal details. It probably didn't matter. After the Drigg demo, the Police National Computer already knew all about her.

"You are reporting a stolen dog?" the voice asked her. "What breed of dog and what is its value?"

"It's a mongrel, a black dog. Her name's Goldie. There's quite a lot of Labrador in her," Elizzabeth replied.

"A mongrel. Not a pedigree dog being kept for breeding or showing?" the woman went on. "What value would you say?"

"Well, I don't know. Money's not the point. The dog's really loved. My friend thinks the dog was kidnapped by someone who was out to get her."

"Where and when did this incident take place?"

"Yesterday evening, at a church hall in Keswick. There was a public meeting going on. My friend was one of the speakers. There were lots of people there who don't like her."

"You said that the dog may or may not be stolen?"

"Yes, that's right."

"You've no evidence the dog was taken? No witnesses present?"

"No, but…"

The conversation was petering out. Elizzabeth had imagined walking into a police station, talking to a Desk Sergeant, showing them pictures of Goldie, showing the tweets which Joan was having to endure. On the phone to a distant call centre, her story was sounding all too implausible.

"I can't give you a crime number," the woman said. "However, I have logged the details you have submitted. An officer may get back to you, but I am afraid this is unlikely to be a priority case." And then the standard wind-up line: "Thank you for calling Cumbria Police today." The line went dead.

Perhaps Joan was right all along about the police, Elizzabeth thought. She got up from the bench and headed towards the hotel where she knew Horsey worked. This time her luck was in. As she approached, Horsey and another man, presumably one of his workmates, were just leaving. Horsey had a pile of leaflets under his arm, prominently printed with the words A New Voice for Cumbria.

"I was coming to look for you, Horsey," Elizzabeth said.

Horsey looked embarrassed.

"Yeah?" he replied.

"Yes, we need to talk.

The other man looked confused. "Who's this, and who's Horsey?" he asked.

"This is Baz's ex. I'll explain later."

"Joan Arkle's dog has disappeared, and I think Baz is trolling her about it. Some of the tweets are really nasty," Elizzabeth continued.

Horsey looked even more embarrassed.

"I dunno. Baz isn't feeling very warm towards you. Or towards your friend."

"Has Baz got the dog? Joan thinks one of you could have taken it last night."

"You're joking."

"You were all pissed."

"Yeah, but do us a favour."

"As a prank?"

"No, I left the hall with the lads, with Baz and Mick, I think Terry was having a slash at the time, and the dog was lying there in a corner with its tongue out. Anyway, I remember because Baz said something like 'next time I'll bring you a tin of Chum'. It was a joke. That was all."

"OK," Elizzabeth was mulling this over. "OK," she said again. "But listen, Horsey, there seems to be a lot of nastiness going on just at the moment. I don't like it."

"I think Baz thinks that all the nastiness is coming directly from you. He's missing you, you know. He'd have you back."

"It's over," said Elizzabeth firmly.

35.

Lindsay wriggled into her wet suit and with some difficulty yanked the large zip up her back. Swimming was the easy bit, compared with this part of the process.

Alongside her another woman was already ready, splashing water from the lake on to her face. "Brr," she said. "It is cold, your mountain water." She grimaced.

"Yes, this is Cumbria, not the Med," Lindsay replied. She had rung around friends in her triathlon circle over the weekend and arranged to borrow a wetsuit that, more or less, fitted Lluïsa. "It'll be fine once we get started."

Lindsay was a planner by background who worked three days a week for a local council as part of a job share. Really, she would have liked a full-time post, but that would have meant leaving the Lake District. It was out of the question: it would have been impossible to leave Phil. And completely impossible to leave the mountains, of course.

Still, her work meant she always had Mondays off. Today, she had persuaded Lluïsa to help her recce one of the swimming sections of the Frog Graham. They'd driven in Lindsay's car up to Keswick and then taken the quiet road on the western side of Derwent Water. This would be the last, and the longest, of the four lake crossings she would have to do when she was doing the Frog Graham for real. Today the plan was to swim just to the little outcrop of Otterbield Island and then on to St Herbert's Island half way across. Lindsay wanted to be sure that Lluïsa was as confident a swimmer as she'd implied.

It was still relatively early, not yet ten o'clock, and they had the stony beach at the edge of the lake to themselves. Lluïsa looked across to Lindsay. "Time to plunge," she said. "U, dos, tres…"

Lindsay watched from the beach as the younger woman launched herself into the water, immediately breaking into a strong front crawl stroke. She needn't have worried: if anything, Lluïsa was a stronger swimmer than she was. She entered the water in turn.

It was true that, even in wetsuits, the water was cold. Still, the suits gave them buoyancy. Lluïsa paused momentarily to let Lindsay catch her up, and they swam side by side away from the shore. In ten minutes or so they were on the shallow approach to Otterbield Island.

"When you do the Frog Graham, you have to get out and run across each of the three Derwent Water islands," Lindsay said.

"Why?"

Lindsay laughed. "That's just the way the challenge was created."

"OK, but now I want to keep swimming," Lluïsa replied. "We can stop on the next island."

"St Herbert's. OK."

In the distance one of the Keswick tourist boats was coming out of Derwent Bay. Ahead of them rose the rocky outcrop of Walla Crag and away to their right was the summit of High Seat. Lindsay matched Lluïsa stroke for stroke. It felt good to be wild swimming in such a beautiful place. It felt good, too, to be doing something physical. It hadn't always been the case in the past, but now Lindsay's body knew exactly what was expected of it, whether she was on a bike, in the water or running in fell shoes over the hills.

"I like it here," Lluïsa said eventually when they had arrived at St Herbert's Island and dragged themselves out of the water.

"How long will you be in England?" Lindsay asked.

"I think I must stay some more time still," Lluïsa replied. "My employer understands, fortunately. They do not pay me, but my job is kept."

"If you're still here next month, maybe we could do the Frog Graham together," Lindsay said. "You told me you ran in the mountains back home."

"Yes, in the mountains behind Barcelona. In the Pyrenees, too. We have high mountains there. You can breakfast in Catalunya, have a picnic lunch in a refuge hut in France and then return for a good meal in a Catalan restaurant in the evening. You must come."

"The Spanish-French border runs along the summits of course."

Lluïsa looked a little pained. "The border between France and Catalunya, yes. We tend not to say Spain."

"Ah, OK," Lindsay replied.

"Your mountains are small, but I like them," Lluïsa went on.

"I'll take you running on the fells next time we're both free. We'll need to buy you some fell shoes though."

"What are fells?"

"The local name for mountains. It's a Viking word. The Norwegians call them fjells."

"Fells," Lluïsa tried the word out. "A nice word. Yes, we will go running on the fells. But first we need to swim back."

"We do. Ready?"

Lluïsa nodded.

Like large ungainly otters, the two women in their wetsuits plunged back into the lake.

"I will race you," Lluïsa said laughing.

"You're on," Lindsay replied.

36.

Had he wanted to, Terry could have joined Baz and Mick on Twitter and given some more traction to the #wheresgoldie hashtag. In his case, though, he would have been able to say exactly where Goldie was. His tweet would have said something like *Goldie is on the M6, in the back of my car, and is driving me crazy by barking all the time. #wheresgoldie.*

But Terry felt no inclination at all to tweet. The day was not going well.

Looking back, he must have been more stoned and pissed the evening before than perhaps he'd realised. At the time, untying the dog's lead and taking her with him as he left the church hall had seemed an entertaining way to finish the evening. His plan was to catch up with Baz, Mick and Horsey who were just ahead of him, and they'd all have a good laugh when they saw his prize. Maybe they'd take a photograph of themselves pointing their fingers as pretend guns at the dog.

Terry hadn't really thought beyond that. But his current girlfriend Trix had told him that she liked animals. He could maybe give her the dog as a present.

Things hadn't gone to plan. Baz, Mick and Horsey had vanished into the Keswick night, so Terry found himself having to drag Goldie back through the streets to the little one-bedroom flat above his shop. Trix was there, already half asleep.

"Where's the dog from?" she'd said.

"I sort-of found it. It looked like it needed a home. I could give the dog to you as a present." Terry was aware that he was not entirely coherent.

"Are you crazy?" Trix said is astonishment. "A stolen dog?"

Terry thought about this for quite some time.

"That's funny," he said eventually. "That makes it a hot dog."

"You'd better take the dog back straightaway where you found it," Trix went on unamused.

"Too late," Terry said. "Tomorrow will do." He took Goldie, still on her lead, into the small kitchen, found a blanket and gestured to the dog to lie down.

"There you are. Good boy. Or good girl. Whatever," he said, returning to the bedroom, taking off his clothes and getting under the duvet alongside Trix.

Goldie started yowling. It wasn't as loud as howling or barking, it was a pitiful noise that was closer to crying. And, having started, Goldie continued yowling. Almost all night.

"For fuck's sake, shut that dog up," Trix said at one point in the early hours. They had both been awake for some time.

"I've tried. I've given it water. I've given it that tin of beef stew I had in the cupboard. What more does the bloody dog want?"

"It probably wants its owner," said Trix pointedly. "You're a complete moron, Terry Venables."

"OK, sorry, I'll make sure everything is sorted tomorrow."

She didn't reply. Trix, still awake, had turned on to her side away from Terry and had yanked as much of the duvet as she could over her head. Finally she must have slept, because the next thing she was aware of was her alarm sounding at half past six. Goldie was still yowling piteously from the kitchen.

"Jesus," she said. Terry was asleep. As every weekday morning, she dragged herself out of the bed and made for the bathroom. She worked morning shifts cleaning one of the Lake District's most prestigious (and most expensive) hotels, situated deep in the Borrowdale countryside. The minibus picked her up outside Booths supermarket each morning at 7.15.

Trix just had time for a bowl of cereal and a cup of coffee before heading out. She gave the dog a token pat as she did. "Goodbye, dog, it's been nice knowing you. Don't come back."

"Goodbye, Terry," she called out in an extra loud voice as she clomped down the stairs making as much noise as she could. "Goodbye," she called again from the front door. The dog was continuing to yowl.

Terry slept on, eventually waking up around eight. With a start, he remembered that he had unfinished business waiting for him, lying on a blanket in his kitchen. He dressed quickly, picking up his mobile phone as he did. Oh shit. The dog's disappearance was all over Twitter. He read the tweets which he knew had come through from Baz and Mick, maybe Horsey too, without amusement. The more that the whole of the Lake District was being asked #wheresgoldie, the less chance he had of quietly getting the dog back unobserved to the church hall. His plan was to tie it up outside on the church railings. Someone would be bound to find it.

What does this Scotsman have under his kilt? It's Goldie, who's playing hide and seek. The tweets were still coming in. *Here's Goldie enjoying a morning out at the Eiffel Tower. She stowed away on a plane from Manchester. Naughty Goldie.*

Shit, shit, Terry said to himself. As if it wasn't enough to read about Goldie on Twitter there was also a What'sApp about the dog which had arrived from Trix, who must be on the minibus. *DON'T do anything about the dog until I've spoken to you. Keep the dog with you. This is IMPORTANT. I'll ring after ten. Xxx.*

Terry was pondering what precisely was so important that he had to endure yet more of the dog's yowling when there was a knock on the front door of the shop.

Bad-temperedly, he went down the stairs. Beyond were two men who, given the circumstances, he would rather not have seen. Or given any circumstances. He let them in.

"Morning, Terry, my old son," said one, a tall white man probably in his early thirties.

"Morning, Terry," said the other, a much shorter man, also white, with close cropped hair. "Long time no see, eh?"

"What are you doing here?" Terry replied. "We agreed you wouldn't come to the shop."

"Ah well, needs must. Our friends in the police have got off their arses over the weekend so there are going to be a few changes around here. Just for today we need to use your flat."

"No, that's not the deal. We agreed that I could help you out now and again when I'm going south in the car, but nothing on the premises. I've got a legitimate business to look after."

"Yes, and how did you get the deposit for the lease? A figure of £5000 as I recall, wasn't it Alan? Perhaps I should remind you who lent you that money. Should I, Alan?"

"I think you should, Rod," the other man replied.

"It was your good friend Rod, wasn't it? Anyway," Rod went on, "you don't need to worry your little head about us. Not at all. Because you need to go to the wholesalers in Preston today. You're right out of eucalyptus-flavoured oil, aren't you? Or something like that. Can't disappoint the customers. Here's the address in Preston where you need to go."

"I open the shop on Mondays at ten."

"Yes, but not today. Look, we've thought of everything." Rod pointed to a handwritten sign which Alan was carrying. *Sorry, we are unexpectedly closed today due to a family funeral*, it read. "It just needs sticking to the front door."

"There's no funeral," Terry replied.

"Well, not yet," Rod replied. "Let's hope there won't be any funerals any time soon."

A loud barking began from the top of the stairs.

"Got yourself a guard dog?" Alan asked.

"Just a dog."

Rod went up the stairs and stopped at the door of the kitchen. "Terry," he said, "Come up here."

Reluctantly Terry followed him.

"I've seen that dog before. In fact, I've seen that dog this very morning on about a thousand Stolen Dogs signs which are all over Keswick. What the fuck is that dog doing here, Terry?"

"Sorry, it's a long story. I found it. I'm going to hand it in today to the police."

"You're bloody not going anywhere near the police today. You'll have to take the dog with you to Preston. It can't be left here with us." He turned to the dog. "Come on, Rover, Terry here is taking you on a magical mystery trip. And in fact he's leaving right now."

"I'm not ready yet," Terry replied.

"Oh yes you are," Rod replied. "Goodbye Terry. Don't come back before six o'clock. And tell your girlfriend the same. You'll have to text her. We don't want to see her, is that clear?"

"Enjoy the sights of Preston," Alan added. "Bye, bye."

37.

A hundred pounds is a lot of money. Or at least it is a great deal of money if, like Trix, you are working very hard for the minimum wage.

It was impossible for Trix not to see the 'Stolen Dog' signs or to recognise the dog in the photograph as she walked the short distance

119

from Terry's flat to the minibus rendezvous place. And it was impossible not to notice the reward which was on offer.

The money was as good as in the bag. She tried ringing Terry, but the call went through to voicemail. The lazy bugger was still asleep. She texted instead. All he needed to do was to keep the dog on the premises until she was back from work at lunchtime.

Once safely on the bus, she texted through to the mobile phone number at the bottom of the Stolen Dog poster. *Hi*, she texted. *Great news, we've found Goldie. My boyfriend found the dog last night wandering aimlessly in Keswick town centre. It was too late to ring the police so he brought it home, and we've looked after her. We've fed her and made sure she was comfortable. Goldie's quite safe. Can you come round to the little vaping shop behind the Alhambra cinema in Keswick at about one? Looking forward to a happy ending!* One o'clock was when Trix would be back from her shift in the hotel. It was, strictly speaking, true that Goldie could have been picked up from Terry's shop before then but Trix felt justified in getting her half share of the reward money. Much as she loved Terry, if she wasn't around when the dog-owner came Terry might feel entitled to claim it all for himself.

The text was safely on its way when a What'sApp came in from Terry. It was not what Trix had been expecting. *Don't under any circumstances come home before six. Old friends have arrived. I'm spending the day in Preston. Dog with me in car.*

Trix messaged back. *I've arranged for the dog owner to come to the shop to pick up the dog at one o'clock. There's a £100 reward!!*

Terry replied immediately. *For gods sake cancel them. Shop shut today. Invent some story. Keep them well away from the shop.*

There was nothing for it, but to send a second text message to Goldie's owner. Trix pondered how she could write something plausible. In the end she typed: *Really sorry. Goldie is absolutely fine, she's a lovely dog. My boyfriend's taken her to Preston for the day because he didn't know about the one o'clock arrangement. We'll fix a new time as soon as poss.*

It was a pretty curious message but, Trix thought, it would have to do. Almost immediately she noticed a phone call coming in from the number she had texted. She let it ring out. She let the three other attempted calls which came through almost immediately from the same number ring out too. Just for a day, she said to herself, Goldie's owner would have to be patient.

The motorway was snarled up just beyond the southern turn-off to Lancaster, and Terry found the traffic ahead of him slowing to a crawl and then stopping completely. A few minutes later an ambulance and a police car both screamed past on the hard shoulder. Just his luck to be caught in a tail-back.

Just his luck to have a snivelling dog with him. Terry didn't know much about dogs, but he was beginning to realise that Goldie probably should have been taken for a morning walk. Somewhere close to the Killington services he had heard the sound of water running on to the back seat of the car. The bloody dog was having a pee.

"Listen, dog," he said, turning round. "We're in a traffic jam. I'm sorry, you'll just have to be patient." He tried passing his arm back towards the dog and giving her a stroke. A low growl met his efforts.

"Oh come on, I'm only trying to be friendly," Terry said.

Goldie moved restlessly round the back of the car.

"Cross your legs, dog," Terry called back.

Slowly, very slowly, the traffic began to move forward again. A short way ahead he passed the police car and ambulance and two cars which were now parked on the hard shoulder. It was a shunt, nothing too serious by the look of it.

A new noise emerged from the throat of the dog in the back of Terry's car, a sort of anxious crying.

"Nearly there," Terry said. The car had just passed the first sign advising that the Preston turn was now a mile away. Terry, in the fast lane doing eighty, increased his speed further. But there could be no mistaking what was happening behind his left shoulder. Squatting in the floor at the rear of his car, Goldie was relieving herself of two very large and very smelly turds.

"You stupid stupid dog," Terry yelled. "You stupid dog."

At some level, however, Terry knew this wasn't quite right. It was he who was stupid.

38

Lunches out with the editor of the Cumbrian Enquirer were not precisely glamorous affairs. Nick and Molly had found a table in a café round the corner from the newspaper's office and settled down with glasses of tap water they'd helped themselves to from the jug by the counter. Molly was opting for mushroom quiche and mixed salad. Nick had ordered a soup-and-sandwich combo. The sandwich promised to be a goat's cheese from the Appleby Creamery over in east Cumbria.

"Tell me the worst," Nick said.

"I saw John last week, along with John and Teresa," she began.

Nick understood. John Wythenshawe was the Cumbrian Enquirer's accountant. John Greet and Teresa Perkins, brother and sister, were the majority owners of the Enquirer, having inherited 80% of the shares from their father. Molly, in hindsight perhaps unwisely, had more than ten years earlier invested some of her savings in the business. She was the third, minority, shareholder.

"We're trading at a hefty loss, but we knew that anyway," Molly went on. "Basically the Greet family now just want to get out. They've put feelers out to the main newspaper groups in the region. But of course this is a bad time for all local papers. I don't think anyone will buy the Enquirer with the intention of keeping it as a going concern."

"Some local papers seem to be keeping their heads above water," Nick responded.

"Maybe, but their circulation area is probably bigger than ours. We've always been squeezed between the Carlisle papers and those coming out of Kendal."

"Could we mount a buy-out of the Greet family?"

"The trouble is that they've viewed the Enquirer for so long as a nice little cash-cow. They'd want far more for their shares than they are really worth. Don't think I haven't thought about this already."

"We know the old business model for newspapers has gone. We're just not getting the classified advertising, or the job adverts, or the property adverts that we used to. What about making the title free, and hand-delivering to everyone?"

"I've thought of this too. I asked John Wythenshawe informally what he thought and he convinced me pretty soon that the figures didn't stack up. I know that there's been a boom in local freesheets but none of them really have proper journalists or pay for contributions."

The food had arrived. Nick began to eat his soup. "The Enquirer's much loved locally," he said. "I think we should look into crowdfunding. Up in Scotland the West Highland Free Press turned itself some years ago into a kind of co-operative. We could do something similar. We could invite readers to invest in the title and become members of a Cumbrian Enquirer co-op."

"Yes, and I like that idea. But: two problems. If we use the Cumbrian Enquirer name, we face the same problem of having to pay off the Greet family. And if we don't, we have to start completely afresh with a newspaper title that nobody's ever heard of."

Nick nodded. "What's the second problem?" he asked.

"The second problem is that even if we raised the capital to buy the business, and maybe we can do that, I'm not sure we could find the income we'd need to keep it going week after week. Well, not as the sort of professional paper that both you and I would want to be associated with," Molly responded.

There was a pause as she cut into her quiche.

"Do you buy newspapers yourself, Nick?" she asked.

"Of course," Nick replied.

"What about your daughter? What about Rosa?"

"No, she just catches up with the news on her smartphone."

"Exactly," Molly said. "Anyone younger than about forty just isn't buying our product any more. We're dinosaurs."

"Yet local papers are essential. For one thing, they're absolutely essential for a healthy local democracy."

"Yes, and maybe that's why people are increasingly disillusioned with politics. By the way, what's the latest with the New Voice for Cumbria irredentists?"

"I gather there's another street protest being planned in a week or two in Whitehaven. To be honest, it's looking more and more like a home for far-right street-fighters and nobody else."

"Hm, poor Phillip Petherton. Nobody to speak Cumbraek to."

"No." Nick took a bite of sandwich. "Maybe we should print the Enquirer in Cumbraek. At least our subscribers would be loyal."

"The Catalan local press seems still very strong. Or at least that's what Lluïsa told me."

"Completely different culture," Nick replied.

"So what's the story about Lluïsa?"

Nick put down his soup spoon. "You must promise not to tell the Spanish police," he said.

"Promise," Molly replied.

Nick briefly told Molly the background. The episode in Girona with the Catalan flag, the Guardia Civil, the need for a quiet bolt-hole for a few months, the letter to Nick from Ana/Anna, the visit from Rosa who had arrived complete with Lluïsa and suitcase. Molly roared with laughter. "Well," she said. "That's a fantastic story."

"Not one to be printed, though."

"Sadly not." Her quiche was almost finished. "Anyway, to get back to the Enquirer. My idea is that we each buy lottery tickets from now on every week and hope something will turn up."

"And if not?"

"You're a freelance anyway. I become a freelance, perhaps. Or maybe I ask Lluïsa to get me a junior reporter's job on her paper in Girona. What's my chance?"

"I think the Catalan word is the same as ours: *zero.*"

Molly laughed. "I've had over thirty-five brilliant years at the Enquirer but perhaps all good things come to an end at some point. Still, in the meantime…. Why are we lingering over lunch? We've got a paper to get out for Wednesday afternoon."

39.

Joan sat in her van in the car park at Dodd Wood, and decided that red squirrels could wait for another day. Her mind was too focused on Goldie to concentrate on photography.

She reread the two texts which had arrived on her phone. The first text had lifted her heart. Come one o'clock, she and Goldie would be reunited. She would go to one of the cash machines in Keswick beforehand to get the £100 she had promised. There should just about be enough money in her account. It would be worth every penny to see her dog again.

The second text, though, was different. *Goldie is absolutely fine, she's a lovely dog. My boyfriend's taken her to Preston for the day.* There was something strange about this message. Why would you take a dog you'd found the night before to Preston, if you were about to return it to its owner? And, more worryingly, why was the person who sent the texts not answering their phone when Joan had tried to ring?

The key question, Joan decided, was whether the texts were genuine. Or was all this just some terrible continuation of the trolling she had been receiving all day on Twitter? Her experience of Twitter showed just how nasty some people could be.

Whether genuine or not, Joan decided that she would check out the vaping shop that the first text had mentioned, and that she would be there at one o'clock just in case. Anyway, she and Elizzabeth had agreed by text that they would rendezvous back in Keswick at half past one. Joan turned the ignition and turned the van left out of Dodd Wood to head back alongside Bassenthwaite Lake towards Keswick.

The shop was easy to find, but it was shut. A sign on the door said that it was closed all day for a funeral. Joan tried to figure out how this information could possibly relate to the texts. It was perhaps just possible, she thought, that the shop owner had unexpectedly had to go to Preston for a funeral. Perhaps they'd thought it would be better to take Goldie with them rather than leaving her cooped up inside the shop. Perhaps whoever the person was who ran the shop was at the funeral service when she had tried to ring back and that's why they hadn't answered. Still, she had learned long ago not to believe everything people wanted her to believe.

The front door gave access both to the shop and to a stairway going upstairs to what looked like a flat above. She hammered on it hard, repeatedly, but nobody came.

She certainly didn't have a sixth sense that anyone was around. All seemed silent. Neither was there, as she had secretly hoped, the sound of familiar barking coming from inside. Oh well, it had been worth trying.

Elizzabeth was already waiting for her in Booth's car park when Joan got there at about twenty past one.

"Jump in," Joan said opening the campervan's sliding door. "I'll put on the kettle. Meanwhile, what do you make of these?" She passed her mobile phone across.

Elizzabeth read the texts.

"Well, the first message sounds very promising," she said. "The second's a bit strange. Did you go to the shop at one?"

"Yes."

"Anyone there?"

"No."

Elizzabeth reread the messages, and suddenly gave a gasp. "Shit," she said, "The vaping shop. I know whose shop that is."

"Yes?"

"It's run by Terry Venables. One of Baz's friends."

Joan pondered this information. "Somebody who was there on Sunday evening?" she asked.

"Yes, he came in with Baz and two other mates. They were the guys who arrived late and were pissed."

Joan was silent once again.

"So Terry could have walked off with Goldie?" she said eventually.

Elizzabeth thought back to her conversation with Horsey. Horsey had been very convincing when she had asked him directly if he and the others had taken Goldie. He'd replied no and Elizzabeth had believed him. But, when she thought about it, Horsey had said that he left the church hall with Baz and Mick. Terry had left separately. She shrugged. "I suppose it's possible," answering Joan's question. "I mean, it's the only lead we've got at the moment. I don't really know Terry, but Baz's friends can do pretty stupid things."

Joan appeared to have come to a decision. "Listen, Elizzabeth, you stay here," she said. "I won't be very long."

It took Joan about ten minutes to walk back to the vaping shop, choosing to make a couple of purchases from an ironmongers on the way there. Once at the shop, she immediately got to work. A newly-acquired paint brush was dipped in a newly-purchased pot of white paint. In very large letters Joan began writing on the window.

Hello, Terry, she wrote. *Where is Goldie?*

The letters took up almost the entire window. She had just finished the final question mark when she was aware that she was being watched by two men who had arrived behind her.

"Hello, sweetheart," said the taller of the two men. He pointed at the window. "I think you need to explain to us what this is all about."

"Don't you dare call me sweetheart," Joan replied, still holding the paint brush and waving it towards the man. "It's patronising and sexist."

The man appeared unfazed. "Most women don't seem to mind," he said.

"Well I do. If people want to call me anything they can use my name. It's Joan."

The man looked at her. "I see, Joan," he said.

"Are you anything to do with this shop?" Joan went on. "I want my dog back."

"No, we're just passing." He looked at his colleague who nodded back. "Still, this looks a very unusual way of communicating with the owner. It looks to me very like vandalism. I think you could get into trouble for this."

"I saw a PCSO just round the corner by the cinema," the other man chipped in. "Shall I go and ask him to come round here?"

"Perhaps you should, Alan. Or do you think we should effect a citizen's arrest? That's allowed, isn't it?"

"It certainly is." Alan appeared to be thinking things through. "Although, in the circumstances…. It's terrible to lose a pet. I had a dog go astray once. Joan's actions certainly seem highly irregular but I think I can sympathise."

"Perhaps you're right," said the first man. He turned to Joan. "I can see you're very emotional about this. Perhaps this time we won't do anything."

Joan's eyes flashed back at him. "I am not being emotional," she said aggressively. "You are patronising me again. You are mistaking anger for emotion."

"Well, my apologies if I have offended," the man responded. "Perhaps we should just be on our way and pretend this time that… that we didn't see your paint-pot. And we will keep an eye out for your missing dog. Is it your dog that's on all the posters on the lampposts?"

"Yes," Joan replied.

"And your contact number at the bottom?"

"Yes," Joan said again.

"That's good. So we'll know how to reach you again, if of course we ever need to," he concluded.

"Let's go, Rod," said Alan. The two men walked purposefully away up the road, and turned the corner at the end. Joan gave one last look back at the shop window. It was a pity she had been spotted at work, but all in all she was pleased with her handiwork. Sometimes direct action achieved things that you couldn't possibly achieve without it.

Terry the shop owner, she felt, knew where Goldie was. Terry would now get the message very loud and clear that he needed to give her back. She headed in the opposite direction to the way the men had gone, making towards the van.

Rod and Alan had turned the corner and then stopped.

"Well, what the fuck?" said Rod.

"Terry has a great deal of explaining to do to us," Alan replied.

"We need to shift somewhere else immediately," Rod continued. "Seven thousand pounds of stock in that building and a fucking great sign painted on the window in white paint for any passing cop saying, 'There's something really odd going on here.'"

"I know. If she'd painted 'Drugs inside. Come and bust us' it could hardly have been more obvious."

"Cut our losses?"

"For a couple of grand, I'd say OK. But seven grand? - not if we can help it."

"Any ideas where we could move the stock?"

"My mate in Whitehaven is working on something. But he says he needs another 24 hours."

"We could leave the goods overnight in the boot of a car."

"Yes, but what worries me is that we would have to go in to shop to bring it out. There's no back door, I checked. If that woman is still around, we'd be done for. In fact, given the way the window is, anyone going past would eyeball us."

"We could remove the paint from the window. That would help."

"Great idea, Rod. The two of us get out some white spirit and J-cloths and start scrubbing away. That really would attract the attention of anyone going by."

"You're right. So we're stuffed?"

"I think we book ourselves into the best hotel we can find tonight. We'll text Terry and tell him to get the fucking dog back to fucking Joan the minute he's back in town. At least that will deal with her. And, once the dog's disposed of, we'll tell him he has to remove the paint too before he does anything else."

"Terry's bringing more stock back from Preston. About five grand's worth. What about that?"

"I guess it has to stay in his flat overnight with the other stock. Tomorrow, provided the paint's gone and the dog's gone, it should be safe for us to go back in." Alan paused. "By the way, Rod, how do you feel to be exposed as a patronising sexist git?"

"Shut it," Rod replied. After a pause he continued, "Do you think she's a client? Potential client?"

"Hard to say. Weed probably, rather than our goods."

"Still, we have her name and phone number. You never know, she could yet be useful to us."

"She's got our names too."

"God, did we use our names when we were speaking to her? That was careless."

"It would have been even more careless if we hadn't used our work names," Alan replied. They both laughed.

"It's alright," Alan went on. She thinks we were just casual passers-by. No reason why she would associate us with Terry or with the shop."

"That's true."

"So. Everything will work out just fine. Except perhaps for Terry, who I think needs a good talking-to tomorrow. Shall we go and look for an hotel?"

"Separate hotels. No need to be stupid."

"You're right. I'll have the best hotel in Keswick and you can take the second best," Alan said.

"Watch it, short-arse."

"Patronising, sexist and sizeist as well. What a guy." He paused and smirked at his business colleague. "Sweet dreams. See you tomorrow."

40.

All things considered, Terry was not having such a bad day. He'd found a car hand-wash and valeting place on the road in from the motorway to Preston and had stopped and asked them to do a proper clean and polish job inside and out. The guys there looked askance at the two piles of dog poo behind the driver's seat but Terry had told them he'd pay them an extra £10 to sort it out. "It's unfortunate," he said, "my dog suffers from a medical condition which makes him incontinent. I'm sure you understand." The £10 apparently was enough to facilitate the necessary understanding.

While the car was being seen to, he'd taken Goldie on her lead for a short stroll along some of Preston's suburban streets. For the first time, the dog seemed prepared to be friendly, even at one stage wagging her tail when Terry bent down to stroke her. Maybe he was a dog person without knowing it, Terry told himself. Maybe he and Trix should get a dog themselves. Maybe they'd choose a dog like this one, black and hairy and slightly scruffy.

Once the car was sorted, Goldie sprang back on to the back seat and Terry looked at the satnav. He had all day. He'd do the pick-up for Rod and Alan after lunch so the goods weren't in the car too long, he decided. In the meantime the satnav was telling him that there was an area of parkland south of the city centre, on the banks of the river Ribble. Why not? The weather was warm, the spring flowers would be out. A morning beside the river sounded ideal.

It was clear that Goldie thought his idea a good one, too. Avenham Park turned out to be perfect for dogs and although Terry worried that, if he once let her off the lead he would never see her again, in the end he allowed her to run free. She bounded around on the grass happily and then, amazingly, came straight back to Terry and let herself be put back on the lead.

The park had a café, too, which enabled Terry to while away a little more time. He took half an hour over a single Americano, checking his smartphone for incoming messages and tweets. The activity over #wheresgoldie appeared to have died away, fortunately. Baz and Mick would both be hard at work doing something electrical somewhere, and Horsey would be getting ready for his lunchtime shift.

In a leisurely manner he began to walk back to his car, on the way allowing Goldie again to run free over the grass. To be absolutely safe (who knew what sort of electronic trails you could leave these days?), he had decided not to use the satnav to find the pick-up address, instead relying on an old-fashioned street map guide to Preston which he'd bought from one of the service areas on the M6. He found the house without problem and within thirty seconds had been given a large Lidl carrier bag. Inside were a series of self-close plastic bags. Terry's role did not extend to the money side of the business – that was all dealt with separately, by somebody else - but a cursory glance inside the carrier bag suggested that the total stock he was collecting was worth several thousand. Even a small quantity of heroin cost a tidy sum. He put the bag on the back-seat.

A Lidl supermarket bag would attract no attention at all, which was fortunate because he still had several hours to spend in Preston before heading back to Keswick. His plan was to mosey round the shops, perhaps checking out Top Man and Next for the summer season goods which by now they should have in stock. Terry liked to dress well, and he was particularly interested in finding a new black cotton jacket which he could wear with a black T-shirt and his best denims. He drove towards the city centre and eventually found a place to park in a multi-storey car park near the main stores.

"Now then, dog," he said to Goldie. "You'll have to be patient for a little while. You've had a nice walk, so curl up and go to sleep." Remembering what he had once seen on an RSPCA advertisement, he opened one of the back-seat windows, not enough for anyone to get a hand in but enough for the dog to get fresh air. He looked back at the Lidl carrier bag – that was fine, no one could ever know what was inside. And then he made for the shops.

He returned just before five o'clock, with a series of shopping bags in his hands. It was OK living in Keswick but sometimes you needed to get out and go shopping in a place with decent stores. He's bought two new jackets, a new pair of Levis, and a pair of retro-style trainers from one of the big sportswear stores which he'd been craving for some time. He was three hundred pounds lighter, but all in all he felt that it hadn't been so bad to be sent to Preston for the day.

He looked briefly at the back-seat. Goldie seemed to be sleeping quietly in the well of the car. Good. An hour and a half should see them safely back in Keswick, and then he and Trix could get the dog safely off their hands. And claim the £100 reward which Trix had been on about in her texts earlier in the day.

Terry had passed the motorway turn to Blackpool and was embarking on the long stretch of the M6 which has no exits until Lancaster when he was conscious that Goldie's breathing had changed. The dog seemed suddenly to be gasping for air. She was also making a pitiful crying noise again.

"Sorry, dog, I can't do anything for the next ten miles," Terry called over his shoulder. "I'll stop when I get to Lancaster services." The bloody dog certainly chose its moments.

Terry accelerated, pushing his speed up to over eighty. He really didn't want to be stopped, not given the contents of the Lidl bag on the back seat, but the dog's breathing was now sounding more and more peculiar. It sounded as if it was struggling to get any air into its lungs at all.

Lancaster services finally arrived. Terry turned off the motorway on to the slip road and parked at the further end of the main car park, where there were very few other cars.

"Right, dog," he said. "I've stopped the car. Let's sort you out."

Terry was aware that his passenger was not immediately responding. He got out of the driver's door and opened the rear passenger door. "Let's see if you want a short walk while we're here," he said.

In the well of the car, curled up, lay Goldie the dog. It appeared to be lying absolutely still.

"Shake a paw, dog, time for walkies."

The dog did not respond.

With terrible growing realisation, Terry understood that the dog did not appear to be able to make any response at all. He touched the fur. The dog was cold. The dog was no longer breathing.

There could be no doubt that the dog was dead.

"Shit shit shit," Terry cried. "What the hell has happened?" he called out to the empty car. How was it possible that he had been unable to drive a healthy dog safely to Preston for the day and drive it safely back afterwards?

Up to that point his gaze had been focused entirely on the dog, lying under the seats. Now he looked up.

"Fuck oh fuck," he exclaimed. One of the self-close plastic bags he had picked up in Preston had obviously not been properly sealed. It had been pulled half out of the Lidl carrier bag and its contents spread over the back seats of the car. It was too obvious what had happened: Goldie the dog had been sniffing, touching and probably tasting hundreds of pounds' worth of a Class A opioid drug.

Terry had two terrible problems, neither of which he knew how to solve. Rod and Alan would certainly expect him to reimburse them for the lost drugs and, given the shopping he had just done, he had little more than forty pounds in his bank account. Secondly, he was the current custodian of a seriously dead dog, which somehow he had to get out of his car and out of his life.

He sent a message through on What'sApp to Trix. "On M6," he typed. "Lancaster services. Dog dead. Any ideas?"

41.

Joan Arkle didn't seem to like paying for parking. Perhaps it was a matter of principle, Elizzabeth thought, although surely Joan's principles would have meant penalising motorists as much as possible for using gas-guzzling cars? Sometime at the right moment she would tackle her about it.

Elizzabeth was thinking about this because Booth's car park, where Joan had parked the campervan, was pay and display. Joan had simply said she wouldn't be long. Now Elizzabeth, alone in the van waiting for Joan to return from wherever she had gone, found herself watching anxiously for a passing car park attendant to come and slap a ticket on the windscreen. Fortunately none came.

Joan eventually returned and clambered in to the driver's seat.

"What's that? Paint of some kind?" Elizzabeth asked, pointing to the fingers on Joan's right hand which were smeared with large splodges of white paint.

"What? Oh yes, must be." Joan proffered no explanation, and Elizzabeth felt unable to press her.

"So what now?" Elizzabeth asked.

"Just let me try that mobile number again."

There was, just as earlier in the day, no reply. Joan tried a text message: *You texted me this morning to say that your boyfriend had found Goldie and wanted to return her. But you've not told me when or where I can pick her up. Please reply. I have the reward ready. Joan Arkle.*

Joan sat distractedly in the driver's seat, waiting for a text to come straight back but still her phone stayed silent. She tried a second more direct approach, again via a text.

I know Terry Venables took the dog. You can have the money. I just want Goldie back.

There was still no response. Elizzabeth looked across: Joan was clearly becoming more and more distracted. She had to think of something they could do to fill in the rest of the afternoon.

"We could go for a walk," she said. "You could take your camera."

Joan looked at Elizzabeth. "I suppose so. What's your favourite Lakeland mountain?"

"I haven't got any favourites. I've never actually been up any mountains," Elizzabeth replied.

Joan looked at her disbelievingly. "But you grew up in Keswick. You must have explored the fells."

"No. My family's view was that all that stuff was for the tourists. We sometimes went to the coast but we never went walking at all."

"OK." Joan looked at Elizzabeth. "So, what have you got to wear?"

Elizzabeth shrugged. "What do I need? Is this OK?" She was wearing a cotton hoodie directly over her bra, a short pair of denim shorts with ragged edges over a pair of black woolly tights and a pair of white trainers. "I've got a few other things packed away." She pointed to the suitcase which she had brought with her when she left Baz the second time and which Joan had stored in the space directly under the campervan's raised roof, the space that you'd use as children's bunks if you had kids to accommodate.

"You'll be cold wearing what you've got on if we go anywhere too high but we could go to Falcon Crag," Joan replied. "I've been meaning all spring to go there to look for peregrine falcons."

"Where's Falcon Crag?"

"About a mile south of Keswick. Your family really didn't get out much, did it?"

Joan drove the van out of Booth's car park and took the B road along the east side of Derwent Water before pulling in to what a sign described as the Great Wood car park.

"This is pay and display too," Elizzabeth said.

"Yes, but it's National Trust. I've got an old National Trust for Scotland card here that will probably do the trick."

Elizzabeth opened the van door, went to the pay machine and fed it with coins from her own purse. She returned and snatched the card from Joan.

"You need to know who we're fighting," she said. "It's not the National Trust."

"Yes, you're right. Sensible Elizzabeth, silly Joan."

Elizzabeth looked at her. "Not silly. Completely crazy, more like."

Joan Arkle smiled back a little ruefully.

They got ready to leave the car park. Joan had obviously been to Great Wood before. She took Elizzabeth along a woodland footpath for a short way before their path emerged on to the open fells.

"Look up there," Joan said.

"Those rocks?"

"Yes, those rocks. Peregrines nest there regularly, and they're already back again this season. There's been discussion on some of the birders' forums on the web."

"Peregrines are a sort of eagle?" Elizzabeth asked.

"No, they're falcons not eagles, but they're big birds of prey. The female's larger than the male, and they're the fastest bird in the world. When they're diving for prey they can reach speeds well over 200 mph. That's much faster than a cheetah runs."

"How do you know this stuff, Joan?"

"I was mad keen on natural history when I was a kid. And don't forget, I make my living photographing wildlife."

"Where did you grew up? Was it in the country?"

"Not really in the country. I grew up down south."

"Whereabouts?" Elizzabeth asked.

Joan paused before responding. "All over the place."

"Your parents moved a lot?"

Again Joan paused. "I was in care. I don't want to talk about it."

"OK," Elizzabeth replied. "But, still, you did OK at school. You told me once you'd got A-levels."

"Yes."

"I only got GCSEs and then I started working. I probably should have worked harder. My teachers told me I was clever. Why didn't you go to university?"

"Oh well, things happened."

"How did you get involved in, you know, demonstrating and protesting?"

"I was with some friends. Protests and stuff. I'll maybe tell you more sometime. I don't feel like talking about myself right now."

"Sorry." Elizzabeth responded immediately to the cue. Joan wanted to close down the conversation.

"Look," Joan said eventually, pointing up. She pulled out binoculars she had been carrying in a backpack and passed across them to Elizzabeth. Far away a bird of prey was making its way across the sky.

"Female peregrine," Joan went on. "Can you see? Whitish flecked breast, and a sort of dark moustache."

Elizzabeth fumbled with the binoculars, raising them to her eyes and failing to find the bird.

"It's gone now," Joan said. "Never mind. We could come back some other time."

"How do you get the photos you take? That was far too far away."

"That's why I get up really early. You need to get as near the birds as you can and then just wait. Sometimes I've waited hours for the right shot."

"I'm not sure I'd have the patience," Elizzabeth replied. "Shall we go back now?"

"Have you walked far enough? I was going to press on."

"Yes, that's probably enough for a first walk. It's nice here though. Good views."

"It's beautiful round here. Elizzabeth, there's some fantastic places I can take you to. You've got the whole of the Lake District to get to know, that's such a wonderful journey of discovery to be starting. Tell you what, tonight, once we've got Goldie back we'll have a nice meal and I'll show you some of my photos. You were planning to stay another night in the van, I hope?"

That was an interesting question. For the past week, since leaving Baz, Elizzabeth had been actively looking for a place she could move into, and through Facebook a friend of an old school friend had offered her a spare room in Penrith. She'd been in touch with Pete in Maryport, too, and he was keen to have her back. On his sofa, he'd said, but Elizzabeth had a hunch that there might very quickly be a double bed going. She wasn't sure if she was ready immediately to start another relationship. Still, a kiss and a cuddle would be enjoyable. They'd already had the kiss, maybe it was time soon to see what else developed?

Joan was waiting for a reply. "Yes, maybe just one more night," Elizzabeth said. Apart from anything else, she wanted to see Joan and Goldie safely reunited before she left. Joan was still on edge. She needed someone's company just at the moment.

"Good," Joan said. "We can celebrate with Goldie. Still, I've got some unfinished business with your friend Terry."

"Not my friend. Baz's friend. And remember this, Baz is part of my past now. My life's changing."

42.

Jem Braithwaite put down a double-four on the table, shielding his single remaining domino carefully behind his left hand.

The man across the table shook his head. "Pass," he said. He turned to a third man at his side. "Your turn, Roger."

Roger shook his head. "Can't go either, David. Luck is with you tonight, Jem," he said.

Jem took a deep draught from his pint mug and gave a crafty smile. He reached down to put the remaining domino on the table. It was a four and a one. "I'm out," he said.

Two fifty-pence coins were pushed across the table towards him.

"I need the money," Jem said. "Did I tell you I had twenty prime hoggs in the Carlisle auction last week? How much do you think they made me?"

"Herdwicks?" David asked. Jem nodded.

His two companions shrugged.

"£85 apiece?" Roger proffered.

"£64."

"As bad as that?" David said.

"The prices this year are getting worse and worse," Roger contributed.

"It's a mug's game we're in," Jem went on. "We do all the work and someone else cashes in."

"The supermarkets."

"Aye, the supermarkets. And the banks."

The three men turned to their pints of beer and drank.

David was the first to speak again. "I had a dog loose today among the lambs in the in-bye below Beckstones. Two walkers. They said, 'Oh, he won't hurt a fly'. I told them if I found their dog loose among my stock again I'd shoot it. And then they had the nerve to shout at me as if it was all my fault."

"Too many visitors. That UNESCO heritage business was a mistake," Jem vouchsafed.

"What did you reckon to the lass last night?" Roger asked David.

"Blue-hair?"

"Aye, that one."

"Harmless but daft," David replied.

"More than daft," Jem chipped in. "She made my blood roil. I was that cross I wrote a letter this morning to the editor of the Enquirer."

"People like her don't understand the way we do things in these parts," David replied.

"Too right," Jem replied, looking pensive. "She's dangerous."

"We've got more to worry about than people like her," Roger suggested.

Jem paused before replying. "Mebbe. But I want her gone. I want her out of my hair and out of Cumbria. I want her gone for good."

43.

"Who the fuck did that?" Terry was with Trix, looking at the front window of his shop.

"I don't know, but almost certainly this Joan woman. She's been ringing me and texting me all day." Trix passed her phone across to Terry, so he could read the messages.

"What have you said?"

"Nothing at all. But… she thinks she'll get her dog back, now you're back in Keswick. And she's got £100 to give us, she says."

It was about a quarter to seven, and Terry had finally arrived back at the shop. It was, he was pleased to see, empty of the two people who had come visiting that morning.

"How was I to know that the bloody dog was a junkie?"

"It wasn't, before it started going on day trips with you," Trix replied.

"Well, anyway, what do we do?" It didn't help that he had been sent a text via What'sApp a short time earlier. It had come from Rod who had given him very clear instructions on what to do as soon as he was back from Preston. He had to clean the window immediately, take the dog back to its owner immediately, keep the stock safe upstairs overnight, and await more information in the morning.

"Let's get the window sorted first. I'll bring in the stuff I picked up and put it upstairs."

"And the dog?"

"Leave it for the time being where it is. It's out of sight."

Together Terry and Trix started to try to remove the paint. In the few hours since Joan had first applied it to the window it had hardened. The job of getting it off the glass was not at all easy. Terry used a knife from the kitchen as a make-do scraper, and Trix scrubbed and scrubbed with warm water and a sponge. "I think we need white spirit," she said eventually.

"Where do we get that?" Terry asked.

"Possibly in the convenience store. I'll go. I won't be long."

Terry, now by himself, continued scraping. This was, he thought, a really shitty way to be spending an evening. God, how Baz and Mick and Horsey would fall about laughing if they happened to walk past. He'd never live it down.

Although actually all this was Baz's fault. Or Elizzabeth's, because if she hadn't met the woman Joan Arkle Terry would never have been at the church hall on Sunday evening. He'd never have unfastened the dog's lead. He'd never have ended up with a stiff black corpse in the back of his car.

Trix came back. The white spirit certainly was an improvement, and after perhaps an hour of concerted effort from both of them the window was more or less respectable. If you looked carefully you could still see the outline of the letters, but what the hell? From a distance everything looked normal.

"What about the dog?" Trix asked.

"Let's have some food first. I'm starving."

"Chinese takeaway OK? I'll order on the app. Let's not bother to cook tonight."

"I'm not sure there's anything in the kitchen anyway," Terry replied. "Or at least, no food. There are some other things there which we'd probably best try to forget about."

It took twenty minutes for the courier to arrive outside with the food, and another twenty minutes or so for them to eat it, and to share the three bottles of beer which fortunately were in one of the cupboards in the kitchen. Eventually Trix spoke.

"There's some unfinished business," she said.

"I know," Terry replied. "I thought we could drive the car over the other side of the river and find somewhere to stop past the old station. It's quiet up there."

"OK, let's do it now before we get cold feet."

Dead animals weigh much more than you might imagine. Terry and Trix pulled the body of the hapless dog out of the car, one carrying its head and the other its back legs and together they lugged it on to the side of the road.

"Phew, it weighs a ton," Trix said.

"That's got to be good enough," Terry replied. They had chosen a place well away from houses and far from the nearest lamppost.

"Just one more thing," Trix said. She pulled a piece of paper and a pen out of her handbag and in deliberately ungainly block capitals she wrote a single word on it: *Sorry*. Then she tucked the paper into the dog's collar.

"It's the least we can do," she said. "It wasn't our fault, but still…"

"It's only a dog," Terry said. "Let's go home."

44

Joan had driven back from Great Wood through Keswick town centre, parking briefly outside the vaping shop and knocking again hard on the front door. As previously nobody came to answer. It was about five thirty, just the time when the shop would normally be shutting.

"I'm still not getting any answers to my texts," Joan said.

"I know. Let's go back to the smallholding. You can always pop back into Keswick later this evening."

It was impossible for Elizzabeth not to notice the added paintwork on the shop window, but she decided to say nothing. Still, that explained the paint-stained fingers which Joan had had all afternoon.

With some reluctance, Joan took the van on to the Keswick bypass and in fifteen minutes she was pulling up on the hard-standing where she had arranged to stay. In a distracted manner, she put the kettle on the hob without remembering to light it.

"I'll make the drinks," Elizzabeth said. "You sit down."

Joan did as she was told. She was obviously wanting to talk.

"Have I told you how I got Goldie?" she said.

"No," Elizzabeth responded. "Tell me."

"It was when I was down at the anti-fracking demos in Lancashire. Lots of people at the protest camp had dogs and I wanted one of my own too."

"For company?"

"I suppose so. It's stupid to say it, because there were always lots of people coming into and out of the camp all the time, but I was a little lonely."

"Goldie's a lovely companion."

"Yes," Joan replied pensively. "I got her from the local animal sanctuary. I can't believe that somebody else didn't want her as a pet."

"Was she called Goldie in the animal shelter?"

"No, I called her that."

"Can I ask you something? Goldie is a funny name for a black dog."

"I named her after somebody. Emma Goldman."

"Who's that?"

"She's dead now. She was an American feminist. Jewish too. She deserves to be remembered."

"I've never heard of her."

"No, nobody wants you to know about people like Emma Goldman. That's why they go on about Henry VIII and people like him in school history courses."

"We studied Churchill and the Second World War."

"That's exactly what I mean. Even most of my friends in Extinction Rebellion haven't heard of Emma Goldman. She was too dangerous for the powers-that-be. *When in the course of human development existing institutions prove inadequate to the needs of man, when they serve merely to enslave, rob and oppress mankind, the people have the eternal right to rebel.* That's what she wrote in 1909."

"You know that by heart?" Elizzabeth was surprised.

"Yes, and lots more. I had a book of her writings which I lost at a protest camp, but I'm good at learning things by memory."

"What more did she say?" Elizzabeth said.

"*Every daring attempt to make a great change in existing conditions, every lofty vision of new possibilities for the human race, has been labelled utopian.* Or in other words, we get dismissed for our ideas because some people just can't see that they make sense. I wish I'd written that. I want to be as provocative and as dangerous as she was in her time. It's not always easy."

"No, I guess not."

Joan was quiet for a moment. "That bastard who has got Goldie doesn't seem in a hurry to get back in touch," she said finally.

"No. Listen, let me cook tonight."

"Can you cook vegan?"

"I can if you tell me what I have to do."

"OK. We'll cook pasta caponata." She corrected herself. "Or rather you'll cook pasta caponata. I've got most of the ingredients. You could start by cutting that aubergine into little cubes. The onion and the celery sticks need chopping too. I'll peel a garlic clove while you're doing that."

It felt very comfortable working at the tiny worktop in Joan's van. Joan darted here and there, getting the ingredients that the recipe asked for, looking down over Elizzabeth's shoulder to check that the oil in the main saucepan wasn't catching or the onions burning, giving her encouragement all the time. "You see, really, you can eat very well as a vegan," she said at one point.

The kettle was boiled to get hot water, which was then transferred into a second saucepan along with the pasta. "Just till it's al dente," Joan said. "Sorry?" Elizzabeth replied. "Don't cook the pasta too long," Joan translated.

Joan's mood had lifted. Elizzabeth was sure that she was still waiting for her mobile to ring with news of Goldie but the food had given her something different to think about and she was obviously enjoying giving Elizzabeth tips on what to do. For the first time, Elizzabeth felt, Joan seemed not just like someone she admired but someone she really liked. And who in turn liked her.

Joan sat down at one side of the portable table that came with the campervan as Elizzabeth piled the pasta dish on to her plate. Then she sat down at the other side of the table, and filled her own plate.

"This looks *good*," Joan said. "Thank you. I need to tweet a photo of it."

"Sorry?"

"I always tweet what I'm eating. Along with the hashtag #VeganLifestyle. Just to show the world what they're missing if they're still stuck on chicken nuggets or bacon butties."

"No other tweets come through, I suppose," Elizzabeth said carefully.

"No," replied Joan.

The plates had been cleared away, the kettle put back on. "I bought some vegan chocolate today as a treat. We can have it with our tea. Or coffee if that's what you insist on."

"Isn't all chocolate vegan?"

"No, usually it's got dairy of some kind. But more and more you can find vegan things in the shops. We're winning the argument."

Joan relaxed in her seat. "I promised to show you some photographs," she said.

"You did," Elizzabeth replied, coming round to sit alongside her. Joan pulled out her laptop, picked a sub-directory and clicked on 'show all'. The slide show began. Elizzabeth watched transfixed as the images appeared – fantastic views of otters, of badgers, of squirrels, of beautiful mountain flowers, of birds of prey.

"That's a peregrine," said Joan at one point. "Like the bird we saw this afternoon. Obviously the bird in the photo was a lot closer to the camera than the one we saw today."

"Is it a peregrine I've got on my tattoo? I've always wondered what sort of bird it was," Elizzabeth said. She pulled up the back of her hoodie.

"I don't know. Let me see properly."

Momentarily, Elizzabeth remembered that Pete had once asked her the same thing. That time she had a T-shirt on which she had simply pulled up. This time, her hoodie would have to come off if Joan was to see it properly. She pulled it over her head and turned so that her back was towards Joan.

Joan made an appreciative noise. "That's a really excellent tattoo. It's a golden eagle not a peregrine. It's really well done."

"Thank you"

"Do you want to see my tattoo?" Joan went on.

"Go on."

Joan removed her top, to reveal the large blue whale on her chest. "I might as well take the bra off too, so you can see the full extent of the tattoo."

"That's amazing," Elizzabeth said. "How long have you had that?"

"Some years."

"Save the humans!" Elizzabeth was reading the little badge that the whale was sporting. "I love it."

Joan appeared in no hurry to put her bra back on. Instead she put her hand around Elizzabeth's back, and kissed her delicately on the right cheek. "That was a lovely meal you cooked me tonight."

Elizzabeth couldn't quite remember afterwards what had happened next. But somehow her own bra had been removed, somehow she found Joan exploring her body with her fingers. And somehow they had both removed their remaining clothes and, fully naked, had tumbled under the duvet together. This was not fucking as Elizzabeth had up to now experienced it. This was something else. This was slow, careful, love-making.

They clung together for a long time afterwards.

"Did I lead you on?" Joan asked.

"I think I wanted to be led," Elizzabeth replied.

"*If love does not know how to give and take without restrictions, it is not love but a transaction,*" Joan said.

"What did you just say?"

"Something Emma Goldman once wrote. The most vital human right is the right to love and be loved, she said."

"I like that."

It was after ten o'clock. It had become all too clear that there would be no phone call or text that evening. "Oh well, I guess everything will become clear in the morning," Joan said with resignation. "Let's turn in."

They pulled the duvet over them again, holding each other. Joan was the first to fall asleep. Elizzabeth heard her breathing become regular. And then she too must have slept.

45.

"We've got this week's front page lead, I think," Molly said to Nick as he arrived on Tuesday morning for in the Enquirer office. "The Cumbria Police press office has just been in touch. Two big drugs raids over the last few days. Apparently they've recovered heroin to the value of £25,000."

"That's a lot. The police will be feeling pleased," Nick said.

"They sound thrilled to bits."

"Who are our police contacts now that George Mulholland has retired?"

"Their press people gave me the name of a Detective Sergeant called Peter Blackford who's been leading on the drugs enquiry. His boss is a woman called DI Chambers. I haven't had a chance to call either yet. Fancy taking this on?"

"If you want. Where were the raids?"

"One in Penrith, one in Keswick."

"The seamy side of the Lake District that the tourists never discover."

"That's true," Molly said. "It goes with the low wages and poor job opportunities."

"So what do we know so far?"

"Penrith was a dawn raid on Sunday. Three white males arrested and now charged with offences under the Misuse of Drugs Act. I gather this was a cuckooing incident."

Nick nodded. Like other local papers across Britain, the Cumbrian Enquirer had over the past two or three years begun to report cases of cuckooing. "How did the police find out?"

"A neighbour reported strange comings and goings. The police are of course keen that we stress this, so that they get more tip-offs like that in the future."

"What about Keswick?"

"Another dawn raid, but this was today. A flat above retail premises somewhere in Keswick town centre, I understand. A white man aged 24 and a white woman aged 23 have been arrested although not yet charged. Several thousand pounds' worth of heroin in their kitchen."

"Another tip-off?"

"Not clear. You never know, the police may just have struck lucky. I've been given the address they raided. As it's only Keswick, it might be worth popping up there and seeing what's happening on the ground."

"Good idea."

"Thanks, Nick," Molly said. "And - I urgently need the story of the Sunday night climate change meeting and the protests."

"I've got more or less all the quotes I need. Ideally I'd like a final comment from Joan of Arc if I can get one. There's been some very curious stuff on her Twitter feed, incidentally. She's either lost her dog or had it taken. She certainly has a knack of attracting some really unpleasant trolls." Since the evening meal with Rosa in Ambleside, Nick had been much more assiduously following @joan_sparkle on social media.

"She seems to attract enemies of all kinds," Molly replied. "Is the dog a material fact for the public meeting story?"

"No, I don't think so."

"In which case forget about the dog and just write me the story as soon as you're back from Keswick."

"What's the deadline?"

"Lunchtime?"

"Oh god. I suppose I could do that."

46.

For once, Joan allowed herself a lie-in, changing the time of the alarm call on her mobile from 5am to 7am. Even so, she found herself wide awake well before half past six. She reached across to where Elizzabeth was lying and made a few exploratory moves under the duvet with her hand.

A very sleepy voice responded. "Mm, that's very nice, but it's too early."

"It's never too early," Joan replied, making a few more moves. Elizzabeth stirred and opened her eyes.

"I'm getting up," Joan said, "but not until I've had my good morning kiss."

Elizzabeth smiled at her. "I hate early mornings," she said. "And for some reason or other I was late getting to sleep last night. But just this once I'll overlook the time." She propped herself up on one elbow, bending towards Joan's body. Their lips met.

"That's encouraging," Joan said. "You still like me. It's not always like that the morning after."

Elizzabeth stuck out her tongue.

The morning routine in the campervan began. Joan, and after her Elizzabeth, headed for the toilet outside. Then both in turn washed and brushed their teeth at the cold water tap. The kettle was put on. Bread was found and put on the table. Joan pulled out a bunch of bananas and two yoghurts.

"Are we allowed to eat yoghurt?" Elizzabeth asked. "Or, what I really mean to say is, are you allowed to eat yoghurt?"

"This is vegan yoghurt," Joan replied. "It's made from cashew milk. Soy milk is the usual, but I felt like a change."

"What's your plan?" Elizzabeth asked, after a slight pause. Joan knew what the question meant.

"Still no messages, although it's still very early. We could call by that shop again as soon as it's a half-way reasonable time." Joan took a gulp of her herb tea.

"What are you tweeting?" Elizzabeth was watching as Joan started typing on her phone.

"That Goldie is still missing. The nasty trolling stuff has stopped, but the problem now is that nobody is using the #wheresgoldie hashtag at all."

"I think you should report the trolling to the police. And those messages about Goldie having been found and then taken to Preston – they were weird. Mention them, too."

"I'm not going to the police, Elizzabeth."

Joan had suddenly turned prickly. Elizzabeth rapidly backed off. "OK, sorry I suggested it," she said.

The moment passed, but Joan remained on edge. This was the time of day, Elizzabeth knew, when Joan was normally out in the countryside, the time of the day when the best natural history photographs were there to be taken. It was, frankly, a problem that the campervan doubled up as both bedroom and motor vehicle. It was a problem, too, that the campervan was parked up each night on land in the middle of nowhere, far from bus routes, and that Elizzabeth had no transport of her own. For the past few days she had been more dependent on Joan than she would have liked.

"I've been thinking. I need a place of my own, so I'm not stopping you doing what you need to do. I've been offered a spare room in a friend's house in Penrith," Elizzabeth said. "How would you feel about running me and the suitcase over there some time today?"

Joan looked devastated. "You're walking out on me?" she asked. "Just like that? After sharing my bed last night?"

Elizzabeth leaned towards her and gave her a big kiss. "Stop sounding so vulnerable. Listen, if I've got my own place it means that you'll have the van for your work. It doesn't mean we have to stop seeing each other. You can drive the van across and stay at my place... If, of course, you want to do that."

Joan's face lit up. "Of course I want to."

A second kiss seemed appropriate.

Eventually Joan broke away. "Time to get the van on the road. Let's head back to Keswick and see if today brings better news than yesterday," she said.

47

Nick had parked in one of the town centre car parks in Keswick and made his way to the address Molly had given him. He joined a group of about half a dozen onlookers who were standing in front of the shop, obviously attracted by the blue and white Police tape stretched across what remained of a broken front door and by the sight of the uniformed police constable who was standing beside it.

Nick went up to the policeman, showed him his NUJ press card, and asked what was happening.

"I'm sorry, sir, I have nothing to tell you. I suggest you talk to the press office," the man replied. It was the response Nick had been expecting. He made his way back to the small group of onlookers.

The shop had been selling e-cigarettes and vaping oils. Nick wondered if Molly knew this, and whether she had ever been a customer there. Once upon a time the Cumbrian Enquirer offices had reeked of stale tobacco smoke, the result of Molly puffing her way, one fag after another, one day after day, through the newspaper's weekly cycle of deadlines. Then, a couple of years or so back, she had had a health scare. The smoking had abruptly come to an end, and Molly's new craze of vaping had begun. These days the Enquirer offices smelled of sickly eucalyptus. It was not very pleasant, Nick thought, but it was still a great improvement.

His eye was suddenly caught by the remains of words on the shop window. It wasn't easy to read but little by little he made out a message. *Hello Terry*, it said. *Where is Goldie?*

He struggled to make sense of any of this. Goldie was the name of Joan Arkle's dog, the one she had apparently lost or had stolen. #wheresgoldie was the hashtag which she had been using on her Twitter feed. So how was it that the same message was now appearing in faint white paint on the window of a shop which had just been busted by the police? And why 'hello Terry'?

Back in his Fleet Street days, Nick had prided himself on being an experienced investigative journalist. What he'd learned very quickly then was that sometimes what could seem like a very significant story was actually not really a story at all. The paint on the shop, he thought, probably came into this category. Whatever it meant, it probably wasn't the effort of trying to work it all out.

He took a few photographs of the policeman and the front door (once upon a time he had just been a wordsmith, but these days the Enquirer required its reporters to take cameras as well), and turned back to find his car to drive to the office. As he turned he almost literally bumped into two women who had just arrived. God, it was her. It was Joan Arkle, with that other woman, the one who spelled her first name with two 'z's.

"Joan," Nick said. "What are you doing here?"

Joan chose not to reply in words. Her look of displeasure at seeing Nick conveyed a response that needed no further interpretation.

Nick turned instead to Elizzabeth. "Hello again," he said. She shrugged.

He tried one final approach. "Joan, I am writing up the story of the Sunday meeting today for the Enquirer". He saw her look at him. "Do you have any final thoughts or comments to give me?"

"No," she replied firmly, walking on.

Joan had parked the campervan on a yellow line near Keswick cinema, and she and Elizzabeth had rounded the corner to walk towards the shop. They both stopped abruptly. Joan's paint had been almost entirely removed from the shop window since they had been there the previous afternoon, but instead there was now police tape across the broken front door and a policeman standing guard. They tried to take this in. And then, at that moment, the bloody Enquirer journalist had popped up from some hole in the ground asking questions. They'd seen him off as quickly as they could.

"Go and ask the copper if a dog's been found in the shop," Elizzabeth said to Joan.

"No way," Joan replied.

"I will then."

Joan watched Elizzabeth march up to the constable and ask him something. She saw him shake his head and gesture to Elizzabeth to step away from the doorway. Elizzabeth came back towards Joan, in turn shaking her head. And at that moment Joan's phone rang.

Elizzabeth heard just one side of the conversation. It went as follows:

....

Joan: "That's right. It was me that put up the posters."

....

Joan: "A black dog, with quite a lot of Labrador."

....

Joan (a cry): "Where?"

....

Joan: "North of the river?"

.....

Joan: "Beside the road?"

....

Joan: "I'll be there as quickly as I can. Give me ten minutes."

The call was ended, and Elizzabeth saw Joan's eyes well up with tears.

"Who was that?" Elizzabeth asked.

"A local dog walker. She thinks she's found Goldie."

Elizzabeth looked up at Joan. "That's good?"

Joan muttered back: "Goldie's body."

48.

The two businessmen had ordered Americanos and a couple of Danish in Booth's supermarket café at Windermere, beside the station. Both were in smart work suits that were clearly bespoke. Both had laid expensive-looking designer briefcases in front of them on the café table where they were sitting.

"The fry-up breakfast looks tempting," Rod said.

"Didn't your hotel offer you cooked breakfast?" Alan asked him.

"Yes, but a lot's happened since breakfast."

"You'll get fat. They'll talk about you behind your back when you go to the gym."

"Everyone knows not to talk about me when I'm at the gym," Rod replied. "Or at any other time."

Alan smiled. "What are you thinking?"

The two men had arranged to meet in Windermere by What'sApp messages on the mobile phones they reserved just for communicating with each other. Rod had heard the news of the police dawn activity in Keswick on the BBC Cumbria breakfast show, had understood immediately what it meant, and had straightaway notified Alan.

"It's a great opportunity for us," Rod said in answer to Alan's question. "OK, we have lost some stock, but the competition has been hit harder. That bust in Penrith will have knocked their distribution network for six."

"We've lost a lot of stock. And suddenly things are quite lively. We could back off for two or three weeks until the heat goes down."

"If we back off, someone else will come and take our place. Manchester are gagging for a share of the trade up here."

"I know, but it's still a risk."

"Yes, but you know what always happens after the police get busy. The price on the street goes through the roof. We can easily make back what we've lost in just a few weeks."

"What about Terry? How much does he know?"

"Almost nothing. OK, that transport route through Preston is compromised now. But he doesn't know anything about us apart from our names. Or what he thinks are our names." They both laughed.

"How did the police know to raid his flat today?" Alan pondered aloud.

"I've been thinking about that too. Any other day of the year they'd have found nothing there apart from e-cigarettes and vaping liquids."

"And yet they picked the one day there was stock to be found. Curious."

"Terry himself?"

"Highly unlikely. He's got a long stretch inside to look forward to now."

"Girlfriend?" Rod asked.

"We don't know much about her but why would she go to the police? She'll be charged, too."

"What about the woman with the dog?"

"That's who I think it must have been. I think there must be history between her and Terry that we don't know about. She dumped him for some reason, let's say, and he retaliated by taking her dog. I mean, why else steal a fucking dog?"

"How did she know we'd left Terry with some sweeties in the flat?"

"She probably didn't," Alan replied. "But she probably knew why Terry was visiting Preston and that he'd have stock with him overnight. So she goes straight to the police. 'Hello,' she says, 'Why don't you make a little visit to this address tomorrow at the crack of dawn? Perhaps smash down the front door when you arrive, and have a look in the upstairs flat?' And just to make sure they found the right shop, because we all know how stupid the police can be, she also decides to paint a dirty great sign in white paint on the shop window. *Hello, Terry,* and all that."

"I think you're right. Terry should be grateful he's in custody. The alternative would have been a little clearing-the-air discussion with us today."

"Should we have stopped to talk to the woman in the street when we saw her with her paint-pot? Joan, that's her name."

"Possibly not. Although it would have looked strange if we'd just walked past."

"Did she suspect us, do you think?"

"I didn't think so at the time, but now I'm not sure. She could give the police good descriptions of us, unfortunately."

"She'll have her dog back by now. And she'll have got her revenge on Terry. So maybe we don't need to worry," Alan said.

"I'm not so sure. Don't forget how she went for me all guns blazing. 'I'm not emotional, I'm just angry' and all that."

"That's true."

"Somehow, we need to warn her off. Ideally get her out of the area altogether."

"Well, fortunately she helpfully gave us her name and her mobile phone number, not to mention a Twitter hashtag. Let's see what we can find out about her. And then let's see what how we choose to play this. There are lots of options."

"There are," Rod smiled. "So, we're agreed? We stay in Cumbria for a few more days?"

"I'll sort out that Whitehaven house today as we'd planned. I'll find myself a hotel over there tonight. Over on the coast they all think I'm a travelling sales rep visiting Sellafield. It's useful cover."

"I'll stay somewhere here in Windermere. I'll WhatsApp you if I need to."

"OK. Everything under control, I think."

"I think so, too."

49

Baz went to the bar to get the round in. It was Tuesday evening and he and Mick were back from work, ready to spend some of the money they'd earned during the day in a fairly futile attempt to sort out the new fire alarm system for the Ambleside hotel they were rewiring. Tonight's round was a cheap one: there were just the two pints of Cumberland for Baz to order. Horsey had texted to say he was working in the kitchen and wouldn't be able to make it. Terry had not responded to their texts.

The early evening local news had been on in the bar when they'd first arrived, with the sound turned right down. The first feature seemed to be something about a group of women care workers who were raising money for charity by taking dips in bath-tubs filled with baked beans. As the women were young and were obligingly wearing bikinis to undertake this feat, Baz and Mick took rather more notice of the screen than they might otherwise have done.

The feature ended, and another news item started. Baz turned away to pick up his pint. Mick, still watching, gave an audible gasp.

"Shit," he said, elbowing Baz so that about half a pint of his beer spilled on the table.

"Careful, you idiot," Baz replied.

"That's Terry's shop."

It was. The television camera pulled out from the name board at the top to show the whole building, along with a uniformed policeman who was standing outside it. Below on the TV screen ran the caption *Drugs raid in Keswick.*

The television changed to show a police officer, someone named as Detective Sergeant Blackford, who was clearly reading from a prepared statement. Baz and Mick strained to hear the sound, but without success. A new caption told them what they needed to know.

Heroin valued at over £10,000 found.

The image on the television changed again, and a photograph of Terry himself filled the screen. It was not a particularly flattering shot. He was lunging towards the camera, mouth open in mid-cry and clutching in his right hand a sign reading 'A New Voice for Cumbria'. The TV company had clearly used a freeze-frame from the footage they'd taken the previous Sunday evening just before the public meeting. Below the image was another caption: *Two charged and remanded in custody.*

Finally Terry disappeared and once again the screen was showing the outside of his shop. The camera lingered on the scene for perhaps ten seconds. And then the news item was over. Back in the studio the presenters were joshing with the weather forecaster.

Baz and Mick looked at each other, their drinks forgotten.

"Terry didn't do drugs," Mick said eventually.

"Well, maybe weed," Baz replied.

"Yes, but not the heavy stuff. We'd have known."

"Would we?" asked Baz.

"We knew him pretty well," Mick replied.

There was more silence between them.

"This is serious," Baz said eventually. "Heroin. They'll charge him with storing and supplying the drugs, not just with possession. It means prison."

"Presumably they picked up his girlfriend too. She'd have been with him overnight."

"Oh god, poor Trix."

Baz thought some more.

"I think the drugs were planted. I don't think Terry kept heroin in the shop. Somebody was out to get him," he said.

They pondered this idea.

Mick broke the silence. "It's possible. By the way, did you see what I saw on the TV? Something very faint written on the shop window?" he said.

"No?"

"It looked like someone had painted a message saying Where's Goldie?"

Baz looked at Mick in amazement.

"Are you mad? I know we asked Terry to join in on the tweeting yesterday, but why would he have painted the hashtag on his shop?"

The #wheresgoldie meme had been Monday morning's activity. Goldie the lost dog had been almost forgotten by them since then.

"Did Joan Sparkle ever find her dog?"

"Dunno," Baz replied, his mobile phone in his hand. I'll check her Twitter feed."

There was a brief moment as he ran his finger up and down the screen.

"Oh my god, read this" he said. "*I am very sorry to have to report that my beloved dog Goldie is dead. Thank you to everyone who tried to find her. #remembergoldie.* That was tweeted this morning. Hang on there's another tweet just below it. *My lovely dog Goldie never did anyone any harm. She was kidnapped on Sunday evening and killed yesterday. I'm devastated. But I know who did it. His name is Terry. Terry, don't think you can ever get away with this. #remembergoldie.*"

"She's saying that Terry took the dog? And killed it? She's completely bonkers."

"Yes, and dangerous too. Why did she think Terry had the dog?"

"No idea," Mick replied.

Baz paused again. "The dog was at the church hall. Terry wouldn't have done something stupid with it after we'd left, would he?"

"Come on, Terry's not stupid."

"No. Although what he kept in his shop wasn't all that wise."

Mick took a swig of beer. "I've got it!" he said. "Of course. Joan Sparkle."

"What about her?"

"It was Joan Sparkle who planted the drugs on Terry. Of course she did. She thought he had taken her bloody dog so she took her revenge by putting heroin in the shop. She probably tipped off the police too."

"Do you think so? I know she's a mad vegan but I didn't have her down as a heroin user."

"She's a hippy, she'll have access to drugs somewhere."

Baz had been scrolling through @joan_sparkle's other recent posts. He suddenly stopped.

"Shit, there's another tweet here from her. Look at it." He passed his phone across to Mick.

"It's a picture of somebody's tattoo. And a message with it," Mick said. He started reading the tweet. *"The last Golden Eagle in the Lake District died around 2016, but Golden Eagles have now been released into the wild not far away in the Scottish Borders near Moffat. Hopefully, we'll soon see this magnificent bird over our mountains again. Meanwhile, you can enjoy looking at this great Golden Eagle tattoo on the back of a friend of mine."* Mick stopped reading the tweet. "Why are you interested in that, Baz?" he asked.

"Because it's bloody Elizzabeth's tattoo. I'd recognise it anywhere. Elizzabeth has been showing off her body to Joan Sparkle. God I hate them both."

He was fiddling again with his phone which Baz had returned to him. "Do you remember I showed you a video clip of Elizzabeth in my bedroom a few weeks back? Enjoying herself with a banana? I think the video could do with having a wider audience." There was a look of concentration on Baz's face for a moment.

"There we are," he said. "I've posted the video as a reply to Joan Sparkle's tweet. It'll go to all her followers. And we might post it on some of our other Twitter accounts and Instagram and YouTube, while we're at it."

Mick read the tweet which Baz had written accompanying the video. *"Why just look at the tattoo? Here's what the woman with the eagle tattoo looks like. And here's what she does in the bedroom. She just has to see a banana to get an orgasm. Keep puckering up those lips, Elizzabeth."*

Mick looked again at the video. "That'll get taken down by Twitter," he said.

"Yes, but not until hopefully half the country's seen it. And posted it all over the place themselves. Listen, as of today, Joan Arkle has demonstrated that she's a really serious enemy of ours. Forget last Sunday evening, that was just a bit of fun and games. Joan Arkle has got it in for us big time, and we have to make sure we get her before she gets us. And Elizzabeth has left us to go over to the enemy. Elizzabeth's in Joan Arkle's camp now."

50.

Father and daughter were engaged in having the worst argument that they had ever known. The mother had made herself scarce in the kitchen.

"I knew what you were doing would end in disaster," said the father. "It's an absolute catastrophe."

"It's a set-back but we will find a way to get over it," said the daughter.

"A set-back?!" The father sounded apoplectic. "It's a hell of a lot worse than that."

"The clip was only on the television for a few seconds. Most people won't even have seen it."

"A drug dealer! Thousands of pounds' worth of heroin! And what was he shown carrying in his hand? A New Voice for Cumbria poster. Are we recruiting members now in Strangeways?"

"I'll check the membership database as soon as you stop having a go at me, but until I do we don't know whether he's a member or not. We're not responsible for people who just turn up to our rallies."

"That rally was a mistake from beginning to end. Basically it was hijacked by yobs, all shouting Immigrants Out and stuff like that. I expect they're all junkies. And that candidate you've got for Keswick. He'll be into drugs too."

"Rick's a sensible guy."

"How do you know? HOW DO YOU KNOW? I wouldn't trust him an inch."

"Listen, I am running our May election campaign. I am choosing the candidates. Just keep out of my business."

"None of the yobs had Cumbrian flags."

"Maybe not, but they care about the same issues as we do. The raw deal people in Cumbria are getting. Poor jobs, low wages, poor housing, cuts in services, cuts in health care."

"Half of them were drunk. They were just looking for a fight."

"Dad, back off."

"No, I won't. This is it. I'm going to close down A New Voice for Cumbria."

"You're what?! It's not your decision."

"I think it is. Who registered the party with the Electoral Commission, filled in the form and wrote the £150 cheque they needed? It was me. And who opened the bank account? Your mother and me. So I get to decide. I'm closing it down."

"Don't be so fucking unreasonable," shouted his daughter.

"Paula! Don't you ever ever use language like that in my house again."

"This is my home too, and I will say whatever I bloody well like. You're completely crazy. I'm trying to organise a sensible political campaign and all you want to do is dress up in stupid costumes and parade around the Castlerigg stone circle at dawn. Jesus."

"You'll have to set up your own party with a new name if you really want to carry on. I want nothing more to do with your election campaign."

Paula Petherton looked at her father. "I want nothing more to do with you. I'll pick up my stuff later. Bye."

She made for the front door, went out and slammed it behind her. At exactly the same time, the future election prospects of A New Voice for Cumbria were slammed tight shut as well.

Her mother emerged from the kitchen. "Oh dear," she said.

51.

The spare room was curiously furnished, with unmatching furniture which was certainly second-hand and had probably come from one of the local charity shops. It was also a very small spare room, with only space for a single bed. Still, Kath had been welcoming to Elizzabeth when she and Joan had arrived in the campervan that lunchtime, and had busied herself putting the kettle on for a brew. And Kath had given Elizzabeth a spare key to the front door: Elizzabeth now had a place to call her own.

"It's going to be intimate in bed," Joan said, eyeing up the single bed. Together they had lugged Elizzabeth's suitcase and her few other belongings up the stairs.

"Intimate is good," Elizzabeth responded. She reached across and gave Joan a kiss on the lips. "I feel I need to get to know your body a lot better than I already do."

"That won't be difficult in this bed," Joan replied.

Kath was a friend of a woman called Maggie who in turn had been a school friend of Elizzabeth's. Kath was looking for a lodger and Maggie had told her that Elizzabeth was looking for somewhere to stay. "She's just split up with her long-term boyfriend," she'd told Kath. "Or rather husband."

It rapidly became apparent to Kath from what Elizzabeth said that Joan was also going to be sharing the spare room some nights. She was a little surprised how quickly Elizzabeth appeared not only to have changed her sexual orientation but also to have found a new partner but, still, good luck to her. Kath herself had been looking for a new man for several months, so far without success. Maybe the answer was to follow Elizzabeth's lead? Although, Kath told herself, despite everything she did rather like men.

Elizzabeth began to put her clothes into the small wardrobe which was in a corner of the room. Joan blew her a kiss. "I'll be back this evening," she said, making her way downstairs on her way back to the van. "It won't take too long to get to Blackpool and back."

That morning they'd driven round together to the quiet roads north of the river in Keswick. And there, lying in a gutter, they had indeed found Goldie's body. The dog walker who had telephoned Joan was there too, standing a little way apart, holding her own dog firmly by its lead and looking anxious. Joan seemed almost preternaturally calm. She reached down to pick up Goldie's body, cradled the dog briefly in her arms and then transferred the corpse into a cardboard box which she put on the floor of the campervan. Elizzabeth herself wanted to burst into tears. But Joan seemed in a zone far beyond that sort of emotion. She seemed to have already resigned herself to Goldie's death. It was maybe, Elizzabeth thought, the way that Joan also tried to cope with the fact that she was living on a planet hurtling towards climate disaster but populated by idiots.

She saw Joan stoop down and remove the little note *Sorry* from under Goldie's collar. She expected Joan to comment, but she encountered only silence. Time enough later to talk things through, she thought. Joan could still be in shock.

"I'm going to ring the dogs' home where Goldie came from," Joan suddenly said. "There's a very friendly vet who works there."

Elizzabeth looked at the body near her feet, and thought that a vet was unlikely to be able to do much at this stage. Joan perhaps guessed what she was thinking.

"I want to know how Goldie died," she said. "I'm going to ask for a post-mortem. It will cost me, but I've still got £100 on me that I drew out from the machine yesterday."

"OK," Elizzabeth said.

"The dogs' home is near Blackpool. I'll go there this afternoon. First I'll take you to Penrith so you can find this room you're renting."

"Please look after yourself today."

Joan understood what Elizzabeth was saying. "It's alright. I'm OK. You learn to harden yourself against the world. I was at a picket at a fracking site last year when a friend had her leg run over by a contractor's vehicle. She was a really good friend. She almost lost her lower leg."

"I'm so sorry," Elizzabeth replied.

"It's a risk you have to take if you aren't prepared to roll over and accept the world as it is," Joan said. There was a pause. "It doesn't mean I didn't love Goldie. Of course I did. I loved her to bits. You knew that." She paused again. "Anyway, let's find this house in Penrith."

It took Elizzabeth not more than a few minutes to unpack. Kath, who had returned home briefly during her lunchbreak to let Elizzabeth in, had gone back to the office where she worked. Elizzabeth let herself out with her new front-door key and decided to explore Penrith. The town might be less than twenty miles from Keswick, but Elizzabeth knew it hardly at all. New town, new start, she thought. Not to mention new lover.

She returned to the house after five to find Kath already home and unpacking shopping. "I'm sorry the kitchen's so small but you're welcome to use it as much as you like. But I thought I'd offer to cook for us tonight, as it's your first evening here. I've picked up some beefburgers from the co-op. She looked at her new lodger and smiled.

"Oh Kath that's kind of you," Elizzabeth replied. "But I'm vegetarian. Or maybe I'm vegan. I haven't quite decided yet."

Kath looked quizzically at her. "No?"

"I've only just stopped eating meat. Joan is vegan."

Kath understood. Everyone learned to make compromises when they started new relationships. Giving up meat was in the circumstances not much of a sacrifice.

"Alright, I'll cook my beefburgers and then you and Joan can have the kitchen to yourselves if you want. When are you expecting her?"

"Any time now," Elizzabeth replied. And as she spoke, there was a knock at the door and Joan was there.

All things considered she seemed to be in surprisingly good spirits. "It's a beautiful evening," she said. "How do you fancy a short trip north, Elizzabeth? There have been otters reported on the river Petteril just north of Penrith, and this time of the day could be a good time for sightings. I need to increase my portfolio of otter photographs and I don't often come over to this part of Cumbria. And anyway Kath needs to cook her evening meal." Joan was eyeing the packet of beefburgers on the kitchen table somewhat disapprovingly.

Together they drove out of Penrith up the A6, once the main trunk road from London to Carlisle but now empty of all except local traffic. A few miles north, Joan turned into an even quieter minor road and eventually pulled in to a lay-by. "I've checked the map. The river's just here and there's a right of way along the bank," she said. "The odds are against seeing anything but you never know."

The footpath was very wet. Elizzabeth, still with only the trainers she'd worn for Falcon Crag, rapidly found herself walking through claggy mud. Walking shoes were going to be a necessary purchase if she spent more time with Joan, she told herself. How much did they cost? Did Workington magistrates allow people to run up debts?

Joan was ahead of her, looking at the ground intently.

"Spraint," she said, picking something off the ground. Elizzabeth looked blank. "Otter poo," she translated. "We're getting warm."

At that moment, Elizzabeth looked a little downstream, to a bend in the river overhung by trees. "Joan, there are some dogs in the river," she said. The dogs bobbed their heads cheekily.

Joan followed Elizzabeth's gaze and laughed. "They can look like dogs, but those are what we've come to see" she said. "That's a mature otter and a juvenile, perhaps nine months old now. I knew we'd have a good chance here."

Very quietly she made her way further up the path, her camera at the ready. Elizzabeth followed her, equally quietly. Silently they watched the otters at play. For perhaps five minutes the animals splashed and cavorted in the river, seemingly oblivious to being watched. And then, all of a sudden, they were gone."

"I think there could be a holt by the overhanging trees," Joan said in a whisper.

"What's that?"

"An otter's home. They live in burrows."

"Did you get any photos?" Elizzabeth asked, also whispering.

"I got some real beauties," Joan replied, checking back on the small screen of her camera. "Not bad for half an hour's work."

"That was magical," Elizzabeth said. "I never thought I'd ever see otters. Thank you."

"Why are you thanking me?" Joan asked.

"Because it's only because of you I've seen them. I didn't even know we had otters in Cumbria."

They made their way back to the van. "What do you want to do for food?" Joan asked. "I could rustle up a vegetable stir fry in the van, unless you want to cook back at Kath's house."

"Stir fry is good," Elizzabeth said. "As long as you promise you really will come back afterwards to Kath's. To my place, I mean."

Joan kissed her. "Is that enough of a promise?"

"It will do for now, but I'm treating it only as a deposit for what's to come later. And now can I tell you my good news?"

"Go on."

"I've got a job. I wandered round Penrith this afternoon, and went into a vegetarian café for a coffee and cake."

"I know the place," Joan said. "I go there sometimes for the wifi."

"Anyway, I plucked up courage. I told them I had just moved to Penrith and was looking for work. And… and I told them I was vegetarian. And, guess what, they said they could offer me a job. It's not full-time. They want me lunchtimes during the week and then for longer on Sundays. But it will mean I will have some money again. I can't tell you how good that feels."

Joan took Elizzabeth in her arms and gave her a big hug.

"Today started so badly, but it's ending on a high," Joan said. She placed two plates full of steaming food on the table. "Let's eat," she said. As always, the mobile phone came out for the necessary photo of the meal and the #VeganLifestyle tweet.

This time, however, the meal was left untouched. The mobile phone was a mistake. It was impossible not to notice that someone had just posted a short video on Joan's Twitter feed. Joan and Elizzabeth watched it in silence. And then Elizzabeth collapsed, howling wildly like an animal.

"I thought I loved him so much," she said. "He was my life partner. I was going to have his children."

52.

"I have bought a new pair of fells-shoes."

Nick was momentarily confused.

"Fell shoes. Excellent, they'll give you plenty of grip on the rocks. Lindsay told me that you had been out running on the hills with her."

"Yes, and she and I have agreed. We are both going to do the Frog. We're going to do it the weekend after next."

It was Saturday morning, and Lluïsa was at Nick's house in Grasmere. As well as the fell shoes, Lluïsa had now acquired a second-hand bicycle which she had used that morning to cycle up from the flat in Ambleside. They were drinking coffee, filling in time as they waited for Lindsay to arrive. Lindsay was driving down from Phil's in Carlisle to join them for another day on the hills.

"Porto un llibre per a tu," Lluïsa said. Since arriving in the Lake District, she had been on a one-woman mission to try to persuade Nick that he could still understand a little Catalan.

"You've got me a book? Why?"

"Perquè avui és el dia de Sant Jordi, és 23 d'abril. A Catalunya, és tradició regalar un llibre als seus amics. Porto un llibre per regalar-li a la Lindsay, també."

"You give people books to celebrate St Jordi's day? That's a really good tradition," Nick replied, thinking that the British book trade could do with something equivalent. He thought ruefully of the piles of unsold copies of his own book *Nuclear Power: Yes Please?* Presumably his publisher would keep them in a warehouse for a year or two and then pulp the lot.

"It is because St Jordi is the patron saint of Catalunya," Lluïsa went on.

"England's patron saint is St George and it's his saint's day today too," Nick replied.

"But, Nick, do not be stupid, he is the same person," Lluïsa replied, deciding that communication might be easier in English.

"Ah, St George obviously travelled around. Dragons everywhere in those days."

There was the sound of a car drawing up outside and a moment later Lindsay came in through the unlocked front door. A third mug of coffee was organised.

"Lluïsa has presents for us," Nick told Lindsay.

"Really?"

"Yes, I have a book as a present for you for Sant Jordi day. I ask my mother to send them to me last week," Lluïsa explained.

The two presents were unwrapped. Lindsay's was a book of colour photographs, with text in English, of the Catalonian part of the Pyrenees. Nick's book was similar but had fewer photographs, more maps and more text. It was written in Catalan: *El Parc Nacional dels Pirineus, un paisatge especial.*

"I like your mountains but my mountains are beautiful too. When I go home again, I want you both to come and visit me. We will visit the Pyrenees. There is great walking and running over the mountains. Perhaps we will run the mountain marathon race there together."

"That's a fantastic idea, Lluïsa," Lindsay said. She looked across to Nick, who nodded.

"First we practise by doing the Frog Graham, of course," Lluïsa said.

Lindsay pulled out a map of the western Lakes. "OK, so let me show you my plan for today's recce," she said. "We'll take one of the cars to Keswick, park it there and then take the bus round to Buttermere. Leg 4 of the Frog Graham starts from there. My favourite section."

Lluïsa and Nick looked on as Lindsay ran her finger over the map.

"There's a stiff climb to start with, up to Robinson and Dale Head," she said. Robinson and Dale Head were two of the Lakeland mountains that closed off the top end of the beautiful Newlands valley. "But once we're over Dale Head we've done most of the hard work. From there, it's really pleasant running more or less downhill all the way to Maiden Moor and Catbells. Lluïsa, you'll love this. There will be some fantastic views today over Derwent Water."

"Why is it called Catbells?" Lluïsa asked.

"Some people say that the name originally meant the lair of the wild cat," Lindsay replied.

"There won't be wild cats up there today. Plenty of people though," Nick said. Catbells is one of the most popular Lakeland hills for day walkers.

"After Catbells the route drops down for the swim across Derwent Water. We recced that the other day so we don't need to do that again," Lindsay went on. "So today we can carry on along the Cumbria Way long-distance path back to Keswick. Or if we're tired, there's always the bus."

The map was folded, the coffee mugs piled in the kitchen sink, the house locked and Lindsay's car started again. Lluïsa, in the front passenger seat turned round to talk to Nick.

"I interviewed Joan the climate protester yesterday," she said.

"Did you?" said Nick surprised. "I didn't know you knew Joan Arkle."

"Yes, I talked with her at the public meeting, remember? She gave me her mobile number. I like her."

"Was she... friendly?"

"Oh yes, very friendly. She told me much about Extinction Rebellion and gave me many useful contacts in other parts of your country. I have a commission from La Vanguardia in Barcelona to write an article on climate change protests in Britain."

"I thought nobody in Catalonia was supposed to know you were here?"

"Well, obviously the newspaper won't use my name. Actually Anna has organised the commission for me."

Nick remembered that Rosa's mother had told him in her letter that she had begun working for La Vanguardia. "Will people in Catalonia be interested in what's happening here?" he asked.

"Oh yes," Lluïsa replied. "We have similar problems to you. Many of our towns have flooding risks which are getting worse as the climate changes. I am going to write about the floods you have suffered in Cumbria."

"It will be some time before people here forget Storm Desmond," Nick said with feeling.

"Yes, flooding is terrible. We worry about droughts and fires, too. The book I gave you, Nick, tells you how beautiful it is to go walking in the mountains. But whole mountain ranges are sometimes closed to visitors in the summers because of the fire risk. All the tourists get turned back by the police."

"We've had bad moorland fires in the Pennines recently," Nick said in response. He looked out of the window. They were by now reaching the outskirts of Keswick. "What else did Joan say to you?"

"She is still upset because her dog was killed last Monday."

"I saw that on Twitter," Nick replied. "I'm sorry for her."

"The animal hospital did tests. The dog died from drug poisoning."

"Really?" said Nick, suddenly taking a professional interest in what Lluïsa was saying.

"Yes, Joan blames the man in the shop who had the drugs. The story you wrote in the Enquirer this week."

Drugs raids rock Cumbria had been the headline which Molly had run in a larger than usual size on the front page of that week's edition of the paper, accompanied by the photograph of the uniformed police constable standing guard outside the vaping shop which Nick had taken on Tuesday morning. Nick and Molly had written the article together. It was one of their strongest front page leads for several months, but Nick felt that there was something more to the story that had so far eluded them. He was still intrigued at why the window of the shop had carried the enigmatic *Where is Goldie?* message. Come Monday morning, he decided, he would see if he could follow this up.

"I don't suppose you mentioned my name to Joan when you were talking?"

"Oh yes," Lluïsa replied cheerfully. "I told him that you were almost my uncle. I told her that you were a good journalist and had written a very good book, too."

"Ah, right," Nick said, not sure whether such an endorsement was quite what would be needed to persuade Joan to talk to him again.

Lindsay brought the car to a halt in the car park next to Keswick's bus station. "Time to stop this chit-chat and to get ready for the fells," she said. "The bus goes in ten minutes. Everybody out."

53.

Jem Braithwaite took the quad bike as far as he could up the hillside, stopping just before the ground rose more sharply towards the high fells beyond. He had fixed an open trailer to the back of the quad, ready for its passenger.

There was a pleasure in being out on the fells which he still delighted in, even after all these years. This was his land, after all. Herdwicks were sheep which, as everyone knew, were hefted to the particular area of the mountain-side which they knew as their home. Sometimes he felt hefted in just the same way, hefted to his three hundred acre patch of pasture and rough grazing high up overlooking the Buttermere valley below.

He had farmed this land since he was twenty-seven, when he had taken over the farm after his Dad's accident. For thirty years he and Betty had shared the work together, all the good times and all the hard times too. And then, when she was still only in her fifties, Betty had been taken from him. The big C. Since then he'd farmed alone. The two lads were making their own way in the world, both working indoors in offices, neither of them prepared to follow their father into the tough life of running an upland sheep farming. It was a common story. According to something he'd read, the average age of a farmer in Britain these days had risen to 59.

Sometime, Jem knew, he would have to give it up. He was 66, the age by which almost everyone else in the country had retired. He was already suffering from problems with his legs. As he knew when he was being honest with himself, he had begun to drink far too much. It helped dull the pain. The bottle of whisky was there for when he returned from meeting Roger and David in The Fleece. For the evenings when he felt alone and lonely.

He scrambled as best he could up the rocky outcrop and found what he had come to collect. The sheep was on its side, already beginning to decompose. The creature had wandered too far along one of the rocky ledges and become cragfast. It was a risk you took when you farmed where he did. Sheep weren't bright.

A dead sheep means lost money, but more than it represents an unpleasant extra task for a farmer. These days you can't just burn or bury the carcass. The rules say that you have to remove it from your land and pay an approved contractor to take it away to be disposed of.

Jem picked up the dead animal by its legs, and only then noticed the small white object which had been lying alongside. It was also dead. The lamb must have stayed with its mother to the bitter end. A further loss.

He dragged the ewe towards the trailer, and then scrambled back to fetch the lamb. Both animals carried the blue smit marks he had himself painted on their fleeces, identifying them as belonging to his stock. He flung the carcasses into the trailer.

He suddenly felt faint. He must have hurried up the fellside too fast. He steadied himself against the handlebars of the quad, and looked back at the trailer. In place of the sheep with their smit marks the trailer was now holding the body of a young women, her close-cropped hair the same blue colour as the paint he had used on the sheep.

Jem rubbed his eyes. The woman disappeared and the sheep returned. He turned the ignition key and set off fast down the hillside.

Wishful thinking, he told himself later as he sat in the kitchen looking across at the bottle. Simply wishful thinking.

54.

There were no blue and green and white flags of Cumbria this time, but there were St George's flags out on the streets of Keswick, in the hands of a group of a dozen or so young men. Horsey had prevailed on Baz and Mick, as well as some of his workmates and a few friends of friends, to join him for a St George's Day rally. It was a good opportunity. The town was full with Saturday morning shoppers.

A New Voice for Cumbria, Paula had told him by email, had decided not to contest the local elections after all. But Horsey's nomination papers had already been handed in to the council. The election was only ten days away and it was much too late to withdraw. His name would be there on the ballot paper, come what may. He decided he might as well make as much of the experience as he could.

A PCSO was watching the demonstrators from a discreet distance. Horsey had prepared a number of hand-produced placards for the occasion, and Baz had picked up the one which read *Cumbria for Cumbrians: keep foreigners out.* Mick had a placard which said *Cumbrian young people need decent homes.* Between the two of them they were trying to get some chanting going. It had to be admitted, though, that there was an absence of energy about the event, certainly compared to the rally they'd staged the previous Sunday evening. Maybe they'd been wrong to hold the event in the morning: late afternoon would probably have been better and would certainly have allowed them to get some beers in first.

There was another reason, Baz thought, and that was the absence of Terry. They missed the leadership which he had been able to provide. It had now been five days since the police had raided Terry's shop and taken him and Trix away, and a couple of days since they'd seen the shop plastered all over the front page of the Cumbrian Enquirer. But Baz still hadn't come to terms with what had happened. He remained convinced that the drugs were planted, and as far as he was concerned this had all the makings of a plot hatched by Joan Arkle. Elizzabeth probably figured somewhere in the story, too, although Baz wasn't quite sure how. He was angry with her. He had put her remaining clothes and the other stuff of hers that she'd left behind out with the rubbish on Thursday.

There had been another unsatisfactory consequence of Terry's arrest as well. Baz had been unable without his friend's help to make contact with Michelle, the woman whom Terry had promised him was hot as hell and would be gagging to meet him. Baz's life was currently empty of both Elizzabeth and Michelle.

The St George's Day rally petered out as one by one the participants drifted away. At the end, Horsey was left with just Baz and Mick by his side.

"Drink?" Baz said.

"Spose so," Horsey said without much enthusiasm. He folded away the flags and left the placards alongside a council litter bin for someone else to take away. "I'm not sure why I'm bothering with all this," he added morosely.

"Don't be depressed," Mick said. "You'll get our votes at least, won't he Baz?"

Baz looked embarrassed. "Sure. I'll need to get on the electoral register, I guess."

Horsey looked at him in disbelief. "You tosser," he said. "It's too bloody late. Didn't you even make sure you had a vote?"

Baz shrugged an apology. "Anyway, one vote never makes any difference in an election," he offered.

They were making their way aimlessly along Keswick's Main Street when Horsey abruptly stopped. "Well well, so who have we here?" he said.

Across the road, a white campervan had just pulled up. From the driver's door was stepping someone last seen on the stage of a church hall the previous weekend.

Horsey called out to her. "Give us a sparkle, Joan."

Joan glared at them.

"Fancy coming with us for a donner kebab?" said Mick.

"Fancy coming with us for a hamburger?" said Horsey.

"Fancy coming with us for a shag?" added Baz. The men laughed.

From the passenger door, another person was emerging from the campervan. Elizzabeth looked across to the small group opposite and immediately turned her back.

"Elizzabeth," said Mick. "Don't walk away from us."

"Yes, we've got things we need to talk about," Horsey added.

"How did you like Baz's video?" Mick called out to Elizzabeth's back.

There was no reply. Both Elizzabeth and Joan had turned the corner.

"The video's been taken down on Twitter," Baz said to Horsey and Mick. "I checked yesterday."

"Yes, but it's up on lots of other platforms. Loads of people have already seen it," Mick replied.

"We need to keep up the Twitter pressure on Joan Sparkle. Make her feel frightened. Make it so that she doesn't feel able to post any more."

"At least we know something now," Horsey said.

"What?"

"We know she lives in a campervan. And I've just taken a photo of the van and the number plate on my phone."

"Let's tweet the photo now. That will freak her out." Baz got to work on his phone. "*Watch out for this campervan, everyone. The woman in it is dangerous. Let's drive the #witchwagon out of Cumbria,*" he typed.

"Witchwagon," said Mick, looking over his shoulder. "I like that."

55.

Whatever Lluïsa had told Joan Arkle had obviously worked. Nick couldn't believe the difference in Joan's manner towards him when he rang her from the Enquirer office on Monday morning.

"Oh, hello, Nick," she said, sounding as if they had been friends for life.

This was almost as disconcerting as Joan's previous frostiness. As a journalist, Nick always found it easier if the people he had to interview professionally were not unduly suspicious of him or aggressive. On the other hand he didn't want them to be his friends either.

Was she available to meet up?, he asked her. She certainly was, she replied: was eleven o'clock a good time?

Once again they agreed to rendezvous at the Dunmail Raise lay-by on the main road from Ambleside to Keswick. And once again, Joan's campervan was already parked in place when Nick arrived at five to eleven.

"Would you like some tea?" Joan asked Nick, as he climbed into the van and took his place at the table. "The kettle's just boiled. I've got some vegan biscuits too. They're good, I recommend them."

Nick took the proffered mug and helped himself to a biscuit. "How has the photography been going?" he began. It was usually a good idea to start an interview with small-talk.

Joan almost smiled in response. "Have a look at this," she said, passing her laptop across the table. "I got this this morning at half past five. I had to get up at a quarter past four, but it was worth it."

"Are they red grouse?" Nick asked, looking at the photo on the screen.

"No, black grouse. Much rarer. I took these at the RSPB reserve over at Geltsdale in the North Pennines. It's one of the best places to go if you want to see a black grouse lek."

"A what?"

"A lek is when the male birds strut their stuff to try to show off to the females. It's about the most impressive thing there is to see in Britain, if you're into wildlife. But you have to be there about dawn to see it."

"There must be about eight birds in your photo."

"Yes, I was lucky. Can you see the way that the birds have spread out their tail feathers into a fan, so they can show off their white under-feathers? And there's the bright red wattle above each of the birds' eyes. It's really distinctive. During the lekking the wattles become swollen with blood. I think it's something to do with the level of testosterone in the birds."

"Some time, Joan, you must really take me out with you when you're photographing wildlife. Would that be OK?"

"Why not?" she replied. "Provided you're prepared to get up early. I could arrange to pick you up at your place."

Nick must have looked surprised. Joan saw his look and went on. "Oh, Lluïsa said you lived just off the main road in Grasmere village. Anyway I saw your address was in the BT directory enquiry database."

Nick said nothing, but privately he was telling himself that he urgently needed to go ex-directory. Once before, when he had been covering the story of a young fell runner who had died during a Lake District race, the father of the runner had found his home address and had come round to his home. It had been an unwelcome visitation. These days you really had to try to keep your personal details, including your private address, off the internet.

Nick had momentarily tuned out of what Joan was saying. He had obviously missed something significant.

"You never told me you'd written that book," Joan was saying.

"Sorry?"

"The book on nuclear power. I thought at first it was going to be saying how wonderful nuclear power is. *Nuclear Power: Yes Please?* The title confused me."

"The title is supposed to be ironic."

"So I gathered. It's good, what you've written. I liked it."

"Thank you," Nick said, slightly nonplussed.

"I mean I didn't read it all, of course. I skipped the business stuff about the nuclear power companies. The boring stuff."

"Joan, that was the material which was central to the whole book. That was my original research. I was trying to reveal the corporate interests which had pushed nuclear power back on to the agendas of governments around the world."

Joan replied with a shrug.

"Well, never mind," Nick went on. "You're one of the very small number of people who've bought my book. You'd be amazed how few copies of a book a publisher can manage to sell."

Joan didn't immediately reply.

"You did buy it, did you? Or did you get it from the library?"

"Yes, sort of. I borrowed it."

An unwelcome thought struck Nick.

"You didn't nick the book, did you?"

"Well, I took it from the bookshop in Ambleside. There was a whole pile there unsold so I didn't think they'd miss one."

"Joan, you shoplifted from one of the small number of remaining independent bookshops. That's a disgusting thing to do."

Joan shrugged. "Yeah, well, nobody was buying your book anyway and at least now I've read it."

Nick grimaced.

Joan smiled back at him. "But I guess you're right. Anyway, I went back after hours and stuck a £20 note through the letter-box," she added.

"Joan, you really are quite extraordinary," Nick responded. He pulled himself together. He was here professionally. He finished the tea and picked up his reporter's notebook.

"Tell me how Goldie died," he said, abruptly changing the subject.

"She was poisoned. Opioid poisoning."

"How do you know that?"

"I got a vet I know to do a post mortem. She said that Goldie had obviously come into contact with an opioid drug. Heroin or fentanyl. Apparently fentanyl is often used to lace heroin. When dogs sniff it it gets absorbed through their membranes into their noses. Basically they overdose and die."

Joan was recounting the story without emotion.

"I've never heard of that happening before," Nick responded.

"The vet said it's a well-known problem for police dogs and sniffer dogs at airports. They can suffer and die from the very drugs that they're trained to find."

"Would... Goldie have died quickly? Don't tell me if you'd rather not."

"Apparently dogs exposed to drugs like fentanyl can stop breathing in a couple of minutes. There's this great antidote you can give them and that's what the police have ready for their dogs just in case. It's called.... Naloxone, I think. But obviously you have to know what's happening and you have to be really quick administering it."

"Joan, this is a terrible story."

Joan Arkle gave her trademark shrug. "Goldie was a wonderful dog," she said. "She didn't deserve to die."

"Lluïsa told me that you think you know who was responsible."

"I know for certain. It was Terry Venables, the man who the police arrested on Tuesday morning. You're welcome to print that."

"I can't just print something on the basis of an uncorroborated allegation. Why are you so sure?"

Joan began to tell her story, starting with the Sunday evening public meeting. Nick's pencil made shorthand marks on the pages of the notebook. "I'd left Goldie in a side room of the church hall," she said. "Terry Venables was there, pissed. I think he took the dog out of spite."

"You only *think?*"

"Then I got this message on my phone the next day." Joan passed her mobile across to Nick. "Telling me I could pick up Goldie from the vaping shop. Except that I then got this second message. That Goldie had been taken to Preston. And I went to the shop anyway but there was no-one there."

Nick was reading the two messages on Joan's phone. He looked up.

"There was a painted message about Goldie on the shop window," he said.

"Oh yes, I did that," Joan replied. "I wanted the man to know that I knew he had the dog."

"How did you know that the man at the public meeting owned the shop? I mean, Joan, I agree the messages are mysterious but I can't print just a load of hearsay."

"A friend told me about Terry Venables and his shop. A friend who used to know one of his mates well."

This rang a sudden bell for Nick.

"Not the woman Elizzabeth with the two 'z's? The woman who was arrested with you at the Drigg demonstration?" Nick asked. He was about to add, "The woman who was the reason why you came into the Enquirer office and chained yourself to Molly's chair that time?" He decided not to mention it.

"Yes, it was Elizzabeth who told me. She used to be the girlfriend of Baz, who was one of Terry's drinking mates. Baz has treated her disgustingly. She's well out of that relationship." Joan did not elaborate.

"You had some really nasty trolling on your Twitter account too, when Goldie disappeared. I saw it."

"Yes," said Joan baldly.

"Who was behind all that?"

"Dunno, but Elizzabeth says that it was Baz and his mates." She shrugged.

"Are you going to the police with any of this? I mean, you've got the vet's report, you've got these phone messages about Goldie, you've got strong circumstantial evidence that Terry Venables was involved."

"Nah, I don't do police," Joan responded.

"Why not?"

"Why do you think? I'm going to be seeing enough of the police anyway a week today. That's the date when my Drigg trial is finally coming up. They'll be out to get me for everything they can."

Nick had forgotten that Joan's trial had been deferred after she had pleaded not guilty before the Workington magistrates. He should probably be there himself on Monday, he told himself.

"You don't want to talk to the police, but you don't mind me running a story in the Enquirer?" It was a question.

"No, if you want to, you're welcome," Joan said. "You can mention my name. Oh, the only thing I haven't mentioned to you yet is this."

She passed a small piece of paper across to Nick. He looked at it, and then looked back at Joan quizzically. The piece of paper had just one word on it: *Sorry.*

"I found the paper inside Goldie's collar when Elizzabeth and I picked up the body. I suppose it was a message to me. I suppose the message meant that they hadn't meant Goldie to die."

"Just the one word *Sorry*," Nick said.

"Not much of an apology for the death of a beautiful dog that I loved and who loved me, is it?"

"No," Nick agreed. "It's not."

56.

Baz had woken up feeling horny. It could have been, perhaps, that the effects of the previous night's video which he had been watching before he went to sleep still hadn't worn off. But it could be because of Michelle.

In recent days he had been having the most amazing fantasies about Michelle. Sometimes she was blonde, with frizzy hair and a pixey face, and with bright red lipstick on her lips. Sometimes she was a redhead, with a mass of wavy red hair that plunged over her neck and down over her breasts. Her breasts were magnificent, proud and tight. She would grab his head with both her hands and pull his lips violently into hers.

Michelle would arrive in his life in various ways. Sometimes he would catch sight of her beckoning him into one of the bedrooms in the hotel where he was working. Sometimes she would be waiting for him in his flat when he came back from work. Sometimes she would be at his front door in the mornings, handing him a letter which she told him had been delivered to her by mistake. And then she would come in, removing as she did the shirt she had been wearing over her bare breasts.

Today, as Baz woke up, Michelle was at his front door again. He was convinced of it. He had heard her knocking as he emerged out of sleep. Today she must have found another letter to hand-deliver to him. She'd be wearing a black bra to match the tight black leather shorts she'd have on. She was so real that Baz nearly went down to his front door to let her in.

He pulled himself together. Enjoyable as the Michelle fantasies were, he'd rather have the real thing, he told himself. Except that today it really did sound as if Michelle was waiting for him downstairs. It really did sound like she was hammering on his front door.

Something was doing in his head.

There it was again. Bang, bang.

Baz pulled on a T-shirt and boxers and investigated.

Michelle was not waiting for him on the other side of the front door. On the other side of the front door were two young male police constables in uniform. One of them showed Baz his warrant card. Baz was dimly aware that he was being asked his full name and date of birth. He must have answered. Because then Baz found himself hearing words he had previously only heard on cop shows on TV.

You do not have to say anything. But, it may harm your defence if you do not mention when questioned something which you later rely on in court. Anything you do say may be given in evidence.

You are being arrested for disclosing sexual images, Baz heard the policeman tell him. We have to ask you to accompany us to the police station for questioning. We will wait while you get yourself dressed.

Baz stood at the front door motionless.

"Go and put your clothes on," the policeman repeated.

"Why are you here?" Baz eventually responded. "It's Monday, I need to get to work soon."

"We need to question you further about an offence you may have committed. You have been accused of having publicly disclosed a private film showing a person depicted in a sexual way without their consent. The custody officer at the police station will explain your rights. You will have the right to free legal advice."

Baz remained silent as he took in what he was being told.

"You're accusing me of revenge porn?" he said.

"That's what some people call it," the policeman replied.

"This is Elizzabeth, isn't it?"

"Just get your clothes on, sir."

"It was only a bit of fun."

"Our police car is here. We will drive you to the station."

Elizzabeth had taken the decision to go to the police station immediately after her first Sunday shift was over at the café. She and Joan were very close to having their first row about it. Joan had told her in no uncertain terms that she was stupid to imagine the police would help. But Elizzabeth had found a determination that she didn't know previously that she had. She'd kissed Joan affectionately and then told her, "It's my decision."

Penrith has one advantage over Keswick, and that is that it still has an old-fashioned police station, complete with police on duty. Elizzabeth pushed open the door. A man on the front desk eyed her as she came in.

"I have been a victim of sexual harassment," she said, in a strong voice. "I'm only prepared to talk to a woman police officer about the details."

"Let me see if someone is available to speak to you, madam. Take a seat," the duty officer replied, disappearing briefly into an office behind the front desk.

Elizzabeth sat on a hard metal chair for what must have been at least ten minutes. Finally a young woman in plain clothes approached her. "I'm DC Rosie Whittaker," she said. "I'm very sorry you've had to wait so long. Let's go somewhere quieter."

DC Whittaker led the way into a small interview room just off the main corridor. "My colleague tells me you want to report a case of sexual harassment."

"My former boyfriend has posted a really horrible video of me all over the internet," Elizzabeth replied. "It's embarrassing and he's doing it out of revenge. But I don't know if it's a crime."

"Revenge porn has been a crime since 2015," DC Whittaker responded. "You've done absolutely the right thing in coming to talk to us."

"The thing is, I originally allowed him to take the video."

"That doesn't matter. The law is clear. If material of sexual nature is circulated when someone involved doesn't consent to it being made public, then that's potentially a crime. The video is in some way sexual, I assume?"

"Yes," Elizzabeth said. "I suppose I have to show you it?"

"At some point yes, but let me reassure you. I work for a specialist police unit concerned with domestic violence."

"I've got Twitter to take it down but I expect it's still on loads of other places."

"Ideally it's better to come to the police before you get the social media companies to take material down. For the purposes of evidence, you see. Or at least try to take a screen shot of what's online before it disappears, as a record. But I know that can be a difficult thing to ask of someone in the circumstances."

Elizzabeth nodded. "Sorry, I never thought of that."

"Let me ask you. Are you prepared to give me a formal witness statement now?" DC Whittaker asked.

"Yes," Elizzabeth said firmly.

"Good. It's really important that we can get justice for you. Otherwise the law might as well not exist."

"I've made up my mind."

"There is one thing I do have to advise you," DC Whittaker said. "I'm afraid the law as it stands does not give you anonymity. A lot of people think that the law should be changed, but at present if your case goes to trial your name may be in the public domain. Some women who have suffered revenge porn have found themselves in the national media as a result."

"I'd prefer to be anonymous, but I don't care, I'm going through with this."

"I admire your courage. You're right," the policewoman said.

She reached across to a jug of water and poured Elizzabeth a glass.

"Let's take your statement."

57

Nick was at his keyboard. Writing an effective news-story was a skill which came with experience. You had to assemble your material in a way which made the story immediately understandable. You had to persuade your readers to keep reading.

His chosen opening paragraph was already on his screen:

Cumbria's escalating trade in illegal drugs has claimed another innocent victim. Goldie, a much-loved pet Labrador-cross, was found dead of drug poisoning on a Keswick street last week.

Nick had shared with Molly what Joan had told him about Goldie's death when he had returned to the office that lunchtime. They'd agreed between them that the story was potentially another front page lead. But it needed careful writing. Some of what Joan had said was still uncollaborated.

The next two paragraphs took shape:

Mystery continues to surround the full circumstances of Goldie's disappearance and death, which her heart-broken owner Joan Arkle claims is linked to the high-profile drugs raid by police on a Keswick shop last week. The post mortem on the dog revealed that it died of exposure to illegal opioid drugs, most likely heroin or fentanyl.

"Goldie was a wonderful dog, a real friend to me," Ms Arkle told the Cumbia Enquirer. "She didn't deserve to die."

As all journalists know, quotes are an essential part of any news-story. If you haven't slipped in a quote by the third paragraph of your story, you're probably going astray.

Nick pressed on. He'd already told readers that Goldie was an innocent victim. He'd reported that the owner was heart-broken. Now to get to the detail.

Ms Arkle last saw her dog on Sunday 18th, at an evening meeting she had organised in Keswick on climate change. She alleges that Goldie was abducted at the end of the evening by a hostile member of the audience who was drunk at the time.

Cruelly, the following day she received an anonymous message that Goldie had been found safe and well. "I was told in a text to my mobile phone that I'd be able to pick her up at lunchtime," she said. "I had already drawn from the bank the £100 I'd promised for

Goldie's safe return."

The text which Joan Arkle received and which she has now made available exclusively to the Cumbrian Enquirer appears unequivocal. It reads, *My boyfriend found the dog last night... Goldie's quite safe. Can you come round to the little vaping shop behind the Alhambra cinema in Keswick at about one?"*

Nick was conscious that, professionally speaking, this oh-so-nearly happy ending to the news-story would make the ultimate tragedy of Goldie's death even more poignant to his readers. He carried on with his work.

However, in a curious twist, this text was followed almost immediately by a second anonymous message. This read *My boyfriend's taken her [Goldie] to Preston for the day because he didn't know about the one o'clock arrangement.*

The shop where Ms Arkle was told she would be reunited with Goldie was the subject of a dawn raid the following morning by the police. As reported in last week's Enquirer, heroin to the value of over £10,000 was found on the premises. The shop's owner Terry Venables was arrested and has now been remanded in police custody.

Joan Arkle alleges that the texts were sent by Terry Venables' girlfriend, who is also in custody. She believes that Goldie died from exposure to illegal drugs which Terry Venables was holding, either in the shop or perhaps on the so-far unconfirmed journey which Mr Venables may have made to Preston that morning.

Without the text messages which Joan Arkle had shown him, Nick would have been very much more cautious in the way he had drafted this part of the story. He was still careful to make it clear that Joan's views were still simply assertions.

It was time to press on to the story's denouement.

Hoping to hear Goldie's friendly bark from inside, Joan Arkle visited the vaping shop at 1pm as originally arranged, and then again twice later that afternoon. However her hopes were dashed. Each time the premises were empty.

Goldie's body was found the following morning near Keswick's former railway station, where it had apparently been dumped. In a final twist to the mystery, a small piece of paper with the single word *Sorry* had been left under the dog's collar.

"It's not much of an apology for the death of a beautiful dog that I loved and who loved me, is it?" Joan Arkle said.

Molly was reading the story over Nick's shoulder on his computer screen. "Good stuff," she said. "We can use that last bit in the headline. Something like *Sorry your dog's dead: Was mystery message left by drug dealers?*'

"Something a bit shorter?" Nick asked.

"Maybe. Let me work on that. What about a photo?"

"Joan Arkle's supplied it," Nick said. "It does the trick admirably." The photo was the one which had appeared on Joan's Stolen Dog posters, showing Goldie with her tongue hanging out.

"Goldie looks like everybody's loveable pooch," Molly said.

"She does," Nick said.

58.

Rod paid for the two Americanos. He and Alan were in Caffè Nero in Carlisle, a suitably anonymous place where two businessmen could get together up for an informal meeting on a Thursday morning. Alan had already made for a very quiet table at the far end of the café. It was the first time they'd met together for over a week.

"All going well over in Whitehaven," Alan said. "Prices are on the up, too, just as we expected."

"Things well with me, too. I've seen off the Manchester boys for the time being."

"So our only problem is this."

Alan put down the latest edition of the Cumbrian Enquirer.

On the cover was a cute picture of a shaggy black dog together with a large headline which read *Drug dealers say 'sorry your dog's dead' - claim.*

"Front page two weeks running. That's one week too many," Alan said.

"Two weeks too many."

"It'll be fine provided we're out of the news from now on. Another week and people will forget things."

"I know. But at the moment our business is a bit too centre-stage."

"The problem is the woman we discussed last time. We both thought she'd disappear from sight once she'd got her bloody dog safely back. And instead Terry Venables in his wisdom delivers her with a corpse. Just what we needed."

"I've been making some enquiries. She's not precisely a shrinking violet, our Joan Arkle," Rod said.

"Go on."

"Lengthy criminal record, for starters..."

Alan raised his eyebrows. "Really?"

"...but only for taking part in demonstrations and things like that." Rod carried on. They laughed.

"She's all over social media," he continued, pulling out a mobile phone. "Here's a photo of the campervan she lives in, which someone's conveniently posted on Twitter. And Miss Arkle herself has helpfully tweeted to tell us where she parks her van. It's at a smallholding somewhere near Ullswater."

"Interesting."

"She's attracting a lot of trolling. There's a campaign going on for people to tweet whenever they spot her van. The hashtag being used is #witchwagon. She's obviously got enemies already."

"Ideal. Who?"

"Some of the trolling may be Terry's friends. Revenge for his arrest and all that. If so, this week's newspaper should liven things up even more. But she's got other enemies. She annoyed a lot of local farmers recently by claiming that climate change will force them to change the way they farm."

"You attack the farming lobby at your peril," Alan observed.

"So, assuming we want Joan Arkle out of the way as quickly as possible, other people are doing our job admirably already. But there are things we can do to help them along."

"OK?"

"It should be easy enough to put a tracking bug on her van. Then we can monitor directly what she's up to."

"Good idea. I know someone who could organise that. A young guy in Workington. He won't have any idea who we are. I'll arrange for him to be paid in kind."

"I want to make Joan Arkle move about more. Somehow we need to get the people who live at that smallholding not to allow her to park there any more."

"A letter to suggest that they are breaching planning law, maybe? Something like that."

"Mr Bean would do that for us. He does the necessary legal language very well. And his letters come on the right sort of headed notepaper," Rod suggested.

"Mr Bean is trying hard not to cooperate with us any more."

"I know. But what a pity we know about his cocaine habit. I think the Law Society might be very interested if we told them."

"Mr Bean it is, then. I'll contact him today."

"I've one more idea."

"Yes?"

"We create an angry Cumbrian farmer. Someone who can't stop tweeting abuse. His Twitter name's Farmer Giles. He wants Joan Arkle out of his hair, out of Cumbria and preferably dead."

"Excellent. Do we know any farmers?"

"We don't, but we can find someone prepared to do the tweeting. We arrange it third-hand. As soon as possible."

"Leave that with me as well," Alan said.

Rod paused and changed the subject.

"Missus all right?" he asked Alan.

"Fine," Alan replied. "How's yours?"

"Fine too," Rod responded.

Sometimes it was better to keep business affairs and personal life firmly separate.

59.

"Did we know this part of the story?" DI Chrissy Chambers asked DS Peter Blackford as they each made themselves a mug of coffee on Thursday morning. The two detectives were reading the front page of the Cumbrian Enquirer which Peter Blackford had brought in with him.

"Not really," he replied.

"I wonder why the woman went to the press and not to the police." She paused. "Joan Arkle, I know that name from somewhere."

"Climate change activist. Arrested at the Drigg demonstration."

"Ah yes." It all came back to Chrissy Chambers. "The woman with the large blue whale tattoo. The woman who stripped off in court."

"Sorry, guv, I'm not with you."

"Don't worry. It's an anecdote I'll share with my grandchildren when I retire from the force."

"By coincidence, Joan Arkle's Drigg trial is scheduled for next Monday. I checked," DS Blackford said.

"I assume it's coincidental." She paused. "You don't think Joan Arkle is simply trying to shift the blame for the dog's death? That she uses drugs herself, and her dog came into contact with her stash? The arrests in Keswick last week would be a good opportunity to try to shift the attention away from herself."

DS Blackford pondered. "Why would she organise a PM for the dog in that case? Surely you'd just quietly dispose of the body and hope nobody asked any questions."

"That's true."

"Her story seems too complicated to have been made up. And, anyway, it's not as though she's frightened of publicity normally. She organised that public meeting on climate change recently."

"So she did." DI Chambers pondered. "Her name's not come up in any of your enquiries, I suppose?"

"No."

"Still, let's keep her in sight."

"Right," DS Blackford responded.

"Where are we now?" Chrissy Chambers continued. "With the drugs initiative, I mean."

"The trail's gone rather cold. I think the big boys have escaped the net this time, unfortunately. If I'm honest, we had luck on our side in Keswick. I was by no means sure we'd find anything in that shop. It was just that something rather odd was going on there."

"I think that's one of the secrets of detective work. Knowing when something is just slightly odd."

As it happened, Chrissy Chambers had been discussing almost

exactly the same thing the previous Monday in a café in Cockermouth. She'd been pleased to be able to meet up with George Mulholland, and he had certainly seemed pleased to see her and to get the latest news from the force. She thought he seemed older than when he had been at work. Retirement could be difficult. You spent decades of your life working your way up the career ladder and then, abruptly, the ladder was pulled away and you were supposed to make yourself a new life cultivating roses or playing bridge. Or doing anything which stopped you interfering in the real world outside which was carrying on without you. No wonder some people found the whole experience of retirement so traumatic.

Nevertheless, Mulholland still had the sharpness he'd displayed as a DCI and Detective Superintendent. He'd given Chrissy exactly the sort of mentoring she had been hoping for. He'd been delighted when she told him that she was now very close to completing her Senior Investigating Officer Development Programme. Her Professional Development Portfolio was already submitted and all that awaited her was the necessary end-of-course interview, or professional discussion as they called it. It was a matter now of days. After that, she'd be enrolled on the register of qualified SIOs, ready at some point to lead her own major enquiry. In some ways that still seemed a scary prospect, but in other respects she now felt prepared for the challenges it would bring.

George Mulholland had been helpful in other ways. He'd encouraged her, for example, to cultivate appropriate contacts in the media and had passed on the contact details for Molly Everett, the editor of the Cumbrian Enquirer. "Molly is an old friend of mine from school days, and she and I have often found it useful over the years to have little chats" he said. "Of course, you must remember that journalists have newspapers to fill and we have criminals to catch. It's not necessarily always the same thing. Once or twice I got very cross indeed with Molly Everett. But, if I were you Chrissy, I would ring her up and have a chat. She's got a sidekick too, Nick Potterton, he's quite useful. Apparently once upon a time he worked for the Sunday Times. I don't know how he ended up working up here."

It was this part of her conversation with George Mulholland that

Chrissy Chambers was thinking about now, as she talked to DS Peter Blackford.

"I think it would be helpful to keep up the media interest in the drugs story," she said to him. "The more we can encourage the public to be watchful, the more chances we have."

"I agree with you. There's been a big growth nationally in the use of AirBnB places and holiday lets as an alternative to cuckooing, and in our part of Cumbria this would be a good message to get across."

"You're right, that's a very strong story to take to the press. What examples have we got?"

"At the moment just that case from Flimby which was linked to the Penrith raid."

"One example is enough. I'll see what our press people think, but I'm inclined to ring the Cumbrian Enquirer editor later today."

60.

"John and Teresa have sold their shares," Molly told Nick on Thursday afternoon. "I've just had a phone call from the accountant."

"Sold their shares? Who to?" Nick asked.

"Who do you think?" Molly gave him the name of a regional newspaper group based in the north of England.

"What happens now then?"

"I have to give all the remaining staffers redundancy notices. And I think I have to give myself a redundancy notice, too."

"God, Molly, that's desperate."

"Technically I think the redundancy notices should have gone out weeks ago, to comply with the law. The redundancy pay will have to come out of the Enquirer's small stash of remaining reserves. And I'm afraid freelances get nothing."

Nick shrugged. "I know," he said. "That's why the freelance day rate I've been charging you has been so enormously high."

"They've sold their shares over my head, so I don't even know what my own shares in the Enquirer are worth," Molly went on. "If they are worth anything."

"How many more weeks?"

"Two more editions."

"Only two? Is that all?"

Molly nodded.

"So we need to start planning to go out on a high. A special final edition which will celebrate all the Enquirer has done over the years and which readers will be able to save as a special commemorative edition."

Molly was shaking her head. "No," she said.

"Sorry?" Nick asked her.

"No farewells allowed. No special edition. The new owners will be using the Enquirer name and want it to seem as though nothing is changing."

"But that's outrageous."

"Yes. This is the only story in all my time as editor where I am effectively being censored. Where the Enquirer is unable to report the news that it should be reporting."

"What happens if we simply disregard that instruction?"

"Apparently I will be receiving a detailed message from the new owner's solicitors about the precise wording they will permit."

"Oh, Molly, I'm so sorry. Somehow we'll mark the occasion."

"We will. By the way, any follow-up on the Goldie the dog story?"

"Nothing from Joan Arkle. She's been quite quiet. Mind you, the trolls on her Twitter feed are as horrible as ever. They are calling her campervan her witch wagon."

"Disgusting." Molly paused. "I had a phone call over lunch from the police. A woman detective inspector who told me she'd been given my details by George. Wants to introduce herself."

"George is still being useful in his retirement then."

"Yes. DI Chrissy Chambers is her name. She says that holiday lets are increasingly being used by drug dealers, without their owners having any idea that this is happening. Owners think they're letting a family have a holiday to remember in the Lakes and in fact they're giving the front door keys to drug traffickers. Given our readership, this sounds a story that could definitely have legs."

"I agree. Although I guess you'd better follow it up pretty soon. If, that is, we've only got two more papers to produce."

"You're right, I haven't taken this in yet. I think I'm still in some sort of shock."

She turned away from her screen. "In three weeks I suppose I'll be able to join George Mulholland and his wife in some gentle retirement pursuit. Got any suggestions? Flower arranging?"

"Let's talk it through. I'll be out of work too. Maybe there will be opportunities for us to do some freelancing together."

"Maybe."

61.

It was Monday, another working week, and Joan had got up at five o'clock. Elizzabeth had stirred, reached across sleepily to kiss her and wish her good luck. Then Elizzabeth had muttered "space in the bed at last", had turned over and had gone straight back to sleep.

It was true that the single bed was companionable but not particularly conducive to sleep. A few times Elizzabeth had chosen to sleep overnight with Joan in the van on the smallholding instead, but the problem then was she somehow had to get back to Penrith in time for her work in the café. Joan had dropped her at the bus stop at Threlkeld or, on one occasion when Elizzabeth was running late, had taken her all the way in to Penrith. Elizzabeth didn't like either option: it made her feel somehow dependent on Joan.

It was still only about twenty past five, just beginning to get light, when Joan let herself quietly out of Kath's house and opened the driver's door to the campervan parked outside. The early start was a deliberate plan to make at least something of the day, given that most of it was going to be a complete waste of time. She was due at Workington Magistrates Court once again at ten o'clock, this time for the actual trial. No doubt she'd be kept waiting for hours. Then the trial would happen, she'd say why she was pleading not guilty, the magistrates would find her guilty, they'd decide her punishment and then everyone would go home. What a charade.

So before spending time with idiotic human beings she had decided to spend much more profitable time looking for black guillemots. Fleswick Bay, on the Cumbrian coast south of St Bees Head, is about the only place in England where this distinctive little seabird nests.

Bird forums on the web had told Joan that they were nesting again this Spring, and although the posts had also warned that you had to be patient to see them that wasn't going to be a problem for Joan: she was happy with the idea of being out in the countryside before most of the rest of the country had even woken up.

The campervan purred sweetly as Joan headed westwards along the A66, turning off just before Workington to pass through Whitehaven on her way to St Bees and Fleswick Bay. The van had become such a part of Joan's life that she could barely remember the time before she'd got it. There was one thing missing this morning, though. There was no loveable scruffy black dog curled up under the passenger seat to keep her company.

Joan felt Goldie's absence intensely. The dog would have been in seventh heaven to have been taken to the coast. She'd have romped up and down the paths beside the sea, chasing any rabbits that were rash enough to appear. And then she'd have happily curled up again in the van while Joan got her camera out and got down to work. Some time in the future, not just yet because the pain of loss was still too great, there might be another Goldie, Joan thought. Some time, not yet.

Joan waited half an hour for the black guillemots to present themselves and be obliging but, eventually, there they were, small black birds with the distinctive white patch on their wings. Joan took several close-up photographs, all of sufficient quality for uploading for her online agency. The fulmars, nesting on the cliff around St Bees Head, were even more obliging, at least from a photography perspective, even if they did spit out their familiar foul-smelling oil as Joan came close to their nests.

All in all the morning was very productive indeed. Razorbills were on the cliffs, as were kittiwakes and herring gulls. There is admittedly rather less demand for images of seabirds than for, say, cute shots of red squirrels or otters, but nevertheless Joan prided herself on the breadth of her wildlife stock photography. She returned to the campervan around nine o'clock exhilarated and cheerful.

Even the experience of walking once again through the front doors of Workington Magistrates' Court couldn't dampen her mood. She was shown as expected to a seat in the waiting room where she took the opportunity to re-read her notes and prepare herself for the occasion.

She'd had the prosecution papers through from the CPS, which said exactly what you'd expect them to say. The CPS had advised her that they would be calling as witnesses the two policemen who'd arrested her.

She was, of course, conducting her own defence. She wasn't going to argue about what had actually happened at Drigg on the Saturday afternoon of their demo. Instead she was going to use the legal argument of necessity. She was going to argue that the evil inherent in breaking the law was in this particular case less than the evil which would have resulted had she obeyed the law. It was necessary, she would tell the magistrates' bench, to break the law to achieve a greater good.

She would point to the evidence that climate change was a reality, and that among other things this meant that there was an increased risk of coastal flooding. She would point out that the Drigg nuclear waste dump was almost at sea-level. She would argue that the effects of flooding at Drigg could be so catastrophic for the nuclear waste dump, and for everyone living nearby, that there was an overriding duty on her to demonstrate.

To make the point, she'd chosen this time to wear an Extinction Rebellion T-shirt to court. The T-shirt sported the familiar hour-glass logo, but no slogan: surely this time not even the most fusspotty magistrate could object.

Joan had used the argument of legal necessity several times before when she had found herself in court, and of course in each case she had been found guilty. She had no illusions that it would be different this time. But on principle she wouldn't plead guilty. She didn't accept that she was guilty of anything, except perhaps a determination to speak truth to those who'd rather hear lies.

There would be at least one other person in court who would hear her defence. She was pleased to see Nick Potterton, the reporter from the Cumbrian Enquirer, arrive just after her. She'd waved at him cheerfully but had then signalled that she was looking through her papers. He took a chair at the other side of the waiting room.

And then, astonishingly, at only about a quarter past ten, she was called into court. Nick Potterton followed her and took a seat at the back.

There was the usual procedures as she was asked to confirm her name, date of birth and address. The court still had her living at Pete's address in Maryport where she had been at the time of her arrest, but she wasn't going to confuse things by saying that she now lived in a campervan. Pete wouldn't mind her using his address for a very modest untruth.

Then the charges against her were read out. She was conscious that something was not proceeding quite as normal. The prosecutor was advising the magistrates that his two police witnesses were not available. There had, apparently, been confusion over the exact date of the trial and the PCs were off on a training course down south. The prosecutor expressed his profound apologies to the bench. He would, he said, be grateful to Your Worships if they would adjourn the trial to another day.

Joan got to her feet. I have fully prepared my defence case for today, she told the magistrates. I have taken time off from my professional employment to attend the trial (this might have been a slight exaggeration, but still, it sounded good). I would suggest that it is the responsibility of the prosecution to ensure their witnesses are present. I wish to object to an adjournment.

The Chairman of the magistrates looked at his colleagues and then instructed the court usher to clear the room. Joan, Nick and the prosecutor trooped outside. Joan settled back in the chair she had left only five minutes earlier.

They had almost no time to wait before the usher shepherded them back in to the court. The magistrates reappeared. The Chairman spoke.

"The view of the court is that delays or adjournments, where these are unnecessary, do not advance the course of justice, and in this instance we have decided not to grant an adjournment. The trial will proceed as planned."

The prosecutor got to his feet.

"Thank you, Your Worships. Given the decision you have made, you will understand that I am not in a position to offer any evidence."

He immediately sat down. Joan looked back at Nick and shrugged.

The magistrates withdrew, returning only seconds later.

"All stand," said the usher.

The Chairman spoke. "Miss Arkle, we find you not guilty of both charges. You are free to leave."

Joan and Nick found themselves together outside the court house. It was not even eleven o'clock.

"Coffee?" asked Nick.

"Coffee, no. Herb tea, yes. So the answer to your question is yes," said Joan.

They made for a nearby café.

"Well, I wasn't expecting that to be over so quickly. Or indeed to end in the way that it did," Nick said.

"I didn't have a chance to make my political statement. It was going to be stonkingly good."

"I'm sorry I missed it. Still, you have been acquitted."

Joan smiled. "The British justice system still stinks. Just occasionally, though, the wheels fall off."

She supped at her mug.

"Any more black grouse to show me today?" Nick asked.

"Black guillemot today." Joan pulled out her laptop. "I was on the coast first thing this morning. What do you think?"

"I think you're an extremely talented photographer," Nick said, looking at the images.

"I'd rather be known as an activist," Joan replied.

"That goes without saying," Nick responded.

62.

Elizzabeth was in the café kitchen loading up the commercial dishwasher when the message came through on her phone.

Not guilty!! Hahaha. Tell you all tonight. Love you. J.

This is the moment, she thought, when I put all the plates and cups down and dance a little jig round the kitchen floor in celebration. Not guilty – they had neither of them foreseen that outcome. Instead the previous evening they'd discussed the fines that they thought Joan would be given and how much, or rather how little, the court might be prepared to accept in instalments each month.

But to her astonishment when the text arrived Elizzabeth found that she had a sudden feeling of resentment. Joan had been the organiser of the demonstration at Drigg, she'd persuaded Elizzabeth to take part, and the outcome had been that the police had collared them both. And yet now Joan was walking away from the court acquitted of any crime. It was Elizzabeth who was left with the criminal record and, to pay for that, was having to stuff £50 each month into the gaping maw of the bloody Workington Magistrates' Court.

In the circumstances, the least Joan could do would be to offer to contribute to her fine, she thought resentfully.

God, Elizzabeth told herself, that was an unworthy thought. Why had she allowed that to come into her head? Nevertheless as the day wore on, she couldn't get the edge of bitterness she was feeling out of her head.

She loved Joan. She wanted them both to go through the same experiences together. If she was guilty of a crime, somehow that meant that Joan needed to be found guilty too.

63.

"We're really sorry, Joan."

It was Patrick speaking. He and Meg were now in their third growing season since they had taken on the smallholding near Ullswater. They'd both moved up from Lancaster captivated by the dream of trying to become more self-sufficient. The reality had admittedly proved harder than the original vision, but they had stuck it out and had more or less managed to scratch a living. The polytunnels they had put up produced a range of seasonal vegetables that they sold primarily to wholefood shops in the northern Lakes. The brassicas had been eaten badly by caterpillars but at least the beetroot crop had been successful.

"If it was up to us, we'd have no issue with you staying in the van here permanently," Meg chipped in.

"The problem is that we are just tenant farmers. Apparently we have no rights under the tenancy to allow any caravans or camping on the land. And they say that that includes campervans too."

Joan said nothing. Patrick had texted her to ask her to call in as soon as possible at the little tumbledown farmhouse where he and Meg lived, and she had diverted off the A66 on her way back from Workington to Penrith, where she was planning to celebrate the result of the trial with Elizzabeth. It quickly became clear why she was being summonsed: in a nutshell, she was being evicted.

"We had no idea that we were doing anything wrong until we got this letter," Meg was waving a letter which had obviously come from a firm of solicitors. "But apparently we face the forfeiture of our tenancy. That's the wording they've used. And that would break us. We've been working so hard to get the polytunnels up and to get the land certified as organic."

"If we lost the tenancy, we'd have worked our arses off for three years for nothing," Patrick added.

"That's all right," Joan said, accepting the inevitable. "It was nice of you to let me stay as long as you did. Don't worry, I won't ever bring the van back up here again."

"Oh thank you so much. I knew you'd understand," Meg said.

"We're really grateful," Patrick chipped in.

"I was worried that you might have nowhere else to go. But then I thought how many people you know locally. I knew you'd be alright."

"Yes," Joan said. "I'll be all right. Don't worry about me."

There was nothing more to say. She went back to the van, started the engine and hooted a couple of times as she drove down the lane. Patrick and Meg waved as she left. She wouldn't see them again.

64.

"She's in the paper again. Our little friend."

Rod passed the new edition of the Cumbrian Enquirer across to Alan. It was Thursday and another week had gone by. This time they were meeting in the café on the platform at Lancaster station.

"*Climate activist acquitted as prosecutor offers no evidence,*" Alan read out the headline from one of the inside pages of the Enquirer.

"*Local climate change activist Joan Arkle was found not guilty last Monday of charges she had faced following the recent demonstration at Drigg nuclear waste site,*" he carried on, reading aloud the opening paragraph. "*Magistrates at Workington Magistrates Court acquitted her of the charges of criminal damage and aggravated trespass after the Crown Prosecution Service offered no evidence in court.*" He stopped, and looked up at Rod.

"Interesting, don't you think?" Rod said.

"Very revealing. I think it confirms everything we thought."

"Basically, a deal struck. Miss Arkle tells the police what she knows about Terry Venables' extra-curricular activities so they can raid his shop just at the right time to find the maximum amount of stock. Our stock. And in exchange they drop the cases against her. It couldn't be any more transparent."

Rod turned to another page in the paper. "There's also a big story here about how wicked drug dealers are, and how they are taking over holiday lets and AirBnB. A quote from a poor holiday cottage owner who got caught out."

"So three major stories in three consecutive weeks," Alan said. "Is somebody trying to warn us off?"

"Probably, but fortunately it's only a local rag. I'm not sure anyone reads it any more. I don't feel like being frightened out of the Cumbrian market, do you?"

"No." Alan paused. "So let's turn our attention back to Miss Arkle."

"She owes us. How much stock did we lose? Well over ten grand. She's got a debt to pay."

"Which she won't pay."

"Which she won't pay in cash. But perhaps we make her pay in some other way," Rod suggested.

Rod and Alan both drank their coffee.

"Farmer Giles has started being a busy man on Twitter," Rod said.

"He has," Alan agreed. "That's working well."

"Mr Bean's done the business as well," Alan went on.

"I know," Rod said. "The campervan has been moved. It's been parked overnight in a side-street in Penrith in recent days. Boyfriend's place, perhaps."

"Perhaps. " Alan paused. "But Penrith's no better," he went on. "We need her out of the Lakes altogether."

"Got any ideas?" Rod asked.

65.

Sometimes the best birthday presents are the presents you give yourself, Elizzabeth decided. She would give herself something to remember turning 25. She would get a new tattoo.

She'd been thinking about this for a while, ever since Pete in Maryport had shown her his Extinction Rebellion tattoo, had stroked her upper arm and said something like "You could have a tattoo here too".

At one stage she'd thought that she would show her commitment to Extinction Rebellion in the same way as Pete. The hour-glass logo had the advantage of being relatively modest – it wouldn't cost too much at all, and it wouldn't be too painful. But Elizzabeth had changed her mind. Now she was planning something different.

It all went back to that evening in the campervan, the evening after Joan had taken her up to Falcon Crag to see the peregrine falcons. Elizzabeth had shown Joan her eagle tattoo and then Joan had shown Elizzabeth her blue whale tattoo. That was an evening which Elizzabeth would not forget.

So the new tattoo was going to be a whale. Elizzabeth was planning something much more modest than Joan's. For one thing, she really couldn't afford at the moment more than a small tattoo. Her plan was for the whale to bend its back delicately up the inside of her left lower leg, just above the ankle. It would match in some sense the ankle-chain that she had tattooed on her right leg. But, more importantly, it would also match in some other sense Joan's tattoo. It was a way of affirming their relationship.

She'd already talked to the tattoo artist who had done her golden eagle, and they'd arranged a time for her to go into the studio to discuss the design in detail. She'd mentioned it earlier in the week to Joan, too, who was enthusiastic. Joan had bent down to feel the skin in the place Elizzabeth had indicated. "Hmm, yes, it would go well here," she said. Then she had slipped her hand up on to Elizzabeth's inner thigh. "Or it could go here," she said, stroking it gently. Elizzabeth felt Joan's hand wander even further up.

"Some people have tattoos here," Joan said.

"That's quite enough. Move your hand away this minute."

Joan laughed. Her hand stayed where it was. Elizzabeth reached across and kissed her.

"OK, just this once keep it there," she said.

"So you're Taurus," Joan had said eventually. "You're meant to be stubborn. And persistent. Are you stubborn and persistent?"

"No, You're the only stubborn and persistent person round here. What sign are you?"

"Aquarius. My birthday is 1st February. I'm supposed to be independent and enigmatic."

"God, you're certainly that," Elizzabeth said.

"We're not supposed to get on. Aquarians and Taureans are supposed to be really incompatible."

"Who says?" Elizzabeth replied. "We get on, don't we?"

"As far as I know we get on," Joan said. That remark, Elizzabeth decided, deserved another little kiss.

Joan got out her phone and went online. "OK, I can tell you more about your personality. Taureans are sensual. You're artistic. You like shopping. Oh, and it also adds here that you like sex. Yes, I think you're a classic Taurus."

Elizzabeth laughed. "Most of the time, Joan Arkle, you talk good sense. Just occasionally, though, you talk bollocks."

"Never," Joan argued back.

Elizzabeth's birthday, May 6th, was a Friday this year. She woke with Joan in her arms in the single bed in which, somehow, they had to try to sleep. "Happy Birthday," Joan said. She had two presents which Elizzabeth immediately unwrapped. One was a delicate necklace which she put on immediately. The other was a vegan cookbook, full of attractive colour photos. "Just to encourage you," Joan said. Elizzabeth laughed.

"I was wondering about buying you a ring, but I thought that might be presumptuous," Joan went on. "But maybe your birthday next year."

Elizzabeth laughed again. Her birthday the previous year had been a pitiful affair, with Baz taking her out for a curry but then leaving her to go home while he went on to the pub with his mates. She was well out of that. Sometime she'd have to talk to a solicitor about properly getting the divorce. But in the meantime, she would enjoy the way that her life was developing. Twenty-five! – how adult that sounded.

66.

Unusually for a Friday, Lluïsa had come into the Enquirer office. She had heard the news of the paper's sale from Nick with disbelief and had volunteered to do what she could to help with the final edition. She was also at a loose end: she had finished her article on the activist movement in Britain against climate change and filed it through to La Vanguardia in Barcelona.

But there was another reason: it was raining torrentially outside.

Lindsay and she had been scheduled to do a final recce for the Frog Graham over Barf and Ullister Hill, a part of the north-western Cumbrian fells that they would have to cross on their way from Bassenthwaite Lake to Crummock Water and which is known as a challenging navigational section. But one look out of the window had been enough to convince them both to abort the plan. A day being drenched to the skin was probably not the best preparation for what would undoubtedly be a real challenge for them both. The plan was to do the Frog Graham for real on the Sunday.

Nick and Molly had agreed that there would be a farewell party for the Enquirer the following Wednesday, immediately after the Enquirer had been finally sent to the printers, and Lluïsa offered to help Nick with the arrangements. Nick and Molly went through their contacts book and emailed out invitations. "Don't forget George Mulholland," Nick said. "Of course I won't," Molly replied.

"Meanwhile, we need to start getting the news pages together. What sort of stories are we likely to have for next week?" Molly went on.

"Local election results," Nick contributed. The elections had been the previous day, the first Thursday in May. "Nothing very surprising there. Except perhaps the utter annihilation of A New Voice for Cumbria."

"Poor King Phillip."

"Yes. His daughter only got 52 votes in Kendal. And the candidate in Keswick, Rick someone, managed only thirteen."

"Unlucky man," Molly said.

"Otherwise, I don't think there is much yet to go on. Have you thought about the front page?"

"Funnily enough, I have," Molly said.

"We're very limited in what we can say, aren't we."

"We are. I have been sent the legally approved text to put in small type at the bottom of the page. All about a new chapter opening in the history of the Enquirer. And a pusillanimous thank you to the retiring editor Molly Everett and her staff.

"Nevertheless I am in control of the front page lead," she went on. "Do you know Dr Peter Chevin, one of the Ambleside GPs? No? Well, he's retiring and moving down to Knott End in Lancashire. I thought we'd lead on this."

Nick raised his eyebrows. "This sounds like a downpage filler on one of the inside news pages, not our final front page."

"Normally I might agree. But not this time. I've already got the headline devised for the story. I intend to run it as bold as I can. Two decks."

"What's the headline?" Nick asked.

"The headline I have in mind is *Farewell, Cumbria*. I think that's ideally appropriate for the GP story, don't you?"

Nick smiled. It was good to work with a really good professional journalist like Molly. "I see what you're thinking," he said.

67.

Baz had a stubby pencil, with which he was doodling on the inside of a cardboard box which had once held a new double electrical socket. It was lunchtime and he and Mick were sitting on the floor of an Ambleside hotel bedroom and eating the sandwiches they'd brought with them. Outside, the rain was beating against the windows.

"OK," said Baz. "Let's set out what we know so far." He wrote a large question mark on the cardboard.

"Let's start with your arrest," Mick prompted.

"Elizzabeth always had a nasty streak," Baz replied. "She'd have loved going to the police." He had spent an uncomfortable day in the police station before being charged and allowed home. The court hearing, he had been told, would be June or July, or maybe August. Or whenever. No-one seemed to know or care.

"You don't know for sure it was Elizzabeth."

"As good as."

"Yes, but think back. We were in the pub, watching the news of Terry being busted. Who was it we worked out had planted the drugs on Terry?"

"Joan Arkle."

"Yes, Joan Arkle. And then what did you do?"

Baz looked blank. Mick helped him out.

"You got your phone out and looked at her Twitter feed."

"Yeah."

"And that's where you found the photo of Elizzabeth's tattoo. On Joan Arkle's feed."

Baz was silent for a moment, while he took another bite of his sandwich. "So what?"

"So maybe Elizzabeth didn't have anything to do with it. Maybe Joan Arkle was trying to get revenge on all of us because, you know, we mucked around at her meeting that time. She tried to bait you. And of course you took the bait."

Baz pondered this. "That was definitely Elizzabeth's tattoo. How would Joan Arkle have got a photo of it?"

Mick shrugged. "I don't know. Tattooists often take photos of their work. Maybe Joan knows the artist who did it and got the photo from them."

"Joan's wormed her way into Elizzabeth's life. More likely that Elizzabeth just showed it to her."

"OK, maybe. But why did Joan choose to tweet it that time, along with some weird stuff about eagles in the Lake District? I think she'd already successfully ticked off Terry on her little to-do list and yours was the next name on it."

Baz poured himself a coffee from the flask beside him on the floor.

"Whatever happened, I think Elizzabeth was in on it, too."

"Perhaps, but we know that Joan Arkle is the ringleader. It was she who got Elizzabeth to go on that demo that day."

They both fell silent.

"The witchwagon hashtag's not really taken off," Baz said.

"No. Basically it's just been you and me using it. Terry... well, Terry can't at the moment. And Horsey has been too busy with his election campaign."

They both laughed.

"I voted for him," Mick said.

"Did you?" Baz replied. "Did he get elected?"

"He got thirteen votes apparently."

Baz shrugged and changed the subject.

"What do we do next?"

"You mean, Joan Arkle? I don't know."

"I saw her van yesterday in Keswick. I thought of letting her tyres down, but it was Booth's car park. There were people about."

Mick was playing with a screwdriver which he had picked up from the floor.

"Vans like that have their engines at the back, I think." He twirled the screwdriver round his fingers. "It would be pretty easy to get at the electrical wiring."

Baz looked at him. "That's interesting," he said.

"Of course, we'd have to find the van first, and at a time when Joan Arkle wasn't anywhere nearby."

"Possibly easier said than done."

"Possibly," Mick responded. He thought about this.

"OK, so for the moment let's just keep going with the witchwagon tag," he went on. "Get your phone out."

Baz pulled out his smartphone.

"Don't use your own Twitter account," Mick warned.

"What do you think I am? Some sort of idiot?"

68.

In the corner of the main bar of the Wetherspoon's in Carlisle were two young men, clearly in no hurry to leave. It wasn't surprising. Nobody else was showing much sign of wanting to leave the warmth of the pub. Outside the heavens had opened.

Mandie was one of the bar staff on duty that lunchtime. She had eyed up the lads as they'd come in, checking to see what she thought. The older one, she decided, had a nice body. While serving them their pints she had removed his T-shirt, albeit (since she was at work and management might have got funny) only in her imagination. Bar work was boring and you needed something to take your mind off things.

Under the T-shirt was – what? The bare chest would be OK, she thought, not too hairy. What about the stomach? She wasn't sure. The T-shirt didn't look as if it was hiding a decent six-pack. She turned away, to ring up the sale at the till.

A little later she'd wandered deliberately close to the two lads, ostensibly to clear up the dead glasses from neighbouring tables. Rob, he seemed to be called, the older lad. She pondered whether to undress him completely. What would she find under his jeans? No, she wasn't sure she wanted to find out. She decided that this time at least she would leave him fully clothed.

Rob and his friend were deep in conversation about something. Aidan was the name of the other one, she heard. A bit too young, she decided.

Still, they had money. Rob had paid for his round with a £20 note from a sizeable wad of notes he'd pulled form his pocket. They were talking of money as she went near their table. It was fine for some.

She wandered back to the bar. Working in the hospitality trade was poorly paid and she was on a casual contract, with no guarantee that the work would continue. Other people seemed to have the luck. Where was her own Fairy Godmother when she needed her?

69.

It rained all day. More than that, the rain came down in a deluge. On the Cumbrian fells, small watercourses became raging rivers. Footpaths became rivers too. The rainwater had just one aim, and that was to run off the mountains to the valleys below as quickly as it possible could.

In Keswick, in Cockermouth, people looked apprehensively as the river levels rose. The Storm Desmond floods were all too recent. Surely Cumbria wasn't going to cop yet more flooding?

Inside the Enquirer office, Lluïsa looked through the window and decided she and Lindsay had made the right decision.

"Plou a bots i barrals," she said to Nick. "That's what we say in Catalan when it rains very heavily. What's the English?"

"We say it's raining cats and dogs," Nick replied.

"But that makes no sense," Lluïsa said.

"No, that's English for you."

"Could you say it was raining dogs and cats?"

"No, that definitely doesn't work," Nick replied.

70.

It was raining just as heavily on the A591 from Keswick south past Thirlmere and the wipers in Joan's campervan were barely able to cope. She was at something of a loose end. She hadn't felt able to leave the van parked outside Elizzabeth's place all day. Had it still been possible, she would have gone back to the smallholding, parked the van and stayed there reading or practising the tin whistle. Her efforts with the whistle had rather slipped in recent weeks.

Instead, she had turned the van south rather aimlessly when she reached Keswick, deciding that she might as well head down to do some shopping in Windermere. Hers was almost the only vehicle on the road. She drove over Dunmail Raise, approached the village of Grasmere and, on a whim, turned off the main road. Lluïsa had described to Joan where Nick Potterton lived. Perhaps he'd be in and prepared to put the kettle on. Joan had recently reposted a tweet from Greenpeace about cost overruns at the new nuclear power plant being built at Hinkley Point, and she wondered if Nick could give her any further information.

She found Nick's cottage without difficulty. It was on the northern edge of the village, the middle of a small terrace which had been constructed of local Cumbrian stone and slate. Joan knocked on the door, but no-one came. She tried the handle, which to her surprise opened: Nick obviously followed local custom of not always locking his front door. Still, she couldn't just go in and make herself at home. She carefully closed the door again, returned to the van and rejoined the main road south.

She hadn't mentioned anything about it to Elizzabeth, but she had a work problem which was turning into a real headache. Several of the best photographs she'd taken and put on her agency's website had been lifted by a small travel company based in Ontario and used without any sort of copyright clearance in a brochure advertising escorted holidays to England. Her agency regularly monitored the web for illegal usage of their photographs and normally copyright breaches were rapidly resolved. Usually the company involved apologised and paid across a slightly larger reproduction fee than usual.

This time, however, the Canadian firm was showing no sign of cooperating. Joan's agency had asked her if she was prepared to consider the costs of a possible legal action in the Canadian courts, to which the obvious answer had to be no. But it was deeply annoying that people could steal her work in this way. OK, amateur photographers might be happy to put their work on the web and allow anyone to download pictures, but she depended on her income from photography. Without the money from reproduction rights she would be unable to live.

She drove on into Ambleside thinking evil thoughts about Canadians. And then her day took another turn for the worse. South of Ambleside, as the road wove along the shoreline of Windermere, she was conscious that a police car had begun to tail her. When the road was clear, the car overtook her and immediately put on its blue lights, flashing to her to stop. She pulled the van up.

"Are you the legal owner of this vehicle, madam?" asked the young policeman who came round to her driver's window.

Joan glared at him. "Yes, I am," she firmly replied. Was this some fishing expedition by a bored cop? Or was this someone who knew who she was, knew about the Workington magistrates' decision and was out to get revenge?

"May I see your driving licence, madam?" the policeman carried on. Joan grumpily produced it.

"Can I ask exactly why you've stopped me? I bet you wouldn't have stopped me if I'd been driving a shiny BMW."

"Your numberplate has come up on our records as belonging to a vehicle which does not have a current MOT, madam. Have you recently arranged for an MOT test?"

"No, I've not had any sort of reminder that the MOT's run out."

"No reminders are sent, madam. It is the owner's responsibility to remember when their vehicle needs testing."

Joan looked at him in disbelief. "You're joking?" she echoed. "No reminders?"

"That is the system, madam. I will have to arrange for a penalty notice to be sent to you, I'm afraid."

Joan glowered. "Great," she said.

The policeman looked back at her. "Technically, you should leave your van here, to be picked up by a breakdown vehicle and taken to an MOT centre." He looked at the rain lashing the windscreen.

"In the circumstances, I will permit you to continue driving to an MOT test centre in Windermere. The nearest one is close to the station. If they can fit you in today and your vehicle passes, you will be at liberty to continue your journey. If not you will have to leave the vehicle there. Do you understand?"

Joan nodded angrily.

"I will advise my colleagues on patrol today to look out for your numberplate. You will be stopped again if you are found driving and the MOT pass has not been recorded on our database."

He returned to his patrol car and drove off. Joan followed at a discreet distance, her windscreen wipers once again struggling with the quantity of rain.

Baz and Mick packed away their tools. It was three o'clock on Friday, and that meant the end of the working week. The contract for the work at the hotel was running late, several weeks late in fact, but that was management's problem.

"Bloody hell," said Mick as he looked out from the main front door at the rain. "Bring the car round here for me, will you Jeeves?"

"Sod off," said Baz. "If I'm getting wet you're getting wet too."

Together they hared across the car park to where Baz's car was parked. Normally Mick drove his own car to work, but he'd had to book it in to the garage for the day. Ironically, given the weather, it was for work on the aircon system.

Baz started the ignition, pulled his car out from the hotel drive, wriggled round the Ambleside one-way system and put his foot down as he reached the northern outskirts of the town.

"A couple of jars in Keswick when we get there?" Mick asked.

"Why not? I'm thirsty already," Baz replied.

They were just approaching Ambleside cricket ground when the car made a spluttering noise and appeared to be losing power. The rain pounded against the windscreen.

"Everything all right?" Mick asked his companion.

The car came to a halt.

"Shit," said Baz. "I meant to fill it up this morning."

It took Mick a moment to take this in. "Don't tell me you're out of petrol. God."

"Diesel, but yeah."

Both men looked at the fuel indicator, which was as far into the red as the gauge would permit it to go.

"Ring the AA or whoever," Mick said. "They'll come out."

"Yeah, I would do if I had breakdown cover," Baz replied. There was a moment of silence. "I think we'll have to leg it back to that BP garage in Ambleside. It's only a mile or two."

Mick looked across at the driving seat.

"You're the driver. I'm staying here. Off you go."

In Penrith Elizzabeth was spending her birthday at work. That's the way it was with birthdays when you were an adult, she told herself. Still, the café was almost deserted because of the weather, so she was able to get away promptly at the end of her shift, at two-thirty. She hurried home as quickly as she could, and retreated upstairs to her little single room. Joan had told her to expect her back around four, and Elizzabeth was anticipating that they might decide to celebrate her birthday by spending the rest of the afternoon snuggled under the duvet together. She was disappointed when a text came through some time around 3.15. *Had a shitty day. Pulled over by police and now in Windermere at MOT garage. Van needs £300 of work. Disaster. Won't be back until around six. Sorry. Xxxx*

Rain beat at the window of Elizzabeth's room. She decided to get herself under the duvet anyway. Happy Birthday to me, she told herself.

Kath was back from her work around five thirty and called up the stairs. "Cup of tea?"

Elizzabeth went down to the kitchen, to find Kath smiling broadly. "Happy birthday," she said. "Joan told me. I've got you a birthday cake and a bottle of fizzy. Just from the supermarket I'm afraid."

Elizzabeth reached across and kissed her. "Kath, you're so kind."

"I'll get three glasses out and some plates. Is Joan back?"

"That sounds like her at the door now."

It was. Joan came in fuming.

"Have I ever told you that I hate police? I hate motor mechanics. I hate every single person living in Ontario. And as for the weather, of course it's going to bloody rain. That's what you have to expect from climate change." She sat down at the table.

"Joan, please cheer up. It is my birthday. Come and have a slice of the cake Kath's bought me."

Joan looked at the slice which had already been cut and put on the third plate.

"I can't eat that," she said abruptly.

"Why not?" Elizzabeth asked.

"It's got dairy cream of course. I'm vegan."

"Please, Joan. Just this once. For me."

"Of course I'm not eating the cake," Joan replied. She had pulled out her phone.

"What are you doing now?" Elizzabeth asked her.

"Checking on the web for the brand of prosecco." She paused. "Sorry, can't drink that either."

"You can't drink the prosecco? Why?"

"It's showing red on my database. It's been filtered using isinglass. Isinglass comes from fish bladders."

Elizzabeth looked at her. "You're not prepared to drink to my health because of fucking fish bladders? God, Joan, sometimes you're impossible."

"I'm sorry, but unlike some people I have principles."

"What's that supposed to mean?" Elizzabeth had started almost shouting.

Joan made a face.

"Joan, sometimes I hate you and your fucking principles," Elizzabeth went on. "For god's sake, can't you live in the real world for once?"

"I'm not stopping you doing anything you want to do."

"No, you're just ruining my birthday, that's all."

They glared at each other. Kath made an excuse and left the room.

"I've just about had enough of you," Elizzabeth started. "You seduced me into joining your climate change group. And then you seduced me into taking part in your demonstration, so that I got arrested and got myself a criminal conviction. And then you seduced me into your bed."

"*I* seduced you into bed? I think you'll find there was consent involved."

"You knew I was heterosexual. You just wanted the challenge of bedding me."

"Fuck you, Elizzabeth."

"No, why don't you just fuck off and let me live my life as I want."

Joan looked at her for a long moment. "Right, if that's what you want, I'm going right now. I won't see you again. And, don't worry, I won't text you again."

Joan marched to the front door, slamming it behind her. Elizzabeth heard the sound of the motor turning and of the van driving away.

And then Elizzabeth burst into tears.

73.

Saturday was as bad as Friday. The weather forecasters were going on about a deep Atlantic low crossing the north of England. As always, the Lake District took more than its fair share of the rainfall.

Lindsay was staying in her flat in Ambleside so that she and Lluïsa would have a head start for Sunday's Frog Graham attempt. They'd agreed that they'd leave Keswick at three thirty in the morning, to give them plenty of time – all being well - to complete the Round before nightfall came. As he'd promised, Nick was on stand-by to join them.

But by tea-time on Saturday, it was clear that their plans would have to change.

"It could be dangerous on the fells after this amount of rain," Lindsay said.

"Yes, it has rained cats and dogs," Lluïsa replied.

Lindsay laughed. "Did Nick teach you that phrase?" she asked. Lluïsa nodded.

"The forecast is better for tomorrow afternoon and Monday's meant to be dry," Lindsay went on. "Let's rearrange for Monday. Neither of us has anything else to do then."

"OK," Lluïsa said. "I will be able to go home soon, and I want to do the Frog Graham before I do."

"We'll do it on Monday," Lindsay said.

The day's delay meant complications. Lindsay had to put calls through to cancel the arrangements with running club friends who had offered to run with them on the Sunday. Most people were working on Monday, but Lindsay managed to garner just enough offers of help to be able to draw up a rota of supporters. Phil agreed to take the day off work and to drive down from Carlisle. His role would be to serve up the necessary food and hot drinks at the road crossing points. Nick undertook to do the first leg over Skiddaw before he went to work.

"We'll be fine," Lindsay told Lluïsa. She was surprised, however, at just how nervous she was feeling.

It was dark at three o'clock on Monday morning, but it was at least dry. The two women got themselves dressed in running tights and long thermal tops, with their waterproofs, spare clothes and wetsuits carefully packed into running sacks. They also had two waterproof drybags with them which they would tow behind as they swam.

Nick was ready dressed for running when they picked him up at his house. "All set?" he said. "Now or never," Lindsay replied.

Lindsay parked her car in a deserted Keswick and she and Lluïsa touched the stonework of Keswick's Moot Hall, as tradition insisted, to signify the start of the challenge. Nick was official timekeeper for the first leg. 3.42am, he announced.

It was wonderful to be out by themselves on the fells. The long climb to Skiddaw seemed easy and as Lindsay had anticipated, the sky was beginning to lighten by the time they reached Dodd Wood.

"Entre el gos i el llop," Lluïsa said.

"Sorry?" Lindsay asked.

"It means it's half-light, so you're not sure whether you're seeing a dog or a wolf."

"No dogs or wolves here," Nick responded. "Just three fell-runners enjoying themselves."

The early morning mist was rising from the fields surrounding St Bega's chapel.

"Less than two weeks and I'll be back here. For the wedding," Lindsay said.

"I'll be back too," Nick said. "Provided I'm still on the guest list, of course."

"I'll have to think about that," Lindsay responded, as she and Lluïsa sat down on the little rocky shore to put on their wetsuits.

There was no solitary woman beside Bassenthwaite Lake today, Nick noticed. He wondered momentarily where Joan Arkle might be.

The noise of two splashes meant that Lindsay and Lluïsa had entered the water. It was six o'clock in the morning. Good luck, Nick shouted after them, and then turned round to run back to Keswick. Lindsay was lending him her car for the day, on the understanding that he was back in Keswick that evening. In time, all being well, for their triumphant return.

It was Phil who had undertaken to keep Nick up to speed with Lindsay and Lluïsa's progress. The first text came through to Nick's phone around 10.15.

They've just entered Crummock Water, it read. *They had some navigational problems at Ullister Hill, but are both running well. Lluïsa in particular is swimming really well.*

Nick had a day's work to do in the Enquirer office. He wanted Molly to have the best possible farewell edition of the paper that could be achieved. Even if the front page was already sorted, there was still all the usual inside news pages to fill with copy. He had to get his head down.

But it was hard to concentrate.

The next text arrived from Phil at 1pm.

They're safely over Red Pike and High Stile and have finished the Buttermere swim. They're both having something to eat before tackling Robinson. Lluïsa is eating Spanish omelette, she says that it's just what you need for a day in the hills. Lindsay is eating rice pud. Lindsay's got a blister but says she's fine. Will text again when they're over Catbells.

Nick had to wait until 4.30 for further news.

They've made it down to the lake edge at Derwent Water. Lluïsa quite tired now, but says she's determined to push on. Lindsay a bit apprehensive about Derwent Water, knowing it's the longest swim. But they've nearly cracked it.

Phil's final text was sent at 5.30.

They've done Derwent Water!! Safely at Calf Close Bay. Another half hour and they should be back at the Moot Hall.

But the text was unnecessary. Nick himself had driven from work, arriving at Calf Close Bay on the eastern shore of the lake at twenty-five to six, just in time to see Lindsay and Lluïsa change for a final time out of their wetsuits into running gear and head off up the B-road into Keswick. See you at the Moot Hall, he called after them. I'm bringing the champagne, he added.

74

Elizzabeth remained furious with Joan all Saturday, and Sunday too. She stomped off to work in the café on Sunday morning. Kath tactfully kept out of her way.

But suddenly on Monday morning her anger disappeared. Suddenly she wanted to see Joan again, to talk things through, to make up, to see if they could be friends again.

She texted Joan. *I'm so sorry. Let's put this behind us. Come and visit me tonight.*

There was no reply.

Later on Monday morning she tried ringing, but her call went through to voicemail.

At lunchtime she texted again.

Joan, I hope you're not annoyed with me. I need to hear from you.

There was no reply to this message either.

Finally, at tea-time, Elizzabeth sent another message.

Joan, I'm really sorry that you haven't responded.

Although she didn't know it, there was a reason why Elizzabeth had received no reply. Joan had taken the campervan that morning over to the Duddon valley, where she had decided to stay and park up for the evening. Mobile coverage in the Duddon valley is very poor. Phone calls and texts don't get through.

75

Joan had taken a decision. It was time to leave the Lake District behind. Tomorrow she'd take the campervan down the M6, down maybe to Devon. She had friends in Totnes.

A long drive would help recharge the van's leisure battery. The gauge was showing that it had almost nothing left. But, anyway, she had come to recognise that her stay in the Lakes had become disastrous. The past few days had been hard, having to move the van every night to some new hidey-hole on a back road among the hills just in case. The abuse and the threats on social media had been getting worse - it was really quite disgusting what some people felt they could say - and for almost the first time in her life she felt unsure of her physical safety. How was it possible, she asked herself, that she could be freaked just by some online trolls? She'd felt no fear confronting police on the anti-fracking demos in Lancashire, no fear at all when taking part in the Extinction Rebellion direct action in London. But now, she had to admit, her life in the campervan was just a little too solitary for her liking. She missed Goldie enormously. Ever since Goldie had been killed, she had felt vulnerable.

She'd driven the van that day over the Wrynose pass from the Duddon valley where she had stayed the night before. She had made her way along Langdale and had finally found a little pull-in to park up on the back road on the lonely side of Grasmere. The lights of the cars of the tourists who were hurrying back from a night out to their hotels and B&Bs could be seen far away across the lake. Nobody came this way at this time of the evening.

PART THREE

76.

Chrissy Chambers sat at her desk in the Major Incident Room which had hurriedly been made available for her at the Penrith police station. It was Wednesday afternoon, less than twenty-four hours since a campervan fire had been reported near Grasmere. It was extraordinary how abruptly your daily work as a police officer could change.

She'd been at home with Tony the evening before, both of them putting their feet up in front of the TV, when the call had come through. It had been her Detective Chief Super ringing. Apologies for the late hour, he'd said. Oh, and congratulations on successfully completing the Development Programme, he had added.

Word had obviously reached police headquarters: it had been just a week since her name had been formally entered on the national Senior Investigating Officer database.

"Now you've done the theory you'll be all ready for the practice," Chrissy's Chief Super had gone on to say.

She'd urgently signalled Tony to turn off the TV sound. "I'm sorry, sir, I don't quite follow you," she'd said.

The Chief Super got to the point. "As of this evening, we have a major incident to investigate. I need an SIO. I think this is one for you."

Forty-five minutes after taking the call, DI Chrissy Chambers had found herself dressed in white protective clothing, looking at an almost destroyed campervan. The fire had been all-consuming, leaving little but the bare metal skeleton of the vehicle remaining. What had once been the floor was completely unrecognisable debris.

The uniformed branch had done their job well. The scene had been cordoned off with two young PCs stationed at either end of the cordon ready to turn back anyone who ventured up the road. The third officer there was an older PC who had taken responsibility for the crime scene and had already summonsed two mobile arc lights. These were now lighting up the night sky.

Chrissy Chambers took charge. "I will need this photographed and videoed," she said to the Constable.

"I've already called for a photographer, ma'am," he replied.

"Good. We'll need specialist forensics called in. I'll want the road and the verges checked as well as the vehicle. I'll organise that."

"Yes, ma'am. The fire service were rather over-keen, unfortunately. Their tenders were parked all over the road and a lot of water was discharged into the vehicle. We arrived fifteen minutes after them so I couldn't do much to secure the site."

"The water shouldn't matter too much. Forensics will be looking primarily for human remains or DNA traces."

"Yes, ma'am."

Chrissy Chambers had been taught that the first few hours of a major incident are crucial. Sometimes the first few minutes can make all the difference – the 'golden hour', some detectives call it. Well, she hadn't been there for that first hour but she was determined now that her investigation would have the best start it could.

"Tell your colleagues not to let anyone enter the site without protective clothing and only with my express permission," she said. "Everyone must be logged in and out. The photographer has my permission to enter. You're working the night shift, I assume?"

The PC nodded.

"All right, thank you for all you've done. I will be appointing a Crime Scene Manager to my team and I will arrange for them to be here early tomorrow."

"Thank you, ma'am."

77.

The Enquirer's farewell party was over. Nick was back home, in the spare room that counted as his office.

He stopped typing and checked the word count: just under 300 words, about the right length. Although he had more or less stopped freelancing regularly for the national press he still retained contacts at The Guardian. He had a story which he simply had to cover. He checked his text through a final time and emailed it to their newsdesk.

A high-profile climate change activist in Cumbria is missing, feared dead, following a devastating fire in the campervan where she lived. Police are working on the assumption that the fire may have been started deliberately.

Joan Arkle, a controversial figure in the Lake District because of her calls for farming practices to change, has in recent weeks been the target of vituperative abuse on social media. Her dog was killed two weeks ago in what Ms Arkle had claimed was a deliberate act of cruelty aimed against her.

The campervan, a VW conversion, was parked on Tuesday evening on a quiet back-road near the tourist village of Grasmere. Locals reported hearing a loud bang and seeing flames at about 8.30pm, and the van was almost entirely destroyed by the time the fire service arrived shortly afterwards.

Police have sealed off the site of the fire and have launched a formal investigation. DI Christine Chambers of Cumbria Police who is leading the investigation appealed to the members of the public who had been in the vicinity of Grasmere on Tuesday night or who had information on Joan Arkle's recent movements to contact the police.

Joan Arkle was in court several times following anti-fracking protests in Lancashire and North Yorkshire and was recently acquitted of two charges arising from a protest demonstration earlier in the year at a nuclear waste site near Sellafield. In a recent interview with a local Cumbrian newspaper she argued that direct action was necessary, given the climate emergency faced by the planet. "Getting arrested the first time may be a big deal for some people, but I've stopped worrying. We know from our history that it is only by breaking the law that things ever get achieved," she told the reporter.

78.

Chrissy Chambers had managed only a few hours' sleep the previous night, and now it was late afternoon on the Wednesday and she was still working hard.

But never mind. So far, so good. Her investigation was getting properly under way. She had over the course of the day assembled the team she needed. DS Peter Blackford was her Deputy SIO. She had an excellent Office Manager in DS Kate Morgan, a safe pair of hands who had performed the same role for George Mulholland during several investigations he had led. Every Senior Investigating Officer knew the value of a good OM.

She'd ensured that the scene of the campervan fire was secured. She'd discussed the House-to-House enquiry strategy and appointed an officer to coordinate that side of things. Unfortunately there weren't many houses anywhere near the scene, but there might have been, let's say, local dog walkers out the previous evening.

She'd started the necessary SIO Policy File, the strategic document in which she had to record all the key policy decisions she was taking during the investigation. She'd also issued an initial press release and done a statement to camera for the local TV news. It was suitably short on detail but it was still necessary. The media could be a complete pain in the arse but they could also be important partners in an enquiry.

The administrative part of the investigation was going well, Chrissy told herself. But she still didn't know what exactly she was investigating. Was this a homicide enquiry? What would be found in the charred wreckage of the campervan?

Even if nobody had been in the van when it caught fire, was this attempted murder? If so, where was the intended victim now? Joan Arkle had not been seen or heard of since the fire. All her social media activity had stopped.

But, Chrissy told herself, this might not be a crime at all. Campervans could catch fire. They had their own potential firebombs in the gas cylinders they carried, even if the cylinders were supposed to be fire resistant. A gas leak? A tragic accident?

Her Chief Super had given her some advice before ringing off the previous evening. "You know what they say: in an investigation you need to create enough slow time to think," he'd told her. He was right. But how, under the pressure of a new investigation, could you find the time you needed?

In half an hour, all her team were coming together for their first full Briefing. She urgently needed to collect her thoughts.

79

In the days since her birthday, Elizzabeth had never stopped thinking about Joan. Her initial anger had dissipated after the weekend but had returned on Tuesday when it was obvious that the texts and phone calls she'd tried to make to Joan were bringing no response.

Together with the anger, though, Elizzabeth felt a deep sense of loneliness and despair.

On Wednesday evening Kath invited her down to the kitchen, made her dinner and sat afterwards talking things through.

"You have to give Joan time," she said. "Joan's lovely, but she's got a strong personality."

"Joan's stubborn and selfish," Elizzabeth replied.

"No, I don't think so," Kath said. "I think she loves you."

"I thought *I* loved her," Elizzabeth said. "But then I thought I loved Baz and look what a disaster that turned out to be. I'm just really bad at making relationships."

"Everyone's allowed to make mistakes and, OK, Baz sounds like a mistake. That doesn't mean you're always fated to pick the wrong partners."

Kath reached for the corkscrew.

"I bought a bottle of wine this afternoon to cheer you up. By the way, no fish bladders were harmed in making it. I've checked."

Elizzabeth gave a wan smile. "OK, you can pour me a glass," she said.

80

Chrissy Chambers breathed deeply. The next forty-five minutes or so were ones that she couldn't waste. She needed to be on the top of her game.

The first briefing was the key moment to set out the shape that her investigation would take. She needed to create the necessary team spirit among the disparate group that, over the past twelve hours, she'd brought together. But this was also, as everyone in the room knew, her first time as a Senior Investigating Officer. Of course, people would be watching to see how well she performed.

The role of SIO is a curious one, with two quite different aspects to it. On the one hand, you lead the investigation. You read the documents that, day by day, the enquiry generates – or at least all the important ones. You think about the case. You are the lead detective, and it is your role to ensure that enquiry leads are followed up. The task is to identify those groups of people who can potentially be suspects, ensure they are interviewed, and then - all being well - reach the point where you catch the actual suspect or suspects you are looking for. And your role continues beyond that if, as you hope, the case reaches the courts, the trial takes place and a conviction results in the safe removal of a dangerous person or persons from society.

Investigation is one part of the job. But a good SIO also has to be a good manager. You have to ensure effective information management systems are established and that the administrative wheels of the enquiry keep turning effortlessly. And this doesn't just mean management skills. Leadership skills are necessary too. You have to lead your team, support the officers working under you, reassure them when things don't seem to be moving forward.

Frankly, managing Manchester City is a doddle by comparison.

Chrissy began the briefing with a set of slides which Kate Morgan her Office Manager had helped her assemble. The presentation itself started with several photographs of the crime scene, complete with the campervan remains, an aerial view of the site, and a map of the roads nearby.

"The 999 call to the fire service, which was made by a local resident who saw flames, was received yesterday at 20.33. We can assume that the event itself – an arson attack, if that is was it was – would have been a few minutes earlier, perhaps around 20.25. The fire service arrived at 20.45, and officers from the Windermere station arrived at 20.57. I myself was at the scene from 22.11," Chrissy said.

"You'll notice that, if this was an arson attack, the arsonist or arsonists had only a few routes they could have taken to leave the scene. They could have gone south towards Elterwater but frankly the obvious escape route is straight out on to the A591 and then either north towards Keswick or south to Ambleside," she went on.

Chrissy looked around at the twelve or so people in the room.

Ideally they'd have moved from the Major Incident Room to somewhere more spacious for the briefing but there was nowhere suitable available. People were perched on desks or standing, looking at her and at the slides. They were attentive, she noted with satisfaction.

"I want to turn now to discuss the victim, or we should say at this stage the potential victim. As you know, her name is Joan Arkle. This slide shows her PNC record with previous arrests and convictions. You will see that she is well known to several police forces, not just our own. All her offences have been related to her political activism and participation in demonstrations.

"She has been high-profile in recent weeks, and we need to be very conscious that this enquiry will attract media and public interest. Here are some recent local newspaper reports about her. You'll find them all already filed in HOLMES 2 as Other Documents."

A series of slides showed the feature and news stories about Joan Arkle which Nick Potterton had written for the Enquirer.

"Joan Arkle has attracted considerable hostility. Here are some comments she has attracted on her Twitter feed, which I think you will find as disturbing as me."

There were intakes of breath from some of those present when the slides came up.

"Her campervan, for example, has been repeatedly described recently as a witchwagon. We will need to investigate where these tweets have originated. There is another question for us to consider. The vast majority of people who receive offensive illegal tweets like these would come immediately to us. Was there some reason why Joan Arkle felt unable to report this abuse?"

The slides were replaced by video footage.

"This has been passed to us by the BBC regional TV news in Newcastle. It shows the demonstration in Keswick on Sunday April 17th at around 19.00 hours outside the church hall where Joan Arkle was staging a public meeting on climate change. It was a rowdy meeting. We need to identify those people who were demonstrating outside. Potentially they could comprise a TIE category."

There were nods in the room. One of the potential tasks facing a SIO as an investigation progresses can be to identify groups which may contain the suspect and then to instruct police officers to trace, interview and where appropriate eliminate each person in each group.

"As well as the demonstrators outside, there were a lot of hostile people inside in the audience. We need to find out who they were, too. This group could also potentially be a TIE category. So we have plenty of work ahead of us."

Again there were nods.

"There is an event which it appears may be linked." A slide of the Enquirer's news story with its headline *Drug dealers say 'sorry your dog's dead' – claim* appeared on the screen.

"According to the newspaper Ms Arkle claimed that her dog had been abducted at the end of the public meeting by one of the audience. She also alleged that she had been sent a text saying that the dog was safe and well in a shop in Keswick but that later she found the dog's body on a back road in Keswick. This all seems, shall we say, a curious story. It turns out that the shop where the dog was supposedly being kept safe was the very shop which was raided by us on the morning of Tuesday April 19th when as you'll recall over £10,000 of heroin was found. I have already issued Actions for the two persons arrested in that raid to be interviewed, to see what they can tell us. Both are remanded in custody, so that is convenient. DS Blackford" – she gestured to Peter Blackford sitting alongside her – "has been leading on the drugs investigation and he will be following up this side of the enquiry.

"We also need to consider a very different possibility. Was Joan Arkle deliberately trying to cover herself by inventing that story and planting it in the press? We must not rule out her direct involvement in the local drugs trade. The attack on her campervan could have been a revenge attack by others in the trade. It could have been her own attempt to cover up her traces."

Chrissy Chambers looked around the room and saw people nodding.

"As always we also need to consider if this was a domestic. We know as yet very little about Joan Arkle's personal life or partners. Or her family background. Are her parents alive? Does she have siblings? We need to find out.

"So as you'll gather Joan Arkle is an elusive person. The crux of our investigation is whether or not she met her death unlawfully in an arson attack on her campervan. The forensic work going on at the campervan is critical to the enquiry, and I am expecting very shortly to have their report.

"If there is no evidence of human remains, we face other questions. If Joan Arkle survived the fire by escaping, or if she was not in the van at the time of the fire, where is she now and why hasn't she contacted us? We may have to consider the possibility that that she has been abducted. If true, this would have very serious implications for the way we progress this investigation. It would also put us under enormous pressure to move quickly.

"So thank you for your patience. This investigation is going to be a team effort, and you all have your part to play. I want to open this briefing out now to your own thoughts."

Chrissy sat down. God, it wasn't easy having the responsibilities of an SIO, but on the other hand this is what she had been trained to do. And, she told herself, this is what she wanted to do.

And so far, things were going OK. Her presentation, she knew, had gone well.

81.

"Hello Nick."

Nick immediately recognised the voice at the other end of the phone call. "Hello, Martin," he replied.

"How's the bucolic life oop north?"

"Martin, if you try to mock the northern accent I will personally come to The Guardian's office in King's Cross, walk up the apples and pears, and punch you in the hooter."

Martin Eveyard was the features editor at The Observer, the Guardian's Sunday stable-mate. Nick had worked with him many years earlier when they were both starting their journalistic careers and once or twice recently Martin had contacted Nick to offer him freelance feature work.

Martin laughed at Nick's response. "Life going OK? How's the

Thirlmere Thunderer?"

"If you mean the Cumbrian Enquirer, the very last issue was put to bed yesterday."

"Oh god, sorry to hear that. Usual reasons why a local paper can't keep going?"

"Yes, the usual. So here I am, a keen but unemployed young hack, ready for all your commissions."

"I'm not sure I recognise that description of you. But I may have at least one piece of work to offer."

"The climate change activist?"

"Exactly. The Guardian is running your news piece tomorrow, but they've also passed it on to me. I want to commission 1200 words off you. This Joan Arkle sounds an interesting character. When will you know if she really was murdered?"

"The police forensics people are apparently working away. The detective who's leading on this implied this afternoon that they'd know very soon."

"For this Sunday's paper then?"

"That might be pushing it, but I'll do my best." Nick paused. "Martin, how would you feel if I worked with my former editor on this? As a two-hander?"

"Fine with me, as long as you don't want two fees."

"You're paying the traditional rubbish rates?"

"The usual rule applies. Think of what you'd have been paid as a freelance twenty years ago and divide it by two. Or maybe three."

A short negotiating session commenced between the two journalists, with Nick pitching his price as high as he dared and Martin gradually whittling the figure down. Eventually they agreed on a rate which Nick felt was at least half-way decent. Although, as he'd be splitting the money with Molly, getting the commission wasn't precisely a cause for a champagne celebration.

"Right, we'll get going first thing tomorrow," Nick said.

"Or even tonight," Martin responded. "No time like the present."

Nick's watch showed that it was already well past eight o'clock. "I don't think so," he said.

"OK, but I need the copy urgentissimo. Keep me updated." Martin rang off.

82

The police investigation was beginning to develop its own rhythm. It was only eight on Thursday morning but already the Major Incident Room was full of people. There was an air of purposefulness as Chrissy Chambers and her team went about their work. The first few days were lived on adrenaline. The difficult time would come later on, if the investigation dragged on without a breakthrough.

She and DS Peter Blackford had made themselves cups of instant coffee which they were drinking in a corner of the MIR. Peter was proving a valuable deputy SIO, even if they were both feeling their way into roles they were taking on for the first time.

"Let me share what we know about Joan Arkle," Chrissy began. "Or rather what we don't know. She is difficult to pin down. She appears to have lived in her campervan in recent months more or less full-time and to be without any sort of permanent address. She isn't registered with a local GP. Her bank thinks her home address is somewhere near Blackpool, but Lancashire Police checked this out for me yesterday and it is the home of an anti-fracking protestor who says she hasn't seen Joan for over a year. No council tax record and not on the electoral roll. Curiously, HMRC don't know of her either. Talk of about flying below the radar." She paused.

"Except when it came to climate change issues, when she was about as high-profile as you could imagine," Peter Blackford interposed.

"I know. You know that old adage that the College of Policing sometimes use in their courses? 'Find out how a person lived and you will find out how they died'. In this instance, it's not proving easy."

Chrissy turned to the desk in front of them. On it was the statement which two of Peter's team of DCs had taken late the previous afternoon from the woman called Patricia Blakeney, the girlfriend of Terry Venables, who had been arrested with him at the vaping shop. Patricia – it seemed she was usually known as Trix – had been forthcoming.

"Her statement would appear to collaborate Joan Arkle's account of what happened to the dog," Chrissy Chambers said. "That the dog really was taken by Terry Venables at the end of the church hall meeting."

"Yes," DS Blackford said in agreement. "And that the texts which

Joan Arkle received on Monday morning saying that the dog was safe and well were sent by Ms Blakeney."

"If the dog's death was caused by Terry Venables during his trip to Preston as Ms Blakeney states, there is nothing to suggest that Joan Arkle had any dealings with illegal drugs herself."

"That's my reading of the evidence, ma'am."

"And that in turn would suggest that we're not looking for a drugs connection to the campervan attack – if indeed it was arson."

"I know. So if the van was subject to an attack, there was some other reason behind it. What about the people who were demonstrating at Joan Arkle's meeting?"

"Nothing very revealing as yet." Chrissy Chambers paused and laughed. "Although I did enjoy reading one particular statement."

She went to the computer and logged in to HOLMES 2. "Read this," she said smiling.

DS Blackford did as he was instructed. *My name is Phillip Petherton,* he read. *I participated in the rally on Sunday April 17 in Keswick because I believed it was going to further the aims of A New Voice for Cumbria, a political party which I established and, subsequent to the rally, I decided to dissolve. I was appalled by the behaviour of some of those who were there. Nobody apart from my good wife and I had Cumbrian flags. I feel that the good name of Cumbria was defiled that evening....*

"I think we can safely eliminate Mr Petherton from the investigation," Peter Blackford said.

83.

Nick rang Molly on her home phone early on Thursday morning.

"Molly, how would you feel about delaying the flower arranging for a few days?" he began. He filled her in on his conversation with Martin Eveyard.

"You could do this commission just by yourself," Molly responded.

"Yes, but somehow I'd prefer to do it together. I thought you could handle the police side of things, and I'll see if I can get more background on Joan Arkle from people who knew her. Although I'm not sure how easy that'll be."

"There's the woman with the two 'z's who was in court with her," Molly said.

"The padlock and chain episode. Yes, Elizzabeth, I'd already thought of trying to find her. We don't know anything about Joan Arkle's family background though. How did she come to take up life as an activist?"

"Well, my husband whom I thought I knew very well suddenly appears to have a keen interest in genealogy," Molly responded. "Paul's got all the software stuff you need to track down family trees. Birth certificates and all that. I don't suppose you've got Joan Arkle's date of birth?"

"It was given out in court in Workington. I'll check my notes." Nick had been trained as a junior reporter to keep old shorthand notebooks, just in case. He reached across to the one he had been using back in late March and flipped through the pages.

"Got it," he said, giving Joan's date of birth to Molly. "That's about all I know, though. Joan hasn't any middle names or if she has she didn't tell the court."

"OK, I will let my super-sleuth hubby see what he can come up with. How long is The Observer giving us?"

"What do you think? They want it as soon as possible, of course."

84.

Pete Rawlinson was recovering from an unwelcome visitor at his Maryport flat. Early on Thursday morning a uniformed police officer had shown up, asking all sorts of questions about Joan Arkle. Pete wasn't at all sure whether Joan would want him to say anything to the police. Last time he'd seen the police at close quarters had been at the Drigg demo when both Joan and Elizzabeth had ended up being carted off to the police station. He didn't trust the police and he wanted as little to do with them as possible.

He decided to be unforthcoming. No, this wasn't Joan's home. No, Joan had stayed with him briefly earlier in the year, that was all. No, he hadn't known that Joan had used his address when she was arrested. No, he lived here by himself. No, Joan lived in a campervan which she parked up near Ullswater.

Yes, he had chaired the public meeting, because Joan had asked him to. No, he hadn't seen her since the night of the meeting.

No, he wouldn't make a statement. If they wanted to know about Joan, why didn't they talk to her directly?

He had shut the door firmly, and had texted Joan to tell her. *The police have just been round asking all sorts of questions about you. Any idea what they're on about? Not still Drigg I hope.*

85.

DS Kate Morgan the Office Manager hurried across the MIR to where Chrissy Chambers was talking to the woman officer she had appointed as the investigation's Document Reader and Receiver, the person whose job was to take in the Actions Reports and Statements from police officers working out in the field.

"I'm very sorry to interrupt, ma'am. Forensics are on the phone," Kate Morgan said.

Chrissy Chambers picked up the phone. "DI Chambers," she said.

There was the sound of someone talking.

"I see," Chrissy said at one point.

More talking.

"Is that finding completely reliable?" Chrissy interjected.

More talking.

"Thank you for letting me know. Please let me have the written report as soon as you can."

She put the phone down.

"Something come through?" DS Blackford her deputy was sitting at the adjacent desk.

"Forensics have found something very curious. They have found the remains of a tracer bug fixed on the underside of the rear bumper. So someone must have been able to follow the van's movements all the time. I am still thinking this one through."

DS Blackford nodded.

"Anything else from forensics?"

There was a long silence. Eventually Chrissy Chambers replied.

"Human remains found," she said quietly.

"I see."

"Not formally identified yet. But a woman's body. Estimated age between 25 and 40."

"Accidental fire? Or – deliberate?"

"Forensics have no doubt. The fire was caused by petrol igniting inside the campervan. The petrol was almost certainly contained in a bottle which was thrown inside."

So…"

"So from now on we are a homicide investigation," Chrissy Chambers said.

86.

Kath and Elizzabeth met over the kitchen table on Thursday morning.

"You're looking a bit more cheerful than last night," Kath said.

"Last night's wine, maybe. I think things will work out. I have a hunch I may hear news of Joan today." She smiled.

Kath smiled back, before hurrying off to her office. Shortly afterwards Elizzabeth also left the house, making her way to the centre of Penrith to go to work in the café.

Her manager, looking anxious, approached her as soon as she arrived.

"Did you see the local TV news last night?" she asked.

"No?" Elizzabeth replied.

"There was a detective reading a statement. All about a burnt-out campervan at Grasmere. It's not your friend's van, I hope?"

Elizzabeth's manager pulled out her smartphone and showed her a still from the transmission which had been posted on the TV company's Twitter feed. The van was unrecognisable. The numberplate however could be read.

Elizzabeth looked at the photo in disbelief, standing motionless. Then she rushed to the toilet. She returned a few minutes later, extremely pale.

"I must ring the police," she said.

87.

Jem Braithwaite opened the front door of his farm house. A uniformed policeman was there. Another officer, a policewoman, was shutting the door of the police car which was parked in the farmyard.

"Mr Jeremy Braithwaite?" asked the policeman, showing his warrant card. "May we come in?"

Jem reluctantly let the two officers into his parlour. He had nothing against the police personally, except for the fact that they represented Authority. Frankly, like many other hill farmers in the Lakes, he liked to have as little to do as possible with any form of Authority.

"Don't take this wrong but I'm just going out," he said. Jem had spent all the previous day sorting the stone from a wall which had collapsed half way up the fellside and today his task would be to rebuild the wall. He needed to start work as soon as possible.

"I understand, sir," said the policewoman, who appeared to be in charge. "May I show you last week's edition of the Cumbrian Enquirer? Are you the author of this letter to the editor?"

Jem looked at the newspaper she was showing him and nodded.

"In which case, I wonder if we can ask you some questions?"

88.

Pete Rawlinson's Thursday was not getting any better. At lunchtime the bell for his flat rang a second time. This time, there were two more police officers at his front door. These two were clearly in no mood for pleasantries.

"Peter Rawlinson? We need to interview you and take a statement. It will be better if you are prepared to accompany us to the police station," said the older looking policeman.

Pete found himself spluttering. "Why are you pestering me today so much?"

"I'm sorry Mr Rawlinson, but we need to take you to the station. That's where we'll be able to talk." Pete found himself bundled into the back of the patrol car.

The interview room was gloomy and pokey and Pete found it intimidating. The interview, it transpired, would be both recorded and videoed. The two police officers who had come to his house sat down facing him, and one began.

They wanted to know everything. They wanted to know when Joan had lived at his flat. The exact dates, please.

Would he describe himself as Joan's partner? No? Had he perhaps had a sexual relationship with Joan Arkle? When had that been? Why had it come to an end?

Pete mentioned the new clutch which Joan had been waiting to have fitted to her van while she had stayed with him. (Thank you, sir, we will check that detail out.) Did he know which garage had she used?

How had he first met Joan?

When had her last seen her? Since the public meeting in Keswick? No? Was he sure?

Had he attended the demonstration at Drigg? He had? Could he describe in his own words what had happened? Who else took part?

(Pete paused. "I'm not sure I should tell you their names. They might not want me to," he had said. The policeman interviewing him paused too. "Sir, we are undertaking an important investigation and we need as many details as we can. We are asking for your full co-operation. We are sure you understand." Pete had muttered a few names. "And Elizzabeth Bowes was there too but you know that because you arrested her," he added.)

The questioning continued. What did he think of Joan Arkle as a person? Was she difficult or easy to deal with?

He had chaired the public meeting, had he not? Could he describe in his own words exactly what had happened?

Did he know any of the people in the audience? How did he know them?

Did any of the audience say anything to suggest that they did not agree with Joan Arkle? What did they say? Would he describe any of the audience as drunk?

Did Joan Arkle have her dog at the meeting?

And so it went on. The interview must have lasted at least an hour. Pete felt completely drained by the time the camera and recorder were switched off.

As he left the interview room, he tried asking a question. "Please, has something happened to Joan?"

The reply came quickly. "That, sir, is exactly what we intend to find out. As soon as we have information to communicate with the public we will do so. Until then I must ask you to be patient."

89.

"Who are you?" The man at the front door in a suburban street in Keswick was aggressive.

"My name's Nick Potterton." Nick was going to add "from the Cumbrian Enquirer" but then realised this was no longer true. He compromised. "I'm a journalist. I'm looking for Elizzabeth. Does she still live here?"

"No." An equally aggressive response. "Why did you think that?"

Nick decided not to mention that he had written down the address Elizzabeth had given at the Magistrates' Court in Workington all those weeks back. This, clearly, was the ex-husband, the man who – at least according to Joan Arkle that time in the office - had responded to Nick's newspiece of Elizzabeth's conviction by assaulting her. This perhaps was not going to be a productive visit.

"I just wondered if you knew where Elizzabeth was living now?" he asked.

"Not a fucking clue, mate. Now why don't you just sod off?"

The front door was shut firmly in Nick's face.

It was ridiculous, but Nick was struggling to get the leads he needed for the Observer's feature. Elizzabeth Bowes was his main hope, but so far he had no idea how to track her down. He hadn't necessarily expected her ex to be very cooperative but Nick had also drawn a blank that afternoon in Maryport. He'd driven all the way across to the address which Joan had given in court to find that this was the home of the young man Pete who had chaired the public meeting. Pete was clearly in shock from a heavy duty interview which, from what he let slip, the police had put him through a little earlier in the day. He wasn't precisely unfriendly, but neither was he particularly helpful. In any case, it rapidly became clear that Pete knew nothing very much at all about Joan's life or background.

Frankly, the commission was getting nowhere. Molly had been in touch to tell him that the woman detective who was leading the enquiry had been unforthcoming. "I will be issuing another press statement shortly," was all she'd offered. It would appear that the police officer was anything but chuffed at the idea that her investigation might feature in a national Sunday newspaper.

If need be, Nick would simply ring Martin Eveyard and tell him that the feature wouldn't be possible. But professionally that would be a frustrating outcome. A beautiful corner of the Lake District National Park had been the location for, potentially, an extraordinary crime: the deliberate targeting of a climate change activist. This was a story which it surely had to be possible to unearth.

90.

Chrissy Chambers was being briefed by her press team. In a quarter of an hour she had arranged to issue a second press statement and to hold her first full-scale press conference. She knew the room would be heaving with journalists.

This time she had some significant new news she would share with them. She would tell them the campervan fire was deliberate. She would tell the media that she was leading a murder enquiry.

She would also take the opportunity to appeal directly to the public. The question she would ask was whether anyone had recently been seen buying petrol in a can. She'd already issued Instructions for uniformed colleagues to visit every petrol station within a twenty-five mile radius to see what CCTV footage was available, but just possibly someone watching the local news or reading the press reports might remember something significant. It was worth a try.

But Chrissy Chambers also had information which she definitely didn't intend to share with the media. That morning a distressed female called Elizzabeth Bowes had phoned the 101 call centre. Conveniently, Ms Bowes was already on the PNC. She had been arrested and convicted of offences at the demonstration earlier this year which Joan Arkle had organised. She'd also reported an alleged case of revenge porn from her ex, a man called Barry Bowes.

The call was a useful breakthrough, Chrissy Chambers felt. She'd arranged for DC Rosie Whittaker who had originally handled the revenge porn claim to interview Elizzabeth Bowes again. The transcript had arrived in the MIR mid-afternoon, and it had been riveting reading.

It turned out that Barry Bowes was an associate of Terry Venables. Elizzabeth Bowes claimed that he, and two other drinking friends, had been the people who were responsible for the trolling that Joan Arkle had been getting. Chrissy had immediately issued instructions for all the three men to be interviewed under caution.

And Elizzabeth Bowes, in between extended bouts of weeping, had told DC Whittaker something else. She'd told her that she had been Joan Arkle's friend. She had paused, and then rephrased what she had said: her lover.

At last, Chrissy felt, her investigation was making progress. She picked up her papers and went through to her press conference. As she expected, the room was completely packed. Never mind, she told herself, I can handle it.

91.

Nick gave Lindsay a big hug when she arrived in Coniston village for the regular Thursday running club evening on the fells. She was smiling broadly and clutching the certificate which had been issued to her by the Frog Graham Round club. "I'm a life member, apparently," she said. "It means I never have to do the Frog Graham again!"

"Where's Lluïsa tonight? Too tired from Monday's exertions?"

"No, she's hired a car and driven to Scotland. Something to do with an article for her newspaper in Catalonia."

"Oh I'd forgotten. La Vanguardia have commissioned her to write about the connections between Scottish nationalism and the Catalan independence movement. She asked me if I had a direct phone number for Nicola Sturgeon in my contact book and seemed a bit put out when I said that I hadn't."

"Yes, aren't you supposed to be a real journalist?"

"I told her to talk to the SNP press office. How long is she staying in Scotland?"

"She didn't say. I only know she's gone because she left a note behind for me in the flat. I've been with Phil since Monday. By the way, I'm sorry I couldn't make the Enquirer farewell party yesterday."

"You weren't the only one."

"Poor turnout? What a shame."

"At least Molly and I have the possibility to write something for The Observer. You've heard the bad news about Joan Arkle?"

"Yes, I saw that policewoman being interviewed on the local TV news tonight before I came out. Joan Arkle was the lone woman we saw down by the shores of Bassenthwaite Lake early that Sunday? I've heard you and Lluïsa talk about her."

"It's shocking news. Joan could be prickly but she was passionate about what she believed in."

"Sometimes it's easy to feel that the whole idea that we're in a civilised and democratic country is simply a thin veneer and we're living on the edge of something horrendous."

"I hope not. Although Joan would have said that we're definitely on a knife-edge when it comes to living on a planet with runaway temperatures."

Nick was pleased to see Lindsay but it was Lluïsa he'd really hoped would have been at the pack run. He needed Lluïsa's help. She'd told him a couple of weeks back that Joan had given her some useful contacts to interview for her article on British climate change activists. His efforts all day to track down Elizzabeth had failed, but perhaps these contacts could give him another avenue to explore. He texted her with the request that he'd hoped to have asked her face-to-face.

He was just locking his car door ready for the run to start when his mobile pinged. Lluïsa had responded immediately. *It's terrible news about Joan*, she wrote. *Have the police discovered anything? Please tell me exactly what is happening. I will be here several more days, maybe a week. Perhaps tomorrow I interview Nicola Sturgeon. Did you know the Scottish Parliament was designed by Enric Miralles? He was a famous*

Catalan architect. When we are independent, perhaps we get a Scottish architect to design a new Parliament for us. The names you want from my article are in my notes in the flat, but I am sorry, it is untidy there. You will never find them without me. I hope you can wait until I am back. Una abraçada Lluïsa. PS I have seen a bagpiper!

Nick got back in his car. He'd been looking forward to his usual Thursday run, but this week the feature for Martin Eveyard came first. Time was rapidly running out. He headed straight back to his home. He'd had a brainwave which just might work out.

Lluïsa, he knew, had already filed her climate change article to La Vanguardia in Barcelona. Assuming it was already published, he might be able to avoid having to wait until Lluïsa was back in Ambleside to get some idea of who Joan had put her in touch with. The article might contain useful leads.

As soon as he was in his office he went online, going straight to La Vanguardia's website. It was in Catalan and Spanish, but he could cope. After much searching, he found what he was looking for. *Els anglesos contra el canvi climàtic* read the headline, with a by-line stating that it was from 'a special correspondent'. The article was illustrated by a photograph of Joan, wearing her Fracking Stupid T-shirt. Presumably Lluïsa had taken it herself.

Nick skim-read the text. As he would have expected from any half-decent journalist, Lluïsa had been in touch with a press spokesperson from Extinction Rebellion. There was a quote from them about the actions which XR had been organising in London and around the country.

Much more usefully, Lluïsa had interviewed two other people. One was a woman called Jennifer Johnson, who lived in Oxford and was engaged in a grassroots organisation there called Oxfordshire Climate Emergency Action. The second was closer to home. Pamela Morrison, Lluïsa's article said, had been a stalwart of the successful fight against fracking in Lancashire and lived near Blackpool. Nick translated from the Catalan the quote which Lluïsa had attributed to her: "We have to keep fossil fuels safely in the ground and generate the energy we need from renewables. Fracking for oil is the very last thing our planet needs us to be doing."

A trip to Oxford might turn out to be necessary, but Blackpool was very much nearer.

Better still, Pamela Morrison even had her number listed in the online BT phone directory. It was getting late, but Nick rang her anyway, introducing himself as an Observer journalist interested in the anti-fracking campaign. Of course she'd be pleased to meet him, she said. When did he want to come? Tomorrow morning? Well, if that was necessary. Say at nine o'clock?

Nick had decided that it would be better tactics to mention his particular interest in Joan Arkle only when he was safely inside Pamela Morrison's house. Phone calls could be a tricky medium if you wanted to extract potentially difficult information. Face-to-face was always better

92.

Rod and Alan were in Preston. It was Thursday evening, but they were in a coffee shop rather than a bar. They'd fixed the rendezvous at very short notice.

"Not my usual paper," Rod said, pulling out a copy of that morning's Guardian. "But read this."

Alan read the news story.

A high-profile climate change activist in Cumbria is missing… A devastating fire in the campervan where she lived … Police have sealed off the site of the fire and have launched a formal investigation…

"So there is a God," Alan said. "Our prayers answered."

"Still…" Rod seemed less sanguine than his business colleague. "It was also all over the teatime TV news tonight. We have a major police enquiry on our doorstep."

"Rod, we've had things like this happen to us several times before and we've always come through them. Business risk, it's called."

"I don't like it. Thousands of pounds of stock lost and now this, all in a few weeks."

He paused. "I've decided I hate the Lake District. Too many fucking sheep and too many fucking police."

"I take your point."

"Actually I hate the countryside full stop."

93.

Pamela Morrison invited Nick into her kitchen and made them both a cup of coffee.

"I didn't know journalists worked so early in the morning," she said.

"Sometimes we do," Nick replied.

"I think I know why you're here," she said. She pointed to Nick's article in the previous day's Guardian. "You're not really interested in our anti-fracking movement at all. That was a ploy. You're here because of Joan Arkle. You should have been honest when you rang me."

Nick paused before replying. "Yes, you're right. It's about Joan Arkle."

"My assumption is that, given what has happened, you're sniffing around for a juicy story. I don't think I want to play ball."

"I'm based in the Lake District and I interviewed Joan a couple of times for the local paper. I also went to the public meeting she organised on climate change. I've grown to respect her for her commitment and passion."

Pamela looked intently at Nick. "How did you get my name?"

"Indirectly. We've had a Catalan journalist on an internship with us recently and Joan passed on your details to her. I know Lluïsa pretty well."

"Ah." Pamela made a noncommittal noise.

"Joan spoke to me of the time she'd spent here in the anti-fracking campaign. It was clearly an important issue for her. That's really why I've come today."

Pamela did not reply directly. "I learned much from our protest. I learned how to make placards and write leaflets. I learned that the police aren't necessarily the loveable Bobbies I used to think they were. I learned what happens when you are arrested." She paused. "I also learned to treat the media with considerable caution."

"I understand that. Although I think your campaign managed the media very effectively. You had some excellent coverage."

"Yes. We learned to. We realised that the media liked the idea that we were mostly mums and grandmothers, normal Northern folk rather than some sort of rent-a-mob. I'm a retired teacher, you know."

"How did you find yourself becoming involved?"

"It was the earthquakes. The first time it happened, the room seemed momentarily to be swaying in front of my eyes. I was worried I was having a stroke or something. But the quakes continued coming. They were not massive, of course, but nevertheless we felt them in this part of Lancashire. It was a clear indication that something was going on underground that we ought to try to stop."

"The company had permission to test-drill, though. Some people would say that they were in the right, not you."

"Oh yes, the government gave the necessary authorisation. The government overruled the county council, which had refused planning permission. Before that happened, we'd campaigned in all the usual ways. We'd lobbied councillors and we'd signed petitions. In the end it became clear to us that all that stuff would never be enough."

"The country needs oil. People could accuse you of putting our energy supplies at risk. You were just a load of NIMBYs." Sometimes as a journalist you had to play devil's advocate.

Pamela smiled a little wearily, as if she understood what Nick was doing. "There's ample energy to be harnessed safely and cheaply. There's wind power. There's tidal power. There's the power of the sun itself. Don't tell me that we need to scrabble around deep underground to bring up fossil fuels which when we burn them will simply add to global warming."

"Joan said something very similar to me once," Nick said.

"Joan knew what she was talking about."

"Can I ask you how she got involved in your campaign?"

"She breezed into our little protest camp one weekday early last year. She was a breath of fresh air. We were all women who were retired or nearly retired, and she was young enough to be our daughter. Maybe even our granddaughter. She and I got on particularly well."

"You felt you could trust her?"

"Absolutely."

"Did she say anything about her background?"

"Ah, now you're being a journalist again. I can tell. You're trying to probe."

"Yes, I am," Nick replied. "But it's a question I have to ask you."

"She didn't say much about herself. I don't think she had a happy childhood. She was brought up in care, you know."

"Yes, she told me that too."

"She mentioned some of the campaigns and demonstrations she'd been involved in. She told us lots of stories of the disappointment felt by all the activists who were in Copenhagen in 2009, when the climate change summit came to an end and the governments hadn't managed to agree to anything."

"It can be disheartening sometimes," Nick suggested.

"It can. You've no idea of the amount of emotional energy you can use up when you're struggling to create change." Pamela paused, as if pondering how much to say. "I had a low moment when I felt I couldn't carry on. We seemed to be making no difference at all. I'd just had enough. I was suffering from burnout. It was Joan who helped me through."

"Joan seems to have an endless supply of energy."

"But Joan also had her moments. I was worried for her once or twice."

"She originally grew up in the South, I think," Nick proffered.

"Yes, we teased her about that. Soft southerner and all that. I think she had some connection with Oxford at one point, maybe with an organisation down there. But to be honest I really knew very little about her background."

"Would you tell me if you did know more?"

Pamela looked at Nick, sizing him up. "Yes, perhaps I would," she replied.

The coffees had been drunk. Nick felt the interview had run its course.

"I appreciate you talking to me," he said.

Pamela smiled. "I don't think I've told you anything Joan wouldn't have said herself. I just hope she's safe and well. She was such a strong person that I can't imagine anything bad could ever happen to her." She showed Nick to the front door.

94.

"Let's take stock of where we are," Chrissy said to DS Peter Blackford early on Friday morning. They found themselves a quiet corner.

"Elizzabeth Bowes, first," Chrissy said. "Have you read the statement DC Whittaker has taken?"

"Yes," Peter Blackford replied. "She doesn't have a solid alibi for Tuesday evening."

"No. The woman Kath whose house she is staying in was out at yoga for an hour and a half at the relevant time."

"But… "

"I know. But…" Chrissy paused.

"She has admitted to a sexual relationship with Joan Arkle."

"Yes, and they had a row. Fortunately, not every row between lovers leads to arson or murder. If it did, we'd be even busier than we are."

"That's very true," Peter Blackford said. "Although -"

"DC Whittaker took the precaution of interviewing her under caution."

"Of course."

"However Rosie Whittaker also told me that Bowes appeared completely distraught that Joan Arkle might have died. I think we need to be looking elsewhere."

"How far have we got with Bowes's ex? And the other two names she gave us?"

"They're in custody. I had them arrested last night and they're being interviewed this morning. I wanted them to sweat it out a little overnight."

"They're friends of Terry Venables."

"They are. Venables has an alibi since he was safely in custody the night of the fire. We will find out very shortly if the other three have alibis or not."

"I have a feeling that you think we're making good progress," DS Blackford suggested.

"You may be right," Chrissy Chambers smiled at her deputy. "But I'm slightly worried that this investigation seems to be going more smoothly than it's supposed to. And we still know almost nothing about Joan Arkle's background. We've got some way to go."

95.

It was not yet eleven. Nick sat in his car outside Pamela Morrison's house pondering his options. His smartphone told him that Oxford was four hours' drive away.

It was a long way to go on the off chance that someone might be in, but on the other hand the Observer needed their article and he had time on his hands. He drove back from Blackpool the same way he had come but at the M6/M55 junction turned south rather than north.

Oxford was a nightmare to drive through. According to the internet, Oxfordshire Climate Emergency Action were based at an address on the Cowley Road but when Nick finally found a way there which avoided the problem of navigating the city centre he found that the office – on the first floor above a wholefood shop - was firmly shut. Nobody in the shop seemed to know who he could contact, and they certainly didn't know of anyone called Jennifer Johnson.

It was by now half past three and Nick felt stymied. Google had brought up a number of references to Jennifer Johnson (including one in the very article in La Vanguardia which he had originally found) but Google was unable to provide any sort of home address or phone for her. Social media had also been unhelpful. She seemed very elusive. He had messaged what he thought was probably the wrong Jennifer Johnson on Facebook but perhaps predictably had had no response.

A wasted journey. Perhaps he had been foolish to even attempt it. Still, now he was in Oxford he decided that he might as well make the most of it. He left his car parked where it was on Cowley Road and took a bus in to the city centre, getting off in High Street in the heart of the university area. He decided to be a proper tourist. He strolled around aimlessly, past the Radcliffe Camera and the Bodleian, and was surprised to find himself passing by Blackwell's bookshop. It is probably good advice for authors not to check in bookshops for their own books, but Nick couldn't resist the temptation. Surely a shop as large as Blackwell's would carry stocks of *Nuclear Power: Yes Please?*

They didn't.

Nick carried on towards Carfax, attracted by the sound of what sounded like a scratch brass band. Somebody had set up a foldable table, with leaflets and booklets arranged on a table cloth. Balloons and a colourful banner were flying in the breeze, and a few musicians were trying to attract the attention of passers-by. Nick, on the other side of the road, decided not to bother to cross. And then he saw what the banner said. By sheer good luck, Nick had discovered Oxfordshire Climate Emergency Action in action.

Behind the stall was a woman about forty who greeted Nick as he approached. "Do you know about our organisation?" she said.

"I do. I've just driven today all the way from Cumbria to meet you," he replied.

"Really?" The woman looked confused. "Why?"

"I'm very keen to talk to one of your members. Jennifer Johnson."

The woman responded with a look of surprise. "I see. Who are you?" she asked.

Nick decided to be honest and to declare himself as a journalist.

"Oh, OK," the woman replied. "Jennifer Johnson isn't here. In fact, Jennifer Johnson doesn't exist. It's just that it's convenient for us to have a name for our spokesperson when we talk to the media, and that's the name we made up. I'm Matty."

"Matty?"

"Mathilda. I'm one of the co-chairs of our group. But why have you come from Cumbria?"

"I don't suppose you knew Joan Arkle when she was in Oxford?" Nick asked.

"Joan. Yes. It's ages ago, though. She'd just dropped out of Uni and was getting involved in environmental politics. She didn't stay in Oxford long."

"She was at university?" Nick asked.

"Yes, she was at St Hilda's here at Oxford. She was supposed to be studying PPE. You know, philosophy, politics and economics. She decided she wanted the practice of politics rather than the theory. She gave up the course after her first year." Matty paused. "What has Joan been doing in Cumbria?"

Nick told his story. He described how he'd first seen Joan, minus T-shirt, in Workington Magistrates Court. Matty laughed. He described how she had invaded the Cumbrian Enquirer's office and chained herself to the editor's chair.

"Yes," Matty interrupted. "That sounds just like Joan. She's great. What's she doing now that's worthy of a journalist's attention?"

Nick completed his story. The uproar at her public meeting, the abuse on social media, the death of her dog. And, finally, the campervan fire.

Matty had suddenly paled. "That's shocking," she finally said. "Oh god, I just can't believe that. I never knew."

"There's a short news story in today's Guardian yesterday which I wrote last night. I think the other nationals will be covering it tomorrow. Probably national TV too."

"I can't believe it," she repeated herself. "And the police say they're treating it as murder?"

Nick nodded. "Joan said very little about her background," he went on. "I've come here because I thought you might know a little more."

"I don't know much, but I know as much as anyone else in our group," Matty replied. "I know she did well at school. Well, obviously she did, to get a place at Oxford."

"And yet she grew up in care," Nick said.

"Did she? I always thought she'd been at some sort of girls' boarding school."

Nick looked surprised. "Did she ever mention parents or siblings?" he said.

"I don't think she ever talked to me of her family. I got the feeling that they didn't like the idea that she'd dropped out of Oxford. I mean, it's not a move that improves your career prospects."

"No," Nick paused.

"Listen, I'm tied up on the stall until five," Matty said. "But let me give you my phone number. Ring me if you want to know anything else."

Nick nodded. "OK," he said. "Thank you for your help."

96.

Molly rang Nick about four o'clock, just as he was about to catch a bus back to his car. "You around?" she asked.

"I'm in Oxford," Nick replied.

"Oxford?"

"I've been interviewing an old activist friend of Joan's."

"Useful?"

"Interesting background info, but I haven't cracked the story yet," Nick replied.

"Maybe I can help," Molly said. "Hubby has been hard at work with the genealogy software. He's found details of Joan Arkle's birth certificate. The right date of birth and everything. She was born in Maidenhead. Her father is recorded as a county court judge and her mother as a legal secretary."

"That's a surprise," Nick said.

"Joan's real name is interesting, too."

"Sorry?"

"Her name is Penelope Bramshaw."

97.

Chrissy Chambers had called another team Briefing for five o'clock and she and her deputy Peter Blackford were together, having a final run-through of what she would say.

The transcripts from the morning's interviews were back. Unhelpfully Barry Bowes and his friend Mick had resolutely stuck with 'no comment' throughout. The other man, who it transpired worked as a chef in Keswick, had been much more forthcoming.

"He's firmly pointing the finger at his mates when it comes to the tweets against Joan Arkle," Chrissy said. "He claims to be completely innocent of everything. He says that the *wheresgoldie* business was their idea. He says that the *witchwagon* was them too."

"Farmer Giles as well?"

"No. He claims that wasn't them."

"Farmer Giles posted some really unpleasant abuse against Joan Arkle on Twitter."

"Yes, and at the moment we haven't identified if that is someone else we need to talk to. One thing I'm sure of is that his name isn't Farmer Giles."

There was momentary silence between the two police officers.

"I have issued instructions to try to trace the type of tracker bug found on the campervan, and where it might have been bought."

DS Blackford nodded.

"The petrol station enquiries are beginning to come back but unfortunately so far there's nothing very interesting," Chrissy continued.

DS Blackford nodded again. There was another moment of silence.

"But I know more about Joan Arkle that I did when you and I talked this morning," Chrissy Chambers said eventually. "Something important."

"Yes?"

"The PNC rather let us down on this but I got one of the civilian staff to do some poking about on public online databases and they struck gold this afternoon. The victim's name is Penelope Joanna Arkle Bramshaw. Parents both dead. Sister lives in Berkshire. I've asked Thames Valley to interview the sister as a matter of urgency."

"That's a really big step forward."

"How much should a detective go on intuition, do you think?" Chrissy asked him.

"Well, that's a difficult question. All our work is evidence-based. On the other hand, sometimes hunches turn out to be right. Do you have a hunch?"

"I do, but I'm not sure whether it's a helpful or unhelpful hunch."

DS Blackford said nothing.

"I think we're still not talking to all the right people," Chrissy

Chambers said eventually.

DS Kate Morgan rushed across from the doorway to the MIR.

"Ma'am, you need to see this," she said, passing a photograph to her senior officer.

Chrissy Chambers studied the photograph. "Where's this from?" she asked.

"One of the PCs has just brought it in. It's from the petrol station in Ambleside. CCTV footage from a week ago today. The man was buying petrol in a can."

Chrissy Chambers studied the photo further, and then passed it to Peter Blackford.

"We know this man," Chrissy said.

"Do we?" her deputy replied.

"He's safely downstairs in the cells at the moment. I was watching the video recording of the interview with him a short while ago."

"He's - ?"

"He's Barry Bowes," Chrissy Chambers said. She paused. "Maybe we stick to the evidence and forget about the hunches."

98.

"What! Joan Arkle's an alias?" Nick asked Molly, holding his mobile close to his ear to cut out the noise of Oxford's traffic.

"It's more complicated. The birth certificate gives her full name as Penelope Joanna Arkle Bramshaw. Arkle was her grandmother's maiden name."

"Your husband is an investigative genius. He should have been a journalist, not a solicitor."

Molly laughed.

"Paul says he has heard of Joan's father. Sir James Bramshaw. Sir James had something of a reputation in the world of the law for being old-school. Not the chap you'd choose to have in front of you if you were a barrister at the Crown Court defending, let's say, a working-class single mother."

"You said he *had* a reputation."

"Retired two years ago. Died last year following a major stroke.

Obits in the Times and the Telegraph. I'll email them across."

"What about the mother?"

"Her name was Judith. She died aged 43 of cancer when Joan must have been about thirteen."

"Molly, Joan Arkle once she told me she had grown up in care."

"Really? It's possible, I suppose. Unless Joan perhaps felt that it was better not to admit to being the daughter of a right-wing judge."

"Perhaps."

"There's one more thing a little odd. The two obits I'm sending you both say that Sir James is survived by one daughter. A daughter called Millicent. No mention at all of Penelope. Or, er, Joan."

"Millicent?"

"Yes. My hubby has found out something about her," Molly went on. "Sir James Bramshaw's will and probate is available online. Did you know the government has an official Probate Search website?"

"No, really?"

"So anyway we have paid the government £1.50 and have got the will downloaded to us as a PDF. Sir James left pretty well all his estate to his daughter Millicent. Millicent Grainger, she is now."

"OK," Nick said.

"Of course, the good thing about seeing the will is that it gives a home address for Millicent as the beneficiary. Assuming she's not moved since he died she lives in a village off the M4 near Newbury. Got a pen and paper?"

Nick scribbled down the address Molly gave him. "That's quite close to Oxford," he said. "Less than an hour's drive. I could try to get there tonight."

"That's all I've got for now. Sorry Nick, Paul is taking me out tonight, so it's over to you. Go ahead and file the story if you get enough information."

"Going somewhere nice?"

"The latest Cockermouth AmDram production. It's an adaptation of Agatha Christie's Murder is Easy. If I pick up any useful tips I'll let you know."

99

Millicent Grainger, née Bramshaw, lived in a large detached house set by itself in woods in the heart of the Berkshire countryside. Her husband, a fund manager for one of the big unit trust firms, was away on business so it was Millicent herself who answered her front door when it rang just after six on Friday evening. There was a man she didn't recognise on the porch.

"Hello," the man said. "It's Millicent, isn't it? I've come about Penelope. My name's Nick Potterton. I'm a journalist."

Millicent looked at him. "You'd better come in. I've been expecting you."

She led him into a chintzy front room which Nick guessed would probably be described as the drawing room and sat him down on a small sofa.

"You've been expecting me?" Nick said in surprise.

"Not you personally. But I've been expecting the press. And the police. You're here first. I expect the police won't be far behind."

"You know about your sister?"

"Just what I've read in the papers and on TV. Someone showed me an article in The Guardian yesterday." She spoke with an educated southern English accent, but she also sounded enormously tired. "Which paper are you from?"

"The Observer," Nick replied. "Although I interviewed your sister for a local paper in the Lake District."

"You knew her as Joan, I suppose?" Nick nodded. "I called her Penny. That's her proper name."

"Have you been in touch with her recently?"

"Recently? Don't be idiotic. I haven't had any contact with her since she left Oxford. That's at least ten years. Nearly fifteen. I'm 37, so Penny must be 34. This happened when she was 21."

"She's never once been in touch? No birthday cards or anything?"

"Of course not. Listen, Penny chose her own route in life and I chose mine. My father warned her of the consequences. He warned her that he would disown her, but she took no notice. So my father severed all ties. And frankly I think he was right."

Nick paused. "Can I ask you about your mother? Her death must have been shattering for the whole family."

"I knew you'd be asking all these questions. I guess sending a journalist to me is Penny's revenge."

Nick said nothing.

"I was seventeen when Mum died, and only a year away from university. Penny was fourteen. I think Mum's death particularly affected her," Millicent continued. "My father was a good man but he was of his time. He thought children needed to be brought up strictly."

"And after your mother's death he suddenly found himself responsible for your sister? Who was already a teenager by then and presumably knew her own mind."

"Something like that. Penny told me once that Father had abused her. Not physically, but just by his behaviour towards her. If I'm honest, sometimes Father bullied me."

"Did - er, did your sister get sent to boarding school?"

"That's right. A fancy pile on the outskirts of Windsor. Boarding fees of £30,000 a year. Father could afford it, of course. I'd been sent to private school too, but as what they call a day-girl."

"Your sister didn't like the school?"

"She hated it. She was nearly expelled more than once. Still, the school got her into Oxford. Four straight A*s at A-level. And then Penny blew it all."

Millicent paused. "She got herself a tattoo when she left Oxford. Did you know? It's a ridiculously large whale. I mean, a tattoo on her chest! Father nearly had apoplexy."

The front door bell rang.

"Excuse me a moment," Millicent said.

She returned a moment later into the drawing room accompanied by two uniformed police officers.

"I probably need to go now," said Nick, getting to his feet. "I'll see myself out."

100

Phil had cooked a lamb moussaka to welcome Lindsay back from work, and they uncorked a bottle of Primativo wine to go with it.

"Friday evening," Lindsay said. "Start of the weekend."

"Which means there's only a week to go," Phil said.

"Until you make an honest woman of me."

"Something like that," Phil replied. "The RSVPs are coming back from our invitations."

"I know."

The wedding invitation list for Phil and Lindsay was not necessarily very orthodox. It included almost all the members of Phil's cycling club, almost all the clubmates of Lindsay in the Coniston and Hawkshead Harriers, everyone from Ambleside mountain rescue, and friends of theirs from work. Phil's brother and Lindsay's mother and her sister made up the family contingent.

The little Anglo-Saxon church of St Bega at Bassenthwaite was going to be bursting at the seams. They'd chosen a very simple ceremony, just an exchange of vows and an exchange of rings. Presumably the vicar would want to preach a sermon of some kind, but hopefully it would be short.

The wedding day proper was set to commence immediately after the ceremony. Phil and Lindsay had planned a mass cycle ride north along Bassenthwaite Lake to Uldale and Caldbeck and then to the Cumbrian village of Hesket Newmarket, where a stop at The Old Crown, a community owned co-operative pub which had become a firm favourite of Phil's, was going to be compulsory. Wedding guests who wanted to opt out (or in other words, the immediate family) were invited to stay put in the tearoom close to St Bega's. Later in the afternoon, a vintage bus was lined up to convey them to a small country hotel in Borrowdale. At the hotel there would be a buffet, some drink, probably a few inappropriate speeches and, finally, a disco.

"A hundred or so have already said they're coming," Lindsay said. "It's not going to be cheap."

"Worth every penny," Phil said. "If I get to spend the rest of my life with you."

"God, Phil, spare me the romantic bit."

"I'm allowed it once in a lifetime. And, do you know what, I do quite fancy you."

Lindsay laughed.

"My first wedding day was the pits. It was family only, in an unpleasantly fancy hotel near Kendal. None of my friends were there. And of course Greg turned out to be a shit," Lindsay said.

"That's all in the past," Phil said.

"It is. I'm older and wiser. And if Greg hadn't been a shit I'd never have met you."

"So what's the plan? Will you cycle in your wedding dress?" he asked her.

"Of course I will. I've got it carefully planned. Cycling helmet, sunglasses, wedding dress, arm-warmers if needed, Lycra tights. By the way, have you warned The Old Crown that we'll be descending on them?"

"Yes, they are asking the co-op brewery next door to brew us a special firkin of ale called Phil and Lindsay Get Hitched. I think that's what they're calling it. It may be Phil and Lindsay Get Pissed."

Lindsay laughed.

She changed the subject, and their mood.

"Did you see the TV news tonight?" she said.

"No. You mean the police investigation?"

"I wondered how the police were progressing. Nick and Lluïsa had both interviewed the woman who's died. Mind you, I gather she wasn't necessarily the easiest of interviewees."

"Still, what's happened is a shocker."

"The police policewoman in charge is very up-beat, but I can't say I'd like to have her job. Such a responsibility."

"It was definitely arson?"

"Yes, the police say it was a petrol bomb that started the fire. They're appealing for people who may have seen suspicious people buying petrol in cans to get in touch."

Phil put down his glass of wine and looked at her.

"What?" he said.

"They say that the arsonists may have been seen buying the petrol in a service station. Basically they're looking for leads."

"I saw two guys doing that when I filled up the car last weekend. At the filling station on the Wigton Road. I assumed they'd run out of petrol."

"When was this?" Lindsay asked.

"Last Saturday, I think. Mid-afternoon. Maybe about four."

They looked at each other. Lindsay was the first to speak.

"It's probably just a coincidence."

"Probably. I'll think about it overnight. I can always ring the police tomorrow."

101.

Nick had gone online and booked himself into a roadside hotel somewhere near Newbury. It was much too late to start the journey back to Grasmere. Besides, he felt that he now had all the information he needed for the feature for The Observer. Martin had already texted him twice earlier in the day, urgently asking for an update on progress. Really it was now or never if the piece was going to meet the deadline for Sunday.

Daughter of posh judge becomes activist wasn't really news. *Daughter of posh judge killed because of her activism* definitely was a story.

The hotel bedroom was appallingly badly lit and the small chair which was provided was the wrong height for the corner desk. Still, it would have to do. Nick pulled out his laptop, and reread his interview notes.

Nick wanted his feature to pay a proper tribute to Joan, to her passion, to her determination and stubbornness and to her remarkable talent as a wildlife photographer. Most of all, he wanted her personality to come alive in the words he wrote. There had been a life-force about her which needed communicating.

There were various alternative ways he could tell the story. Nick took a sip from the small bottle of mineral water the hotel had provided and tried out a couple of possible openings. He came to a conclusion. He would start the piece in Workington, that morning in the court when Joan had revealed her whale tattoo to the startled magistrates on the bench.

I don't find my T-shirt offensive, Joan had told them. Fracking is what's really offensive, she'd added. But don't worry, I'll put my T-shirt on inside out.

Once started, the article rapidly took shape. At about half past eight, Nick took a final look at the word count, called up Outlook on his laptop and sent the email off to Martin Eveyard's Observer address. It was, Nick felt, a competent piece of work. He might be living these days far from his London life of old, but he still had the skills he'd learned years back when he'd started off in journalism. He didn't need Martin to tell him the piece was good. He knew it himself.

102.

A police investigation is full of hard, unrewarding, tedious work, most of which turns out to have been utterly unnecessary.

Just occasionally, it feels like there's a breakthrough. Chrissy Chambers had returned home on Friday evening feeling positive. But Saturday morning wasn't going to plan.

She had allowed the Keswick chef, Rick Logan, that was his name, to go home, advising him that she was releasing him under investigation. He looked blank, but he also looked delighted to get out. The other two lads were still a floor below her, in the cells. They'd got themselves solicitors some time in the previous twelve hours, or maybe they'd simply accepted the duty solicitor.

Nevertheless, despite this, Barry Bowes was still saying 'no comment' to everything, except for muttering now and again under his breath that he'd been properly set up by Elizzabeth, the bitch. The other man, Mick, Michael Chatsworth, had begun to be communicative, however. He'd admitted that he'd taken part in the trolling of Joan Arkle on Twitter. Both the *wheresgoldie* and *witchwagon* material. However, like Rick Logan he'd adamantly denied knowing anything about Farmer Giles.

More interesting – in fact, more disturbing – was something else he'd said while under caution. Chrissy had arranged for the DCs undertaking the questioning to bring up, in a suitably roundabout fashion, Barry Bowes' purchase of the petrol at the Ambleside petrol station the previous Friday. Chrissy had expected Mick either to tell an obvious lie or to fall back on 'no comment'. But he hadn't.

"Oh yeah, that," he'd said. "Baz was taking me back from work and the idiot hadn't put enough fuel in the car. Diesel it was, actually, not petrol. I told him I wasn't walking back to the filling station so in the end he had to go. He got completely soaked. What a tosser."

Chrissy read this through on the transcript several times thoughtfully and then rang her lead officer in forensics. He'd confirmed what she had thought. Then she accessed the DVLA database to check the vehicle which Barry Bowes was recorded as keeping. It was a second-hand Honda Civic saloon and sure enough it was listed as a diesel model.

Petrol is highly flammable. Diesel is combustible, but put a lighted match in a pool of diesel fuel and very often it will just fizzle out. Almost certainly it was petrol not diesel that was lobbed into Joan Arkle's campervan, Chrissy told herself with a sigh.

Of course, she knew that Barry Bowes had bought a fuel can. He could easily have taken it a second time to a filling station somewhere and this time put petrol in it. But at the moment the evidence for this wasn't there.

On the other hand, what had come through that morning were two phone calls to 101 from members of the public. A woman said she had seen an older woman filling a fuel can the previous weekend in Barrow. A man had rung with a message that he had seen two young men at the Wigton Rd garage in Carlisle, also filling a fuel can.

Barrow! Carlisle! Why had she decided only to check out petrol stations within twenty-five miles, Chrissy asked herself? The issue for her now was whether there would be CCTV footage of the relevant forecourts (likely) and whether the CCTV would still have been retained after a week (touch and go).

She put a call through to the CID in both Barrow and Carlisle and arranged for officers to be dispatched immediately to the filling stations. She instructed them to let her know as soon as they could if the CCTV was available and, if it was, to tell her what showed up for the relevant times.

While she was waiting, she worked her way methodically through some of the statements and reports which had come in. Was this how she had anticipated spending a Saturday when she had first decided to do the SIO Development Programme? Probably not. Tony was being very understanding. He'd floated the idea at breakfast of them both driving up to Housesteads, the Roman fort on Hadrian's Wall, to take a stroll along the wall. He'd seen her face and immediately told her it didn't matter.

The morning wore on. Most of the rest of her team were also in the MIR, but she detected a slightly different mood in the room. The early enthusiasm had begun to dissipate. Now she felt her colleagues were digging in for the longer run.

Chrissy remembered what her Detective Chief Super had told her. Make slow time. Well, time was certainly passing slowly. She went across to the kettle and made herself her second instant coffee of the day. Someone, Kate Morgan perhaps, had brought in a packet of chocolate digestives. Chrissy helped herself to one.

The call came back from Barrow first. No CCTV footage available and the staff said they'd never be able to remember back to the previous weekend. Sorry, they'd added.

Lunchtime came and went. Eventually the call came through from Carlisle. Two males had been seen buying petrol at 16.11 on the Saturday. CCTV close-ups of their faces available. The footage would be passed to her as soon as they could access the recording. Chrissy allowed herself a very tiny smile.

103.

The What's App message came through to Alan at about two on Saturday afternoon. It was a message from Rod.

"The dog's been taken ill with a stomach bug. I'm taking him to the vet's in Warrington at five tonight. I'll have to cancel the evening out we'd arranged."

There was no sick dog and no evening out arranged. This was Alan's business partner advising him in the way that long ago they'd planned that something urgent had cropped up. They needed to rendezvous. Rod was telling him to be at the main Starbucks in

Warrington in three hours' time.

Rod was already there, sipping a latte, when Alan arrived. Alan looked quizzically at his partner.

"The campervan fire," Rod said baldly.

"Fortunately, that was nothing to do with us."

"No. Well, not exactly."

"What are you telling me?"

"It's slightly complicated."

"Yes?"

"I'd put the word out that it wouldn't be too disappointing if the van suffered an accidental fire. Obviously only when there was nobody inside."

Alan looked in amazement at Rod.

"What?"

"We'd talked about the need to get Joan Arkle out of Cumbria."

"Yes, but not in that way."

"The stupid fuckers cocked up," Rod said. "The two lads who did the fire didn't check the campervan was empty."

Alan thought for a moment. "Rod, you amaze me. Instead of an accidental fire in a tatty old van which nobody gives a monkeys about we have a fucking inferno and a murder investigation."

"Well… something like that," Rod admitted.

"Can we be linked to it?"

"It was all arranged at four removes. The lads involved know nothing about either of us. They're clients, but they're small fry. The guy who put them up to it and paid them doesn't know us either."

"OK, so why am I in Warrington this afternoon?"

"I've heard word from Carlisle. There's a dispute going on about whether the lads should get the money. It's…. it's causing ripples in the business."

Alan pondered this. "So…"

"We're out of Cumbria anyway. We agreed that on Thursday."

"There are other options. North Wales is looking promising," Alan replied. "I've been putting feelers out in Rhyl and Llandudno. Some Liverpool boys are there already, but there's scope for us too I think."

"Are there any bleeding climate change activists with hairy dogs in North Wales?"

"There are lots of people living in shitty accommodation looking for something to make their lives better and wanting to be our customers. What's not to like?"

"OK, boyo," Rod said. "Bye-bye Cumbria. Wales it is."

104.

Sunday, ten am.

Chrissy Chambers was back in the MIR, waiting impatiently. The two young men on the CCTV footage had been identified and arrested in their homes very early that morning. They had been transferred from Carlisle and were now downstairs undergoing questioning.

Five past ten.

DS Peter Blackford rushed into the MIR and hurried over to where Chrissy was sitting.

"We have a confession," he said.

"Yes?" Chrissy replied.

"From one of them. The other one is saying nothing but the younger lad, the one called Aidan Pickering, has cracked."

"Go on."

"They were offered £500 and a generous supply of heroin."

"To do what?"

"To buy petrol and to set fire to the campervan. They were told on Tuesday afternoon exactly where they would find it parked."

"By whom?"

"Man called Richie Markham. He's someone we've been interested in for the county lines enquiry."

"£500 to commit murder? That's shocking."

"Aidan Pickering says they got it wrong. They were supposed to torch the van when it was empty. He says that, in his own words, they got a right bollocking afterwards from Markham. But he says they were nervous."

"They were nervous? And because of that someone innocent dies?"

Chrissy Chambers stopped and looked at her deputy.

"Team briefing as soon as possible. Press conference ditto. Days off all round tomorrow."

"Yes, ma'am."

She looked down at her desk, slowly and methodically putting the paperwork there into one single pile.

"So," she said eventually. "This counts as a successful first investigation for both of us, I suppose."

"I suppose so."

"What a nasty job we've chosen to do."

105.

It was on the following Thursday that North Wales Police put out a short statement to the media.

The statement reported that two white males, one aged 34 and the other aged 33, had been arrested early that morning in police raids on separate hotels in Bangor and Conwy. The statement said that the men had been charged with offences under the Misuse of Drugs Act and were being remanded in custody. Additional charges were expected to follow.

A police spokesperson was quoted as saying that the arrests were viewed by the police as a significant step forward in the fight against the organised drugs trade.

106.

The Saturday of the wedding was a day to remember.

"I do," said Phil in St Bega's chapel, at the right time in the ceremony.

"I do," said Lindsay, a moment later.

The vicar pronounced them man and wife. They kissed. A cheer went up from the packed chapel. Only half the wedding guests were inside, the rest having to wait in the grassy churchyard outside. A hundred or so bikes were parked together a little way away on the main road.

The morning had begun with a swim in Bassenthwaite Lake. This had been Lluïsa's idea. Lluïsa had got back to the Lake District the previous Thursday after her week in Scotland, and had been adamant that the swim was essential. For old time's sake, she said. Lindsay had persuaded a few of her triathlon women friends to join them and in the end there were about eight women who took the plunge.

"God, look at my hair," Lindsay said when they got back on shore. "Brides are supposed to have immaculate hair."

"Phil won't mind," said Lluïsa.

"He'd better not change his mind now," Lindsay replied. She had by this stage stripped out of her tri suit and was in her underwear, towelling herself vigorously. One of her other friends was holding her white bride's dress, ready for Lindsay to slip it on.

"This is simply a ridiculous way to prepare for a marriage," Lindsay said. "It's all your fault, Lluïsa."

"Sorry, I do not speak any English," Lluïsa replied.

Lindsay laughed. In the end, all was ready. "Am I as radiant as brides as supposed to be?" she asked Lluïsa.

"Gorgeous," Lluïsa replied. "Molt maca."

The service was at 2pm. Just before three the gaggle of cyclists took to the road. At 3.45, the first pints of Phil and Lindsay Get Hitched were being poured in the Old Crown. At five o'clock the third and final barrel of the special brew had been drunk dry and the cyclists returned back the way they had come. And at half past six everyone was in the hotel, tucking into the buffet.

Nick found himself cycling alongside Lluïsa on the journey back, Lluïsa still riding the second-hand bike she had picked up cheaply when she had first arrived in the Lake District. The wedding was to be Lluïsa's farewell to the Lakes. She'd no sooner arrived back in Ambleside on Thursday than she'd announced to Lindsay that she was planning to return to Catalonia immediately after the weekend. Things had quietened down in Girona, Lindsay gathered. With any luck, Lluïsa wouldn't find the Guardia Civil at the airport ready to arrest her. It was time to go home.

"We'll miss you, you know," Nick said.

"I'll miss you," Lluïsa replied.

"You are almost certainly the only Catalan woman who will ever complete the Frog Graham Challenge."

Lluïsa laughed. They cycled on companionably on the quiet Cumbria country road.

"There is just one person missing today," Nick said.

"You mean Joan," Lluïsa said.

"Yes. I know it's stupid, but at the wedding I looked across from St Bega's to see if she was standing beside the lake. But she wasn't."

"I didn't really know her but I still miss her," said Lluïsa.

She paused. "I've done a short news update about it for La Vanguardia. They've run that photograph of Joan again."

"I've got a short feature in tomorrow's Observer," Nick replied. "It's a sort of obituary. I found it almost too painful to write."

They fell silent. There was just the sound of cycle wheels turning.

"The world is full of beautiful countryside," Lluïsa said finally. "I have asked Lindsay and Phil to come to the Pyrenees with me for Midsummer. We will go into the hills to a little hostel which is run by friends of mine. We call it *ecoturisme*. It'll be wonderful. We have special Catalan cakes we eat every year the evening before St John the Baptist feast day."

"Have Lindsay and Phil agreed?"

"Yes, but on one condition. That I persuade you to come as well."

Nick laughed. "I don't know if I can," he said. "I may have work to do that week."

"But you have no excuse. Your newspaper has closed. You can spare a few days to see me again. And anyway I bought you the Pyrenees book."

"That's true," Nick said. He laughed. "I suppose I've no choice. I'll come."

107.

Elizzabeth Bowes returned home to Kath's house late on Monday afternoon. A month had passed. She was beginning to come to terms with the fact that Joan Arkle had left her life. She still felt a terrible emptiness inside, and an irrational guilt that somehow she had been responsible for Joan's death. If only she could turn back the clock, she thought. But the past is forever gone and Elizzabeth knew that she had to think of the present.

The event they'd organised in Joan's memory the previous day had gone well. Pete and his new partner Becki had done most of the preparatory work but Elizzabeth had also worked hard to get the word out. There'd been environmental activists and XR people arriving from all over the north of England and in the end well over a hundred were there. They'd chosen to go down to the Drigg boundary fence again, but this time it was agreed that the event would be a completely silent vigil. Everyone carried placards with a single slogan: For a Future for the Earth and its People. The police had been told of the event but had deliberately kept themselves as unobtrusive as possible. The detective who had led the investigation had even appeared briefly and left a bouquet of flowers, before hurriedly making herself scarce.

And then afterwards everyone had unwound at a nearby village hall which had been prevailed on to provide space for a pop-up exhibition of some of Joan's wildlife photography.

The event felt like a turning point for Elizzabeth.

That Monday morning she had been to one of the firms of solicitors in Penrith to start the necessary steps to divorce Baz. It had been a young woman solicitor who she had seen. At the end of their discussion, she found herself coming out with a question she hadn't anticipated asking. "How do you become a solicitor?" she asked.

The woman looked at her. "Normally you do a law degree and then the Legal Practice Course. Then you do a period of what's called recognised training. Why?"

"No particular reason. Except that I think I could be a solicitor,"

Elizzabeth replied. "For various reasons I've got quite interested in the law over the past few weeks."

"It would be great to see more women in the legal profession. I'm sure you could do it. Have you got a degree?"

Elizzabeth shook her head. She didn't like to admit that she hadn't even got A-levels.

"That doesn't necessarily matter, provided you're prepared to put the work in. Hang on, somewhere here I've got a booklet from the Law Society." The woman scrabbled around in her desk and eventually produced a small brochure which she handed to Elizzabeth. "Listen, if you want to talk anything through, I'd be happy to meet you and try to help. Pro bono of course."

"Pro bono?" Elizzabeth queried.

"No charge," the solicitor translated. "I was the first generation in my family to go to uni so I didn't find it easy to enter the law. I had a lot of help when I was qualifying. It would be good to give something back."

Elizzabeth read the booklet, which had been entitled *Mature students and career changers*, several times over the weekend. The task which she would face if she were to try to qualify seemed enormous. The cost appeared prohibitive. But she'd taken a decision: she would at least give it a try. The first stage appeared to be to get A-levels. She'd checked online and found a local college that would enrol her for the following September. She'd study English – she'd always been good at English. She'd study Law. And, partly as a tribute to the influence which Joan had played in her life, she'd study Political Science.

One decision taken. There was however a second thing she needed to get right.

She'd changed her mind about her new tattoo. It wasn't going to be a whale. She would always associate a whale tattoo with the memory of Joan and she had decided she wanted something different.

She was going to arrange for her new tattoo to show otters. There'd be a pair of them, splashing in a river. One would be a mature adult and the other would be a younger animal. Just as she'd seen them on the river Petteril.

108

Rosa was driving. To her right, in the passenger seat, sat her father. Behind Nick in the back seat was Rosa's partner Becky.

They had left Barcelona late in the afternoon of June 23rd, taking one of the main trunk roads north towards the Pyrenees. They skirted Vic and passed through the small Catalan towns of Ripoll and Camprodon.

"We must be nearly in France," Nick said at one point.

"Nearly but not quite. This is where we turn, I think. Another 5km or so up a track, or so Mum said on the phone. We're getting very close to the mountains."

"Glad you're driving," Nick responded.

Rosa had picked up her father at Barcelona airport and taken him to the Gràcia area of the city. Rosa had relocated to the city for her work the previous week, her employer arranging for her to move into a spacious first floor flat in one of Barcelona's most elegant areas. Becky was already there, pottering about in the kitchen as Rosa and Nick arrived.

"Hola!" she said, coming across straight to Nick and giving him an enormous hug. "I'm so pleased you could make it. I've not seen my father-in-law for ages and ages."

"Hola is the only Catalan she knows," Rosa told her father. Becky pulled a face.

Nick had had serious second thoughts about this trip. Lluïsa's invitation had seemed attractive at the time it was offered, but the more Nick thought it through the more problems he foresaw. The eve of St John the Baptist, *la Revetlla de Sant Joan*, was a very important festival in Catalonia, celebrated in style. This would undoubtedly be a family get-together.

That had implications for Nick. Lluïsa's uncle was Jordi; Jordi was the partner of Anna, the woman who had left him, breaking his heart. Nick wasn't sure how well he would cope.

It was the news that Becky would be there too that had swung it. Rosa had told Nick on the phone that Becky was going to take a few days off work to come and see Rosa's new flat for herself. Becky felt like a second daughter to Nick and this seemed an opportunity not to miss. Besides, he'd been worried in recent months for them both and it was good that Becky was making the effort.

"I expect we'll be there before Mum," Rosa said as the car continued on ever-narrower roads. "She's driving back from her work to Mataró to pick up Jordi. Anyway, Mum keeps southern European time."

"How is Lluïsa getting here?"

"She's coming with her parents Patrícia and Artur. And her brother and his wife are coming too. I've not met them. They've got two children, Pere and Ester."

"Lindsay and Phil are driving straight from Girona airport, I think," Nick said.

"Yes, that's what Lluïsa said."

Rosa slowed down, beside a sign which said El Refugi de l'Àguila. "Here we are," she said peering through the rapidly disappearing daylight. "The Eagle's refuge".

The centre was a cross between a youth hostel and a climbing hut, equipped with a rustic farmhouse kitchen, a large communal lounge dominated by a long table, a series of dormitories and a small number of single and double rooms. It was run, Nick gathered, as a co-operative venture by a young couple from Girona called Xavi and Meritxell. Xavi greeted them warmly, practising his English as he did.

"Welcome to the Pyrenees," he said. "Please, you must make yourselves at home," he said.

Phil and Lindsay had already arrived and had bagged one of the few double rooms. "Fair's fair, we are just married," Lindsay said. Nick smiled, and did a round of introductions.

"We've been here for a good couple of hours. It's really beautiful. The mountains are right outside," Lindsay said.

"I've got my fell shoes. Have you got yours?" Nick replied.

"Of course I have," Lindsay replied.

There was the sound of more traffic outside. The main door burst open, and Anna and Jordi came in. Anna made straight for Nick, and gave him a very large hug. "Nick," she said. (It came out as always as *Neek*). "It's so good to see you. We are so very grateful to you. Thank you for looking after Lluïsa so well."

Jordi in turn hurried up to Nick, shook his hand and then

embraced him in a bear hug. "Thank you," he echoed.

"How is Lluïsa?" Nick asked, and then deciding to change into Catalan. "Com va la Lluïsa?"

"Bé, molt bé," Anna replied, moving on to kiss Rosa and then Becky, her daughter-in-law, very warmly. "We are having a great evening together," she carried on, in English.

"We are going to have a great evening together," Rosa corrected her.

"That's what I already say," her mother replied.

There was more noise outside and a sudden influx of new arrivals. Lluïsa came in first and did the introductions. "My mother Patrícia. My father Artur. This is my big brother Miquel and my sister-in-law Núria. And Pere who's four. And Ester who's two."

The party settled down. Xavi emerged with several bottles of cava, and a series of small bowls with tapas. The evening meal, Nick knew already, would be some considerable time coming. The secret was to pace yourself.

Lluïsa came over to where Nick, Lindsay and Phil were talking. "There will be fireworks later. It's a tradition. And we will all eat coca de Sant Joan. That's a tradition too. That's a special cake we eat just tonight."

"Mm, I can't wait," Lindsay said.

Nick had been sitting quietly. "It's weird, I know this is the festival of John the Baptist but when I hear people talk of Sant Joan I think of Molly at the Enquirer and what she used to call Joan Arkle," he said.

"Saint Joan."

"Exactly. Someone who said things people didn't want to hear and suffered because of it."

"She would have loved the mountains here," Lindsay said.

"She would have." There was a moment of silence between them.

Beside Nick, Becky had settled down in a big armchair. Pere was on the floor at her feet, playing with bricks. Becky was bouncing Ester up and down on her lap.

"One, two, three," Becky said to Ester, holding up three fingers.

"U, dos, tres," Ester replied.

Becky repeated what Ester had said and then held up five fingers.

"U, dos, tres, quatre, cinc," Ester said.

"U, dos, tres, quatre, cinc," Becky responded hesitantly.

Anna came across to her daughter's partner. "You're learning, Becky," she said. "You're not quite as fluent as Ester though."

There was a comfortable atmosphere in the room. A young puppy had been frisking around but had now curled up in front of a large wood fire. The sounds of two languages being spoken merged. At one end Lluïsa's parents were chatting with Xavi and Meritxell who had emerged from the kitchen. Jordi was chatting with Lluïsa's brother and his wife. Anna was pottering around, putting plates out on the table. She sensed Nick looking towards her and gave him a big smile. Really, Nick thought, it feels curiously as though I belong here.

Pere was still on the floor, playing. Becky had begun to read Ester a child's picture book, making up the English text as she did. Lindsay and Phil were talking to Rosa. Nick found himself next to Lluïsa.

The evening moved to a new phase. The little puppy in front of the fire was making whiffling noises in its sleep. Artur had begun singing quietly at the other end of the room. Patrícia, Xavi and Meritxell joined in. Ester was asleep in Becky's arms. Phil and Lindsay were together, chatting quietly and holding hands.

Lluïsa had gone into the kitchen and now returned carrying a large pastry on a plate. She called for quiet. "This year I used a new recipe to make the coca de Sant Joan. It's got no butter and no cream and no eggs. I wanted to make it this way for someone special I met in England.

"When I interviewed Joan for my article we talked about our lives. I told her of our demonstrations in Catalonia, and she told me of the things she had done as an activist. We have had very similar experiences. So now we eat Catalan coca and we drink Catalan cava and we remember her."

109.

The party had not finished until well after midnight, but Lindsay had suggested an early start. Nick crawled out of his sleeping bag reluctantly at seven the next morning and put on his running gear. Lluïsa was also already up, dressed for running. Phil was still asleep in the double room. The rest of the hostel was silent.

"The early part of the day is always the best," Lluïsa said as she led the others up the footpath which rose rapidly from the back door of the hostel into the mountains.

"Just imagine we're doing another early morning recce for the Frog Graham," Lindsay said.

"I don't remember Skiddaw being this steep," Nick replied.

Marmots were what Lluïsa had promised them when they'd discussed a morning run the night before. "You'll find them all over the hillsides," she had told them.

She was leading the way, her nearly-new fell shoes bought in Ambleside once again coming into their own. Lindsay was next, with Nick bringing up the rear. The path they were following rose steadily up and up.

"Amazing countryside," said Nick. He stopped to take in the view. The high Pyrenees mountains were all around them now.

"It's so wild and so beautiful," Lindsay said.

"Yes, it is," Lluïsa agreed. "But the landscape is changing. Lots of glaciers are disappearing. Year by year the snow is further up the mountains." She paused. "Xavi and Meritxell are active in a local campaign. Our land is under threat. Climate change."

"It's a global issue," Nick responded.

Lluïsa nodded.

They ran on, further up the mountain path, and the vista changed. Now the very highest peaks had come into view. Nick, Lindsay and Lluïsa paused again. Nick reached to pull a water bottle from his backpack. As he did, a massive dark shape came in from the corner of the mountain ahead of them and swept the sky close above where they were standing.

"Wow. What is it?" asked Lindsay. "Eagle?"

"Yes, Golden eagle," Lluïsa replied. "It is not common here. We are very lucky to see it."

They watched the bird silently. It circled several times above them, as if trying to ensure that the humans below could appreciate it properly. And then, finally, it flew away.

For a long moment nobody said anything. Eventually Lindsay spoke.

"Fantastic," she said.

"Fantastic," Nick echoed.

"Yes," Lluïsa said. "We live in a beautiful world.

Also available from Gritstone Publishing

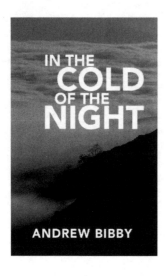

In the Cold of the Night, by Andrew Bibby

The staff at Greensleeves residential park are undertaking the Three Peaks Challenge for charity. But their attempt to climb the highest peaks in Scotland, England and Wales in one weekend goes badly wrong. As they begin the walk up Scafell Pike in the Lake District their boss disappears. Next day his half-naked body is found in a moorland bog, miles off route.

As the police begin their enquiry Nick Potterton, once a successful London journalist but now a struggling part-time freelance for the local press, also investigates. The 'Body in the Bog' story becomes the paper's front page lead and it falls to Nick to try to find out exactly how Richard Meade met his death.